PROPHETS OF

DECEPTION

A NOVEL

RICHARD I. LEVINE

ISBN-13: 9781530370627
ISBN-10: 1530370620

A RAY SILVER ADVENTURE

CDC is a troubled agency. There have been four separate scathing federal studies about CDC. All of them together and separately paint a picture of an agency that has become a cesspool of corruption.

—Robert F. Kennedy Jr.,
Speaking to the Vermont Legislature, May 5, 2015

Vaccination is expensive and represents a cost of one billion dollars annually. It therefore benefits the industry, most notably the multinational manufacturers. One sells the vaccines. The other then provides the arsenal of medications to respond to the numerous complications that follow. Their profits increase while our expenses go through the roof.

—*Dr. Guylaine Lanctot, MD,*
Author of the Best-Seller The Medical Mafia

Their poison is like the poison of a serpent: They are like cobras who refuse to listen.

—Psalm 58:4

Acknowledgments

The fictional characters, corporations, and events depicted in this book are a creation of the author. They do not exist. Any resemblance of these fictional creations to an actual entity, event, or person now living or dead is coincidental and unintentional. **The information put forth in this novel is for entertainment purposes only and is not to be a substitute for medical opinion or advice.**

Any mention of real people—either living or deceased—real products, corporations, or works of art (paintings, motion pictures, photographs, music, or published literature) are incorporated within the narrative for entertainment purposes only and out of respect and/or admiration of those entities and in no way is meant to infer any endorsement of this work and/or the opinions of this author.

I wish to gratefully acknowledge the many brave natural healers who have dedicated their lives to speaking out, educating the public, and providing safe, effective, affordable, and commonsense health-care solutions in defiance of powerful corporate pressure, mainstream media ridicule, and political and regulatory agency threats brought by those who value profit over the common good. With that being said, this novel is dedicated to the growing number of outspoken natural healers, be they DCs, DOs, MDs, NDs, and PhDs. Thank you, **Toni Bark, MD; James Chestnut, DC; Patrick Gentempo, DC; Suzanne Humphries, MD; Christopher Kent, DC; Joseph Mercola, DO; Jeanne Ohm, DC; Sherri Tenpenny, DO; Barbara Loe Fischer of the NVIC; filmmaker Jeff Hays;** and the thousands more frontline field practitioners from the natural healing arts community. Also, a big thank-you to the real heroes: the countless parents of vaccine-injured children who have educated themselves and, to the dismay of the true Prophet$ of Deception, are educating the public and making a difference.

A shout-out to whistleblower **Dr. William Thompson**, a researcher at the CDC who in 2014 shed light on the willful omission and cover-up of research data showing a strong link between MMR and autism—by his superiors at that federal agency. As of this writing he continues to ask Congress to conduct hearings so that he may testify under oath. Also, a very special nod with love and admiration to **Dr. Andrew Wakefield**—a brilliant, caring medical professional disparaged by the moneyed interests but still held in high esteem within the healing arts community because he dared to explore and found enough evidence to suggest the need for further study on a possible link between MMR vaccination and autism, and as such became the target of a vicious character assassination. Andrew is a man of conscience and integrity, and I pray that as the coauthors of his research have been exonerated, so, too, shall he.

And finally to you the reader:
It's because of the fact that your body's ability to heal is greater than the medical-pharmaceutical complex has ever permitted you to believe that you owe it to yourself and your family to be informed, to ask questions, to demand answers, and to be allowed access to viable options outside their realm of understanding. You do have the right of refusal, too. No medical procedure should be performed upon anyone without his or her informed consent or without the informed consent of a legal

guardian, for to do so is unconstitutional and is nothing less than tyranny. That is why it is important to have a health-care professional in your corner who understands the difference between promoting and maintaining your health, and promoting and maintaining the health of the disease-care industry.

1

McTavish Labs
White Plains, New York
January 2008

Ray checked the time on his cell phone for the third time in five minutes. Making sure he was safely in the shadows, he looked over at the large metal door, lit by a single halogen flood, and spied the red power light on the security camera mounted just above it. A rustling of snow-laden branches from the other side of Haarlem Avenue grabbed his attention as quickly as it did his breath. He watched, frozen in place, exhaling long and hard when he was sure there was nothing there. He watched the condensed vapor rising up from his mouth and wondered if it was visible to the camera. Off in the distance a lone siren broke the predawn silence, at first becoming louder—eliciting protest from a stray dog—then fading off until it and the canine could no longer be heard. He glanced back at his phone. *"It's three o'clock—where is this guy? She said he'd be here at three."*

He heard another rustling followed by a series of short piercing cries of what sounded like a music student torturing the scales and saw the shadows of two cats stretch across the road before melting into the darkness. *"Don't chase after the pussy, you fool. The first rule of dating is, you let her come to you."* Ray gave in to a laugh—his first in a while. At any other time the sounds of the night would have gone unnoticed or perhaps would have tricked a willing subconscious into adding a new dimension to an evolving dream. But with his senses amplified by adrenaline, anything that broke the calm seemed louder than usual and made him uneasy. *"If you're not used to this stuff by now, Ray Silver, you need to give this shit up once and for all."* He narrowed his gaze on the service door as if it might pop open by the force of his will.

No matter how many times he had reviewed the plan, studied the online satellite images of the company grounds, or looked over Paige's drawings of the main building's interior, Ray was still anxious—anxious enough, in fact, to ignore the throbbing sensation from the gash he'd sustained to his knee when he crested the twelve-foot fence. He cursed himself for not having executed this a week earlier when his anger had fully suppressed his other emotions. He cursed the additional downtime that allowed him to become distracted with the trivia now competing for his attention. *"Stop thinking about that stuff."* Ray was convinced he would have been completely focused on the task at hand and easily able to do whatever had to be done in order to get the information needed to exact his pound of flesh...had they not waited. *"Too many distractions! Just gotta stay focused. I can still do this. I can. Just gotta stay focused on the mission...on why I'm here."*

The mission was designed to finally expose the fraud, corruption, and cover-ups, as well as the corporate insiders at government agencies who were making life-and-death decisions based solely on one critical component: profit. Regardless of the consequences, he wanted to shed light on every ounce of it. And if he got caught, there would be plenty.

Unlike his previous exploits, this mission wasn't government-sanctioned, nor was it orchestrated by a quasi-independent agency subgroup. This undertaking was self-created. This one was personal. Ray was just a private citizen—a "whack-job alternative health-care provider," as some in the press had called him—taking the law into his own hands. There wouldn't be a well-placed handler at the CIA or the NSA standing by to clean things up, not even his son. Even if Jimmy had offered, Ray would never consider jeopardizing his career. He had to admit that without the broad shoulders of Uncle Sam propping him up, his bravado felt a lot less bulletproof. Success or failure, this one was entirely his—and Paige's. And as far as he was concerned, failure wasn't an option.

The delay had given doubt the opportunity to plant a few seeds of hesitancy—just enough to make him think what his life would be like if Leigh Anne were no longer a part of it. He knew she could only put up with just so much of what she called his "insatiable need to risk life and limb," of that there was no doubt. Ray had come very close to losing her the last time, and he now worried he would go home to find out she really had had enough. He could only hope she truly understood that what he had to do was every bit as important as their relationship. He hoped that after all was said and done she would be there for him. He knew if he had moved sooner, it wouldn't have changed the situation at home—but also that he was deceiving himself that he wouldn't have allowed it to become a distraction. Now that it was, he hoped she would allow herself to be seduced by the insatiable lust he had for her, which always made her feel guilty for even thinking about leaving. *"She has every right to be angry. After all, this is the third time I'm breaking a promise to never do anything like this again…and yet here I am."* The extra week spent in the Rockies had given him ample time to relive their debate, second-guess and reconstruct his argument, and question the validity of his solution. *"A little late to worry about that now, Ray…put it to bed so you can focus!"* He scolded himself for his lack of discipline and for being careless enough to have lost his grip while climbing the ice-covered fence, which made him think of his knee.

Ray looked down at the stain on his torn trousers and then noticed a few drops of blood in the snow. *"Shit!"* As he quietly dug his heel at the ice crusted surface—covering up his mess just as a cat would work a litter box—he thought about the time when he was ten years old and came home with a rusty nail embedded into his right foot. His mother had nearly fainted when she saw the trail of blood leading from the front door to his bedroom. She screamed about lockjaw before dragging him off to the doctor's office for a tetanus shot. "You can't get tetanus from rust, Ma," he'd said. Remembering, he shook his head at the old wives' tale. "*Stay focused, damn it!*" He tied a handkerchief around his right knee. "*If this is going to work, then you need to maintain discipline…and stay focused.*" He continued to scold but couldn't keep his mind from wondering, a blessing in disguise as it kept him from thinking about the cold. When the wind kicked up, he again checked the time and cursed. "*Damn it, Paige.*" The delay challenged his patience, just as the weight of the snow challenged the tree branches along Haarlem Avenue. His mind danced back and forth between Leigh Anne, his children, Paige Motz, and everything in between—replaying almost every bit of minutia Paige had shared. "*Where the fuck is this guy? Maybe he's not coming. Maybe he had second thoughts.*"

Had he known his imagination would take advantage of him, just as a politician does a tragedy during campaign season—and he should have known, given his recent past—he would have insisted they stick to the original date. But there had been enough suspicion to believe their plan had been compromised.

"*I'm telling you, Ray, we have to push the date back until I get some reassurances from my guy at McTavish.*"

"*We both know this whole op is risky, but to delay because of an e-mail from a former coworker is not—*"

"*Several e-mails from a few former coworkers.*" She waved a number of pages in the air.

"*Giving nothing more than cryptic warnings. You said so yourself. You would think they'd come right out and—*"

"*Their e-mails could be monitored. They can't risk it.*"

"*And how do they know you're even planning a visit?*"

"They don't. But they're not stupid. I've been asking a lot
of questions and perhaps they—"
"Perhaps they told security?"
"Which is why we should hold off until I hear otherwise."
"OK, fine. And in the meantime, what? Sit here in the
middle of the forest...in the freakin' cold?"
"Just until I hear from Ambrose."

* * *

Former White Plains police officer Ambrose Martin had been a night-shift security guard at the lab for slightly over thirty years. He had taken a liking to Dr. Paige Motz during her short time at McTavish and treated her like a daughter because she had always treated him with kindness and respect—unlike the other researchers. And even though he had assured her of his help, she remained cautious. Paige was familiar with the rumors of how he'd been forced out of the police department for disappearing whenever a fellow officer needed immediate assistance. One rumor frequently mentioned by the other security guards had him passed out, stone-cold drunk, while still on duty. The rumors embarrassed Ambrose, but she never asked if they were true. She knew he liked to drink and reasoned that if it had been a problem, the drug company would have never hired him, let alone kept him for thirty-plus years.

Paige was more concerned the bosses had been aware of his fondness for her, witnessing on many occasions the way he rushed to carry boxes from her car or escort her from the building with an umbrella on rainy days. She appreciated the sweet gestures from the kind old man and made it a point to remember birthdays with his favorite Irish whiskey and plenty of holiday cookies at Christmas. "Let's just hope it doesn't come back to bite us in the butt," she had told Ray. It wouldn't be beyond the McTavish hierarchy to threaten the old man's employment if they suspected he had information of her whereabouts or even her activities. If for nothing else, Paige's experiences with them had taught her to be skeptical as well as vigilant. So at her insistence, she and Ray had remained at her cabin until Ambrose could help her confirm or deny the cryptic messages from former coworkers appearing sympathetic to their cause.

* * *

Neatly tucked away in the Colorado mountains, half-way between Loveland and Estes Park, the old log cabin was a simple structure perched on a heavily wooded hilltop facing the valley below. It had been strategically built so that any approach by foot or horseback—and nowadays by four-wheel drive or snowmobile—had to come straight on from the east. The only exception would be a helicopter, but the engine and rotor noises echoing across and down through the trees gave plenty of warning. Surrounded on three sides by dense forest, steep cliffs, deep crevasses, and fast-flowing rivers of bone-chilling water, for the weekend woodsman there were no safe approaches from the north, south, or west. And while the winter snow made the landscape all the more beautiful, everything blanketed in white also made things deceptively more treacherous for the inexperienced. But Paige was experienced, and she had remembered the abandoned place from when she and her brothers hunted caribou, elk, and deer—often taking refuge in the rundown cabin when the weather unexpectedly turned bad. She had long dreamed of restoring it and making it her home, and was grateful it was still there and unclaimed when she'd abruptly left McTavish two years prior. And she was even more grateful that her brothers had helped to make it a decent place to live.

At first her departure hadn't been cause for concern to anyone at the pharmaceutical giant until she began making noise on new-age websites and at several alternative health-care expos—preaching to the choir about falsified research data, bribery, corruption, the revolving door between industry and government, and the willingness of the mainstream media to pimp for one of their best advertisers. The few times McTavish representatives were faced with questions about her appearances, they publicly laughed off her accusations of impropriety and painted her as a disgruntled ex-employee who had to be fired because of chronic carelessness and other behavioral issues.

She had hoped they would be satisfied with just destroying her reputation, but it wasn't until she found her car vandalized beyond repair and her Fort Collins home ransacked that she understood they had something more sinister in mind. She was convinced of it when the natural gas line to her house was loosened—on the inside of her home. It was then she knew she had no other choice but to head for the cabin. The memory of a former colleague disappearing after he claimed to have evidence of a secret biological experiment was never far from her mind. Paige knew McTavish company statements that he'd left the country when they suspected him of embezzling were completely manufactured for the authorities as well as the press. But it served its purpose, getting local law enforcement to abort any search for him or his remains. Thus, she decided to take up residence in the mountains. It was unlikely that anyone hunting for her would ever find the hideaway that had been frequented by outlaws of the once untamed West. But just in case they did send people, she would be able to see and/or hear them with enough time to react. For Paige, fight or flight was more than just a physiological response; it was a conscious choice.

* * *

Ray was growing impatient waiting for the night watchman. His toes were becoming numb—not because of his knee injury but from the cold. Had it been just his right toes, he would have been concerned about possible nerve damage. New York winters weren't just cold, they were a deep-down-to-the-bone damp cold, and he'd been outside long enough that he was starting to feel the ache. Yet he thought it odd that he still couldn't feel any pain in his knee. *"Perhaps I did cut a nerve? Nah, the gash isn't deep enough, and I can still flex my foot...I can, right?"* He moved both feet up and down, back and forth to prove it and to get his circulation going again.

"Don't think of the cold. Don't think about the feet. Think of anything but the cold. Go over the plans...that's it, review the plans step by step." Instead, his mind began replaying his eldest daughter's youth. The images of Casey running, laughing, and learning to ride her bicycle were so vivid it was as if he'd witnessed them just weeks before. Every stage of her life from childhood through college flashed through his mind like a slideshow, always ending with the ear-to-ear grin she had displayed when he'd pinned on her lieutenant's bars at her commissioning ceremony. He found it hard to think beyond that point, but he knew he had to balance just enough of the sentimental things to keep the fire burning...yet not so much for it to become one more thing competing for his attention. She was, after all, his motivation for being here in the first place. On top of everything else racing around in his head, thinking about Casey kept Ray thinking about the evidence he needed—the evidence he strongly suspected had always existed and was reassured by Paige he would find at McTavish.

"Geez, Ray, stop worrying, OK? The stuff will be there."

"I'm not worried...I'm concerned. I wanna be absolutely sure, which is a lot different than being worried."

"Borderline."

"Yeah, right."

"You are, admit it. You're walking a fine line between being concerned and being worried."

"Far from it...and look who's being antsy."

"Then stop asking me about it, for God's sake."

"Can you blame me? It's kinda boring up here. I mean, if it weren't for the satellite feed connecting us to the outside world, I think I'd go nuts."

Suddenly aware of his shadow, Ray pressed back into the darkness. "How the hell did I miss that?" he reflexively blurted out loud as he looked up at the security camera. Again he checked the time, now wondering if he had the correct door, or even the correct building. The possibility that changes had been made since Paige's departure had been a real concern. Certain things such as the file cabinets and boxes containing all her work could have been relocated to not just another part of the building but to another section of the compound. Locks could have easily been changed, and even security could have been upgraded. Technology certainly had advanced in the past few years, and with corporate espionage always a threat, the billions in yearly drug sales would make the expense of any upgrade a mere drop in the bucket for McTavish. Mere pennies when compared to yearly donations made to federal and local political campaigns—an investment that worked in their favor, as the money and gifts bestowed upon Congress yielded more political appointments and lucrative contracts from the grateful body of lawmakers. With those contracts came secrets, and with the kind of secrets hidden inside this compound, there could have been, should have been, systems in place that even Paige's elderly security friend wouldn't have been aware of.

The thought of enhanced security around the grounds wasn't lost on Ray now as he scanned fence posts, light stanchions, and rooftops for anything that remotely looked like a camera or an infrared beam. The fact that he'd made the fifty yards from the fence line without setting off lights, bells, or whistles gave him little comfort, as grabbing him now would only bring charges of trespassing. *"Perhaps,"* he thought, *"they are waiting to add breaking and entering, theft, destruction of private property, or maybe even espionage."* But in spite of all the what-ifs, he was still going to carry out what he'd come to do. Nothing was going to stop him, especially now that he was here—especially now that he'd left his DNA in a trail from the top of a fence all the way to the backside of building number one. As if all that weren't enough—and just as he'd convinced himself he could stay focused—the echo of Leigh Anne's words began to bounce around in his head:

"I thought you were going to tone things down, Ray, but since you got back from Seattle you've actually cranked it up a few

degrees…I don't want you to do this, Ray. This is all happening way too fast, and you're not thinking clearly."

"I've thought this out, and I can assure you my thinking is very clear," he whispered into the darkness. He could hear her reply: *"Considering what you stand to lose, I don't think so."*

"I've built up the clinic and made it everything I said I would. And haven't I arranged my own hours so you can still teach at the university?"

"Yes, of course you have, but what was all that for? Were you doing it because you wanted to, or were you doing me and the girls a favor…just making a deposit of goodwill in order to spend it on one more wild adventure?"

"That isn't fair. This isn't any wild adventure; this is something that needs to be done. Regardless, you still do agree with me on how we choose to raise our girls, yes?"

"I'm their mother, and I'm going to do what I think is best for them. And the way we handle it now is our personal life-style choice…at least it should be. I remember a time when you offered your opinion only when it was asked for and, more importantly, only within the confines of your office. Over the past couple years and especially the past six months, you've gone way beyond that, and you know it."

"The facts back me up…I have an obligation to share what I know, and you know that."

"The facts, Ray, are inconclusive. You've really been sticking your neck out."

"Speaking out to the community is not sticking my neck out. It's not!"

"You don't realize what kind of pressure this puts on me."

"That's just it, Leigh, I do know."

"You feel blindsided by Casey, don't you?"

"Now is not the time to bring up my daughter, not when I'm about to break into this lab."

"You didn't want to see because her being in the military had always been part of your dream. And as far as we know, the link you talk about...it's still just a theory...your theory. You can't be sure there's a connection."

"OK, you're gonna stay in my head about this? Fine. It doesn't change the end result. And I know you're going to say there's no evidence, but I say there is, and that's why I'm standing here at three in the morning in the freezing cold."

"Because it's personal."

"Yes it's personal."

"I'm afraid. I'm afraid that you're going to escalate this beyond searching for answers, beyond searching for proof or exposing those responsible. I'm afraid that you're going to take this thing beyond that. I'm afraid you're out to seek justice on your own terms. I see it in your eyes, and I hear it in your voice."

"Justice? There is no justice for what they do to people."

"If you do what I think you're planning on doing, it amounts to an act of premeditated revenge...and if you do this—"

With each rattle of the perimeter fence, his heart rate jumped. Ray's throat tightened when the bushes rustled with more vigor. Again he held his breath, and again he squeezed himself against the wall—hoping the darkness wouldn't betray his presence. *"It's ten after three. Where the hell is this guy?"* He thought he saw something or someone move in the distance, but he couldn't be sure. He stared past the fence at the end of the long driveway, beyond the empty street and beyond the parking stalls, zeroing in on the thick rows of neglected vegetation that masked the Metro North Railroad platform. At that moment, all he could hear was the heaviness of his breathing, not realizing that the more he tried to control each breath, the louder each one seemed to be. Clumps of snow fell from several of the trees—the impact silently swallowed by the thick layer of fresh powder blanketing the street. Ray still wondered—hoped—it was just the wind kicking up, or maybe it was the stray dog that had been barking just minutes before and was now looking for comfort under a bush. He didn't dare leave his cover to investigate. A sharp stabbing gust of wind whipped around the corner of the building, and as he tensed from the assault, the tightness in his throat eased. *"It's definitely the wind."* He had pressed so hard against the wall he felt the rough brick scratching at the back of his head.

Ray thought it was colder than normal for January, colder than he remembered from his New York childhood. But after spending the past two weeks on the eastern slopes of the Rockies, it wasn't the cold that now bothered him but rather the perspiration generated by the flood of stress hormones rampaging through his body: the beads of sweat rolling off his forehead to sting his eyes or down the back of his neck, intensifying the bite of the cold against his skin. He couldn't understand how he could generate so much water while his toes felt so frozen.

The seconds seemed like minutes, the minutes felt like hours, and the waiting was made all the more intolerable each time he looked at his phone. *"Twelve after...where the fuck?"* He lurched into a defensive posture at a blackened figure racing toward him, relaxing slightly when he saw it was Paige. Before he could say anything, she forced him back against the wall, her hand over his mouth. He halfheartedly resisted, and she pushed back harder, her thigh now pressed tightly in between his, her eyes burning through to the back of his skull.

"Do you want to blow this whole thing?" She held up his fleece cap.

He firmly grabbed onto her hand and moved it off his mouth, whispering "What the...where'd you get—"

"It was by the fence. You didn't feel it come off?"

Ray grabbed the cap, then rubbed the back of his head, realizing why he had felt the bricks scratching him. "If I had, would I have left it there? What are you doing here so soon?"

"Your cell phone."

"What about it? Did I butt dial you or something?"

"You kept looking at it. You're like a teenager who can't spend a few minutes without texting someone. What are you doing, and who the hell were you talking to?"

"I was talking to myself...and I was checking the time. It's twelve, make that thirteen after. Your guy is late."

"Well, each time you check the damn time, the display light gives you away. Are you sure you've done this kind of stuff before?" She said this sarcastically.

"As if you didn't know."

"I'm beginning to have my doubts," she retorted.

"Well...they weren't exactly like this though."

"I thought you said...never mind." Paige heard a chain rattle and glanced over to the service door.

"Hey, I just admitted that this is a little different from the other things I've done, but you've never done this at all."

"But I worked here and—"

"And it's been a few years."

"Yes, it has, but I know the layout, and I know where they've got my research locked up. And I know the layout of the CEO's office. So I'm going in with you."

"Which brings me back to my question, what are you doing here so soon? I thought you were going to get files from the animal lab while your body—" They both realized she was still pressing into him, and they separated. "I mean, while your buddy Andy got me started in here."

"They moved it." She was barely audible.

"What?"

"The animal lab—they moved it."

"Whaddya mean they moved it?" His voice rising. "Moved it where?"

"Not so loud! OK you're right, it's been a few years. But I'll ask where it is, and we'll go there after we get done with this."

"But that—" he started, but she slapped her hand over his mouth.

"Will you lower your voice, or do you really want us to get caught?"

Again, Ray grabbed her by the wrist and pulled her hand from his face, continuing in a forced whisper, "But that wasn't the plan. You were supposed to wait for me when you were done."

"Yeah, I know, but obviously the plan has changed, and the more I thought about it, the more I couldn't let you go in by yourself and I also realized there are additional files we'd better get."

"Like?"

"Like the files of politicians on the company payroll and former McTavish employees appointed to key positions at the FDA, CDC, and NIH. Like the files they have on surgeon generals who came from the pharmaceutical industry and like the files they keep on former researchers who've mysteriously disappeared."

"Yeah, sure, but we're not gonna get anything if your friend Andy doesn't open that door."

"Amby. The guard's name is Ambrose—you know this already. What's wrong with you, Ray?"

"What...ever. He's still late, and let's not forget that you're public enemy number one to these people, and because of that you can't risk being seen anywhere near here. You do remember telling me that, right?"

"Right, but—"

"No buts, Paige. I just spent two weeks in the North Pole eating Santa's reindeer so you could instruct me on what to do."

"That was the best venison you've ever had, and you know it."

"It was the only venison I've ever had, but that's not the point. You weren't supposed to be here...too risky. But then you said it was important to get evidence out of the monkey lab and that it was best for you to do that. So now you're here and—"

"Ray, stop it! What's your problem? You scared? You having second thoughts?"

"Your guy is late, I'm freakin' freezing cold, and you're talking about venison. That's my problem. Yes, I'm a little—"

The lock on the side door clicked, and the low squeal of a rusty hinge stopped their conversation. Ambrose's pudgy face and red bulbous nose peered through the opening as if he were the burglar and not the security guard. "Dr. Motz, is that you?"

"Over here, Amby."

Paige and Ray stayed pressed to the wall.

"It's OK; I killed the power to the camera," he said, smiling as he pointed above the door. "Quick, you two. We don't have much time. Follow me."

"Amby, wait." She could smell whiskey on his breath. "You've been drinking."

"Just a little, Dr. Motz…just a nip or two to stay warm."

"I hope it was just a nip…or two. We might need you later, got it?"

"Yes, ma'am. You know I don't get drunk on the job. You know that, right?"

"Yes…I know that." They nodded at each other.

"You two better follow me," Ambrose said.

"The other guards, where are they?" She tugged on his arm.

"I had to wait till they were outta the way. Stipo is sleepin' as usual. McClure is over in buildin' two watchin' a replay of the Rangers game. And Adams—"

"He's giving a tour of the animal lab to some high school girl?"

"They do love them little bunnies, but actually he took this one down to the cafeteria." He was embarrassed. "We got us a new soft-serve frozen yogurt machine down there. It's got all the fixins', too. The girls like that sort of thing as much as they like the animals. And that's a good thing for you, Dr. Motz."

"In a sad way, it's good to see that some things around this place didn't change. By the way, where'd they move the lab?"

"It's in the basement of buildin' four, in the middle of the compound. They moved it away from the street 'cause sometimes the mornin' commuters could hear the monkeys screamin' durin' the drug trials. I thought I told you that."

15

"No, you didn't. What about Patane and Vadella?"

"They're cleanin' up a little chemical spill on the other end of the buildin'. I asked 'em to move one of those big fifty-five gallon drums, and some of the stuff got spilled. I guess I forgot to tell 'em the lid was loose or that there was some grease on the ground." He winked. " Now there's stuff all over the floor in the loadin' dock area. It's real slippery, too. They'll be busy for a while, so there's nothin' to worry about."

"I can smell it, Amby."

"It's kinda strong, Dr. Motz, but I wouldn't worry none."

"Can you tell me if anything else has changed?"

"Let's see." He looked up at the ceiling to help him think. "Animal lab, soft serve...we got all new computers now...a whole new system."

"What kind of new system?"

"Beats me. I just know the big mucky mucks kept sayin' the operatin' systems kept gettin' that blue screen of death stuff. The things were goin' on the blink all the time. Don't you remember? It was happenin' when you was here."

"I remember."

"And there were some people who kept tryin' to get in through some kind of back door."

"Hackers?"

"What?"

"Nothing, go on."

"Anyway, they brought in all these techie people from Silicone Valley." Ambrose looked at Ray, who laughed at the mispronunciation. "If you ask me, they looked like they was from one of them rock 'n' roll groups. Anyway, we got all new stuff now...the works."

"But my stuff...I had printed copies of all my work and kept them filed away just in case the old system was ever compromised."

"You and Janice Hughes, I mean Dr. Hughes, were the last two who did stuff like that. Did ya hear that she's left the company?"

"No, but I'm not surprised. She was just as disgusted about all the lies and the other bullshit...more than me, I think."

"The bosses had us shred all the paper copies of your stuff. Whatever work you did, it's only on the computer now...all of it." Ambrose was apologetic.

"Why all digital?" Ray was curious.

"Easier to edit or destroy on a moment's notice is my guess," Paige said. She clearly wasn't happy. "At least everything will be in one place and easier to transport. Amby, just give me the keys to an office with a workstation. I'll also need a user ID and a password."

"I'd better come with you," the guard insisted.

"It would be better if you patrolled the hallways. Go check on that spill."

"I don't know, Dr. Motz. I don't' think that's a good idea," he protested.

"Ambrose," Ray interjected, "listen to Dr. Motz. If for some reason we get caught, we don't want you getting in trouble, too. You've done enough, and I...I mean, *we* appreciate it."

"That's all well and good, but if what you and the doc say is true, then I wanna help."

"You've helped us more than you know. Now the best thing you can do is resume your patrol, and if you run into any of the other guards, you can steer them away from us."

"He's right," Paige confirmed. "You've done more than anyone could have asked for. Let us take it from here."

"OK, Dr. Motz. If I think you're gonna get caught, I'll pull a fire alarm or somethin' like that. That should distract everyone long enough for you two to get outta here...and if it means anythin', now it all makes sense why they fired you. You knew too much. You knew they were lyin', didn't you?"

"They didn't fire me, Amby...I quit...because I knew too much, and I couldn't be a part of what they were...what they *are* doing."

"That's what I meant to say...you quit, that's right."

"Keys."

"You might as well use your old office. It's been cleaned out for a while now, and as far as I know, no one uses it. You'll be safe in there."

Ambrose resumed his rounds leaving the two to make their way down the corridor. The formaldehyde smell was stronger than Paige remembered. It reminded Ray of the cadaver lab from chiropractic school.

"Wow, that's pretty potent. They must've spilled the entire drum. Doesn't this place have any kind of ventilation?" His eyes began to itch and water.

"I don't remember it being this bad...except the one time they did have a large spill on the loading dock and it got into the air intakes. I'll bet that's exactly where the spill is, by the air intakes."

"What's with that stuff anyway? I thought all the manufacturing was done at the Puerto Rico facility?"

"It is, and while most of the formaldehyde that's here is used on the lab animals, McTavish maintains a small manufacturing line here for when they run off a few test batches of an experimental drug or vaccine."

"Experimental?"

"That's right...for testing."

"On the animals? On the military?"

"As far as I know it's for the lab animals, but that's what we want to find out, right?"

"Right...and the formaldehyde is used as a preservative in the vaccines, right?"

"In all vaccines." She came to an abrupt stop, looked up and down the hallway, and then unlocked a door. "Welcome to my former home away from—" She was taken aback by the emptiness.

"Just as sterile-looking as the hallways," Ray said.

"Well, it's not mine anymore. When I was here, I had it nicely decorated with Apache and Arapaho artifacts from back home, and some nice photographs, too...stuff like that. I was actually hoping that it would still been here. Not that we could have taken any of it."

"You left it all here?"

"I left in a hurry and didn't have time to…I'll bet the bastards had it destroyed and…damn!" She stared at the computer monitor.

"What?"

"I didn't get an access code or a password, nothing. And even if I did, we didn't bring anything to back up the data."

"Whaddya mean you didn't bring…how could you not bring anything?"

"Well, did you bring anything to back up this shit?"

"Well, no. I thought we were looking for actual paper files."

"Exactly!"

"Exactly…OK, not a problem." Ray got quiet and slowly paced around the room.

Paige waited for his solution. "Any day now." She stared at him.

"Give me a sec. After all, I'm not a tech guy from Silicone Valley." He mocked and cupped his hands on his chest. "Can you e-mail those things? I mean, is this system only internal, or is it tied into the web?"

"It should still have net access. The files are probably encrypted, but yeah, I think we can e-mail them."

"Then let's do that, and we'll worry later about finding someone who can decryptify them."

"Decryptify?"

"Decryptify, unlock…you know what I mean."

"Great. By any chance do you have a password or username to get into this thing?"

"Oh yeah, that. Why not try your old one?"

"Like that's gonna work." She rolled her eyes.

"You have a better idea? Maybe I'll go wander the halls to look for Amby."

Paige began typing, skeptical that she would still have access after all this time and surprised that she still did. "OK, this is a little weird. Now why didn't they wipe me from the system? Unless—"

"Unless they just didn't think to do it?"

"Or unless they wanted me to access the files remotely and then—"

"And then they can trace the IP address to find you."

"For someone who isn't a tech guy, you sure know a lot."

"I saw it in a movie. So let's think about this for a sec...if what you say is true, that they wanted you to access it remotely, then theoretically once we send the files in an e-mail, they'll be able to figure out where we access it from. Am I right?"

"I don't know, but I think they can get a fix on a general area. To be safe, we'd better find a neutral site like a public library. We can download the files from there."

"The hotel by the airport," Ray said. "We'll access your e-mail and download the data from the hotel business center."

"No good. What if they can find the hotel? Then they can easily find us."

"We registered under a false name."

"Picture ID. If any hotel staff can identify me from a picture, then McTavish security will go right to the FBI."

"OK, then, we'll...better still, *I'll* go to a public library or an Internet café. I can be in and out so fast that even if they had my picture, which they don't, nobody would remember seeing me."

"Fine. I'm gonna get started, and you check the drawers and some of those cabinets...see if there's a flash drive lying around."

"What makes you think there'd be a flash drive, and why do we need one?"

"Just check, OK? I'm either getting a bad feeling about this whole thing, or I'm getting a headache from the formaldehyde, Ray, but it's beginning to seem way too easy."

She tiptoed to the door and checked the hallway. Ray looked through the drawers and found pens, a pad of paper, and a few compact discs, and in a small box there were several drives.

"Just as you thought." He held them up for her.

"Certainly no coincidence."

"There's other stuff in the drawer, so someone's been using this office."

"Maybe."

"Hey, look, if you think we're being set up, then let's abort right now."

"We're already here, and you're the one who wanted to do this." Paige searched the network for her files.

Ray paced around the office, occasionally opening the door to check the hallway. "Can you hurry it up? The smell is getting worse out there."

"I'm going as fast as I can."

"I thought your friend Ambrose—"

"He's not my friend!" Paige snapped, annoyed at the interruption. "He's just a security guard, and he wouldn't be involved in a setup like you're probably thinking."

"I wasn't thinking that, but now that you mention it, let's just go over what we know. He was late letting us in, and he offered up your old room, which is farther into the building than some of the other offices we could have used. Think about that. An office closer to the back door or even near the old storage rooms would have been better for us. Your old access code is still valid, and blank flash drives just happen to be sitting in an empty drawer in an office that's just as empty."

"It's got a new computer and a desk and some stuff in the drawers, so it's not empty. And maybe he did or didn't leave the drives for us, but he probably doesn't even know what a flash drive is. Would you please let me do this?"

"You're the one who said you had a bad feeling about this."

"Stop distracting me. We'll discuss this later."

Paige worked as fast as she could, but it still took her time to navigate the new network. Finally, she exclaimed, "Pay dirt! Everything is here: my stuff, the politicians, the list of corporate insiders at the regulatory agencies, internal memos about fast-tracking...all of it!"

"Experimental stuff for the defense department?"

"There's a DOD file! No time to look at it now. I'll e-mail it, and we'll go through it all later." She sent off the e-mails and then began downloading onto a drive.

"Forget that part, and let's get going."

"No, we need these. If we were set up, chances are we could possibly get nailed before we leave the campus. That's why we'll split up. I'll go over the north-side fence that borders Bond Street, and you go to the south side of the compound and hop the fence onto Glenn. We'll meet up by the car on Cloverdale. If they nab you and find the flash drive, they won't suspect that we also e-mailed the files...at least not until they have their IT guys check their servers."

She pulled the drive, downloaded files onto the second one, and slipped the first into Ray's pants pocket.

"Are you kidding me? You take it."

"Ray? They could nail either one of us or both. Why take a chance?"

When she finished, she made sure the desk was exactly how they found it. "OK, ready. Let's go."

"Uh oh...you hear that?"

"Hear what?"

"Shhh, listen." A faint ringing sound echoed through the hallways. "You don't suppose—"

Strobe lights flashed, sirens screamed and simultaneously they said, "Ambrose!"

"We gotta get the fuck outta here!" Paige headed for the door.

"Wait! What if it wasn't him?"

"What?"

"What if it's because of the chemical spill?"

"Then everyone's on their way to that side of the building. Let's go!"

"And the White Plains police and the fire department hazmat unit are on their way here, too!"

"All the more reason to get going before they get here."

She eased her head through the office door, only to come face to face with security guard Stipo. Ambrose Martin was nowhere in sight.

2

Just like any other weekday at the Kailua Center for Natural Healing Arts, the reception area was buzzing with activity. Assistants escorted patients to and from the various treatment rooms while front desk personnel scheduled appointments; rang up sales of supplements, essential oils, and alternative health literature; and directed invited guests to one of the lecture rooms to learn about the many services offered by the center. The clinic had been steadily growing since Ray reopened the multidisciplinary facility, but when he purchased and leveled the house on the adjoining property and turned the one-acre parcel into a lush garden filled with tropical plants, a koi pond, and a Zen garden, it became the ideal place for him and the staff to meditate, as well as the perfect setting for the clinic's outdoor yoga and tai chi classes. It wasn't long after the last stone had been laid and the last flowers planted that the amount of people coming to the center nearly doubled.

Each time he stopped to take it all in, he marveled how almost three years earlier a powerful congresswoman with a personal vendetta had been behind an armed FDA raid that had all but destroyed his dream practice—a practice now bigger than he had ever dreamed possible. And in spite of his success, he didn't lose sight of the fact that there were still plenty of politicians and pharmaceutical industry-connected bureaucrats willing to take action against any outspoken natural health-care practitioner. However, Ray did take some comfort in the belief that his past exploits had won him a few adherents in Washington, DC. It was a belief feeding his growing bravado—that and the attention he was getting from the local media. Although he denied enjoying all the free publicity, his wife Leigh Anne, along with a few of their closest friends, made a concerted effort to keep Ray grounded—something that was hard to do since his ongoing criticism of official health policies went without so much as an unofficial "cool it" from the few people he did know within the government.

To look at the fully staffed facility and to see an office busier than Ray could have ever imagined was to see the true testament of the dedicated teamwork that had helped him and his longtime office manager, Leilani Onakea, resurrect what had been and is once again the windward side of Oahu's fastest growing center dedicated to holistic healing principles. With the recent addition of Leilani Blacque, a disabled veteran hired as the clinic's head receptionist, the entire team had been impressed with how smoothly she fit in. Ray and his office manager sometimes argued over who should take credit for bringing her onboard, but ever since Leilani "B"—a.k.a. "Lani" to avoid confusing the patients—was hired to run the front desk, the two women clicked as if they had been working together for years. If Leilani had any issue with Lani, it was over her support of Ray's vocal antivaccination stance. He often joked they were like an old married couple—always finishing the other's sentence or correctly anticipating the other's next move.

The only difference was that he or one of the other staff members became the surrogate "spouse" whenever the women butted heads over the way Lani encouraged Ray—which thankfully didn't become an issue that often. But when it did, Ray would be the one the ladies picked on first, unless he brought his daughters to work: the four-and-a-half-year-old twins Ronnie and Abigail, and three-year-old Sandy. Ray had taught the girls well: the twins keeping "Auntie" Leilani busy, while Sandy was insistent she be allowed to sit on "Auntie" Lani's lap for free rides as she navigated her wheelchair around the clinic.

On this particular day, Mileka Johnson, a television news reporter from Honolulu, had been waiting for Ray to finish taking the center's morning tai chi class so she could interview him about a measles outbreak in the island chain. Unlike some of the other local reporters on Oahu, she was welcome at the natural healing arts center. Ray felt she had been one of his media allies, reporting the real reason for the 2004 FDA raid—something that had helped keep his reputation intact as well as guarantee her an interview when an alternative health perspective was needed. Ray had reason to be skeptical about the news media presenting his side of things in a fair way, but he appreciated the fact Mileka never distorted his comments—editing them a little for broadcast time, but never distorting them—unlike one seasoned journalist trying to spark new life into a fading career by heavily editing Ray's remarks, taking them out of context, and reusing several of the clips in unrelated stories. The segments made Ray look as if he was uneducated and a little crazy. After several protests to the station's management went unanswered, that reporter and anyone else from his station never got past Team Leilani again.

Mileka happily sat in the reception room biding her time, admiring the 250-gallon saltwater aquarium or interviewing the patients while she waited. She enjoyed the fresh morning breezes flowing freely through the open slider doors at each end of the room. Perfumed scents of passionflower and the wisteria-covered bamboo-framed arbors lining the pathway from the parking lot made an impression each time she visited. To her, Ray's place was the antithesis of the sterile white-washed environment of traditional medicine. It was warm and comforting—unlike the typical doctor's office, which she once described as "as cold and impersonal as a routine pelvic examination." Unaware that Ray was now watching her from the main entryway, standing with his hands on his hips as if he were Yul Brenner's King of Siam, she eagerly jotted down quotes from a number of patients, and her cameraman filmed those willing to be recorded. As with previous visits, she was not only taken with the environment but told the staff how impressed she was with the testimonials—so much so that she was almost tempted to become a patient herself.

"Mileka Johnson!" Ray turned many heads as he surveyed the reception room, his volume in sharp contrast with the Zen-like appearance of his clothing. He caught Lani wagging a finger along with her disapproving look for his being so loud. He mouthed "sorry" to her, then lowered his voice. "The last time I saw you…it had to be that personal injury trial."

"You mean that big personal injury trial? It was six months ago. Is your side still savoring the victory?"

"Not my side, but the side I testified for. And if I remember correctly, your station almost lost Colonial State's advertising business over that piece you did."

"They didn't appreciate me airing your post-trial attack against them, and I did get scolded by my editor for not running the piece by him first."

"Well, they did accuse a family of faking injuries and cut off all medical benefits. Colonial deserved the harsh words—what can I say?"

"And of course they weren't faking, right? The dad and mom didn't milk it along…not even a little?" she baited.

"They almost died in that accident. You were there for the whole trial. You saw the evidence and heard all the testimonies, not just mine. They weren't even close to faking. What's more, the insurance company never sent them for an independent exam, which, by the way, are never 'independent.' But when they do make people go for those dog-and-pony shows, they're never done in full view of an impartial witness and it's usually when the patient is about ninety percent improved. So, naturally, the hired-gun exam doc can't find anything significant at that point and comes to the conclusion that the person was never injured. I still can't believe they tried to claim fraud."

"It does happen, you know, and that's why I was sent to cover the trial. Insurance fraud is a growing problem. But your on-camera comments afterward were priceless and got the folks at Colonial pretty mad at me."

"Well, it was the truth, and the 'expert' witness for the defense was nothing more than an insurance whore." He looked around to see who'd heard him. "Please excuse my French."

"Excused. But those were the comments you used, all right."

"Well, there was, *is* a scam going on, and it's the insurance companies closing legitimate claims, running from their contractual obligations, and screw—, I mean cheating innocent people out of money needed to pay their medical bills. Trust me, even though I wasn't the treating doc on that case, I was thrilled to be asked to appear on the plaintiffs' behalf, and I'd do it again."

"I believe you would."

"Are you sorry you aired my remarks?"

"No."

There was a moment of awkward silence.

"So…you ready to make an appointment for your initial exam?" Ray sat down next to his six-year-old patient, Anuhea. Mileka quietly watched the child hand him a crayon drawing she'd made of herself on an adjusting table. Then she gave him a big hug and whispered into his ear.

"I love you, too, little one," he responded.

"That's me and you, Dr. Ray. You see? You're giving me my 'justment."

"I see that, sweetie. Did you really draw this picture?"

"Tha's right, I did."

"This is a beautiful work of art, and you're so talented, Anuhea. Should I hang it over my desk, or should we pin it over there on the bulletin board so everyone can see it?"

"Bulltin board."

"Bring it over to Auntie Lani, and she'll help you put it up there." They smiled at each other, and she ran off.

"Wow, what an honor. Do all of your patients present you with such wonderful artwork?"

"Not the adults." He grinned. "But some do bring freshly laid eggs or veggies from their gardens. A lot of the artwork out here comes from the kids. They like to do stuff like that for us. There's nothing better than taking care of the *keiki*, ya know what I mean?"

"Wait a minute. Do you mean to tell me your patients bring you food?"

"Our mission is to serve the community regardless of a person's ability to pay. These people...the *Kama'aina*...they have a great deal of pride and will pay for their care with whatever they have. And to refuse them would be an insult. It goes to show you how much they appreciate what we do for them, especially for the *keiki*."

Being a Hawaiian native, Mileka knew what he meant about pride. "Do you see a lot of kids?"

"We're mostly a family practice—you already know that. But we do take single people, too. So how about it?"

"I'd like to, but I'd have to drive the Pali from Honolulu for every appointment...round trip no less." She laughed.

"I thought a rich TV star like you lived in Kahala or Lanikai."

"Yeah, right. A five-million-dollar beachfront property? Don't I wish."

"I don't know how you put up with all the noise and traffic, and all those tourists in Honolulu, but big city life is your choice. Regardless, it's only fourteen or fifteen miles one way, so no big deal. Leigh makes that drive to the university several times a week."

"Yeah, but she's driving to her work."

"Look it, you make the short drive and get a massage, or maybe a little Reiki session before your spinal adjustment, and I'll even throw in some cranial therapy. You'll feel years younger by the time we're done with you."

"I'm only twenty-five—how much younger do I need to feel?"

"I guarantee you'll be thanking me. And when you're done with your appointment, you can stop off at Kimo's in Kailua, pick up a nice plate lunch of *ahi pokki* and *masubi*, and take it across the street to Kailua Beach Park, or stop at the Pali Lookout for a nice relaxing lunch before you get back to the station."

"Masubi? You of all people are recommending Spam and white rice?"

"It's got nori, too. Hey, I'd never eat it, but I figured a *kama'aina* like you...unless living in the big city's got you lookin' down your nose at the stuff." He chuckled.

"Having grown up in the shadows of Schofield Barracks sharing a bedroom with two brothers and a sister, I can assure you I'm no big-city snob," she said as she glanced over to the reception desk. "Look, Dr. Silver, it sounds great, but the drive...and then I spend my days chasing down stories all over the island."

"Which means that a couple times a week you're already in the neighborhood, Mileka."

"But I'm working, and I'm with a crew."

"Excuses. Look it, each of us here at the clinic have patients...or who I like to call practice members who come from Honolulu or drive down from Haleiwa. Heck, they fly in from Maui, Kauai, and the Big Island, too. I even have one gal who flies in every other month from California. She comes for the four-day healing and spiritual retreat that we do. But if twenty-eight miles round trip is that much for you—"

"Don't you think the other news stations would claim I was biased whenever I interviewed you for a health story?"

"Ah, so now we get down to the real reason. Do you have an MD?"

"Yes, doesn't everyone? I take that back...you probably don't."

"We have a naturopath here at the center." Ray laughed. "Have you ever interviewed your MD for a story?"

"Yes."

"And no one has ever accused you of being biased toward medicine, right?"

"Right...but this is different."

"No, it's a double standard. But if it bothers you that much, they wouldn't know you were a practice member here unless you bragged about the clinic during your newscasts."

"Oh, and you wouldn't brag that you're taking care of me?"

"Hang a picture of the two of us next to Anuhea's? Maybe if you were on the national news," he joked.

"Not funny." She frowned

It took Ray a few seconds until he remembered that she had recently been passed over for an opening with a major network because of the Colonial State story.

"I know the staff would like to tell everyone you were coming here. The networks may think you need more mainland exposure before they'll take you, but you're still a big celebrity to the locals." They laughed. "And we do have to abide by the privacy laws, and we take that stuff seriously. But if you gave us permission, I could post a picture of you on our website."

"And then my competition would accuse me—"

"So we'll keep it a secret." He stood and motioned for her to join him. "Lani, I'm taking Ms. Johnson back to my office. Call 911 if we're not done in—" Ray looked at the reporter.

"Fifteen or twenty minutes?"

"Lani, call for search and rescue if I'm not back in twenty minutes." He smiled at Mileka's eye rolling.

"By the way," she said to Ray while staring at Lani, "I really like your aquarium."

"Did I ever tell you about the first one?"

"Yes, it got destroyed three years ago during that FDA raid. I covered the story, remember?"

"Weren't you the reporter who said it was because I was interfering with people's medical care?"

"Stop it! You know quite well that I was the one who reported what really happened...that it was all a setup by that congresswoman."

"That was you? Hmmm, I thought it was Setsuko Yamata from channel—"

"Oh my god, Setsuko? Are you kidding me? That's not even funny, pretending to confuse me with her, Dr. Silver, especially after the way she roasted you like a pig at a luau."

"She did, didn't she?"

"Yes, she did. And if she were doing this interview today, she wouldn't mention that you might want to change out of your tai chi clothing. After all, it does look a little too new age for the audience."

"I'm not a suit kind of guy. My standard work attire is an aloha shirt and khakis. Why do you media types only give credibility to a shirt and tie?" he said just as Leilani turned the corner with a white shirt and tie.

"And he's in flip-flops." Leilani looked at him and shook her head. "I really do need to talk to your wife."

"You don't like what I wear? Since when?"

* * *

The built-in shelves filled with volumes of official-looking books in Ray's private office provided the perfect backdrop for conducting interviews. But more than anything else, there was one framed picture sitting in the middle of a display of diplomas and other certificates that impressed Mileka Johnson as well as her cameraman—that of Ray and Leigh Anne with President Jack Walker. And it wasn't one of those staged photos performed for big campaign contributors. This was a candid shot of them in the Oval Office having a private conversation while drinking Hawaiian beer. Its placement wasn't accidental, either, as it was in plain sight behind Ray when he was seated at his desk, his khakis and flip-flops safely out of view.

With the sound and lighting checks done, and Mileka comfortably sitting across from Ray, she was ready to launch into her interview when his phone buzzed. He stared at the number on the caller ID and hesitated. "Excuse me, this is important."

He forced a smile and then took the call before she could respond.

He listened mostly, only answering with one or two words before becoming frustrated enough to dismiss the caller. "I appreciate the update...Stel, not now...do you really...do you really want to do this now? Stel...look it, I'm going to have to call you back."

Mileka noticed an odd change in his facial expression. She stared at him a moment longer, not sure what, if anything, had just happened, but the smile was gone, the softness of his cheeks now tight as if he were clenching his teeth. And he seemed distant, his eyes somewhat cold.

"So—" She stopped briefly to study his face a few seconds longer, noticing he was staring right through her. "So," she began again but felt uncomfortable. "Are you OK?"

"Yes, I'm fine...can we do this now?" Ray's tone was no longer welcoming. "I'm sorry...I'm distracted, and I just remembered I've got other things that I need to be doing."

"But you said we would have time for this today."

"I know...and I always keep my word."

"Just so you know, I've already recorded the lead-in to this story, and I'll finish up my remarks during a live shot on the news this evening. So for the interview portion, I'm just going to ask you a few questions from this camera perspective, and if you don't mind, I'd like to get different angle shots for some of my other questions."

"Whatever." He waved his hand at her to get on with it.

"OK, then." She looked at her cameraman to begin recording and then turned back to Ray. "So as you know, the Department of Health has announced that there is a measles outbreak in the islands, and they've issued a warning that everyone should immediately bring their children in to get vaccinated. What do you—"

"Why?"

"What?"

"I asked you why?"

She signaled her cameraman to stop recording, but having also noticed the change in Ray's demeanor, he decided to keep the camera on. "What are you doing, Dr. Silver?"

"It's simple—I'm asking you a question."

"I know you're asking me a question, but I'm the one doing the interview, remember? So please let me do the asking," she politely said.

"Why?"

"What? Because I'm the reporter. What is this?"

"I know you're the reporter, but I meant why is the Department of Health issuing such a ridiculous warning? Seriously, why are they scaring people like that?"

"Whaddya mean by 'ridiculous'? It's because there's a measles outbreak."

"Yes, I heard. There are six confirmed cases."

"As of this morning, there were seven."

"OK, fine, seven confirmed cases out of, what, a population of about a million and a half people?"

"Seven cases among a million and a half is a lot, for your information, three of which are on Kauai. And don't forget about the tourists." She was concerned the exchange was going in a direction not anticipated. She glanced at her cameraman, who gave her a thumbs-up.

"Yes, plus all those tourists and still only seven cases. So the Department of Health wants all the tourists to get vaccinated as well? On Kauai and all the other islands, right?"

"No, just the residents...the children...the ones who didn't get their MMR shots. The ones responsible for the outbreak. And why are you being this way all of a sudden? Was it that phone call?"

"No."

"Then what? I can understand you wanting to be business-like for the interview, but now you're—"

"Wait a second! Do you know for sure that those seven confirmed cases occurred in unvaccinated children?"

"Are you telling me that immunized kids are the cause of this?"

"Are you telling me that vaccinated kids are immunized?"

"Are you telling me they're not?"

"Well, if they are 'immunized' and therefore protected, then why does the school board make the unvaccinated stay home during an outbreak? Assuming the 'unprotected' will actually come down with anything, are they really going to harm the vaxed kids? How about themselves? They are, after all, unvaccinated by choice, and the parents know and accept the risks."

"I suppose it's possible the kids who got their shots could still get it. That's why herd immunity is so important. But I would think that the unvaccinated can give it to one another."

"So assuming that anyone who didn't get their shots will definitely come down with measles, or any other infectious disease for that matter, are you saying they need to ban these kids from school because it screws with herd immunity?"

"It's a proactive step, yes. That's what's been done in the past, and it seems to have reduced the spread."

"Really? From my memory, they've never been quarantined to their homes. Those kids still went to the local malls, playgrounds, and restaurants, didn't they? From what I've read, herd immunity is an unproven theory."

"Well, then, I guess they're sent home to protect the teachers who aren't up to date with their shots."

"Think about what you just said, and if that's true, then consider that if vaccines really do immunize, then what is completely unknown is for how long. You see, unlike people like me who actually got measles when we were kids and acquired lifetime immunity, people getting those shots may be protected for several years or maybe even just several weeks. They really don't know, because as far as I can tell, no study has ever been done to determine that."

"That doesn't change the fact that they need to be protected from the noncompliant ones."

"So the teachers who haven't had their shots or their boosters, they're not screwing with herd immunity? Are you saying they shouldn't be held to the same standards because they don't pose a threat to anyone?" he asked in a sarcastic tone. "And what about people from my generation? We've only had three or four vaccinations, and that was decades ago. Are health officials saying we're not compromising the herd?"

"OK, I never thought about it like that."

"Does anybody?

"You bring up a good point…but getting back to the current situation, the health department…they issued a press release—" She flipped through the pages of her notepad.

"And people react out of fear, without any critical thought and without ever asking any questions. When it comes to the news media, you guys just repeat what you've been spoon-fed. Then you guys come around to people like me looking to stir up trouble by asking all sorts of questions based upon nothing more than assumptions."

"Not true."

"You assume they're telling you the truth, and you assume alternative health-care providers don't know anything."

"Again, not true."

"And you demand that we're the ones who provide the evidence."

"Yeah, OK, that part's true."

"But even when we provide it, you guys dismiss it out of hand and then go on the offensive, attacking and disparaging the messenger."

"That's not, I've never—"

"And more importantly"—he leaned forward as his voice grew slightly louder—"without ever seeing or asking for any evidence from the medical community, you automatically assume those shots are safe and effective. You guys are always quick to report that it's the unvaxed who are responsible for an outbreak, and you never doubt or question the source of that information!"

"That's not fair, Dr. Silver," she shot back. "That's not fair at all. And I can't believe you're on the attack and you're aiming it at me. Fifteen minutes ago in your waiting room, you were this warm and fuzzy loving person I thought I knew, and now you're...excuse me, but what bug crawled up your butt all of a sudden?" She was practically out of her chair, her cameraman proud of her counterattack.

He *had* been on the offensive, and Ray knew she was right to try to put him in his place. Something did crawl up his butt, and it was this very topic. He saw the confusion and the look of betrayal in Mileka's eyes, and he felt bad. She was his ally, his media connection, his friend, and he'd just walked all over her. His rant about this subject, about reporters like Setsuko Yamata, and about the media in general had been something he had wanted to get off his chest for quite some time. Mileka Johnson just happened to have been a convenient target. He felt bad, and he wasted no time in telling her so—continuing their conversation in a softer, friendlier tone only after she assured him that he was forgiven.

"Every time I see little Anuhea, I think of her brother Keoki...and then I think of Leigh's first daughter, Mahina. Anuhea had a younger brother who died when he was just five months old, a month after his second round of shots. It wasn't as if it was unexpected, either. The pediatrician should have known. That's what gets me mad and—"

"Why, what happened?"

"He was two months old when he received six shots at once, just like the CDC schedule says. Within hours, the little guy started screaming. He had a sustained high fever and a rash that covered his entire body, and then his eyes rolled back into his head and the seizures started. They lasted for a few weeks. The parents were told it was because of an unrelated infection. A 'coincidence' the doctor said. Can you believe that? A coincidence? Then at four months he received five more vaccines, and it happened again...almost immediately. This time there was cerebral swelling and hemorrhaging from the outset. After several days of convulsions, the baby went into a coma and every system in his little body began to shut down. He was on life support until all brain activity ceased a few weeks later."

"That's...that's so—"

"Tragic?"

"Yes."

"Yes, it is…not just because of what happened, but also because it could have been avoided. It's tragic because this happens to other children as well, and it's always a 'coincidence.' I'll bet the doctor wouldn't have been so careless if he wasn't protected by the Vaccine Injury Act. And on top of all that, the hospital tried to insinuate the cerebral hemorrhaging was due to shaken baby syndrome. They hadn't even buried their infant son, and the hospital puts the parents through hell. And as if that wasn't enough, then they tried to take Anuhea away from them, those bastards!"

"Were they ever charged?"

"The parents? No. I'm surprised you didn't hear about this."

"I remember a little, but I think I was preoccupied with your clinic being raided."

"You're right—it was about the same time. Anyway, after they received a hospital bill for $150,000, they threatened a multimillion dollar lawsuit against the medical center, and the administration eventually backed down. But they still issued a death certificate that stated: 'Death due to natural causes.' Can you believe that?"

"And this Vaccine Injury—"

"The National Childhood Vaccine Injury Act. A federal law passed in 1986 after strong lobbying by the pharmaceutical industry. No vaccine maker or doctor can be held liable for a vaccine-related injury. If they could, you can bet little Keoki would've never received that second round."

Mileka sat quietly writing for a few moments. "And your daughter…what happened to her?"

"Leigh's daughter, from before we met. Mahina died after she came down with Kawasaki disease, and it had been misdiagnosed as an ordinary viral infection."

"But not vaccine related."

"That's the big unknown. There's nothing about it in the literature, I admit that. And as far as I know, there's no research being done to see if there's a causal relationship. But she did develop the disease about two weeks after she had a series of shots."

"I hate to use this word now, but could it have been a coincidence?"

"Maybe. But we'll never know. You see, they never even considered it because of the ten-day rule."

"The ten-day rule?"

"Yeah. Some jackass in the federal government somehow decided that if there were no adverse reactions within ten days of a shot, then any negative health event couldn't be considered vaccine related."

"And that isn't based on the science?"

"Are you kidding me? It's based on limiting the government's liability. If a pack-a-day smoker quits the habit after twenty-five years and then two weeks or even two years later is diagnosed with lung cancer, is it unrelated?"

She didn't answer.

"Mahina's case doesn't stop me from wondering, and although she never says anything, I know it doesn't stop Leigh from carrying a burden like so many other parents who put their faith and trust into a profession that holds itself out there as the supreme authority on health care. And because of that, people simply hand their kids over for a medical procedure without being told all the facts, without knowing any of the risks and...and because they're pressured by societal guilt into doing so. And as you can see, it pisses me off to no end. So once again please know that I'm sincerely sorry I took it out on you, I really am. I was out of line."

"I told you you're forgiven. Please, let's forget about it and move on, OK?"

"Sure, but if I can urge you to do one thing, it would be to talk to the people at the Department of Health."

"They've issued their press release. What else are they going to tell us?"

"Did you or any other reporter interview anyone down there?"

"But they—"

"Did you request any records?"

"No."

"Please, go do an interview. Ask if the seven cases were among the vaccinated, and if they tell you they weren't, then ask to see the proof. Just don't take their word for it."

"I don't know—"

"Why not? Because they're the government and they can be trusted? Considering the last three measles outbreaks—the one in California several years ago, the one in Saint Louis, and the one on the East Coast somewhere—even though the CDC and NIH sent out dozens of press releases putting blame on vaccine refusers, those outbreaks were among kids who had been fully vaccinated. Look it up; it's in the public record. The health department here may be denying it now, but we'll see that these seven cases, like the other outbreaks, started among those who had gotten their shots. It may take a few months, but the truth will eventually be revealed, just like in the other outbreaks."

"And where will this truth be revealed—in the alternative health media?"

"Yes, because the mainstream lives or dies by how many ad dollars they get from the drug makers, so they'll never bite the hand that feeds. Nonetheless, the CDC did acknowledge the facts in those past cases, and they'll eventually acknowledge the real facts in this one. They may not come out and say it publicly, but it'll be in the record."

Mileka quickly turned to her cameraman. "Are you getting this?"

He nodded. "Every word."

"You don't believe me, Mileka, do you?"

"I hear what you're saying, I do. But it goes against everything we've ever been told."

Ray stood and moved about the office to stretch his legs, the camera now following his every step. He motioned for them to follow him out to the lanai.

"Years ago when I was a young kid, pregnant moms were told that Thalidomide and Diethylstilbestrol were safe medications

to take during pregnancy, medical doctors were still appearing in cigarette ads telling us how smoking improved lung
function...hell, just recently in Congress tobacco execs were
testifying there was no proof smoking caused cancer. The government used to tell us that DDT sprayed on our food was safe.
That might have been a long time ago, but you know as well
as I do that over the years we've seen many examples where
the public has been misled or just plain lied to. In recent years
it's been nonsteroidal anti-inflammatory medications that
we were told are safe, and look how many people died from
those drugs before the FDA removed some of the prescription-
strength versions from the market. Please go ask the people
down at the DoH, and like I said, ask them to show you the
hard data. With only seven cases, it shouldn't be difficult for
them to comply with your request. You have a legal right to see
that information."

"Trust me, I know what my rights are. But if what you're
saying is true, then why wouldn't they volunteer the information in the first place?"

"That's a good question. I could easily tell you why I think
they withhold it from the public, but you or someone else will
accuse me of being one of those conspiracy nuts. Look it, I'm
not claiming there's a second shooter on the grassy knoll, OK?"

"Actually, that's exactly what you're doing."

"If that's the way it appears, then perhaps it's because I
refuse to blindly accept the growing amount of autism cases,
crib deaths, and childhood cancers as mere coincidence. Look
at the stats on autoimmune diseases over past twenty or so
years. The numbers are skyrocketing. You wanna tell me that's
coincidence?"

"But why would anyone continue to advocate a policy that
was contributing to something like this? It just doesn't make
any sense."

"Greed."

"Seriously? Greed?"

"Yes. Just look at all the money industry lobbyists spend on
Congress. I wouldn't be surprised if they're into local politics as

well. I truly believe they fail to disclose all the facts because of a conflict of interest...financial interest. But if you really want to know why they don't volunteer any information, then you should be asking them, not me. And if they won't tell you or give you any records, then as far as I'm concerned they really do have something to hide. Whether or not you want to investigate, that's completely up to you, but in either case I'd still go over to Kauai and interview the parents of the kids who came down with measles—they'll tell you."

"So are you saying vaccines don't work at all?"

"That's another good question, and that's data I don't have...not that I haven't searched for it, I have. But whether or not they work is not for me to prove or disprove. I'm just looking at the available facts and calling them to your attention."

"But if you're going to make an accusation, you should at least be able to back it up, and you can't back up any of this, can you?"

"I agree on that point, but it's not like I have an industry insider in my back pocket. And do you see what I mean about a double standard?"

"I fail to see how asking for proof is a double standard."

"If they're claiming vaccines work, if they're going to claim that they're safe, shouldn't they be asked for proof?"

"So I ask you again, are you saying vaccines don't work?"

"All I'm saying is that in past 'epidemic' scares, the outbreaks began in vaccinated populations."

"Every time?"

"Call the CDC if you don't believe me. They just don't make the stats available unless requested under the Freedom of Information Act. If you want to know if vaccines work then ask them to show you the proof. Ask the drug companies to show you the research studies. Better yet, ask the FDA to show you the independent research...if there is any."

"Are you saying there isn't?"

"Two years ago, there was a congressional hearing on the possibility of a link between autism and vaccines. Now talk about spoon-feeding. The committee members threw softball questions to the officials from the CDC, and they sat before that committee and testified that without a doubt the vaccines were safe and effective, and that there was no link whatsoever to the increasing rates of autism."

"So how does a hearing on an autism link prove your point on effectiveness?"

"It doesn't. But what it does prove is that bought-and-paid-for members of Congress, like the news media, give government agencies like the CDC or the FDA a free pass on just their word. They've become pretty autonomous if you ask me. In that autism hearing, the CDC didn't present one study, not even one reference that backed up any of their claims. Not one. They freely attacked and discredited any researcher who claimed otherwise but still offered no evidence to back up any of their claims. The director, a former drug company executive, sat before the committee and lied with a straight face. He knew there was no proof to back him up, and he knew that no congressional representative was going to ask for any. Wait! I do have something here."

Ray zipped back into his office and looked through a stack of unorganized papers in his bookcase, finally pulling one. "It's only one paper, but here's a study by the medical school at Empire State University in New York. It was on a 2005 mumps outbreak and was published last year in the *National Journal of Infectious Diseases*. I'm quoting now: 'Vaccine failure accounted for a sustained mumps outbreak in a highly vaccinated population.'" He paused, then repeated it again for effect.

She took the paper from him and briefly scanned it before continuing. "Can I have this?"

"Lani will make a copy for you."

"Are you against all vaccines?"

"If they don't work, or even if there's limited effectiveness, is it worth injecting all those toxins into a little body? Heck, just the logic alone is flawed. First they tell you that a newborn's natural defenses aren't developed enough to protect against infection, which is what breast milk is for, by the way. Then they tell you that overloading an infant's immune system with all these shots is OK because it can easily handle being injected with all that stuff. Seriously, does that make any sense to you?"

"Toxins? You mean viruses?"

"Viruses? Have you ever looked at a product insert that comes with those vials? Have you ever looked at the list of dangerous chemicals in those things, or the possible, I mean *the very real* side effects caused by those substances?"

"No, I haven't."

"No one has. Some people are more concerned about food labels than they are about what's being injected into their kids. We're talking about formaldehyde, aluminum, acetone, polysorbate 80, MSG, and aborted human fetal cells for heaven's sake. Hell, the hep B vaccines and even flu shots still contain mercury."

"And yet they're all approved by the FDA."

"Maybe so, but being approved doesn't mean it's safe. Even approved food additives have been found to cause cancer. And before you jump on that, I have two points to make about FDA approvals. One, when an approved food additive such as polysorbate 80 has been injected directly into the blood of test animals, it has caused serious disruptions to normal cellular physiology. It's caused blood clots, strokes, heart attacks. It's even been used as a spermicide."

"You've got a copy of that study?"

"No, but you can get it online. That's where I read it."

"And in humans?"

"As far as I know they haven't studied it, and if they did, they're keeping the results quiet."

"Now you're sounding conspiratorial, Dr. Silver."

"I'm not making accusations; I'm just stating what I know."

"Then I suppose there are studies done on MSG?"

"There've been a number of them, actually. Used as intended, as a food additive, it's a known neurotoxin, meaning it's toxic…poisonous to the nervous system."

"You're giving me a lot to investigate."

"Good."

"And your second point?" She sighed.

"Each year they remove dozens of drugs because of serious life-threatening side effects caused by those drugs, some of which have been linked to hundreds if not thousands of deaths, and that's when used as directed...like the anti-inflammatories I've already mentioned. Those are drugs they had to 'approve' in the first place, which to me begs the question of competency or, once again, conflict of interest...which is why I have absolutely no trust in that agency."

"So that's why you tell your patients to refuse vaccines, because of food additives and recalls?"

"Believe it or not, I've never told my patients to refuse vaccines. Don't get me wrong, I would certainly love to, and not because of food additives or recalls. But I'm not stupid. If I were to tell them that, or if we were to make health claims on any of the natural methods we use here, or if any natural healer here had a cure for cancer, then the inquisition begins. It could cost me my license, and the last thing I need is another jack-booted raid like the one the FDA did on me three years ago. What I do—what all of us here at the health center do—is present the facts."

"Some will say that you're presenting circumstantial evidence."

"We present the facts as we know them so we can educate people about the very real dangers, and that's as far as we go with this subject. We provide resources that people can use to gain further knowledge, and it's then up to them to make a choice...an informed choice. And that, Ms. Johnson, is an option that is never given to them by the mainstream."

"So I take it your children are not vaccinated?"

Ray hesitated. "I've never taken any of my kids to be vaccinated. Not my two adult children or my three little ones. And keep in mind that my two older kids never missed a day of school due to illness. Not one cold, not one viral infection, and not so much as an earache."

"Then you obviously don't think you've endangered them."

"Right now there are forty-nine doses of fourteen different vaccines for kids by the time they're six years old. That's forty-nine doses of formaldehyde, aluminum, acetone, and a number of other toxic chemicals that are injected directly into these little kids. Don't you think that's dangerous?"

"I hear what you're saying, but I'm sorry, I'm still not totally convinced. I have to believe that if vaccines weren't safe—"

"If they weren't safe, then the government wouldn't allow them?"

"Yes."

Ray sat and leaned back into his chair, shook his head, and stared at the ceiling for a brief moment. "I feel like we're on a hamster wheel. OK, then, let's suppose industry lobbyists weren't throwing cash and gifts around like every day is Christmas on Capitol Hill, as well as in every state legislature. Let's ignore the track record of corruption that our government has. Let's not even consider the fact that executives and attorneys for the drug companies are hired by the FDA and the CDC to write and administer official health policy. Do you remember I mentioned the National Vaccine Injury Act?"

"Yes, you said drug makers and physicians are held harmless in cases of vaccine injury."

"But it's more than that. Back in the eighties, insurance companies refused to indemnify the drug makers against injury claims due to vaccines. They're still insured for all their other products, and they get taken to court for all sorts of drug-related injuries. There isn't a day that goes by that you don't see some law firm advertising on television about a class-action suit for some kind of bad drug...and the claims are legit, too. So why no private insurance coverage for vaccines? If the science is solid and these things are safe, then why'd they go running to Congress to protect them for that one sector of their business?"

They were interrupted with a hard knock on the office door, and Lani wheeled herself into the room. "Consider me search and rescue. It's been way more than twenty minutes, and you have other obligations on your schedule, doctor."

"Thanks," he said, noticing Mileka and his receptionist staring at each other. "Hey, Lani, did you know that Ms. Johnson grew up near Schofield Barracks, too?"

"No," she said, still looking at the reporter. "I had no idea."

"I'm just mentioning it because you two are close in age and I thought maybe you guys might have run in to each other on the playground or something."

"There were lots of army families that came and went quite frequently," she said as she turned to wheel herself away.

"I'll wrap this up, Lani. Thanks. I'm sorry, Mileka, but I really need to end this. I've got a phone call to return and patients to see."

"Did you know that there's a school district meeting in Honolulu tonight and this topic is on the agenda?"

"Yes, I know. They want the state legislature to do away with personal and religious exemptions. Typical knee-jerk reaction, if you ask me, and a clear violation of civil rights."

"I trust you'll be there to voice your concerns?"

"You'd like that, wouldn't you?"

"So is that a yes?"

"It was already on my calendar. It's one of the reasons why I got so worked up when you began the interview."

"And it had nothing to do with that phone call?"

"That's another issue. But going to talk before the school board—"

"Why? You're an old pro at this."

"It's human nature to take comfort in a belief that allows you to be accepted, to be part of the group. A herd mentality, if you will. When that belief is challenged, then it's easier to attack the challenger than to examine the validity of what the herd holds to be true. That's what I'll face tonight when I challenge the school district. I trust you'll be there to cover it?"

"You can bet on it." Mileka started for the door, hesitating just a second. "You know, I'll give you this much: you make a good case, you bring up a lot of good points, and you raise a lot of good questions. But one could easily dismiss all your arguments as coincidence or even overreach. And without proof that these things are dangerous, people will just look at you as a fearmonger."

"Now isn't that ironic?"

"How so?"

"That's exactly how they peddle the flu shot every year, through fear. Like I said earlier, there's a double standard and a human desire for safety in numbers...even if it's psychological."

"One last thing...you hesitated. When I asked if your children were vaccinated, you hesitated before answering."

"I'm concerned about an irrational reaction by some of the parents at the preschool I send my three little ones to."

"I understand. But aren't both of your older children former marines? Or was it the navy?"

"Navy, that's right."

"And if I'm not mistaken, the military vaccinates everyone, yes?"

"It's standard operating procedure. Shut up, line up, and then get stuck like a pin cushion."

"So they were."

"So it seems."

* * *

The lanai at the back of the clinic was a private little paradise unto itself. It was quiet and had a great view of the valley and Kailua Bay. Ray loved it and often went there for lunch breaks or short meditation sessions during his workday because he could be all alone. He seldom spent time there after hours unless he had a planned evening mastermind session with the rest of his staff. Most days, by the time his last scheduled patient was off the table and being checked out at the reception desk, Ray was in his Wrangler sailing down the Kamehameha highway to get home to Leigh Anne and his little girls.

Tonight was different, though. After the abbreviated presentation he gave at the school district meeting, he returned to the office and his private little paradise for some time to decompress, to think, to analyze, and to cool down. It wasn't

47

the back and forth that went on between him and some of the board members that bothered him, nor was it the way he was abruptly cut off midway through his prepared remarks. He already knew that regardless of the few published papers he offered up in an attempt to validate his argument, no matter how many peer-reviewed studies or statistics he could have quoted proving his points, the members of the school board would remain steadfast in pushing forward their agenda. He knew from the outset he wasn't going to suddenly bring those people to the promised land—especially when one board member, a former pediatric nurse, proclaimed: "The science on vaccination is settled, and any suggestion to the contrary is irresponsible. I find it insulting to me, this board, and to the concerned parents in the audience tonight that the owner of an alternative clinic is quoting from papers written by some obviously disgruntled and no doubt discredited scientists." It was quite theatrical on her part when she stood to proclaim how proud she was that she'd personally vaccinated tens of thousands of babies during her career.

Although Ray had known about her position from the outset, he never suspected opposition to this degree. *"She's clearly perfected her political skills,"* he thought. And then it was Josh Kimmel's turn, Channel Two's attack-dog health reporter. He went off on a personal attack—not just of Ray, but of the natural healing arts altogether. Kimmel began ranting how parents should be imprisoned for not vaccinating their children. The post-meeting interview was contentious for sure, and he knew his responses to some of Kimmel's outrageous remarks would be edited for the eleven o'clock newscast. It was all par for the course as far as he was concerned. He could deal with the fallout. What bothered Ray now as he sat alone was what Mileka Johnson had said at the end of their meeting earlier that afternoon:

> *"One last thing, you hesitated. When I asked if your children were vaccinated, you hesitated before answering. Both of your older children are former marines? Or was it the navy?"*
>
> *"Navy, that's right."*

"And if I'm not mistaken, the military vaccinates every-one, yes?"

"It's standard operating procedure. Shut up, line up, and then get stuck like a pin cushion."

"So they were."

"So it seems."

He put his feet up on to the cushion of the wicker ottoman and looked out at the twinkling lights of Kailua in the valley below while savoring each sip of his second ice-cold Pipeline Porter. Surrounded by an array of anthurium, white birds of paradise, orchids, and a few varieties of miniature palm plants, it only took a few minutes of listening to the wind chimes dancing in the gentle breezes coming off the bay to help quiet his mind. Without looking behind him, he guessed it was Leilani who had come outside to chase him home:

"I already called Leigh, and she knows I'm here chillin' for a bit. And by the way, what are you still doing here? Shouldn't you be home getting crazy with your new boyfr—"

"I actually called your house, and your wife told me I'd find you here."

Ray laughed at the sound of Mileka's voice, impressed but not surprised she'd sought him out. "I hope you won't repeat that to Leilani and that your being here is an informal visit."

"Informal?"

"Off the record...because my brain is toast, and I don't want to be held responsible for anything I say right now."

"Like when you told that school board member she should stick to drinking the Kool-Aid and stay away from the formaldehyde?"

"I didn't mind that she wasn't going to listen to anything I had to say, but the fact that she kept cutting me off midsentence and kept referring to my views as being on the fringe or better still that I was militant in my thinking...I wasn't going to let her get away without at least one little bitch slap."

"You should've stopped after you asked her if she bought her antidepressants in bulk."

"She deserved it…and I bet she does. Maybe if she got laid once in a while she wouldn't be such a frustrated old prune." Ray winked. "Are we off the record?"

"Let me see if I got this quote correct: 'Maybe if she got laid once in a while—'"

"Seriously?"

"We're off the record, and uh…I also won't say anything to Leilani."

"Then help yourself to a beer and pull up a chair."

"Don't mind if I do. Got any Castaway in that cooler?"

"Pipeline and Longboard."

"Longboard's fine." She dug into the ice until she found one and sat opposite Ray. He tossed a bottle opener to her. "It got a little heated tonight, didn't it?"

"During the meeting or afterward with Josh Kimmel?"

"Definitely afterward."

"I guess when he realized that my office manager wasn't around to run interference, he decided to go on a kill mission."

"Yes, he did. And you should've known he was going to. Or perhaps you did know."

"I wasn't going there unprepared, that's for sure."

"You had a pretty strong counteroffensive."

"I'll give you some of the credit for that."

"Ah, yes, our interview this afternoon."

"Yeah…the interview…but I really thought I'd get double-teamed from him and our friend Setsuko. She actually surprised me with the softballs she was throwing."

"Don't let that soft touch and her short skirt fool you. She's nonconfrontational to your face, but she'll do her dirty work during her newscast. Now, Kimmel, he's the reporter you tossed from your office last year."

"Yeah, Leilani won't let him come anywhere near the place."

"Then too bad you didn't bring her along tonight."

"She would've kicked his little ass. That would've been fun to see."

"He's been anti alternative health care his entire career, and he'll never let facts or common sense get in the way of a good hatchet job."

"So you know about him, huh?"

"I checked him out when he got hired by Channel Two a few years ago. He's a journeyman. Lands at a small-market station that's typically looking for the next Geraldo to get the ratings up. After he's crucified enough people and the public gets wise to his angle, the complaints go up, the ratings begin to go down, and he's let go, eventually winding up—"

"Here to make his mark against me."

"Don't take it personally. You're a convenient target, and he's just doing his master's bidding."

"Oh?"

"Rumor has it he started his career working in public relations for the pharmaceutical lobby and he's keeping that door open just in case his TV gigs run dry. Since your clinic has become the most popular on the island and you are getting the airtime, you're definitely in his sights. He's a—"

"Jerk! A real asshole if you ask me."

"I was going to say opportunist. If you want my advice, I'd ignore him. He's only baiting you to get you to react. And when you do, he wins. Next time just walk away from him."

"I might just bust his—"

"And when you do, he'll get it all on camera. He'll edit it, too. He'll make you look like one of those violent cultists waiting for the mother ship to arrive."

"Well, I can just imagine what I'm going to look like on his newscast tonight, which begs the question—"

"Why am I here and not at the station?"

"Yeah."

"I already recorded my piece on the meeting tonight. It's short, sweet, and to the point. I cover the meeting and some of the comments posed by concerned parents. And we filmed you getting verbally attacked by Kimmel, along with some of your 'unedited' remarks."

"Seriously?"

"Seriously. But the station won't air that portion of it, which is why I'll have the whole thing posted on my personal blog. I'll get you a DVD of it so you can make as many copies as you want. Play it in your office, give it away to your patients, or use it as material to get back at Josh Kimmel. It's important that people get to see what really went on. Dr. Silver, I hate that guy just as much as you do. Exposing him and his agenda is also good for ratings...my ratings."

"Thanks. I guess I owe you another beer."

"I'm more than happy to take you up on that." She raised her bottle in a toast.

"There's something I just don't get about you. With the heavy influence that big pharma money has over what you news people report, why are you bucking the mainstream when it could totally end your career? Your station is as dependent on that ad money as your competitors are."

"I'm not as naïve as I look. My station wouldn't air half of what I could put together on this."

"So then why?"

"I've been thinking about doing an indie film...a documentary."

"I could see it playing at Park City. What you're doing is risky, but I give you a gold star for thinking big."

"You might want to take it back after what I'm going to say now...you're going to lose." She stopped when Ray shifted his gaze in her direction. He waited while she took a drink. "Don't take this the wrong way, but you are going to lose big. You're fighting a war, Dr. Silver. You're fighting a war against the insurance companies, against the drug makers, and against politicians who rely on corporate money, and you're fighting a war against bureaucrats who are looking to land a private sector job once they retire from government."

"I know who I'm going up against."

"They've got a bigger arsenal than you."

"I know that, too. Look it, they may be big, but so was Goliath. I'm speaking out against a system that is filled with corruption, cover-ups, and hypocrisy...against fraud...against junk science. I'm speaking out against the cavalier attitudes they have toward people whose children have been injured. People deserve the truth, and they deserve a product that has actually been proven to be safe."

"Maybe so, but you're jousting at windmills. You're one little person kicking the shins of big giants. No disrespect intended, but right now you're just an annoyance, and if you keep kicking they just might become angry enough to step on you. You're a nice guy, doc, and you mean well—I get that. But why not leave it alone? Why not play it safe and tend to your practice without calling all this attention to yourself?"

"If I did, you wouldn't be able to make your indie film."

"I'm serious."

"How does that song go? Don't worry be happy? Bobby McFerrin, right? I often ask myself why I can't just let it all go. Leigh's been asking me that, too…a lot lately. It would be easier to put in my nine-to-five and not care. I guess I do it because there aren't too many lemmings who survive the fall and that bothers me…actually, it pisses me off to no end. I'm speaking out, I'm speaking up, and each person who hears the message and doesn't jump with the others…that's one more victory. One of the founding fathers of my profession, Bartlett Joshua Palmer, once said, 'It is better to light one candle than to curse the darkness.' I'm lighting one candle, and then another one after that, and so on, and I'm doing it because of…because it's become personal."

"In what way?"

Ray brought the bottle of Pipeline back to his lips, stared out at the glittering lights in the valley below, and debated answering her.

3

Wahiawa, Hawaii

Between listening to her voice mails, returning phone calls, and watching children chase one another in the playground, Mileka continued to review her notes about her conversation with Ray while his words were still fresh. She also thought about the dirty looks Lani Blacque had been giving her, not quite sure if they were expressions of protection for her boss or distain for her. As much as she kept telling herself the reason for spending the past thirty minutes in her car was to catch up on her work, she knew the temptation to relive childhood memories required the sights and sounds of her youth. She looked out across the playing field as much as she read the words in her notebook. A child's shout caught her attention, and she turned in time to see a soccer ball hit the side of her new convertible. Mileka jumped out of the car to inspect her passenger door, worried she'd acquired her first dent. "You kids should be more careful," she blurted out while assessing the damage.

"I'm sorry, lady." A young girl not more than ten held out her arms in an attempt to retrieve her property. "It was an accident, honest."

"This is a brand-new...I just picked it up this morn—" She looked at the frightened face. "I mean, what if my car wasn't parked here? Your ball would have gone into the street and you would have chased after it. It's pretty dangerous out there, ya know?"

"I wouldn't have chased after it. I know better. I'm sorry about your car." They both looked at the small scuff mark, Mileka running her index finger over it.

"It's not that bad. I bet I'll be able to rub it out." She smiled at the little girl, who motioned with her hands for the ball when her friends began yelling:

"Come on, Keilani!" they called out. "We wanna play!"

Her eyes pleading for clemency, the little girl held out her hands. Mileka smiled and returned the ball, and the girl ran off, leaving her to brush her fingers over the scuff mark as she drifted back to her own childhood:

"Come on, Leilani, go get the ball."

"Why should I get it? You kicked it last, Leka."

"Yeah, but it hit off your leg and bounced into the street. You were the last one to touch it, so you have to get it."

"I'm not allowed to go into the street by myself, and you know that."

"Who's gonna tell? Not me, OK? So go get the ball because those are the rules."

"Well, I think that rule stinks. It wouldn't have bounced off my leg if you didn't kick it so hard. And it hurt, too!"

"If you can't take playing with the big kids, then maybe you shouldn't play with us at all."

"You're mean to me. All you big kids are mean to me."

"If we were mean to you, we wouldn't let you play with us."

"You guys let me play with you because I promised to pay you a dollar."

"Just get the ball, Leilani, and stop being a baby."

"Get the ball, Keilani!" Mileka heard the kids yell and turned to catch the errant soccer ball just in time. Once more little Keilani came running.

"I'm sorry again, lady. It wasn't my fault."

"I'm worried that someone is going to put a real dent into my car."

"We'll try harder to keep it away, OK?"

"I'll tell you what. I'm going to be here for a little while. So if you can keep the ball in the playground until I leave, I'll give you a dollar, OK?"

"What about my friends? There are six of us, ya know?"

Before she could answer, Lani Blacque's minivan passed them and turned into the driveway of the Palms of Paradise apartment complex. Despite the name, the cookie-cutter flats were far from a paradise, but they were decent and an affordable place to live for the civilian employees working at nearby Schofield Barracks Army Base. The Palms were relatively new, and compared to a lot of the older homes in the town of Wahiawa, they were much nicer and certainly a far cry from the house Mileka had lived in as a child. *"All things being equal, I guess they could be considered a paradise,"* she thought. She turned her attention back to the little girl. "One dollar, take it or leave it."

"I'll take it." She held out her hand.

"OK, I'll pay you when I get back and after I inspect my car. If there are no more marks on it, then the dollar's yours." Mileka laughed and kicked the ball back into the playground.

Guessing it would take Lani a few minutes to work the motorized side-door lift gate, Mileka took her time crossing the street. She smiled at the memory of having played on the same field until she saw the scuff mark down the length of her new shoes. *"Damn it!"* The resiliency of her pumps wasn't the only thing she'd underestimated. Lani had been performing her mechanical extraction for quite some time and had long mastered the controls as well as maneuvering her wheelchair within the small confines of the custom-made van. By the time Mileka made it up the driveway, Ray's receptionist was already waiting for her.

"Stalking me?"

"Need a hand?" Mileka asked, ignoring Lani's question.

"Do I look disabled to you?"

"I was just being courteous. Why the attitude?"

Lani let her chair roll a little closer and looked up at Mileka. "Let's see...you show up at our office yesterday without an appointment, you practically dared Doc Ray to go to that school board meeting last night, you got a great interview for the evening news, and now you're here to...wait, let me guess...a social visit, right?"

"You've only worked at Ray Silver's office a few months and—"

"Six months tomorrow."

"Excuse me. You've worked there six months and it's 'our' office? And how do you know that I baited him to go to that meeting? And who says I can't pay a social visit to my sister?"

"I heard the tail end of your conversation yesterday. In fact, it was so interesting that I waited outside his office door a few extra minutes before coming in. And since when do you come back to the hood, girlfriend? If I remember correctly, you couldn't wait to get out of this little army town."

"What I don't understand is that with so many beautiful places on this island, why did you choose to come back here? I know receptionists don't make a lot of money, but with your military disability check, I would think you'd have enough to rent a place closer to your job. And by the way, how exactly did you get that job?"

"I applied for the position after I saw the interview you did with Doc Ray...the one after that big injury trial."

"But why? Of all the health-care offices on the island, why Ray Silver's place?"

"Because I thought by working there I could get treatment on a regular basis and hopefully, finally get some real help. And for your information, believe it or not, I am starting to get a little feeling back in my feet. It's not much, but it's encouraging. But even if I don't regain my ability to walk, I really like working there. He's a great guy, Leilani Onakea is a wonderful office manager, and the practice members are some of the most wonderful people I've ever met. So I just might move closer to the office, but only because the commute is getting kind of old."

"You might move? Ha! I don't think so. I think you're too attached to this place, and I know why."

"You think it's because dad was a career soldier and I have fond memories of living on the base, coming into town on weekends, and all that mushy sentimental stuff?"

"Exactly."

"Exactly wrong. Well, maybe not exactly wrong. But not totally right, either."

"Just like your accusation that I'm not here for a social visit."

"Leka, you've never done anything social with me, and you know it. You're here for information. Well, let me save you some time. I don't know anything. I'm just a receptionist, I'm happy to be just his receptionist, and I don't want him knowing you're my sister because I don't want to lose this job."

"For your information, Ray Silver likes me and he trusts me."

"He trusts you?"

"Yes, he does, because I tell the truth about him. If he or your office manager knew we were related, I think it would be a bonus for you."

"First off, I don't need your help. I've been managing quite well all by myself. Second, I think you're using him, and when he finds out, which won't be because of me, he'll be very pissed off at you."

"Using him? How can you say such a thing?"

"You showed up for that interview yesterday morning in order to get him to go to that school board meeting. You did bait him, and you know you did, so don't deny it. And don't forget that I could always tell when you're hiding your intentions. You do that funny little flutter with your left eyelid." Mileka reflexively brought her hand up to her eye. "You wanted him to go so you could get a great story. And because he feels you're his ally, he'll always be willing to talk to you at length. And I might add that I think what you are doing is dangerous. You're pushing the boundary being his advocate and airing his full remarks."

"How so?"

"Geez, Leka, it doesn't take a rocket scientist to see the drug bias on the other news stations. You giving favorable coverage to the natural health side of things is going to eventually get you fired."

"First of all, I'm not planning on keeping that gig long term."

"What, are you nuts? That's all you ever talked about when we were growing up. You used to do those pretend newscasts, where you were this big famous news anchor and all that. What's changed?"

"The potential to get in front of a wider audience through film making. Documentaries."

"Documentaries?"

"Exactly. Documentaries that expose fraud, corruption, hypocrisy. And I'm starting off big. I'm using this job to gain access to your boss and his crusade against the drug companies."

"So I was right—you are using him! Well, don't you dare! Don't drag him into your dreams of an Oscar. I don't want him getting hurt, and I certainly don't want to see his clinic get destroyed in another FDA raid."

"Are you kidding me? He's doing this all on his own. He's doing this whether I'm involved or not. I just want to get him on film to explain why. And don't be fooled: there are plenty of health-care providers out there who have a ton of information, and they're dying to share it...literally. I've already interviewed a local pediatrician who won't even vaccinate his own kids let alone his patients. Whaddya think about that?"

"I know who you're talking about. He's one of two that Doc Ray has referred patients to. He's a good guy. He does his homework and refuses to blindly follow what the drug reps are always telling those guys to push. But he's been threatened. His clinic's been targeted."

"Ya see? This is the kind of stuff I'm looking for."

"Back up a sec...whaddya mean when you say 'they're literally dying to share'?"

"Over the past year, there have been several outspoken alternative doctors and researchers who had suspicious accidents...fatal accidents."

"I told you, Doc Ray and the rest of the staff don't share this kind of stuff with me, and I know I don't want anything to do with it, OK?"

"One had been using a natural therapy for curing cancer, another had evidence of—"

"I said I don't want to know. Now stop." She began to wheel herself away.

"You know...I'm also doing this for you, sis."

"Ohhh god. Tug on my heartstrings, why don't you. You're doing this for me?"

"We both know why you're in that chair."

"I'm in this chair because I...because when I was in the army, I volunteered for something I shouldn't have. I'm in this chair because I didn't do my homework, I didn't have all the facts, and because I made an error in judgment."

"If you made an error in judgment, it's because they withheld all the facts, and that is still going on today...and not just in the military. You may not like it, but I'm doing this because of you. Just because we ran in different social circles as kids doesn't mean that I don't care about you. You're my sister, and you are my motivation and not some critic's choice award at a film festival. This project is just the first, but it is personal so it is very important to me. What happened to you needs to be told so that it doesn't keep happening to others. Isn't that what Ray Silver is doing on a daily basis at his natural health center?"

"Shut up and get the door." Lani handed her sister the keys. "I've got about a half hour of laps in the pool. If you're staying for dinner, the takeout menu for Mama San is by the phone...and you're buying."

4

Lanikai, Oahu

As much as Ray loved the peaceful healing environment of his clinic gardens, he enjoyed his weekends away from the office just as much if not more. Weekends were a combination of family and personal time, and they almost always started on Friday morning. Technically, Fridays were supposed to be dedicated to babysitting duty so Leigh Anne could spend a full day teaching classes at the university. For all intents and purposes, they were. Leigh Anne taught her classes without interruption, and Ray took advantage of the free time afforded him thanks to a morning preschool and the after-preschool playdate schedule. Knowing he'd have all day Saturday and Sunday to play house dad, the Friday routine allowed him several hours of guilt-free "me" time, which usually meant a hike, some kayaking, or spending time in the kitchen preparing the fresh-caught fish and produce he had purchased from the local farmer's market.

But whether or not it was his turn to host the playdate, Friday morning always began with his girls sneaking in on him and Leigh Anne at the crack of dawn, followed by a leisurely breakfast of pineapple macadamia nut pancakes topped with shaved coconut and mango syrup, and one more chorus of "Wheels on the Bus" during the drive to the school. Every fourth Friday, when Ray had the after-school duty, he'd load up his car with six to seven little ones, take them to Sea Life Park, and deposit them in the "little minnows" daycare to play with starfish and sea urchins in the interactive tidal pool, help feed the dolphins, and watch the sea turtles get their weekly bath. That's when he would take a solo hike up the mountain to Makapu'u Point, indulge in a light lunch he'd pick up from the new cold seafood buffet at Kimo's, and then meditate in the warmth of the Hawaiian sunshine.

The moms were happy, the kids were happy, and Ray was very happy. "Just livin' the dream," he'd say—but not this particular Friday. And it wasn't the fact that he was home with just his three little girls. The four of them could have more fun and get into more mischief than he cared to admit, but he hoped the girls would one day watch all the videos he had taken of their escapades and remember their father's goofy antics with fondness. Ray laughed every time he thought of Leigh Anne coming home to find the four of them, the Jeep, and the front yard totally covered in car-wash suds, or how he thought she would lose it the day she found a trail of white footprints leading from the front door to the kitchen dusted over with flour. Not a word was spoken when she first looked around the room. She'd then shaken her head, sat down on a powdery kitchen chair to eat the overcooked coconut curry chicken potpie they had made for her, and without missing a beat simply asked, "Do anything fun with the girls today?"

He definitely didn't mind having an entire afternoon to be with his princesses, but he did take exception to the abrupt way the playdate group had canceled on him. He knew the excuses were phony, as the moms had hurried away from him in the preschool parking lot as if he had some sort of infectious disease. A frazzled Alice Mayweather usually couldn't wait to deposit her hyperactive boys off at someone's house, and for her to suddenly say she wanted more time with her spirited kids was certainly out of character. He knew Betty Torres did not develop a case of memory loss and forgot that it was Ray's turn to host this week, as she'd kept telling everyone how her daughter couldn't wait to get back to the aquarium.

And then there was single mom Kathy Kotter, a fiery red-headed former lingerie model who kept telling Leigh Anne how lucky she was to have a husband fifteen years her senior: "I've heard that older men are so passionate and they really know how to please their women in bed. And by looking at how good a shape Ray is in, honey…well, no wonder you always look so tired, you lucky girl." Whenever it was her turn to host, Kathy would wear her tightest yoga ensemble and fabricate all sorts of excuses in an effort to get Ray to stay and help. Leigh Anne, annoyed at the suggestion that she always looked tired, warned Ray about her reputation and half-jokingly cautioned him that under no circumstances should he go into her house without parental supervision. But now, three days after Josh Kimmel excoriated him on the evening news, Kathy Kotter and the other moms couldn't cancel fast enough.

Ray knew that when Leigh Anne found out, she wouldn't be happy, as this would affect her weekday afternoons as well. The only questions now were, how long would she be upset, and would he have to start bringing the girls to the clinic each afternoon? The more he thought about it, the more he actually liked the idea. He had always considered playdates at the other houses to be quite toxic, and no matter how many times he'd protested, it seemed that candy and doughnuts would remain the standard afternoon fare. At least now the girls would no longer be coming home bouncing off the walls on a sugar high. He also realized that having his daughters at the clinic would keep Team Leilani off his back.

Ray looked out into the backyard, keeping an eye on the girls as he prepared an *ahi pokki* salad for his lunch. As he cut two-inch-thick strips of the raw tuna into smaller cubes, he felt Magic, his calico, rubbing in and out of his legs—her purring almost as loud as the big-band music playing on the antique radio. He set aside a few chunks for the cat before committing the rest to a large bowl filled with his farmer's market mix of greens, herbs, and spices. He inhaled deeply, sighed "heaven, pure heaven," grabbed his favorite porter from the fridge, and started out to the lanai to feast—stopping midstride when the phone rang. He answered, thinking it was his oldest daughter Casey.

"Hey! Kiddo, I've been trying to get you—"

"Ray? This is Carrie Dunsmore."

"I somehow knew you'd be callin' sooner or later, Carrie." He set his food on the counter and turned down the radio. "I missed you at the preschool this morning. I understand your little girl is...sick again?"

"She's not sick; she just needed a mental health day."

"Of course," Ray said sarcastically.

"Ray, I'm a little concerned about that interview I saw the other day on the news."

"Did you actually see the interview, or were you talking to Alice? And the reason I ask is because Alice saw the Kimmel interview and then began calling everyone in our little after-school care group."

"Alice did call me and—"

"And she got your mind racing. I'm telling you like I've told the others, Carrie, the woman is off the reservation, so please don't allow yourself to get sucked into her circus."

But, Ray—"

"Listen, there's nothing to be concerned about, honest. The reporter has an agenda, and I'm his target of choice."

"Some of the other moms have been talking, and they just don't think it's safe."

"No, of course not. Especially since Alice has the tendency to blow things out of proportion, and you know exactly what I'm talking about. Doesn't she stir the pot each time your daughter is sick...I mean, 'under the weather'?"

"She gets excited, I admit that."

"Alice lobbies to have you dropped from the group, or did you forget how she called your daughter a walking petri dish?"

"I feel bad about this, Ray. I really do." She ignored his question.

"I'm sure you do, Carrie." His dismissal sounded unconvincing.

"I mean it. Leigh Anne is a friend and all that, and we just adore your little girls, and—"

"Carrie, stop a minute, just stop, OK? If you really care about your friendship with Leigh, then I want you to do two things. First, go online and look up the interview that Mileka Johnson did with me that same night. She'll also have an uncut version of the interview that Josh Kimmel did. She had her film crew tape it because she knows he's dishonest in his reporting. You can see for yourself how he omitted or twisted almost everything I said. Then I want you to ask yourself a question. And keep in mind that your daughter seems to be needing mental health days...hell, we both know she's getting good and sick quite often. So let's be honest and ask yourself, why is it that your little girl is always coming down with everything from colds and sore throats to ear infections while my three kids haven't had so much as a sniffle? Shouldn't I be the one afraid to have my girls come in contact with your kid? And yet I'm not, am I?"

Carrie was silent.

He briefly waited for a response, then continued, "When you figure that out, and if you're still interested, I'd be happy to have a logical conversation about it...away from Alice's hysteria. Until then, jumping to conclusions based on rumors and innuendo serves no one and hurts everyone, yes?"

It was still silent on the other end.

"Carrie? Carrie? Understand this. I'm not passing judgment on the way you choose to raise your daughter. You're an intelligent person and, in my opinion, one of the more intelligent members of our little group. I'm just asking you to watch Mileka's piece before you pass judgment on me."

"OK, I'll watch."

"With an open mind, OK?"

"With an open mind."

"Thank you." He let out a long breath and then looked at his lunch. "If there's nothing else, I've gotta go take care of something very important. We'll talk soon."

Ray hung up, and for a few moments he stared at his daughters playing in the backyard. *"Fucking Alice Mayweather... that woman creates more problems. I just hope this shit doesn't get outta hand,"* he thought, then picked up his bowl, stepped out onto the lanai, and stretched out on the recliner, hoping to enjoy his lunch.

The afternoon skies were bright blue, and had he not been distracted, the gentle winds teasing the palms could have easily caressed him into a nap. He hoped Carrie Dunsmore would be rational after watching Mileka's piece. And he was right that she was intelligent. Unfortunately, she often surrendered to peer pressure—going along in order to get along. But if anyone in their group other than Leigh Anne had the ability to think rationally and calm the others, it was Carrie. Still, there was the very real possibility that Alice Mayweather would be making noise at the preschool—reacting more from an emotional need for attention than from anything else.

Then there was the girls' teacher. Although she was one of his patients, he would still need to make a preemptive visit to make sure she was still in his corner. In spite of her personal beliefs on natural health-care, Ray understood that her business decisions would be made to avoid financial loss—which could very well happen if parents began withdrawing their children.

It wasn't long before he was joined by four drooling mouths: the cat and three hungry little ladies who weren't being very ladylike.

"Come on, you guys, stop, OK? You all had your lunch already; this is mine." He tried to fight them off as best he could until the phone began to ring. *"Casey, finally!"* He jumped from the recliner. "OK, fine. Lucky for you three, your big sister's on the phone. And don't make a mess; your mother will kill me. Not that she's gonna need another reason." He surrendered the ahi salad and the lounge chair, and watched the feeding frenzy as he beelined for kitchen.

"Casey! Hey, it's Dad."

"Sorry, Dad, it's just me."

"Jimmy...I'm sorry, I was expecting your sister."

"Sorry to disappoint."

"No, are you kidding me? I'm not disappointed...it's just that I've been trying...have you heard from her?"

"No, not this week, but then again, I've been so busy at work and with Jenna being pregnant I haven't called her. But I know you've been calling, yes?"

"Several times. I've left messages, but I hadn't heard... when the phone rang just now, I just assumed—"

"She's not avoiding you. She's probably busy with—"

"Yeah, I know. Maybe you can call someone in your Seattle office to...never mind, forget I said that. So how are things at the NSA anyway? What's new in the spy biz these days?"

"Come on, Dad, you know I just do legal work for the agency. Stop with the spy biz talk, OK?"

"You had a perfectly good job being a navy lawyer."

"It was limited, and with Jenna's job in New York and now with the baby, I didn't wanna be overseas. And I think you're still not happy that Griff Kelley hired me."

He tried changing the subject. "And speaking of Leigh's baby sister, how is your wife?"

"Dad...he hired me, and I haven't seen him since. I'm one of many lawyers working for the agency, and he doesn't have time to waste on me."

"And speaking of Leigh's baby sister, how is your wife?" Ray repeated.

"Jenna's great, Dad. I'll give her your love."

"Ya know, it hit me the other day that this baby of yours... he or she will be both my grandchild and my nephew...or niece...and we're not even from App—"

"Please don't say it."

"—alachia. Jimmy, I'm not stupid. Why'd you really call?"

"We saw that interview."

"In New York? You saw a local Oahu newscast in New York?"

"We see everything in New York, Dad. Everything. I don't need to tell you that."

"Then don't. I know what I'm doing, so no lectures."

"You've stayed out of trouble for the past three years, Dad. Do you really want to do this?"

"I've got enough on my plate right now, so no lectures, kiddo, OK?"

"Sure. Everyone is good over there?"

"Yeah, we're all good. Come visit?"

"If we can catch a break. Do me a favor and call me if... when you hear from Casey."

"You do the same."

With little hope of salvaging his salad, Ray saw that Magic had gone off to nurse her newest litter and he put the girls down for an afternoon snooze. Still craving his tuna, he foraged through the refrigerator, thinking more about his son and their short conversation than he was about lunch. He tried to call Casey once more.

He had never been thrilled with Jimmy's career choice because he suspected his son did more than just legal work for the agency—a claim made in true conspiratorial fashion. But to keep peace in the family, he knew he would have to stop his badgering. His daughter's career was less stressful for him. A former battlefield and surgical nurse with the navy, she now worked at the Veterans Administration in Seattle. He had wanted her to come to work at his natural health center, having had lengthy debates of the pros and cons about working together. But no one could deny that father and daughter had become a great deal closer after their exploits in Iraq had almost cost Ray his life—something she downplayed each time he sent her another care package filled with Hawaiian treats and a note expressing his eternal gratitude for having risked her life to save his. Except for those notes, the two never spoke of the incident; however, they did speak about her health—a topic that was now frequently on his mind. After leaving several voice mails, he hesitantly thought about calling his friend, Casey's nursing supervisor, Stella Leone.

Stella had become uncharacteristically critical of his growing frustration, and their last few conversations had been peppered with tit-for-tat insults. Had he not been preoccupied,

Ray would have questioned her combative disposition. He paced the kitchen weighing his options, knowing if he did call he would get scolded: for worrying too much and for asking her to act as a substitute parent—which she was already doing.

Ray finished leaving another message on Casey's voice mail. *"She's gonna be pretty annoyed at me for sure."* He then stared at the rotary-style wall phone and picked up and replaced the receiver in the cradle several times before proceeding to dial his friend.

"Didn't I tell you I would call if anything changed?"

"Yeah, Stel, but I've been calling her for a couple days now and haven't heard back. I'm—"

"Worried?"

"No...well, a little. I am her father after all."

There was a palpable awkward silence on the other end of the phone.

"Stel? You still there?"

"Ray, you caught me in the middle of something. Is it OK if I call you back in let's say about five minutes?"

"Sure. I'm at the house, not the office."

"I know, it's Friday."

Even though he hung up, his hand never left the receiver. He alternated his gaze between the clock above the sink and everything else in his retro-style kitchen. He loved the simplicity of it all. It was basic, uncomplicated, and a constant reminder of a world long lost to the conveniences of preplanned obsolescence. Five minutes turned to six and then seven. He jumped when it finally rang.

"Stella?" The connection wasn't as crisp as it was before.

"Like I was saying, Ray, there's no need to worry. She's been busy with work and with more...tests."

"New tests, or repeating the ones they botched?" He struck the first blow.

"Botched? Nobody botched anything. There were a couple of new ones but a few repeats just to make sure there were no false negatives."

"False negatives? In other words, they have no clue and they're scratching their heads, right?" His tone was now prosecutorial.

"In other words, they're being very thorough and careful, making sure they don't come to conclusions without all of the facts," she counterpunched.

Ray noted but ignored her emphatic tone. "And the results were the same, right?"

"Same results, correct. Nerve conduction remains intermittently erratic, sometimes spiking with hyperactivity, and sometimes the action potentials are significantly reduced, and other times—"

"They're just fine, I know. It's like an electrical system that's going through power surges and brownouts. But why?"

"They still don't know, and because of that, they don't know how to treat it."

"Even if they did know what name to pin on it, they still wouldn't have a treatment for it."

"That's not true. What about MS? What about Parkinson's? And then there's—"

"What I meant to say is, they might prescribe a treatment that will mask or lessen the symptoms—"

"Which will make her life easier."

"What's that supposed to mean? Are things getting—"

"No, Ray, not at all! Stop trying to escalate this thing to a level that doesn't exist."

"Stel, please…I'm just trying to get answers."

"I'm just saying in a general sense that once we know what the condition is, we have treatments that can make things easier for people."

"Yes, assuming the side effects don't make them more miserable or create a new disorder."

"Damn it, Ray!"

Again it was quiet on both ends of the phone. After what seemed like a minute, Ray calmed himself, continuing at a level just above a whisper.

"And even though the test results are the same, how is she doing? The truth."

"Hold on one sec, Ray."

As he waited, he heard her speaking to someone. The conversation was hard for him to make out; it was obvious the mouthpiece had been covered. To him it sounded as if she was being ordered about, and her halfhearted protest gave way to the commands of a muffled voice that somehow sounded familiar. He tried to recall the people he knew at the medical center to see if there was a match. He couldn't come up with one. He abandoned his internal search when Stella's voice was once again directed toward him.

"Where were we, Ray? Oh yes, she was the same as the last time you spoke to her. Her legs tend to get a little weak or tingly on occasion. When she loses feeling in her feet—"

"She's losing feeling in her feet?" His volume increased once more. "Since when?"

"It only happened twice, the last time a few days ago. Her feet got a little numb. Just like when you've been sitting for too long and you've reduced the blood flow, and the feet fall asleep. It was like that," she said defensively. "She was in the break room having coffee with some of the other nurses. When she went to get a refill, she lost her balance. She said it was because her feet had fallen asleep."

"But she hadn't been sitting for a long period, had she?"

"No...I don't know. I'm not sure."

"How's all this affecting her, Stella? I mean, how's her spirit? She doesn't tell me anything."

"Because she knows you'll...she's doing fine, Ray, honest. She's still socializing with the other nurses, and she doesn't stay out too late."

"You're waiting up for her? Geez, and you give me a hard time for worrying?"

"No, I'm not waiting up for her. I'm already up, OK? And just be thankful I let her live with me, which makes it easier to keep an eye on her...rent-free, by the way," she tried to joke.

"In my old house that I gave you an amazing deal on, by the way. And yes, we both appreciate the free rent."

"She's a strong woman, Ray, very strong, and she's optimistic, as am I, that the docs will figure out what it is."

"Well, I'm not so hopeful that they'll figure it out, which is why I wanna make sure she continues seeing my chiropractor friend in Wallingford."

Before she could respond, Ray heard that background voice once more. It was low but it wasn't muffled. Seven simple words spoken in two short sentences: "There's the opening. Jump all over it." The voice was male, older, commanding, and familiar, but he still couldn't place it.

Stella let out a big sigh. "Oh my god, not that again! This is a serious health—"

"Yes, that again. I hope you're not discouraging it? You allopaths—"

"I haven't been discouraging her, but you vitalists think everything about health starts in the spine. Really, Ray?" The annoyance in her voice was evident.

"You're just jealous because we fully understand how the body works, and it certainly doesn't become healthy or stay healthy from all the toxic chemicals you people hang your collective hats on." Now he was the one counterpunching.

"Are we really going to get into this now? I told you, she's going to your friend, OK? Somebody please shoot me already." Her exasperation seemed over the top. His was.

He grabbed a coffee mug, catching himself before launching it across the room. *"You'll wake the girls. Calm...be calm...breathe."*

"Ray? Are you still there?"

"OK, that's good...that she's strong, that is...and she's optimistic," he said, deciding not to keep pushing back. "Listen, there's a holistic medical practice over on Bainbridge Island. I'd like her to go see that guy as well."

"So we are going to get into this again, aren't we? You just don't know when to stop this nonsense."

"I don't understand what's gotten into you lately? I really don't. I mean, you almost got me to lose my temper, but I won't let you get to me. I know you guys don't believe in natural medicine, but I do," he calmly stated. "And in spite of what you think, it works just fine."

"'And it works just fine, blah blah blah,'" she mocked. "Unscientific bullshit, Ray!"

"Stella, the guy on Bainbridge is a Harvard med grad who just so happens to have seen the light."

She continued to attack. "From the mother ship calling him home."

"Chelation therapy is great for blood and liver detox, and I know your people never consider that."

"With good reason."

"Yeah, because Visor Pharmaceuticals can't patent it, and we 'alternative' health-care providers can't give you all Caribbean vakays as a thank-you for selling the damn sh... stuff." He squeezed the coffee mug, fighting to keep his anger in check as his volume slightly increased. "So in the absence of anything else medicine has to offer, I would appreciate it if she got checked out by him."

Stella remained quiet for a few moments, listening to the heaviness in Ray's breathing.

"You know, Ray, I only have so much patience for this kind of talk."

This hadn't been the first time she'd baited him like this, and he couldn't figure out why. She was once a loyal friend, but now he had to bite his tongue lest he say what was really on his mind. He still needed her help and couldn't afford to lose her altogether "Do me a favor...truce, OK?

"I'm perfectly calm, Ray. I'm perfectly calm."

"OK, good, very good. Calm is good. We should both be calm. Could you tell her to call me? Better yet, can you give her some time off so she can come here? I'd actually like to have the people in my clinic do some work on her. I also think a little break to enjoy the surf and the sun will do her good."

"I honestly can't give her the time off right now." Stella was now more civil. "I know the rest would help her. Even though we're shorthanded, I've got her on light duty and reduced hours."

"Not even for a few days?"

"No promises, but I'll see what I can do."

"Thanks. Stel? I have one more question. I asked about this a few weeks ago, and I need to ask it again. It's been on my mind for quite some time, and I already know your view on this, but you need to be a little open-minded here."

"I know what you want to ask. Is her illness the result of all the vaccines she got when she first joined the navy?"

"Yes. That, and then all the ones they gave her when she did her first tour in Iraq."

"No way."

"How can you be sure?"

"That's easy...because they're one hundred percent safe and effective like the CDC tells us they are, and second, because there'd be others."

"How do you know there aren't others? Did you or anyone check with the other VA centers around the country?"

"No. But I haven't seen any others here."

"Why would you? You're not in the neurology department, and you're not in the infectious diseases department. You're just an orthopedic nurse."

"Just an orthopedic nurse? Truce over!"

"Here we go. Stel, I didn't mean—"

"If I didn't know any better, I'd say you've been spending too much time listening to that discredited crackpot researcher," she yelled.

"Who are you talkin' about? What crackpot researcher?"

"The one you told me about a couple years ago. That gal who was abruptly fired from the pharmaceutical company in New York. You know, the one who went rogue and is making all those wild claims about falsified research data and possible experimentation on people. That gal who's hiding somewhere in the Rockies. Patty something or other. Patty...no, Payton, Paige, Paula Mott?"

"Paige Motz! Experimental drugs...I remember that. I haven't thought about her in a long time."

"Oh, great! Me and my big mouth."

"I read one article and saw one lecture that she did…on the Internet of all places."

"Well you certainly sound like you've been watching a lot more of her stuff."

"I wish I had been. I'd forgotten all about her. Paige Motz, of course. Thanks for reminding me. She'd be a great person to talk to. I just wish I knew how to find her."

"That's all we need," Stella said.

"I'm serious, Stel. She's no crackpot. The woman knows her stuff."

"Then why is she living in a cave in the Rockies and making videos as if she were Bin Laden?"

"I'm sure that's what you and your people want to believe about her; this way you can write off what she says as incoherent babble."

"Me and my people? Now what's that supposed to mean?"

"You know exactly what I mean, and before this continues to go to the point of no return, I need to go."

"So you can look for your cave dweller?"

"You know what gets me, Stel? Your people have no idea what's wrong with my kid. You do all your tests with all your high-tech gadgetry, and you still have no clue. And with no idea what's attacking her, you guys still insist on doing drug trials on her as if she were some sort of lab rat. You're throwing darts in the dark…and blindfolded, no less. For all we know, your experimentation could very well be making her worse. And the one thing that all of you refuse to even consider is the possibility that perhaps some of the toxic crap that got stuck into her is the spark that lit this fire in the first place."

"Now hold on just a minute."

"And on top of all that, the way you've been treating me lately…you know something?"

"I know that my patience is beginning to wear very thin. After all, a girl can only put up with just so much of your new-age extremist rants."

"New-age extremist rants? Really? So it finally comes out," he yelled "I suppose you've been humoring me these past few

years by pretending to support what I do for a living!" He recognized Abbey's cries from the other room. "I've gotta hang
up; you woke my kids from their nap."

"I woke them up? If I didn't like you, Ray Silver, I would've
hung up on you a long time ago."

* * *

Stella kept the phone to her ear for a full minute after the
call ended. She stared at the bulletin board but focused on
nothing—wondering. She worried that things between them
would deteriorate further as time and Casey's condition pro-
gressed. She thought about the conversation and became
angry: not at Ray, and *not* at herself. She spun around and
looked directly into the eyes of her ex-husband Griff Kelley.

"Are you happy now?"

"Yes," he said bluntly.

"I don't know why I'm always doing favors for you."

"You're not doing them for me; you're doing them for—"

"For my country, yeah, sure," she said in disgust while toss-
ing her cell phone onto her desk. It slid across the surface
and fell onto the floor. She didn't care. "I hope you realize
this jeopardizes my relationship with Ray, right? Or don't you
care?"

"Stel, the only thing this jeopardizes is your hope to get him
into bed someday, which we both know will never happen."

"And you're just jealous that you'll never have me again...
ever."

"Maybe." He laughed.

"You fooled me twice. It won't happen again...unless the
reason you flew out here from DC was to do more than just
strong-arm me into helping you and the NSA fuck over Ray
Silver. What, you want to do me again, too? What's the matter,
Griff? Things not going so well with the new trophy wife?"

"Wow, you really are mad."

"Ya think? Griff, why can't you leave Ray alone? Why do you
keep dragging him back into agency business?"

"Me? Whaddya mean me?"

"Yes, you...or would you rather I just say the agency. You're one in the same, you know. No matter how you cut it, you are the NSA, and the NSA is you. And don't get me started about the CIA."

"I have nothing to do with that group of clowns."

"Stop it, Griff. You know exactly what I mean."

"You stop it, Stella. You know damn well that his very first time...that little ocean voyage to the Philippines...that was all him. NSA wasn't even involved in that one until I got a phone call from the president. If you remember, that's how I met Ray in the first place."

"OK, fine. I'll give you that one, but—"

"And you know quite well that incident opened up a door that was better left closed. Had he not opened the damn thing, he wouldn't have gotten drawn into those next two...incidents. And as nostalgic as all this is, I'm not going to get into the details of those operations."

"Fine, you're not the evil bridge troll always waiting to pounce on him. But why now? Why lure him back in when his daughter is going through all this."

"Are you kidding me? It's because of what his daughter is going through. He wants this, Stel. He needs this. He needs this as much as I need him at this point."

"You're nuts, Griff. He doesn't want this, and he definitely doesn't need this. But you're right about one thing: you *do* need him at this point."

"Don't kid yourself. And don't keep buying into his average Joe chiropractor persona living the quiet laidback Hawaiian family life."

"I take him for his word."

"He may say all those things and he may do all those things: living near the beach, the snorkeling thing, and the kayaking stuff, and—"

"The wife, the kids, and all the—"

"Yeah, all that stuff. But he's conflicted inside. There are two Ray Silvers. There's the one filled with all that aloha and coconuts. Then there's the one who wants to live like he's a character in a Vince Flynn adventure novel. I'm telling you, Stel, he wants this. Deep down inside, he really needs this action."

"Oh, I see it all clearly now. You're his guardian angel setting things up for him to fulfill his deepest desires. As far as I can see, you're just setting him up."

"Say what you want, think what you want, but you know him as well as I do. Go take another look at what Casey is going through."

"I see what she's going through. I see it every day. More importantly, he knows what she's going through, and he certainly doesn't need me or you pushing his buttons until he explodes."

"His buttons have been pushed, Stel, and not by me. I just want to direct his energy so that he doesn't explode."

"This is going to get out of control, and I'm worried, Griff."

"Don't be. You've helped me plant the seeds. All I want is for him to find our little cave dweller. That's all I want from him, that's all he's gotta do, and I'll make sure he feels he's done his part. And, Stel...as angry as you are right now, keep in mind that you agreed to help me."

"Meaning what?"

"Meaning I need you to see this through. Otherwise, things won't go as we've planned. I don't want this whole thing to fall apart."

"Tell me, Griff, when was the last time an NSA operation went as planned?"

5

Veterans Medical Center
Seattle, Washington
October 2007

Casey Silver tried to act as if her molasses-like progression out of the operating room was by design. She was relieved the session was over, amazed she even made it through to the end. Her legs felt rubbery and heavy, her level of cognitive thought boarding on punch-drunk, as if she had just gone the distance in a prize fight. A ring of perspiration circled the neckline of her scrubs. The T-shirt she wore underneath was soaked even more. *"Outta shape,"* she thought. *"It's only been a month and I'm already outta shape."*

What used to be a routine and boring day for her was now a rare exception since the neuropathy that had been affecting her lower extremities became noticeably worse over the past few months. Once she'd begun to experience intermittent episodes of shooting pain or extended bouts of pins-and-needles sensations in her legs and feet, Stella reduced her operating room schedule. When Casey's knees buckled on her a couple times, occurring when she was fatigued but each time without warning, she was forced off surgical rotation altogether.

"You can't be serious, Stella. I'm fine."

"You're not fine, and I can't afford to have you collapsing in the middle of a surgical procedure."

"I was tired. It was a long shift, and I hadn't eaten all day. So I felt a little weak, and my knee buckled on me. What's the big deal?"

"What's the big... are you kidding me? You had a tray full of surgical instruments that went flying when you suddenly went down."

"And I picked up every one of them."

"Including the scalpel that landed blade first into the mattress of a gurney?"

"It was unoccupied."

"Fortunately for you."

In spite of her protests, she found herself assigned to a desk to perform data entry—a task more mind-numbing than a seemingly endless day of hip replacements and knee reconstructions. However, the reduction in physical stress seemed to also reduce the number of her weekly episodes—at least for a little while. And what little benefit she'd enjoyed from the mandated respite she quickly forfeited in the trendy new nightclubs of Seattle's Ballard neighborhood, the pubs around lower Queen Anne, or the rowdy sports bars of Pioneer Square. As long as her stamina held up, she willingly went wherever her nursing colleagues dragged her. They thought she was the much-needed after-hours spark plug they had been looking for, the life of the party when they egged her on—appearing as if she drank too much on several occasions while blaming her impaired state on her undiagnosed condition or the side effects from her medications.

Stella was beginning to doubt the excuses, as Casey didn't seem to experience the same "side effects" while at work—at least not that she could tell. Casey argued that she knew better than to imbibe while medicated. Still, Stella worried that Ray's daughter was beginning to binge—perhaps as a means to alleviate her boredom or, worse, running from the possibility of having an incurable illness, a charge that Casey quickly dismissed by protesting the mothering and coming close to insulting Stella's judgment. Nonetheless, she accepted the challenge to talk to a counselor in order to quiet her father's overprotective friend.

She was hot, her T-shirt now cold and sticking to her skin. It made her uncomfortable. She wanted to begin to undress right there in the corridor but was painfully aware of her surroundings. Every sensation seemed to be magnified: touch, smell, and that of being watched. Hospital staff seemed to move past her in slow motion as she made her way down the hall. Voices and footsteps echoed in her head as blurred, elongated faces scrutinized her stares. She had to stop, bracing against the wall to gather herself—the distorted sensations feeling more intense than ever before. *"So you don't think these meds cause side effects?"* she said silently to an imaginary Stella. Casey fought to hold herself together. *"This will pass. It always does. Just need…to sit and rest."*

She knew she had experienced a similar feeling once and tried to deny the connection to the operating room. *"Iraq!"* she heard her mind say. *"No, not Iraq. This is different…or is it? The marine? No, this isn't about him. This guy is not him. Why'd you think about him? That's easy—they look the same. Stop thinking about it; stop thinking about that marine. I'm just dehydrated…I think. Maybe it's the medication. That's what it is…yeah, that's all it is."*

She forced a swallow in an effort to moisten her mouth. A small amount of bile shot up from her esophagus without warning and burned the back of her throat. She immediately thought of the water fountain in the nurses' shower room. It had the coldest water in the orthopedic ward. *"It's all those fucking drugs…side effects…it's…Stella."* Her thoughts raced back and forth. *"That's right. This wouldn't be an issue if Stella hadn't stuck me on a desk. I wouldn't be so outta shape."*

Had there not been a shortage of surgical nurses that week, she would have never been asked to fill in. And even with the few sessions she did work, it was still too risky for her to do so, as the onset of each episode had been unpredictable. But the newest surgeon on the orthopedic wing hadn't been aware of her situation. And with Stella being off duty, Casey wasn't about to say anything. *"All I have to do is pace myself, stay hydrated, and keep from getting stressed."*

The final surgery of the day had seen a number of unexpected mishaps, which made for a drawn-out, stress-filled session. First, the air conditioning system failed, causing a quick rise in room temperature. Then an IV bag somehow sprung a leak, causing one of the nurses to slip on the wet floor, spraining her ankle. Then a malfunctioning heart-rate monitor had half the surgical team thinking the patient had flatlined midway through the procedure—the surgeons demanding someone initiate CPR, the nurses insisting he was breathing and still had a pulse. And finally, thanks to an anesthesiologist who was preoccupied with his latest romantic conquest—a new hire in the dialysis ward he'd christened the "tight tail from Tacoma"—Corporal Hanks began to wake before the surgeon had finished suturing his knee. It was physically and mentally draining for everyone, but especially for Casey, and the lack of stamina bothered her. She had easily handled much more demanding days and had been through a lot worse in Iraq. Prior to this last session, she'd been complaining about the lack of adrenaline.

"That's what's missing around this place. It's the lack of excitement and the rush you get from the unexpected!" she'd once stated.

"You're right, Silver. This work is so boring…if we could only get that spizz without going back on active."

Many of the nurses on her shift openly complained about the boredom and the monotony. One surgeon lost count of how many of the "cut and paste" procedures he had performed and often joked how he longed for the unpredictable excitement of a war-zone field hospital. And while Casey and some of the staff agreed that a little more unpredictability would make the day interesting, the thought of going back to war was the furthest thing from her mind. It had been two and a half years since she was discharged from active duty, and all things considered, she had to admit this was a welcomed change from the drama of life and death that had played out before her eyes. She'd seen more than her share of bodies that had been ripped apart like a tattered stuffed child's toy being wrestled from the jaws of the family dog. When she had her energy as well as her wits, she knew she was better off with the monotonous repetition of medial meniscus repairs or fending off the unwanted advances of a male colleague who was convinced that one night with him and she would permanently lose interest in women. "Great!" she'd respond. "I've got something to add to my Christmas list."

The walk from operating room to locker room was a struggle. She felt she could have easily made it to the end of the long hallway if not for the exhaustion compounding a longer afternoon of nausea—another side effect in a long list of side effects from her medications. And if feeling ill before the final surgery hadn't been enough of a challenge, when she'd entered the operating room and taken one look at the patient, a flood of emotions had triggered the rush she'd long desired but which was now a distraction. Her heart began to pound, and she felt the heat fill her cheeks—grateful for the surgical mask that hid her face. What was supposed to be a standard knee replacement on a veteran soldier became an unscheduled trip into the deep recesses of her memory. Images came flooding back as if someone had pressed the reverse button on a DVD player—the surgeon's words nothing more than a muffled garble as she gazed at the patient.

"Check this out, nurse. This guy had been medically discharged because his knee was blasted into ground beef, and for three years the VA kept him waiting on the nonpriority list," the surgeon said, getting no response. He then turned to the room. "OK, people, this is the last one on the schedule. So everyone—especially you, Silver—let's stay alert and give him our best so we can send him home in good shape. More importantly, we'll be batting a thousand tonight."

"And we'll be batting a thousand tonight," Casey had said under her breath.

She thought she was hallucinating when she'd laid eyes on the former ranger who bore a striking resemblance to a young marine she had worked on during her first tour of duty. The emotional jolt gave way to or quite possibly triggered an electrical shock like pain that shot through her body. Her legs became weak, and her knees buckled slightly, but she caught herself. Bracing against the gurney, she quickly surveyed the room—relieved that everyone else had been busy, and the patient, already groggy from medication, had been the only witness.

She hadn't thought about the marine in years, but the instant she did, she couldn't stop thinking about him instead of the patient before her. She was on autopilot for most of the procedure, physically performing her job while mentally reliving the war. When the surgeon finished, he complimented her on a flawless assist. *"Wish I could've been there,"* she thought. Afterward, as she shuffled out of the operating room, she thought she'd collapse from the physical and emotional stress that came on with a vengeance and began to overwhelm her.

The cold water from the fountain washed away the taste of bile and soothed the back of her throat. She alternated between large gulps and circling her face through the stream, trying to remember if she'd soloed the last fifty yards down the hallway or if anyone had helped her into the nurses' locker room. Her vision and hearing seemed to normalize, her nausea subsided, and she briefly considered going to sit in post-op with Corporal Hanks—deciding against the idea, as she needed to distance herself from further recollection, now laughing at the futility when she found herself sitting in front of her locker unable to stop thinking about the marine in Iraq. Bits and pieces of that operation kept coming back. Half resisting but yielding to the images, she remembered the look in his eyes and the feel of his hand in hers just before the anesthesia took him into a sleep from which he would never return:

"Nurse, am I gonna—"

"Shhh," she said, *leaning over to comfort him. "You're gonna be just fine, marine."*

"Nurse, please don't lie to me. If I'm gonna die, I have a right to know."

"If you were gonna die, I'd be the first to tell you. You're in good hands. Dr. Terembes is one of the best surgeons we have."

"She's telling the truth, marine," the surgeon confirmed.

"I'm the best they have because the others were smart enough to stay in the States. I understand you're from Philly?"

"That's right, sir," the groggy marine answered.

"That's where I studied: at Geno's on South Ninth Street."

The wounded marine smiled back and thought of chees-esteaks as he faded off from the medication.

"Geno's?" Casey asked.

"Philly cheesesteaks, lieutenant. Couldn't study for an exam without one. OK, people, let's get this kid fixed up so we can send him home along with the others, and we'll be batting a thousand tonight."

She sat there staring at the floor, the surgeon's words echoing in her head. She tried but couldn't remember the last time she'd thought about the young marine, and she felt a little guilty. Not for forgetting him—there had been too many faces to remember—but for having lied to him. "He deserved the truth," she mumbled, rubbing her forehead, trying to wipe away the memory of the desert heat with an imaginary bottle of ice water:

"At least it's August," commented a fellow nurse who was also trying to decompress after the long surgical session.

"Why, it gets worse than this? How can it get worse than ninety degrees at eight in the evening?"

"It doesn't, unless the shamal, *the summer winds, become more intense."*

"I guess you're right, but I've already got dust and sand in my hair, my food, my mouth, and even in my underwear."

They both laughed, knowing how uncomfortable it was to have sand infiltrating every orifice.

Casey took a long drink, then wiped a tear from her eye.

"There was too much damage, Silver."

"They were just a few klicks up the road."

"He lost too much blood before they got him off the line."

"You're right, I know. It doesn't make it any easier, though."

"There's gonna be more of them. You can't let it get to you."

"I know. In the past few months, I've seen plenty. I'll be OK. I just gotta get used to looking 'em in the eye when I lie to 'em. That's what's hard."

"He deserved to be told the truth," she said aloud. Her hand trembled a little as she brushed it across her forehead once more, as if wiping away beads of sweat.

"Hey, Silver, you OK?" a colleague called out. "Who needed the truth? What happened?"

"What?" She looked up at Hannah Baker. "Nothing...nothing. I'm just talking to myself. It was a long day today, and I'm tired...brain-dead tired is all."

"You're just not used to being in the OR since Nurse Ratched put you on the desk."

"Don't call her Nurse Ratched. She was just doing her job."

"Because you told off a surgeon in the middle of an operation? I wish I could've been there to see it."

"He deserved the tongue-lashing," she said, continuing the lie she'd been telling. "And being chained to a desk is actually kinda nice. When no one's around, I get to surf the net."

"Looking at porn, no doubt."

"Ha-ha, very funny."

"Well, you need to pull more shifts in surgery, because you've obviously lost your stamina from all that sitting. I hope you're not gonna poop out on us tonight. We've got great seats for the ballgame."

"Don't worry about me. I'll be there."

"I hope so. It might have taken you a while to start hangin' with us, but since you joined the group, we've been batting a thousand for wild evenings." Hannah laughed. "Can't break the streak, right?"

"Batting a thousand, right. Everybody wants to bat a thousand."

"What's that?"

"Nothing…nothing at all. I'll be there as soon as I'm done with Gibson."

"Are you still seeing that creep? And he is a creep. I hate the way he's always leering at us."

"Yeah, no kidding. Stella's makin' me go. It's because I came home drunk one night."

"Only one night?" Hannah mocked to Casey's glare. "I'm kidding. Did ya ever think about moving out of her house?"

"Yeah, but the rents in this city are getting outta hand."

"Move in with one of us. Unless, of course, you like being treated like a child."

"I live for the abuse. But, hey, she's giving me a free room, and while she's been a little too much of a mother hen lately, she does mean well…at least, I think she does." She sat in front of her locker, rubbing the sides of her legs.

"Well, don't just sit there. Get going, will ya?" Hannah urged. "First beer is at six and the last one to get there buys."

"OK, OK, I'm going." She laughed, forcing herself up. Her legs trembled, and her feet were heavy and clumsy. "Jeez, I can't believe this."

"What's up?"

"Ya know how your legs get all pins and needles when you sit for too long?"

"Yeah…I know exactly what you mean."

"It's been happening to you, too?"

"No…why? It's been happening to you?"

"Ah…no, not really," she lied. "But damn…right now… it's…pretty intense. Wait…OK good, it just stopped. That's what I get for letting myself get dehydrated."

"Well, force yourself to walk around anyway…you know, to get the circulation back. And hurry up, or you'll be buyin' the brew."

The paresthesia in Casey's legs might have stopped and her fatigue seemed to lessen a bit; however, it was still an effort to change out of her scrubs. Even a quick shower and getting dressed afterward required motivation. *There's no way I'm gonna meet up with the girls. Maybe I can sack out on the couch with an egg-plant marinara from Pusateri's Market. But Stella will be home. The last thing I need now is for her to hover over my butt, asking questions. Fuck it, I'm going to the Hawks game."* Then she remembered her appointment with Dr. Gibson, groaning at the thought. "He's gonna make me late. Screw his session; it's not worth being on the hook for a round of beer," she said defiantly, flinging her locker door closed. As it bounced back open, a photo fell off the inner panel and floated to the floor. Casey stared at it for a few seconds, then closed her eyes.

Since her discharge from the navy, her work at the VA and the familiar surroundings of her hometown had eased her transition back to civilian life. But the loss of her partner still hurt. And while she didn't expect to ever forget Sandy and everything she had meant to her, Casey was surprised how little innocuous things triggered flashbacks of the day she lost her soul mate. Sometimes it was an article of clothing stained with blood, the sound of a helicopter flying overhead, a simple sarcastic comment, or a coworker's facial expression. And now the simple downward spiral of a photograph triggered thoughts of that final flight all over again—the sights and sounds of her working to save her father as Sandy piloted the badly damaged helicopter as vivid as they ever had been:

"Sponges!" she yelled.

"What?"

"Gauze, cotton, anything to soak this shit up. Stat!"

Casey found herself looking around the nurses' lockers as if she were still on the chopper making a quick scan of the cabin for a medical kit—again seeing the package of rolled gauze that had been shoved in front of her face.

She reached out and grabbed for it, ripping it open and stuff-ing as much as she could into the incision she had made into her father's right flank.

"Retract. I mean, hold it open so I can see."

"With what?"

"With your fingers. Watch, just like this."

The scenario played out—the sights and sounds now heightened by the smells of burning engine oil and hydraulic fluid coming from the battle-damaged engine. Slicing into her unconscious father to stem the flow of blood from a renal artery torn by a shrapnel fragment. Breathing a sigh of relief with her success.

"He's got as chance, but he'll lose the kidney for sure."

And then she saw the blood dripping down the side of the pilot's seat.

"Sandy, you've been hit."

"Really? I hadn't noticed."

"Are you all right?"

"No, I'm not...I'm really not, Case."

"How much longer?"

"We're about five minutes out. I'm beginning to lose altitude, and I'm beginning to...pray that we make it."

Baker's voice brought her back to the locker room. Casey didn't answer, but her coworker was persistent—calling out from the shower. "I said, were you talking to me?"

"No, Baker, I didn't say anything."

"Just making sure. It's hard to hear anything with the water running, and I could've sworn I heard you calling out."

"I was singing a little; that's what you heard."

"Well, if that was singing, then don't give up your day job."

"You're a real comedian, Baker."

The psychiatrist at the VA had told her she'd been suffering from a mild form of post-traumatic stress disorder, but Casey had disagreed.

"They're just vivid recollections is all."

"Which is common with PTSD."

"I admit that her loss was traumatic for me...I loved her, and I witnessed it."

"Exactly. You were in the same helicopter when it crashed. Very traumatic."

"The memory is still fresh...the void is still there."

"Is that why you go out almost every night and get drunk?"

"Is that what Stella told you? Look, I like Stella and all that, but she's as old as my dad, and like him, she sometimes treats me as if I were some wild high school girl. I go out almost every night to be with my colleagues, people my own age."

"And you drink... to excess."

"Not even close, doc. Not even close. I have one beer, non-alcoholic, so I feel like I'm part of the crowd."

"And your impairment?"

"Some of it's an act, and some...from those stupid meds."

Casey rolled her eyes. "Screw that shrink. I'm definitely not going."

She took a few steps and then began to lose her balance—quickly forcing herself back into a row of lockers in an unsuccessful attempt to steady herself. Hannah Baker heard the noise from the other side of the locker room.

"Geez, Silver, was that you?" She peered around a corner, her voice echoing off the tiled walls. "Don't tell me you already started drinking? Silver? Come on...Silver? Stop playin', girl. Are you OK? Silver?"

6

Lanikai, Hawaii

eigh Anne watched the taillights of the last car disappear at the end of the street, then turned to catch the last of the sun hugging the horizon. Ray had hoped she'd feel a sense of relief because the meeting had gone well, but deep down he knew she still felt uneasy. She once described the emotional roller coaster she'd experienced when he'd run halfway around the world because he believed his son had been in danger. The expression on her face then was the same one he saw now. Although she hadn't said much in the past few weeks, he could tell her uneasiness was not just due to the fallout over his outspoken views but because of an unpredictable edginess that had him content one minute, then grumbling as much as Mount Kilauea the next. For the most part, he had been keeping his troubles to himself—shutting her out because of the guilt he felt each time he looked at her. The mounting social pressure she was now dealing with was his doing, and he knew he owed her the time to air it out.

Ray stepped out onto the lanai, careful to not let the screen door bang shut, and let out a long sigh as he sat back into the soft, thick cushion of the bamboo-framed deck chair. He was relieved the meeting was over—happy that he'd taken a back-seat to his wife's diplomatic skills, only adding in a point or two when absolutely necessary. In spite of her discomfort, noticed only by Ray, they both knew that as an experienced educator she had been the obvious choice to arrange and lead the get-together. She would be the one to calm the fears of the other moms and to dispel the aggressive image they had of Ray, earned in part to his appearance at the school board meeting and his defensive rebuttals to some of the verbal attacks that ensued. And as if she were teaching one of her classes at the university, Leigh Anne would need to educate, or in this case, disarm them with facts, logic, common sense, and the link to the unedited interview posted on Mileka Johnson's website—all while being able to relate to them as a responsible mother no different than they were.

"Do you think Alice Mayweather will be angry she wasn't included tonight?" she asked without turning around.

Ray didn't answer right away. Thanks to the glow of the one streetlight on Kaneapu Place, he was too focused on the out-line of his wife's body sneaking through the porous stitching of her white linen sundress. When the ocean breeze was strong enough, it pressed the material against her, leaving nothing to the imagination. He traced the outline of her body down to the hem and continued to follow the curve of her freck-led thighs and calves—imagining his mouth and tongue gen-tly nibbling and sucking as he inched his way back up. Leigh Anne asked a second time, and he came out of his trance. "Just shy of heaven," she heard him mumble. He reached for his drink and wondered how long they would be talking about the meeting. While he'd much rather have Leigh Anne sitting on his lap softly nibbling away at his neck. But the floor was now hers, and she was going to review the past several weeks, as well as make sure he knew and understood the fact that in spite of appearances they may not have dodged the bullet.

"Are you even listening to me, Ray?"

"Huh?"

"Did ya hear me, or are you fantasizing about—"

"Yes, and yes. I heard your question, and I'm also fantasizing about carrying you off to bed, tying you to the bedposts, and making you squirm and sweat until the sun comes up."

"I'll bet that Kathy Kotter was thinking about doing the same thing to you," she half joked.

"I am an irresistible magnet, I'll give you that." He feigned arrogance. "But I'll bet that Kathy Kotter thinks about doing that to a lot of people...you included."

Leigh Anne turned around in disbelief.

"Yeah, that's right. Now pick your jaw off the floor. I've seen the way she looks at you."

"Get out. She's not—"

"How do you know she's not?"

"Stop it, Ray. She's not interested in me."

"I'm just telling you what I noticed when you were walking back and forth, and your perky—"

"I'll give you some perky."

"You always do, and I'm appreciative and grateful, but she was looking at you as if she were a cat waiting to pounce on dinner."

"If she was—and I'm sure she wasn't—then I'm sure she was thinking about what it would be like to have me out of the way in order to get to you."

"You flatter me, ma'am." He tipped his imaginary hat. "But the last thing she'd be thinking about is hitting on a married guy about to turn fifty."

"Ma'am? You're calling me ma'am? Am I suddenly over the hill, old man?"

"Old man? Come over here, college girl, and I'll show you what this old man can do!"

"We've got three kids; I already know what you can do." She reluctantly laughed.

"And with that body, you don't look anywhere near thirty-five." He patted his lap and waved her over.

"In my entire life, Ray, I've never known anyone so preoccupied with sex as you are...not that I'm complaining."

"But you're about to."

"No, not about that. But if you don't mind, it's time to get serious."

"Ah yes, you wanna debrief. Let me just say that I do owe you that courtesy."

"Yes, you do, and thank you for acknowledging it."

"You did a fantastic job tonight, Leigh. Seriously, you really did." Again he patted his thigh, but she held her ground.

"I think we were lucky the four of them were willing to listen with what I hope was an open mind. But I'm somewhat skeptical that they're not going to let Alice influence the way their kids and our kids interact. This isn't over by a long shot, and I'm still worried."

"Why?"

"Call it intuition. Still, I think luck was on our side that they even listened to what we had to say."

"I don't think it was luck. We both know that had I been the one to take the lead, they would've been totally focused on the meeting being more about damage control for me. Instead, they focused on you and your message. It actually felt good to be the backup...and for the most part, to be an observer."

"You sure spent enough time observing Ms. Kotter."

"Stop it. I gave everyone equal attention—that is, when I wasn't focused on you."

"Maybe so, but now you're gonna have me feeling self-conscious every time I've gotta deal with her."

"Just make sure you don't go into her house without parental supervision," he mocked.

"So getting back to Alice Mayweather. Do you think—"

"Sure, she'll be pissed, but so what? She's a troublemaker. She's always been a troublemaker, and she always will be. The past few weeks should convince you of that. And on top of all that, she's a backstabber. I don't know why you moms let her into your group in the first place."

"Because no one else would have her, and we felt sorry for her. Her kids are well behaved."

"Yeah, when they're on their meds. Otherwise, they're bouncing off the walls from all the sugar she feeds them."

"Now you stop it. You promised me you were gonna tone it down. You promised you weren't going to be so...so—"

"Judgmental? Militant?"

"Those are your words, Ray. But, yes, you promised that you were going to keep your opinions on health-care and life-style choices to your patients and—"

"Practice members," he corrected her. She ignored the remark.

"And if anyone from the preschool wanted advice, you were going to talk to them in your office, in a private setting."

"Yes, I promised, but I'm not giving up the weekly health talks we do at the clinic. I'm not going to stop inviting the general public to attend, and I'm not going to alter what I know to be the truth. But I promise that I'm not going to be so 'out there' with my message that you or the kids are treated as outcasts. I think we...you...made that point. The moms heard loud and clear that I think the world of ER and trauma center docs, and the great lifesaving work they do. But it was equally important that they understood that lifesaving medical procedures are not the same thing as disease-care management—which, I might add, is also not and shouldn't be confused with the restoration of health. There is a very distinct difference between them."

"You don't have to lecture me, and you know that I'm right there with you about the natural healing arts...to a point. There is a limit, as far as I'm concerned, Ray."

"And I'm well aware of that."

"But most people—"

"Sheeple," he interjected.

She rolled her eyes. "Most people have bought into the conventional approach, and that's all they've ever known. So as much as you'd like to wake them up, you already know that when the student is ready, the teacher will appear. And you, I might add, are not anointed by God to be everyone's teacher, let alone force them into the classroom before they're ready to listen."

She walked over to him and ran her fingers through his hair. He, in turn, leaned his face into her abdomen—inhaling as if he hadn't drawn a breath in hours.

"Lavender?"

"Yes, and don't change the subject."

"I love it when you wear lavender...and sandalwood."

"You did have a great line for Carrie Dunsmore, though." She gently pushed his head back. "Did you rehearse that one?"

"You mean the one about my generation having had only three or four shots when we were kids and yet we're not dying from all those viral infections we're told will kill our kids?"

"No, not that one. When you said, and in a very polite way, I might add, 'I'm not going to tell you that you're wrong for being provaccination, because I know you've done your home-work...unlike those people who blindly accept what they hear on the news. That's why you should feel safe in the knowledge that since your child is fully protected, then my children pose no threat to them.' And then she got extremely quiet."

"I had to get that one in. I knew she wasn't going to accept the fact that her little girl is always sick with one thing or another. After listening to your approach this evening, I knew that getting her to feel that her kid was fully protected was just one more way to solidify your message and to get her to reject the hysteria that 'Mayhem' Mayweather is continuing to whip up."

"She's not the only one who's been whipped up lately."

"Are you talking about me?"

"Let's face it. These past several months, with all the letters you've been writing to newspapers and the interviews you've been giving...this is all about Casey's health challenge, and don't you deny it. It's understandable that you're concerned, even worried about her, but it's more than that. You're frus-trated because you think you know why she's having problems and you think it's some sort of medical conspiracy to cover it up."

"I am worried...I admit it. And I'm pissed because they won't even look at the possibility that—"

"And the fact that you're pissed is what worries me, Ray. I feel as if you're getting ready to—"

"Leigh...I—"

"Don't say anything, Ray."

"Hear me out."

"Ray, you've been all worked up thinking that your daughter is a victim. A victim of the military or some pharmaceutical experiment. And I know you wanna go running off to be with her, to help her. OK that's fine…and you should be there for her. But I can tell that you're chomping at the bit to go run off and take out the bad guys. And I'm saying that you just can't keep doing stuff like that. Even if there are bad guys, you can't keep doing that kind of stuff. Not anymore. Not to us, and especially not to the girls."

"Leigh, it's been three years since the last time I—"

"Yes, three years since you ran off to Iraq and almost got yourself killed. And you promised me you were done with all that sort of stuff."

"As I was saying, it's been three years since the last time I allowed myself to get caught up in something like that, and you have to believe me that I really am done." He stood up, placed his hands on her waist, and pulled her in tight. "I admit I've been more outspoken lately, but it's because I'm frustrated with what's happening to Casey. I'm speaking out so that it does bring a spotlight on medical procedures that aren't as safe as we've been led to believe. I'm doing it to channel my energy so that I don't suddenly go running off to save the world."

"Or explode like a volcano?"

"Yes."

"We promised those moms that you were going to tone it down."

"Yes. But if I have to go Seattle to help my daughter, I will."

"Fine. But in the meantime, you'll behave."

"And in the meantime…having learned my lesson…and being that guy who never stops thinking about sex, I should be content to stay here in paradise doing all sorts of sordid things to you."

Ray's cell phone rang, interrupting his advance on Leigh Anne's neck. A quick glance at the caller ID had him shaking his head.

"You're not answering?"

"It's Stella. I seriously think she's going through meno-pause and she has no one to take it out on but me. I'm no longer surprised she can't stay in a relationship."

"Stop it, Ray, just stop it already and answer the phone!"

"The hell with her. She's probably calling to continue insulting me, so no, I'm not answering."

"Ray, it could be about Casey."

7

Seattle, Washington

Ray sat at the window table in Pusateri's Market and took an occasional sip on an espresso—his second—while appearing to watch the world pass by. He looked down at the eggplant marinara, now cold from neglect, and felt guilty for having ordered it. Where he normally wouldn't hesitate devouring the entire plate, he debated taking a few bites only to avoid insulting his host. He hadn't been hungry when he arrived ninety minutes earlier but thought that if he asked for his daughter's favorite dish, it would somehow give him the comfort he'd been hoping to find.

Pusateri's had always been a safe harbor for him, having come to the market on a regular basis during the twenty years he had lived in the affluent bedroom community of Eastridge Heights. He'd often found himself staying an hour longer than necessary—eating, drinking espresso, kibitzing, and generally taking a break from the pretentious facade of what he commonly called the "uppity eastside." The store—it's fixtures and the service—was a step back in time. It looked almost as it did when it had opened sixty years prior, with the framed photos lining the walls serving as a "Where's Waldo" for patrons, who could entertain themselves trying to find the changes from one year to the next.

He was a Bronx boy at heart, and Pioneer Square was the closest thing to that environment the Pacific Northwest had to offer. He couldn't explain why he never thought about it when he was in Hawaii with Leigh Anne, but whenever he came to Seattle, this section of town, especially Pusateri's, immediately called out to him. Whether it was the old-time atmosphere or the smells coming out of Anthony's kitchen, it didn't matter to Ray. When he was there, he felt like a child who had sought the safety of his mother's apron strings when bothered by the imaginary monsters hiding in a closet or peeking out from under a bed in the dark of night. But in spite of the abundance of familiar olfactory stimulants that had easily seduced him during past visits, there was no psychological comfort to be had. Ray found himself growing angry over the fact that those imaginary monsters were now real, and he wondered what, if anything, he could do about it. He entertained a number of possibilities while dosing up on caffeine, each seeming plausible at first but concluding that most would likely result in his incarceration.

He looked around the deli, ready to focus on anything that would take his mind away, even if only for a brief moment. He looked down at his plate and dared himself to take a bite. As far as he was concerned, Pusateri's home-style cooking served up more than a satisfied appetite but also the warm memories of his early childhood and the Saturday grocery shopping he did with his mother: first to the Italian markets of Arthur Avenue, where the shop owners stuffed him with samples of different imported cheeses sliced thick off the wheel, chunks of pepperoni, and little white paper cups filled with tricolored Neapolitan ice cream. And then to the Jewish delis and butchers on the other side of the borough, where his freckled face won over just as many hearts—yielding a bounty of samples that always filled his belly. In the humid heat of a New York City summer, he became so lethargic that he often dozed from the rhythmic rocking of the subway cars on the ride home.

"No, don't do it," he warned himself. *"Don't get off topic. Stay focused on Casey, not on me."* Had he allowed it, the recollection would have helped to ease his mind. But his stress hormones were in overdrive, and he refused the distraction of a sentimental journey—at least that's what he told himself.

Again he looked at the plate of food and closed his eyes, now remembering his daughter bursting into the house after a long cheerleading practice at the high school, starved for dinner and diving into her mother's homemade fresh out-of-the-oven eggplant marinara. He finally picked up his fork and made a halfhearted attempt at cutting through a corner piece before aborting the effort. *"It's no good,"* he thought. *"I can't even pretend to be hungry."*

"I'd offer you an anisette, but you didn't even touch your food. Not even a bite. If you'd like, I'll wrap it up for you." Anthony reached for his plate.

"How long have you been standing there?" Ray said over his shoulder.

"Long enough to know that you're very troubled, my friend...very troubled."

"I'm sorry, Ant, it's just that I—"

"No need to explain. I understand...you don't like my cooking," he joked.

"I'm going to lose her, Ant...my little girl, I'm going to lose her, and there's nothing I can do."

Anthony sat down beside Ray, wanting to comfort him but not knowing what to say.

"Ant, they grow up too fast."

"I know, my friend, I know."

"I look at my three daughters back home in Lanikai, and I pray they stay that young and innocent forever. I wish I could turn back time and relive those days when Jimmy and Casey were that young." Ray looked over at Anthony's son working behind the counter. "You're a lucky man, Ant. Little Anthony and your daughter Bella...they're still young, they're beautiful kids, Ant, and most importantly, they're healthy. You and Joy are very lucky. Don't ever let those kids out of your sight...at least for as long as you can."

Anthony smiled and patted his friend's shoulder. "We'll do our best, Ray. Tell you what. I'll wrap this up along with another portion for you, no extra charge. You can bring them over to the hospital. This way, if your daughter comes out of her...I mean, when she wakes up, she's gonna be starved. This way you two can have a meal together."

"That's kind of you, but I don't think—"

"You want her to eat that hospital food in the condition she's in? Better you should give her my stuff. There's enough garlic, rosemary, and basil in here to cure anything." Anthony smiled.

"OK, sure thing, buddy. Wrap it up for me."

As he swirled the remnants of his espresso, Ray began to notice his fatigue. Since his arrival a couple days prior, he had done nothing but hover over his daughter, fixed on the monitoring equipment by her bedside, scouring the pages of her medical chart, looking for the slightest sign of movement, waiting for her to regain consciousness, and annoying Stella to no end—peppering his friend with questions she couldn't or wouldn't answer. In either case, and in spite of her giving him some latitude because of his emotional state, she had begun to find his uncharacteristic acerbic remarks pushing the weakened boundaries of what was left of their friendship. Her inability or unwillingness to be forthcoming with answers fueled his frustration with her, the Veterans Medical Center, and the medical profession as a whole. Stella's patience had also begun to wear thin, and she'd lectured him on a couple occasions for his threatening comments to a pharmaceutical salesman he accosted in a hallway and for getting in the way of hospital staff.

As it was, Ray was already an unwelcomed guest at the hospital. His brief stint at the center a few years prior found him rebelling against bureaucratic micromanagement and butting heads with career administrator Peter McCain over everything from utilization to the monotony of submitting weekly, monthly, and quarterly reports. But it was the physical altercation with

an orthopedic surgeon in the middle of a senator's highly pub-
licized visit that he was remembered for. So it was no surprise
that McCain had a visceral reaction when he saw Ray for the
first time since his official resignation. Nonetheless, he did
draw pleasure from watching an angry Stella Leone order him
out of the building.

"You've been like this for the past few months, Ray. I take
that back: a few months ago, you weren't as disrespectful to
me. You're treating me as if I did this...as if I'm the enemy.
Now you're just—"

Just tryin' to get a straight answer out of someone...any-
one. But all I get are talking points and a big fat runaround.
Especially from you, Stel. Just who the hell are you protecting?"

"Especially from me? Who am I protect...how dare you!
How fucking dare you! I've told you what I know."

"Which is absolutely nothing. You know as well as I do that
this is probably related to her military service. Every time I've
talked about it, you've avoided any attempt at an intellectual
response by insulting me, by calling me, and I quote, 'one of
those fringe cave dwellers.'"

"Geez, are you on that kick again?"

"Whaddya mean 'again'?"

"OK, then, *still!* You're still on this wild nonsense? You still
quote those disgruntled malcontents who've been discredited
by the scientific community. And speaking of cave dwellers, are
you still looking for that quack?"

"You see? You just proved my point. You're deflecting
the conversation by going on the attack. Well, let me tell you
something: she's certainly no quack. And by 'scientific community,' do you mean the same scientific community that
regularly changes its research data to please their big pharma
benefactors?"

"There you go again, you and your conspiracy theories."

"Damn it, Stel! My daughter is lying in that room down the
hall in a coma, and you people can't figure out why, and you
all refuse to look at the very thing that might have done this
to her!"

"We've been through all this before, Ray. If that were true, then there'd be others."

"Did ya ever follow up with what I asked you to do? Did you or anyone even check with the other VA centers around the country? No, you didn't, and why? Maybe you're afraid that there are other cases."

"You're totally wrong."

"Wrong? Well, did ya contact the DoD to see if there's stuff going on with active duty members? Don't answer, because we both know you didn't. You never had any intention of trying to help me investigate the possibility because you're afraid that I'm right. And I'll bet that when you were on active duty, you administered thousands of those shots to the troops, and just the thought that you participated—"

"That's it, I've had enough!" she yelled, grabbing for the first thing she could get her hands on. "You better get the hell outta here before I slap this bedpan across your face."

"I'm not leaving."

"Yes, you are, either under your own power or with assistance from security. What'll it be?"

McCain and Stella were the least of Ray's concerns as he sat in Pusateri's, waiting for them to end their workday. He was going back to the hospital to be with Casey, but not until they were gone. He was also waiting to hear back from Jimmy. Regardless of what NSA stuff he was in the middle of, the news of his sister's illness would surely get his attention. What he didn't expect was for his son and Stella to be converging on the Italian deli at exactly the same time.

8

Veterans Medical Center
Seattle, Washington

Before Jimmy could come to a full stop, Ray was out of the car and zeroed in on the hospital entrance. Stella was not far behind.

"Ray, slow up!" she shouted, to no avail.

He ran as if possessed, almost knocking several people to the ground as he flew through the lobby door. Not even an outstretched security guard falling out of his chair could block his path, nor break his stride. And any hope of stopping him began to quickly fade after Stella crashed into the dazed and confused watchman.

"Ray, damn it, wait a minute!"

The elevator door closed just as he got to it. Frustrated, he slapped it several times before searching the hallway for a stairwell. He turned to check the opposite direction only to find Stella—her clothing stained from the guard's cup of coffee—limping down the corridor.

"Leave me alone, Stel; just leave me alone."

He moved to his left, and she shifted to her right.

"Listen to me, Ray Silver, just listen to me for a minute before you go barging up there."

"Or what, you'll have me thrown out again? No, I got it… you'll call your ex-husband at the NSA and get him to order a hit on me. Griff's the director over there, and I know he does that sort of stuff. He'll do that for you, right?"

"Ray!"

"My daughter's finally awake, damn it. For how long, we don't know. So let me see her…let me be with her and talk to her while I still can." He turned back to the elevator, vigorously pushing the call button and then slapped at the door once again. "Damn these things!"

"Ray, she flatlined! Do you hear me? Did you hear what I just said? She coded, Ray. They brought her back with the paddles…twice."

"I know that. I heard you in Pusateri's and again in the car. You're like a fucking broken record for Chrissake! She coded, she was dead, I got it, OK?"

"Ray, it's the only reason she came out of the coma. She may not be able to talk to you, and if she can, she may be too drugged up at this point to be coherent. She may not even know it's you."

"Fine, I hear you. Now just let me get to her, and leave me alone."

"Ray, you're all fired up, and the last thing she needs is for you to go storming in there."

"And if she's gonna code again and can't be brought back, I want her to know that I was right there with her. I wanna be able to tell her—" His voice trailed off for a moment. Looking straight through Stella as if she weren't there, he continued just above a whisper: "I wanna be able to tell her what to expect on the other side."

"Yes, of course. You've been there, haven't you?" She raised an eyebrow.

"That's right. Not that I expect you to believe me."

"Now's not the time for—"

"You're damn right, it's not." Again he pushed the call button for the elevator, then dashed around Stella—racing for the stairs at the far end of the hallway, leaving her to wait for Jimmy.

He got several flights up before he realized that the floor numbers at each landing had been painted over. He stood with eyes closed, trying to recall if he had climbed three of four levels. *"Come on, come on, just decide."* He didn't have to. The door flung open, startling both him and the attendant on the other side.

"ICU?" he yelled. "ICU, where is it?"

"One flight up."

He bounded the next sixteen steps by twos, maintaining his pace down the hallway until he stopped just shy of his daughter's room—gasping from anxiety, the lump in his throat making it hard for him to breathe or swallow. Ray felt his heart pounding harder than he had ever experienced. In spite of stares from passersby, he gathered himself as best as he could, stepped into the doorway, and stared at Casey lying motionless. His eyes darted between the monitors, understanding enough to know that the active brain scan indicated she must have been dreaming. Still, he watched his daughter and waited for her chest rise and fall a few times before he allowed himself to believe the digital readouts. He studied her face, and like so many times before, he was reminded of his ex-wife. Mother and daughter had looked almost identical, especially when they smiled—something that Mary Jo did little of the last few years she was alive.

"The doctor has her sedated, so she's in and out," a nurse said, adjusting the flow on an IV drip. "But when she is awake, she can communicate…a little anyway. She asked for you."

"What did she say?"

"She wanted to know if the surgeons at Ramstein were able to save your kidney. She wanted to know if the blood flow had been clamped off too long."

"What? She knows they did. She was told that her quick thinking in Fallujah was what saved it and me," he explained, as if the nurse knew what he was referring to.

"She's having some wild dreams…from all the drugs, I suppose. Apparently, she's been reliving the war, along with a bunch of other things."

Ray nodded and pulled a chair alongside her bed, hesitating before taking her hand. It was moist and cold. Her face grimaced a little, and again he thought of Mary Jo.

"*Are you OK, Jo?*"

"*Considering I just went through eight hours of the most intense...I should've done the epidural.*"

"*I'm sorry if you felt pressured not to.*"

"*No, I just didn't think she'd give me such a hard time coming into the world. Jimmy's birth was a breeze compared to this.*"

"*She was breach, and the chord was wrapped around her neck. She came out all blue.*"

"*I know, silly; I was there, remember? But look at her... little Casey is warm and pink. And she's resting so peacefully now. She looks just like an angel.*"

"*She looks just like you, Jo. Especially that smile...or is that gas?*"

"*Stop it, Ray. I can't believe you just said that. It's a good thing Jimmy didn't hear you say that. He's beginning to repeat everything you say.*"

"*I almost forgot about, Jimmy. He's out in the hallway with your folks. Don't go anywhere, Jo; I'm gonna go get him so he can meet his new sister.*"

"*Don't worry, I'll be right here.*"

"*Jimmy?*"

"I'm right behind you, Dad."

"What?" Ray turned toward the door. "Jimmy!"

"Don't worry, I'm right here. I'm not going anywhere."

"Where's Stella?"

"She's over at the nurses' station...thought it best not to come in."

"Good. Lately she's been a real—"

"Dad, Casey." He pointed to his sister.

In spite of the sedation, her face showed more signs of distress—her lips curling down and her eyelids tightening as Ray now felt her light squeeze on his hand.

She peered out of the Blackhawk's open side door and watched the other air ambulance descend through enemy fire to pick up the wounded. Her pilot again told them to abort.

"Dustoff 17, hold until the Cobras arrive," ordered Bill Graff, Dustoff 18's pilot.

"This is fucked, Billy. Those guys are gonna die down there if we don't get 'em back to base."

"I know, Craig, but patience. They'll be here any minute."

"Nah, I'm going down."

"Craig," Graff called out. "Abort! There's no place to put her down."

"Just gonna tap the front wheel on one of those mud walls, Billy boy."

"Abort, Craig! It's too—"

As the 17 descended farther, a rocket-propelled grenade came streaming out of nowhere and the 18's sister ship lit up like a fireworks show, going down in a ball of flame and exploding on impact.

"Fucking shit! God damn it!" the 18's copilot screamed.

"Listen, kids, it's way too hot," Graff told his crew. "I'm gonna back off a little until the Cobras get here."

"No good," responded Casey. "We've gotta get those guys outta there."

"Did you see what just happened to 17, Silver?"

Casey didn't answer but instead locked her harness into a big yellow hook just outside the cabin door.

"Whaddya doing?" A surprised team member looked at her like she was crazy.

"Lower me," Casey said, stepping out of the chopper. She was instantly suspended one hundred fifty feet above the ground. Dangling in the air, she stared back into the cabin and pointed her thumb downward, calmly repeating the order.

"Jesus Christ!" the copilot shouted. "She's on the cable."

"Silver! Are you fucking nuts? Get back in!" Graff commanded.

"Three of those wounded down there are still alive, one just barely. This is what we came here for, isn't it?"

"Silver!"

"Well, isn't it? Now lower me down before I get my ass shot off."

The chopper danced and swayed as she descended—Graff doing his best to maintain position while avoiding gunfire so Casey didn't swing back and forth any more than she had to. Combatants on both sides fought hard as she got closer to the ground, landing hard. She was within a couple of feet of one of the wounded but still needed a few seconds to orient herself, a result of having spun completely around a few times during the drop. She crawled over to check the soldier's vital signs.

"This one's gone," she reported into her microphone.

She spun to her right and located another wounded soldier. Bullets pinged, bounced off rocks, and dug into the dirt around her feet as she ran to him, hugging the ground as she moved. She immediately checked his vitals.

"He's got a head wound, but he's conscious," she called to the chopper above. "Leg wound, too. Get ready up there."

She removed her harness and secured it around the man's waist, talking to him as she worked. "Can you hear me, soldier?"

"Yes."

"What's your name?" she asked, assessing him for signs of brain injury.

"Jackson."

"What unit are you with?"

"126th Infantry, Oregon National Guard."

"No shit! I'm from Seattle. We're neighbors."

"You're not from Seattle. You're an angel sent from heaven into this living hell."

"I thought there were only fallen angels in hell."

"No, I didn't mean—"

With the harness firmly strapped, she threw herself on top of him in a bear hug, shielding him from further injury. "It's OK, I know what you meant. Now hold on to me while I spread my wings." She looked up toward the helicopter. "Bring us up, Johnny."

* * *

When Ray woke, it took him several minutes of checking between the wall clock and the darkness outside to figure out that it was 5:00 a.m. and not 5:00 p.m., but it didn't take him long to realize that his back was stiff and sore. *"Fuckin' cheap chairs."* He shifted a little to ease a cramp, and a turkey salad sandwich fell to the floor. *"Where'd that come from?"* The last thing he could recall before dozing off was Jimmy heading down to the cafeteria before it closed. *"Thank God I was more tired than hungry,"* he thought, but he could no longer ignore his stomach's complaints. He hadn't eaten in twenty-four hours and now found himself debating the pros and cons of eating a mayonnaise-based sandwich that had been resting in his lap since the evening before. After a quick glance at the laundry list of preservatives and other chemicals listed on the package, he concluded that there were probably enough genetically modified ingredients in the sandwich that it could have easily survived for months without refrigeration. *"All of these chemicals are more of a health threat than the risk of coming down with food poisoning."* In spite of the protest being lodged by his digestive system, he tossed the sandwich into the red wastebin marked "Danger Biohazard."

Ray stretched and looked around, only to find his son at the opposite end of the room slouched in a chair of equal quality. He turned back to his daughter, wondering where she had been and where her drug-stimulated subconscious was taking her now.

"I'm sitting right here, kiddo," he reassured her. Not yet fully awake and too stiff to get up, he did his best to appeal to her. "I'd love to talk to you, sweetie. It's been too long. Promise me…promise me that you won't go until we talk, OK?"

Her eyes fluttered a little, then opened, and she tried to manage a smile when she noticed her father. He had no idea if she knew it was him, but that didn't stop Ray from trying to sit up to have that talk—and then sinking back into his chair when she drifted back into sleep. He'd lost count how many times his eyes had shifted between the monitors to reassure himself that he still had a chance for a conversation. With the numbers declining each hour, he now acknowledged it was a slim chance, but that was better than no chance at all. He leaned his head back, closed his eyes, and began to pray, begging over and over for her to be blessed with a miracle recovery.

"She grew up too fast," he said before he, too, fell back to sleep.

"Come on, Dad, game's over. Let's go home."

"It's not totally over yet, young lady. Go back with your team and wait for the coach's talk."

"Daad? Do I hafta? It's the same ol' stuff each time. He tells us we all did good, even the kids who struck out or dropped balls. Heck, Dad, Jack Bourla made three errors...and that was in the first inning! 'Remember, Yankees, you're all winners,'" she said as she mocked her coach's encouragement.

"Well, he's teaching you kids good sportsmanship, Casey. And that's important to learn in T-ball as it is with all things. It's an important life skill."

"It doesn't take skill to know that T-ball sucks, Dad. Why can't I play real baseball with kids my own age?"

"Casey!"

"I'm just bein' honest. They put me on this team because I'm a girl. I'm ten years old, the ONLY girl on this team of eight-year-old boys, and I'm better than any of them. And this stuff about always playing so the game ends in a tie is just stupid. When I play a game, I wanna win; otherwise, what's the point?"

"We'll talk about this at home, OK? Now go back for the coach's talk and the team cheer."

"And that's another thing, Dad. 'Yippee I Yankees?' That's pretty lame."

Ray laughed in his sleep. The dream was so real that he felt the warmth of that late afternoon summer sunshine all over again...until Casey reached out to squeeze his hand and a cold shiver ran through his body.

"Daddy...I—" Her voice was hesitant.

"What are you doing out of bed?"

"Daddy, I've got something I need to say before—"

"Shhh, save your strength, kiddo."

"Daddy, please. I...I don't have much time."

"Don't be silly, Casey doodle. You're going to be just fine."

"You haven't called me that since I was a little girl."

"I know. That was my favorite nickname for you, and I'm gonna start calling you that again when—"

"Daddy, please listen to me...please." She tried squeezing his hand a bit harder.

"What?"

"I'm sorry."

"Sorry? What do you have to be sorry about?"

"I never meant to make you feel bad about missing the Dads, Daughters, and Doughnuts Day at school."

"What? That was years ago when you were a little girl... when you were in third grade. Why are you thinking about that now?"

"Because I made you feel bad for being the only dad who didn't show up."

"No, no, honey. I was the only dad to not show up that day, and I never forgot how much it hurt you. I let you down that day, and that's why I felt bad...because I disappointed you. I let you down."

"But I kept reminding you about it whenever I was mad at you—"

"And you had every right to, so let's just forgive each other, OK?"

"I forgave you a long, long time ago, Daddy. I just never told you."

"It's OK, Casey, it's OK. When we get you home, we're gonna do a special Dads, Daughters, and Doughnuts Day. Just you and me, baby...is that OK with you? And we'll make the doughnuts ourselves."

"Daddy, I'm scared. I'm not ready. I'm not ready to go."

"Sweetie, you're gonna be just fine."

"Do you remember when you were wounded in Iraq?"

"I remember waking up in the hospital at the Ramstein Air Base."

"Before that...when I was operating on you in the helo... on our way from Fallujah to TQ. Do you remember that special place you said you were when you left your body?"

"Yes, Casey, I remember."

"I was just there."

"But that doesn't mean anything. It was probably the drugs, honey. It's all the drugs they have you on and...and the fact that I told you all about my experience. Your unconscious mind was just looking for a safe place to go."

"Daddy, my body is shutting down. It's all broken inside and...I'm tired, Daddy. I can't fight anymore. I don't have the strength. I'm scared, not because of what lies ahead, but because I'll be leaving you and Jimmy."

"Please, Casey, don't—"

This time when Ray's eyes opened he battled a bright light that filled the room. His neck hurt as much as his back, and it took him a couple of minutes to realize he had dozed back off and it was now just after noon.

"Casey?"

"Dr. Silver, please move out of the way." The nurse's voice was polite but commanding.

The chattering and abrupt movements that woke him had nothing to do with his dream.

"What's that?"

"Please move away from the bed...please, we need to work."

Two doctors and a couple nurses were attending to his daughter—their movements fast but controlled. Her movements were faster, almost demonic. The numbers on the heart monitor had been high at first glance but were now crashing.

"What happened? What's going on?" Ray shifted left, then right, then left again in an effort to see past the medical team.

"Don't worry, Dr. Silver; she's having a seizure is all." The nurse firmly moved Ray farther away from the bed, almost making him trip as he backpedaled. "I asked you to give us some room. Now please let us work!"

He continued to watch, worried as their pace became more frantic—not noticing both Jimmy and Stella standing behind him, not hearing them pleading for him to step out into the hallway.

9

VA Medical Center
Seattle, Washington

"**D**uring the short period I worked here at the VA hospital, I came up here to the roof a couple of times...usually when I took lunch. It was kind of quiet, and you could be all alone and just stare out across Puget Sound. Depending upon the air temperature and the humidity, the Olympic Mountains would sometimes seem a lot larger than they appear right now. Come take a look at this view."

Ray sat on the metal steps leading to the helipad, his shoulders slumped, his voice low and monotone.

"I know you're upset and all...I am, too...but you were pretty disrespectful to Stella. She was only trying to comfort you, Dad."

"The best part though, to me anyway, was watching the ferries coming in or going out of the Coleman Dock. And then I'd watch them slide across the water. It was so peaceful, or at least I remember it being peaceful, not like it is now. Can you believe all the noise coming from the freeway. It's funny, because I don't recall it being that noisy. Anyway, I remember this one time I watched this ferry sail across the sound toward Bainbridge Island until it was barely a dot and—"

"She was pretty upset with the way you blew her off, and please stop ignoring me."

"After what we just witnessed, is this really what you wanna talk about?"

Jimmy didn't answer.

"All right, then, you wanna do this? OK." Ray stood up, dusted off the back of his pants, and walked toward the west-side facade facing Elliot Bay. "I don't need or want her comfort. She'd been nothing but an obstacle during this whole ordeal. Every time I had a question or a concern, every time I asked her to check something out for me, all she did was ignore me or attack me, my profession, my sanity…anything but answer my questions. Every suggestion that I'd make, any help that I offered…she'd twist and distort my words, my intentions, my… she'd turn every conversation into a fight."

"It takes two."

"I did my best to ignore her."

"That's hard to believe."

"Are you calling me a liar, Jimmy?"

"No, of course not, Dad, of course not. I'm just surprised. I thought she was in your corner. I thought she was a friend."

"I thought so, too."

"So what now?"

"This isn't finished."

"Come on, Dad, leave her alone."

"I'm not talking about Stella. That's finished! I don't want anything to do with her from this day forward."

"Then what are you talking about?"

"Casey was betrayed…by her own country she was betrayed."

"Whaddya mean betrayed. How? By whom?"

"I don't know. By the navy, the DoD…I don't know exactly, but I wanna find out."

"Whaddya talking about, Dad?"

"I just have this feeling that she was used like a guinea pig, an expendable lab rat."

"What? When she was in the navy? That's crazy."

"I know you don't believe me. But I keep thinking about Desert Storm and Gulf War Syndrome. It was seventeen years ago. I don't think you'd really remember it. I think about all those guys who got sick during and after that conflict. Keep in mind that not everyone who went over there got sick. You could have a hundred, two hundred guys, maybe more, in one unit or together in one location, but only some came down with the syndrome. Why? Some guys and even gals who weren't even stationed in the Gulf came down with it as well. Now, I'm not the only one who thinks the sick ones had been singled out to receive some sort of mystery vaccine."

"And you're saying that Casey was on the receiving end of some kind of experimental shot? That's totally nuts. What proof do you have?"

"None. But every time I asked Stella or anyone else here at the VA to consider the possibility, to look into her service medical file, to look for some link, some autoimmune reaction...they either laughed at me, attacked my sanity, or just outright ignored me."

"So let's say for the sake of argument you're right on this. How are you going to prove it? How are you going to get proof?"

Ray starred at his son while he thought about his options.

"No, Dad, I couldn't start digging—"

"I'm not asking you to get involved...although with you working for the NSA, you would have access to what would be restricted information. No, forget I said that. I don't want or expect you to get involved in this. I don't want you to jeopardize your job at the agency, especially now that your wife is pregnant. Nope, I'll just have to take care of this on my own."

"You mean like the other messes you've gotten into over the years?"

"Those were different. I've got to figure this one out on my own. But rest assured, I am going to look into this, so don't worry about it."

"You know I would help you if I could. It's just that I—"

"No worries, kiddo, really. I already told you I understand. I got this. So don't you dare feel the slightest bit guilty. I understand how sensitive things can get for you at the NSA. So let it go. This is my thing. This is what a father does for his kids. Like when I thought you had been kidnapped in Iraq and I found a way to get over there…to look for you…and I caught that RPG fragment…and—"

"OK, OK, stop it already. What can I—"

"Just a little information to get me started. Then I'll do the rest."

"As long as it's just a little information."

"I'm hoping to find someone who might know what, why, and how this happened, and if it's happening to anyone else."

"Do you even know where to begin looking?"

"Colorado."

"Colorado?"

"Yeah, but here's that one little favor I need from you."

"You want me—"

"To go back to your office in New York."

"To do what exactly?"

"Keep in mind that the person I need to find doesn't wanna be found."

"Dad?"

"From what I hear, she's *persona non grata*, so she's not going to be just wandering the streets of Durango or some other small mountain town."

"What am I supposed to do? Come up with a name and location out of thin air?"

"Look it, kiddo, I don't know the whole story, but I need to find her because I'm sure she can help me get some answers…and if she's not the one who can do it, then she can direct me to someone who can. Beyond that, if you want to look into her history, then that's up to you. And you gotta keep this to yourself. You can't let anyone at the agency, especially Griff Kelley, find out anything, because he'll be all over you like flies on—"

"You're the last person Director Kelley wants to hear about. You got a name?"

"I've got a name. I just need you to find out where she's hiding."

10

Avenue of the Americas
Manhattan
Mid-November 2007

I t had been a couple weeks since the winds of an Indian summer blasted through the cavernous cross streets of glass and steel, assaulting pedestrians as they reluctantly ventured out of their climate-controlled offices to attack the international delicacies offered up by any number of vender carts lining the city sidewalks. Jimmy took advantage of the cooler weather and the tease of the late morning sun to people-watch outside the Coxx television studios. The blending aromas of falafel, hotdogs smothered in sauerkraut, and thick loaves of Italian bread stuffed with piping hot sausages competed for his attention while he waited for his wife to finish her post-news-program duties.

He was happy her cohost assignment and the newsroom location had been ideal for the both of them, unlike her job as a DC-based political correspondent frantically chasing down leads and interviews at all hours of the day. Now she simply rolled out of bed and into a waiting chauffeured car for a short predawn commute to sessions with professional makeup artists, hairstylists, and wardrobe consultants. If that didn't spoil her, he knew the convenience of working within a couple blocks of Radio City Music Hall, the Eugene O'Neill and Majestic Theaters, and her favorite, the Museum of Modern Art would certainly do the trick—not that he didn't have a hand in the pampering with his downtown office being just a phone call and a subway ride away. He'd said, "I don't care what time it is or how busy I am at work, Jen. If you start having contractions or even if you need anything, you call me." And that she did.

The smells coming from the different food carts made him hungry, and he wondered, with a buffet lining the sidewalks as far as the eye could see, if she'd still insist they walk all the way to the Carnegie Deli on 7th and West 55th. For the past few weeks, she'd had an insatiable craving for pastrami on rye topped with spicy brown mustard, a heaping mound of coleslaw, and a double order of garlic pickle—a feast that could only be washed down with an extra-large cream soda. And though the timing of her cravings had been unpredictable, he knew better than to argue with the physiological demands of pregnancy.

"I know I shouldn't be eating like this, Jimmy, but I just can't help myself. It's all I think about."

"Trust me, I know. I don't mind making the trek up here from Lafayette Street in the middle of the morning, but—"

"As if you needed an excuse to get out of work." She laughed.

"You got me there. I'm always happy to take a break from all that reading, but it's getting harder and harder to drag myself out of bed to make a cross-town deli run at two in the morning."

"It's good training for you in case I go into labor at two or three or—"

"If the baby is anything like you, I'm sure he'll decide to show up in the wee hours of the morning... not that I'm complaining, but it is stressful worrying about you going into labor when I'm chasing down garlic pickles and coleslaw... and on top of worrying about my dad these days—"

"I know. I spoke to Leigh Anne the other day. She says he's been on edge, and he's been obsessing over this thing."
"Which is why I never mention your diet."
"Oh my god, don't you dare! That'll really send him over the edge."

As busy as Manhattan streets were, 6th Avenue (a.k.a. the Avenue of the Americas) was probably among the busiest. Someone once joked to Jimmy that there were probably more cabs and limos clogging the streets than there were pedestrians. And in Manhattan, black limos were surely plentiful, which is probably why Jimmy failed to notice NSA director Griffin Kelley getting out of the one that had just pulled up to the curb.

"You're a long way from the office, lieutenant."

Jimmy continued to watch a scantily clad full-figured brunette walk down the street.

"Silver?"

"General Kelley! I didn't see you, sir."

"Then it's a good thing you're not a field agent, Jimmy. I can see you get distracted easily."

"No, sir. I mean, yes, sir. I mean…it's been a few years since anyone addressed me by my naval rank. I didn't know you were speaking to me. I wasn't expecting—"

"Relax, Jimmy, just relax. It's good to see you again."

"You too, sir. It's been a while."

"Indeed. I assume you're waiting for your wife?"

"Yes, sir."

"Everything OK with the pregnancy?"

"Yes, sir. Just joining her for a midmorning deli craving."

"My first wife…the one before Stella…she used to get these weird cravings all the time. I remember this one time she woke me up at three in the morning because she wanted sauerkraut. Can you believe that? The woman could eat a full jar within minutes."

"I didn't know you'd been married before Stella. I didn't know you had children."

"It was a short marriage, and we didn't have any kids. And I'm not going to have any with wife number three."

"Oh...I'm sorry."

"Don't be. My first wife hadn't been pregnant. She'd just had these weird cravings all the time. Which was one of several reasons it was a very short marriage. My new wife, as young as she is, knows better than to ask for any kids. I'm too old for that now. Before I forget, I wanted to mention how terrible I feel about your sister."

Jimmy nodded his acknowledgment. "Stella called you?"

"Yes. She told me everything...even the falling out she and your dad had. Jimmy, I was honored to have been able to see your sister in action with the 705th Medevac Unit. She was a credit to the uniform. Is there any chance—"

"Unfortunately no."

"I see." There was a moment of awkward silence. "So... short workload at the office?"

"It's been quiet, yes, sir."

"Hit a roadblock trying to find information on Paige Motz?" The question caught Jimmy by surprise. "Yeah, I know you've been searching for her, and I know you've been doing it for your father."

"How?"

"We're the NSA, kid. We keep tabs on everything going through the Internet. Didn't you think we'd keep tabs on what's going through our own servers?"

"I know, but Dr. Paige Motz? She's just a former vaccine researcher, right?"

"She's an infectious disease expert, and the agency has a special interest in her. The first time you typed her name into the search bar, it was brought to my attention and I've had you monitored ever since."

"That was three weeks ago. You've been having me watched for three weeks?"

"That's right."

"Every online search?'

"Every last key stroke."

"Everything I've been doing at work has been monitored?"

"At work, and everything you do from your home computer as well."

"And you're first coming to talk to me about it now? Can I ask why?"

"To see how long you'd keep trying and to see if you could come up with anything we didn't already have archived."

"Then you know I didn't get very far, sir. Except for a couple of videos of her speaking at alternative health conferences—and even then she was speaking from an offsite location via webcam. Anyway, I was just doing a favor for my dad. He wants to locate her, to talk to her about—"

"I know why he wants to find her. We've been trying to find her, too."

"I'm sure the agency's reasons are quite different."

"Not completely, but you're correct. There are other reasons."

"Can I assume it's not because she's been bad-mouthing pharmaceutical companies?"

"Let's just say she has information that could compromise national security."

"What, are you sure? No, I know you're sure. Is this why you flew up from Washington?"

"I've got some other business here, but yeah, I wanted to talk to you about this, and it's better to do it face to face."

"I'll stand down, general. No problem. I'll just tell my dad—"

"No, don't stand down. In fact, I want you to help your dad find her." He handed Jimmy a small manila envelope. "Put this away until you're alone."

Jimmy glanced at it, taking note of the handwritten *"JS for your eyes only—Dr. PM"* across the front before folding it in half and stuffing it into his back pocket.

"You mean you want to use my dad to get to her?"

"Exactly."

"I was under the impression the two of you were done with each other. After the Iraq thing, he made it clear that he wanted nothing more to do with the agency and, no disrespect intended, he wanted nothing further to do with you."

"I'm fully aware of his wishes...and how he feels about me."

"He doesn't dislike you, sir."

"No, but he does distrust me, which is probably why he's not happy with you working for us."

"It was my understanding that you didn't want him getting involved in agency business as well. So, if I may ask, what's changed, sir?"

"As I said, Jimmy, this is a matter of national security. And what I'm going to ask you to do goes beyond your normal duties as an NSA lawyer. But it needs to be done."

"I've had one experience as a field operative, and you knew when I took this job I didn't want to do anything like that again. I hope you're not expecting me to—"

"No, and don't even talk about that out here on the street. You know we've got people for that sort of stuff. But this isn't even going to go that far. We just want to find her and bring her in...for questioning and for her safety."

"Not to mention arrest, trial, and imprisonment? But if she intentionally violated national security, then she should get what she deserves, I guess. And you need my dad because?"

"Because he's been bringing a lot of attention to himself over the past few months and it's been all over the news. And since the subject matter is right up her alley, she'd have to be living on the moon somewhere to not have seen any of it. So we're pretty sure she knows about him, what he looks like, all that stuff. She also knows we've been looking for her, and she can smell us coming from miles away...which is why, I'm sorry to say, we can't find her."

"She's that smart?"

"Smarter. But if your dad is looking for her and if he gets close enough, there's a good chance she'll let herself be found."

"I don't understand. Why would she do that?"

"Out of fear her location will be compromised. So he'll be looking for her, and she'll make contact with him...that's when we grab her."

"And then she'll think he was an agent all along."

"Not that it matters at that point, but she'll probably just think he was careless enough to be followed."

"Outside of those videos, I can't dig up any information on her. It's almost as if everything on her was wiped clean."

"Not to worry. That envelope has all the info you need. It's actually all the info we've got: from her former employer to her place of birth, where she went to school, recreational interests. There's a list of some small towns your dad can go to look for her."

"And if she doesn't take the bait?"

"We think she will. And, Jimmy...he's not to know any of this. He's not to know that we're following him to get to her. There can't be any hint of hesitancy on his part; otherwise, she'll sense it. If he's totally surprised, she'll see it in his face."

"Personally, sir, I don't want him to be used this way. It isn't right, especially now because of what he's going through."

"Jimmy, this needs to be done...and as much as I don't like it either, he owes me."

"Did you forget he almost got killed in Iraq while trying to save your life?"

"Did you forget he went there illegally because he thought you'd been kidnapped?" Griff asked to Jimmy's silence. "I didn't forget what your father did for his country, for the agency, or for you and me. And it's because I haven't forgotten that I've been protecting him."

"Protecting him?"

"With all the commotion he's been making over the past year, he's been pissing off a lot of people. People with a vested interest."

"Senators? Congressmen?"

"And media moguls, to name just a few." Griff nodded toward the Coxx building. "I've gone out of my way to squash two attempted IRS audits and another FDA raid...all of which were ordered in a retaliatory effort to shut him up."

"I didn't know...I'm sure he'll be grateful once he—"

"He's not to know about this, either."

Without missing a beat, Griffin Kelley changed the subject when he saw Jenna Grant approaching. "And I think it's wonderful that you came up here from the office to have lunch with your beautiful bride. And speaking of Jenna." Griff flashed a grandfatherly smile. "Ms. Grant, it's so good to see you again."

"General Kelley, what a surprise! What brings you up to New York?" She gave him a hug.

"I was asked to tape a segment for one of your network's Sunday shows."

"Really? That's great. What about?"

"With the uproar over our new domestic surveillance program, the president thought I should do a little PR."

"I'm surprised you had to come up here to do the taping. All the Sunday political shows originate in DC. But I don't have to tell you."

"Jenna, you will always be an investigative reporter. I like that about you, young lady. I had business here in the city, and this was the only time I had available, so the producer of Coxx News Sunday asked me to stop by here to tape the segment."

"Well, that certainly makes sense."

"Listen, you two, I've got business to attend to, and you, Ms. Grant, better get your pastrami sandwich so your husband can get back downtown and earn his paycheck."

* * *

Jimmy reached across the table to wipe a small smudge of mustard from Jenna's cheek. He showed her the yellow stain on his index finger, and when he reached for the napkin, she grabbed his hand—laughing as she licked it clean.

"You don't know where that finger's been, Jen."

"You mean since I got out of bed this morning?"

"Just eat your sandwich."

"Look who's embarrassed. If you want, I can do my Meg Ryan imitation." She tipped her head back, closed her eyes, and started to moan.

"Now that I know pastrami gets you that aroused, I'll be bringing it home by the pound for those nights when you're too exhausted to fool around...like after the baby arrives."

"And what makes you think that'll ever happen?"

"You're about to be a mother...it'll happen. For starters, you'll get tired from waking up in the middle of the night, and that alone is going to make you cranky."

"So I guess you're saying that all of your interrupted sleep is the reason you're starting to act like a mother? Or should I say *mutha?*"

"Excuse me? Are you referring to the other night when—"

"When you went ballistic on that messenger guy."

"You're kidding me, right? He was flying down the street and almost hit you with his bike. And all I did was just—"

"Get your badass on. Yelling and screaming as if you wanted to kill the guy. You should've seen your face."

"I wasn't that bad."

"You were the color of this pastrami. You definitely had your badass on. And I like it. I like it when you get all, you know, gangsta wit dat attitude, boy. It makes me hot." Making faces and hand gestures as if she were a street tough, Jenna extended her leg to make contact with the inner portion of his thigh.

"I was protectin' my bitch, yo." He played along with her. "You likin' that sammich?"

"This is really hitting the spot. Are you sure you don't want some?" She pushed it toward him, then smiled before pulling back and attacking it herself.

Jimmy took notice of the other customers watching them. Jenna laughed at his embarrassment.

"Slow down, girl. I guarantee it'll be more pleasurable if you give your taste buds a chance."

"Trust me, I can taste it. I've been dying for this since breakfast."

"Which was?"

"The leftover sandwich from yesterday, but that was at three this morning. So you see, I'm already getting up in the middle of the night, and surprise, surprise, I'm not cranky!"

"We'll see."

"But speaking of surprises...why did General Kelley come up to New York?"

"He told you...to tape a segment for one of the Sunday shows."

"No, he said he was taping the segment here because he had other business to attend to."

"Yes, he did say that. However, the director of the NSA doesn't usually disclose his business to an ordinary agency employee like myself."

"OK." She took a bite of her pickle.

"Just like that you're saying OK?"

"Yeah, why? If I ask you again, you'll change your answer?"

"No."

"So he didn't come up here to talk to you about your father?"

"Why would he do that?"

"Your dad has been in the news lately...quite a bit, as you know."

"Yes, but his issue has nothing to do with—"

"It had nothing to do with being in the national spotlight until—"

"My sister."

"Yes. Because an innocent interview about vaccine safety turned into him making claims about military personnel being used as unwitting test subjects."

"Yes, I saw a clip of that interview...on your network, no less."

"I've gotta tell you that the higher ups have been giving me some pressure."

"To do a story on him?"

"Yes. And they don't want it to be flattering, either. And I'm sure you know that Leigh Anne has been feeling some heat as well."

"From your bosses?"

"From her friends...I mean, the other moms from the pre-school. Your father's ongoing rant about this whole thing is making people very uncomfortable, and she and the girls are being treated as if they were lepers. Did you hear that someone painted 'child abuser' across the hood of your father's Jeep?"

"Yeah."

"And 'contagious' in red paint across the door of Leigh's car."

"Yeah, I heard about that, too."

"And then there was the road rage incident."

"It wasn't road rage."

"Jimmy, he chased a guy for five miles through the streets of Kanehoe just because he flipped off your dad."

"It was five blocks, and the guy threw an egg into the car and all three girls were in the backseat. My dad drove after the guy while he phoned it in to the police."

"Still, you really need to talk to him. You need to get him to calm down."

"Yeah, but you know my dad. He's just an activist, and your prior experience with him should tell you that he doesn't just rant without cause."

"I'm serious, Jimmy. Some people can really get fanatical and crazy, and I don't want Leigh and the girls, or your dad, to get hurt because some nut case goes too far."

"I know. I've been keeping up on what's been happening, and I know."

"You'll talk to him?"

"Yeah, I'll call him when I get back to the office. You're not going to do any story on him, are you?"

"Not a chance. They know better than to ask me."

"But they did ask you."

"Do you know how many hundreds of millions of dollars the pharmaceutical industry spends on advertising each year? They don't like it when somebody starts stirring the pot like your father's been doing. When the drug guys come to the media for PR help, they do so with the not-so-subtle threat that all that ad revenue could be in jeopardy if we don't do a thorough job."

"Like that Kimmel character out in Hawaii?"

"He's at the far end of the spectrum, but yes."

"So why are your bosses pressuring you?"

"For one thing, they know I'm related to your father."

"Was your position at the network threatened?"

"No, but—"

"But they knew if they pressured you we'd be having this conversation, right?" Jimmy sighed

"So you'll have a conversation with your dad?"

"Oh, we're going to have a conversation all right."

"And he'll listen to you?"

"He'll be hanging on every word of what I'll have to say to him. I guarantee it. What was the second thing?"

"Because of that latest measles outbreak in Hawaii, there's been talk of growing support in Congress for a bill to take away all vaccine exemptions, both religious and philosophical."

"That's part of what my dad's been arguing against."

"Well, the guy who's been leading the charge on that is Patrick Moffett, the head of McTavish Labs."

"What's that got to do with you?"

"He's making the rounds to all the news programs in a couple weeks. If you ask me, it's all a big push to whip up the fear and get the general public to call Congress to urge support for the bill. He'll be on my program, too, and I've been warned not to deviate from the script that Moffett himself wrote for the appearance."

"And he gets to do that, write his own script?"

Jenna nodded.

"And what does that tell you?"

"Besides the fact that money talks…maybe your dad is on to something. But, Jimmy, please don't say anything to him about this."

"I've got enough to deal with right now and certainly don't need to throw this into the mix."

"Thank you, sweetie. You don't how much this means to get them off my back."

"Anything for my girl."

"Anything?"

"Anything."

"In that case, I want—"

"Another pastrami sandwich...to go?"

"OK!" She smiled. "But what I really want is to know why General Kelley came up to New York."

11

Colorado

After five days of driving from one town to the next and asking questions at health-food stores, farmers' markets, pharmacies, and taverns with nothing to show for it, Ray was tired and becoming discouraged. Breckinridge was a dead end, but it was a beautiful town. It was in the mountains, which he loved, and it was a place he could almost see himself living—save for his addiction to warmer temperatures and an unpretentious Hawaiian lifestyle. And then there were Loveland, Boulder, and Westminster—all a complete waste of time as far as he was concerned.

In the places Paige Motz had once been known to frequent, people acted as if they had no idea who she was. *"Maybe they didn't know her. And then again, maybe they did."* He played devil's advocate in his own mind. *"Maybe they're new to the area and they really don't know anything about her. But if she's here, somewhere somebody's got to know her."* He rationalized but continued to debate as he drove off to the next town on his list. However, it wasn't lost on him that there had been a few who had shown no interest in talking once her name was mentioned. *"Unfriendly, that's for sure. Well, not so much unfriendly as they were acting more protective than anything else. I'll bet they've been here long enough to know exactly who she is. I'll bet they've even seen her lately."* He shook his head when he drove passed a posted sign at the edge of town thanking him for visiting. He pulled off to the shoulder to consider his options. *"I should've pressed harder. Maybe I should've hung around just to watch and see what happened next. There's always that one person, the close friend or a friend of a friend, who locks up his or her store and races off to spread the word just after the snooping stranger leaves."* He pulled a U-turn and drove about a hundred yards before pulling off the roadway one more time. "Ray, Ray, Ray, you're beginning to lose it, man!" he lectured out loud. "That shit only happens in the movies. In bad movies. That shit only happens in bad movies, Ray." He grabbed the map from the passenger seat and traced his fingers across a long stretch of Colorado highway. *"Let's go, cowboy...on to the next stop. If that doesn't pan out, I can come back here, or I could drive all the way over to Durango. That would be a long shot for sure, but Jimmy says she has a cousin over there. It's a long drive, but these places haven't given me much. What am I saying? They haven't given me anything. I don't wanna drive to Durango."*

In spite of being forewarned that the information was old, Ray had given Jimmy credit for doing his best to come up with something, even though that something was starting to look like nothing. At this point he knew it would be a lucky roll of the dice to get so much as one solid lead. But with each dead end making him feel as though he were rolling craps, a few hours after arriving in Fort Collins he was ready to pack it in, and his mounting frustration was taking a toll on his gratitude. *"I've been kidding myself. This has all been a wild goose chase. I just hope Jimmy didn't do this to me on purpose. No, no, no, whaddya sayin', Ray? He wouldn't do that, and if he did, why? To get my mind off...? Stop! Stop it right now. He wouldn't do that to his own father."*

Ray sat and watched the endless stream of students parading up and down the street. *"Back and forth they go. That's exactly what I've been doing, going back and forth and back. Look at them all...like an endless army of ants walking from campus into town and back again."* A flicker of hope filled his eyes. *"The college, of course! She taught here. She did her research here! Students, faculty, students…someone's got to know where she is or at least have a better clue where to look.* "

With a welcomed burst of energy, he made his way down the block, showing Paige's picture to anyone who looked his way. Initially the responses were the same, and those who did speak insisted they had never heard of her. After a while he lowered his head *"Strike three."*

The afternoon was disappearing fast, and his attention turned to more immediate needs: a cold beer, a warm meal, and a hot shower in a hotel room with a halfway decent mattress where he'd rest up before a morning drive back to the Denver airport and a flight to Seattle. With resignation came permission to indulge his thirst before he did anything else. As luck would have it, there were plenty of pubs by the university, and although he didn't know it, he just happened to step into the one tavern that had been Paige's favorite.

He had barely taken a sip of his draught when the bartender took a slight interest in the photo he'd purposely left out on the well-worn bar.

"I hope the hell you're not gonna sit here and start cryin' into your beer," she said.

"What makes you think that?"

"The picture. She break your heart or somethin', buddy?"

"What? Who her?" The lighting was poor, so Ray flipped the photo closer to give her a better look. She didn't shift her eyes.

"Just curious is all. You're looking like your dog died, and you're staring at—"

"No, it's not that."

"Sure, whatever you say. It's OK, you don't have to tell me, but trust me, as a woman"—she leaned into his ear—"I can tell just by looking at you that you've got a broken heart."

"No, really, you don't understand."

"No, of course not, because your story is special, right? Well, go ahead and lay it on me, because I'm sure I've heard 'em all."

Ray laughed and shook his head. "You've got it all wrong, she's not my—"

"Sure. Listen, friend...the name's Saharah, and you look like you needed to talk to someone. I didn't mean to bully you."

"Trust me, you didn't bully me."

"Just the same, you go ahead and enjoy your beer, and maybe after you've had a couple...if you wanna talk, I'll be right here." She winked and patted his hand.

"Look it...if you must know I've been trying to find an old friend. We haven't seen each other since college days, and I heard...I heard she'd been teaching at the university, but no one seems to know her." He pushed the photo closer. "Perhaps she used to come in here?"

"Looking for that old flame, huh? So you probably did just get divorced. I knew it. You see, I can always tell these things."

"Yeah, I guess you had me pegged. Does she look familiar to you?"

"Let me see that. Just so you know, they never look like they did when—" Her eyes widened. "An old friend you say?"

"From college days."

"Don't go away, buddy." Saharah took the photo. Ray watched her walk the length of the battle-scarred mahogany bar and hand it to the other bartender. Glancing back and forth between the picture and Ray, they talked before Saharah's coworker came over.

"She's not here, pal. She hasn't been here in a quite a while...a very long while."

"So you guys do know her? How can I find—"

"She used to be a regular customer and then she stopped coming in, and no, I don't know how to find her. So finish up your beer and—"

"You'll excuse me, but I saw the reaction on Saharah's face and I saw the way you two were talking. She's more than just a customer. People don't react the way you guys did over just a customer."

"Look, pal, I have no idea who you are or what you want with Paige, but—"

"So you do know her!"

"I'm getting tired of this crap, so tell me who you are and whaddya want before I come over this bar and—"

"Calm down, will ya? I already told Saharah, I'm an old college friend. We had a thing a long time ago, and now that I'm single again I wanted to…you know?"

"Do I look that stupid to you?"

"I'm serious. If you don't wanna help me, then—"

"You're not the first guy to come sniffing around here looking for Paige, so don't think I'm gonna believe one word of what you're saying. I think it's time you leave."

"If you don't wanna help me," Ray raised his voice, "that's your business, but I'm telling you the truth. Now if you know her, then I'll bet other people in this bar know her, too, and I'm gonna stay here and ask questions until I find someone who can help me. So if you want me to leave, then you're gonna have to knock me unconscious and throw me out into the street." He prayed his bluff was believable. After a minute, the bartender relented.

"If you so much as cause a commotion or get any one of my customers angry, I will make you sorry you ever came in here."

Ray saw people gaining interest during the forty minutes he made his way around the room, but he never saw the bartender make a phone call. Several students and professors knew Paige Motz, and for a round of drinks they spoke freely about the former faculty member. *"Perhaps it isn't strike three. Amazing what alcohol can do."* And while the conversations hadn't yielded anything solid, he hung on every word in hopes of a clue. Some said they knew of her but hadn't seen her in years. Others remembered her fondly, even going so far as to recount a personal experience. Outside a handful of pleasant memories and a small measure of hope, there was still nothing to go on.

As he gathered his stuff to leave, Saharah stopped him at the door.

"You weren't kidding about knowing her, were you?"

Ray hesitated, feeling guilty for having lied. "No, I wasn't kidding."

"Did you get anything from the people you were talking to? Were they able to help?"

"Outside of a few shared experiences, they hadn't seen her around."

"Dakota...the guy workin' the bar with me...he told you we hadn't seen her."

"Yeah, I know. Tell me something, will ya? Why is he so protective of her?"

"They were engaged once. But that was years ago."

"And he's still—"

"She used to come in when she was in town. They were still friends...you might say they were friends with benefits. But now after she's disappeared, you come waltzing in hot on a rebound, and you're looking to hook up with someone he's still fond of and very worried about. You see the problem?"

"Yeah, I see the problem. Is there any place else I can check?"

"So assuming you find her, do you really think that after all these years you're just gonna walk right back into her life?"

"No, I don't. I guess I was just looking for a familiar shoulder to cry on."

"Take your pick of any place on the street, but you still won't get anywhere. She's gone, and she doesn't wanna be found. When you realize that," she gave him the once over for the third time, "come on back. I've got a shoulder you can cry on."

After he was referred to a woman claiming to be a psychic healer, he was convinced Saharah had been right. When the healer told him he was unable to find Paige because his chakras were blocked, he was certain he had been the victim of a college prank.

"I don't normally start reading people in a bar, but I felt an immediate connection to you as soon as I saw you. I'm quite confident we knew each other in a past life. I see a strong Egyptian leader when I look at you."

"Egypt?"

"Yes. By any chance do you have an affinity for pharaohs or pyramids?" she asked

"No. Nor do I have a desire to chase Hebrew slaves into the Red Sea."

"I was right: your chakras are definitely blocked. I can see you need my help."

She then offered to cleanse his aura in a back booth for fifty dollars, or for one hundred she would take him back to her place for an in-depth healing that would definitely clean out his energy fields. As she pressed on, he couldn't help but notice a familiar-looking face in the crowd. It was hard to be sure, as he was weaving and bobbing in between people and was just far enough away to prevent Ray from getting a clear view. Still, he wondered if he recognized him from two other stops. *"Call me crazy, but I think the old guy is following me."* When Ray finally caught his stare, the homeless-looking man broke eye contact, and to the relief of the patrons around him, he hurried out of the bar. With his curiosity now piqued, Ray excused himself from his past-life princess in mid sales pitch for an evening pleasure cruise along the Nile.

Once outside, he couldn't find the old man. He was disappointed at first, but Ray realized this had allowed him to escape the pub with his energy fields and chakras still intact. He walked up and down the crowded street, and while there was no sign of the stalker, the University Inn did catch his eye. *"Maybe I imagined the little booger. It's a little after four now, I'll get a room, a quick shower, early dinner, and a good night's sleep."*

"Giving up so soon?"

Ray turned to find the man stepping out of the alleyway. "You're following me."

"You're asking a lot of questions about someone."

"Do you know her?" He studied the man, filthy and in need of a bath.

"I heard you asking questions about someone."

"In two other pubs. Yes, I saw you there. And I saw you in this one, too. Why are you following me? Do you know Dr. Motz?"

"Who's Dr. Motz?"

Ray studied him for a moment more. *"Forget this old man... the guy's a drunk. I don't have time for this nonsense."* He turned to leave until he felt the man's hand on his shoulder.

"Dr. Motz, yes!" He laughed. "Dr. Motz...doctor—" His voice stopped as he felt the anger coming from Ray's eyes and slowly retracted his arm.

"So you do know her?"

"Who's Doc...tor Motz?" He smiled nervously.

"Look, buddy, I don't have time for games. Do you or do you not know her?"

"That's the name you've been asking about. Do I know her? I...I don't know her. I don't. Do you know her?"

"You poor old drunk. I'm sorry, but this is a waste of time." Again he began to walk away.

"OK," he yelled. "If you say so. That means I can't tell you, but I have to tell you."

"Look it, damn it, I've spent a number of days looking for someone. I'm tired, and I'm in no mood for games. And why the fuck am I explaining this to a drunk?"

"Yes, I know. You're looking for Dr. Motz and that *is* the game." He stared at Ray.

"OK, pal, I don't know why I'm bothering, but one last time. Why were you following me, and do you know her?"

"No, I keep telling you I don't."

"Either you're drunk or stoned, or I must be, right? Sure, that's it. I'm stoned and I'm hallucinating, or my chakras are fucking blocked. Well, I'm done. Tell you what, whaddya say I give you a few dollars so you can get yourself a bottle to keep this adventure going without me. Here's a few bucks...now please just go on your way."

"Yes! I'll go on my way, and you won't find your Motz. You lose the game." He furrowed his brow, his hand went into his pocket, and Ray thought he was going to produce a knife or a gun.

"Yes...the game. I want to win the game. I want to find Dr. Motz, that's right," he said in a cautious tone. "Do you know her? Can you tell me where she is? Can you help me win the game?"

"The big guy. Ask the big guy—he knows. When you see him, you must give him my best. Tell him I did my job. He didn't think I could do it. But the small guy had faith. Tell him I did my job." He winked and pulled his hand from his pocket. Ray jumped back.

"I've got a note for you, you see?"

"Thank you. If you're Mr. Big Guy, then let me ask you—"

"I'm not the big guy! The big guy didn't think I could do this. Don't you listen?" The man's eyes were now wide with anger.

"I'm sorry, sir, I'm sorry. I didn't mean—"

"The note...I insist." He shoved a crumpled piece of paper at Ray. "It's my job."

"I'm not sure I'll even find her, so I'd rather not. Maybe I'll go speak to the big guy."

"Oh, but you must take the note. I insist. It's from the little guy, not the big guy." He forced himself on Ray, shoving the note into his jacket pocket. The man smelled so bad, it made him gag and recoil. He backpedaled as fast as he could, trying not to trip over his own feet, but he ended up flat on his back watching the old man skip down the street, calling over his shoulder, "The big guy didn't think I could do it, but I did. You go to him and tell him I did, and talk to the little one...he's the one who knows!"

Ray shook his head. *"Jeez, I almost wet myself!"*

12

Fort Collins

Tired and frustrated from hitting dead ends, being short on time, and stressed because of news from home, he still wanted to find this outspoken infectious disease expert, or at the very least find someone who had contact with her if only to deliver a message—even if it was only his name, number, and a plea for her to call him. Dealing with a delusional drunk wreaking of vomit and urine was not the payoff he had expected.

When he'd spoken to Leigh Anne the night before, she'd reported two more flat tires on his Wrangler and a rock thrown through a window at his clinic—the second one within the past few weeks. He never mentioned the first rock, which was found lying on the reception room floor just shy of the large aquarium. He figured Leilani must have called Leigh Anne about this latest incident. The insults and minor acts of vandalism notwithstanding, Ray knew it was just a matter of time before some zealous fanatic would cross the line and go after his wife and daughters. *"Face it, Ray, it's time to take care of business in Seattle and then get your ass home to protect the family."*

He sat on the edge of his bed at the University Inn, twice calling the airline to change his flight and twice hanging up before he did. He was tense, his mind all over the place. A hot shower would certainly help him unwind, but he couldn't stop thinking about the odd little man. Then he remembered the piece of paper shoved into his pocket.

* * *

It was quarter past six, and he sat in the corner booth nursing a beer just as the note instructed. He looked around the pub trying to see if any of the faces looked familiar. They didn't. Ray closed his eyes to get a clear picture of the odd little drunk and was almost certain he was not among the other patrons. He concluded that given the man's age and the way he'd been dressed and smelled, it was unlikely he would have been a customer in this kind of place, nor would they have allowed him in. *"Then again, he did get into the other places...not that he was a regular, but he did get in. What if it was a disguise? Nah, he stunk so bad. What if he cleaned up? I certainly had the time to shower and change. Sure, a shower, a shave...he could be here and I wouldn't recognize him."*

So Ray looked around the pub for what felt like the fifteenth time, if not for the mysterious messenger then for anyone who might have been watching him. The patrons were mostly college students, and they all looked the same. He read part of the note again. *"The Ram Pub, across from CSU on Laurel and South Mason, 6:00 p.m."*

He didn't know if it had been a prank of some sort. He briefly wondered if perhaps someone other than Dakota didn't like him sniffing around asking all sorts of questions about her. *"OK, message received."* He'd had enough. He was going to go back to Seattle and then home to Oahu, convinced he would never find her. *"Maybe Leigh was right. Maybe I'm just doing this to avoid Seattle...to avoid the inevitable."* Ray crumpled the poorly scribbled paper, stuffed it into his glass, and slid across the bench seat, only to be met by a stiff arm to his shoulder. The body on the other end of that arm was huge. He knew he was exhausted when, after looking at the red plaid shirt covering the massive frame, all he could think of was the picture of a giant ax-wielding cartoon character logger on the can of beef stew—at least he felt as if he'd been hit by a can of the stuff. He rubbed his shoulder, shook the image, stared up at the Aryan-looking tree-chopping hulk, and wondered if he could force his way to his feet. *"The big guy!"* he thought. He felt the man's arm stiffen against his halfhearted attempt and felt himself sliding back into the booth. *"Yup, he's definitely the big guy."*

"Giving up so soon?"

"On trying to push my way through a tiger tank?"

"On your search?"

"Sorry, don't know what you're talking about. So if you don't mind—" He pushed against a locked arm that felt more like a steel girder.

"I do mind." He slid right up into Ray, and another man sat on the opposite side. He was a slightly younger and much smaller version of the giant. Same features, but closer to Ray's size.

"You wrote the note?" Ray looked up at the weathered face.

"I wrote it," the smaller of the two answered.

"I guess the big guy doesn't have that skill?" His response was not meant to be audible. *"Damn, I always do that."*

"If I smack you, wise ass, I promise you won't get up until next Tuesday," the big guy said, leaning a little more into Ray.

"Probably into next month. Look it, I'm sorry...I'm tired and...I've had a bad few days. If you don't mind, it's a little hard to...breathe." Ray tried to push the guy back without success. "Hey, I didn't mean anything by it...so could you please resist the temptation to use me as a seat cushion?"

"You'll watch your comments, understand?"

"Understood." With a nod of a head, Ray felt his ability to inhale return. "I don't remember running into you two today."

"You didn't."

"And the note...I take it you're the little...you're the guy who's gonna help me?"

"Oh?"

"The old drunk on the street said, and I'm quoting him, 'Ask the little guy, he knows.'" Ray's guests looked at each other, shook their heads, and laughed. "The guy's a local drunk. He only knows us by that description."

"And you trusted him to deliver the note?"

"It's pretty amazing what some people are able to do for the promise of a bottle."

"Had I known that, I wouldn't have bought him one. So who the hell are you guys?"

"Does it matter?" The smaller of the two took control.

"Yes, I think it does."

"You're looking for someone very close to us."

"You mean Dr. Paige—"

"Lower your voice."

"Motz?" Ray whispered.

"Yes. Why? Who are you, and whaddya want with her?"

"I have some questions."

"So do a lot of people, especially her former employer, along with some people in the government. What kind of questions?"

"About vaccines...I have questions about vaccine research, possible military experiments, stuff like that. I heard her speak a few years ago."

"So did—"

"A lot of people, especially her former employer and some people in the government...I know."

"The way you're going around looking for her is not very smart. You can and will jeopardize her safety."

"And mine?"

"That's still a possibility."

"Listen, it's not my intention to do that, to jeopardize anyone's safety. I need help. I need answers."

"Who are you, a reporter? An agent? Who do you work for?"

"I'm not with the government or any news agency, if that's what you're worried about."

"We're waiting," the big one said.

"My name is Ray Silver. I'm a chiropractor from Hawaii, and I—"

"Let me see your driver's license and your airline ticket."

"My driver's license?"

"And your airline ticket. Let's see them right now."

Ray slid his license out of his wallet and watched the bulldozer carefully scrutinize the laminated card. He handed it over to his partner.

"I assure you it's real."

"The airline ticket?" He stretched his hand across the table without lifting his eyes off the license.

"I checked-in online. I only had a boarding pass, which I chucked once I got to Denver…honest!"

"You're the guy who made an ass of himself in that TV interview."

"Excuse me?"

"Yeah, we saw it. You should do your homework before you put yourself out there to the public. You not only made yourself look stupid, but you give the rest of us who are standing up to medical fascism a bad name. That interview you did is just the kind of thing that gets replayed whenever the news media wants to paint us as nut jobs."

"That piece was edited…heavily edited. The reporter has an agenda against natural health-care providers."

"If you say so."

"Yeah, I say so. Who the hell are you, and do you know where I can find Paige Motz? Yes or no? If not, then I hafta—"

Ray felt the man's full weight lean back into him.

"If you don't lower your voice, I'm gonna hurt you, understand?"

"Yes…now please stop doing that."

"We're her brothers and her first line of defense."

"How'd the Broncos miss you?"

"You just don't stop, do you?"

"OK, OK, I'm sorry. Please don't crush me. I've gotta meet her…to talk to her. It's very important to me."

"You can talk to us."

"No, I need to talk to her."

"Or what?"

"Forget it, just forget this whole thing. I don't have time for this shit. I've gotta get back home because whacko fanatics are painting names on my cars, slashing my tires, throwing rocks through my office windows, and scaring the hell out of my wife and kids because—"

"OK, calm down."

"Or you'll sit on me again? I can't calm down, OK?"

"You better calm down so I can give you directions." He looked across the table to his brother, who nodded.

"Just like that?"

"Yeah. I'll give you directions, and you follow them to the letter, you understand?"

"Or?"

"Or you'll get lost up in the mountains," he said in response to Ray's skeptical look. "I'm not writing any of this down for you, and as you can see, it's dark. If you don't pay attention to where you're going, you can get stuck on some out-of-the-way muddy back road. Gets kinda cold up there at night. This isn't Hawaii, you know? You could even take a wrong turn and end up in a ditch…after a fifty-foot drop… been known to happen."

"OK, I get it."

"It's a bit of a drive from here, about an hour," said the younger brother. "I'm going to give you my jacket and cap."

"Are you kidding me?" Ray looked at both men.

"I can give you mine, but you'll get lost in it. My little brother is more your size. Put the stuff on. You'll be taking my pickup. It's parked out back."

"I have a rental out front."

"Yes, a bright yellow one…nice choice, easy to follow. I'll take it, and I'll keep your license as well. Don't worry, you'll get 'em back. I'll leave both for you at the general store in Glenn Rock. Sometime tomorrow morning, Paige will escort you half-way down the mountain. You go the rest of the way on your own, and once you get to the road, you walk back to the store. Once you get there, go in and order a coffee and a bear claw."

"Coffee and a bear claw?"

"Yeah...and not that fancy latte stuff 'cause he don't have that. Just ask for coffee, hot and black."

"And then what? Is that the secret code or something?"

"Yeah, if you want Heinrich to give you your license and car keys."

"And no one else will ask for coffee and a bear claw."

"He'll know everyone else. He won't know you."

"You think I was followed, don't you?"

"We're not taking any chances, but yes, I'm pretty damn sure you were. Especially after spending several days asking about her all over Boulder, Loveland, Breckinridge, and here in town. You're as bad an investigator as Magnum P.I."

"Thank you."

"When you leave here, you're gonna head south on 287 and then to 34 west. Just past the north fork of the Big Thompson River, you'll make a right onto Route 43 heading toward Triangle Mountain. Pull into the parking lot of the Glenn Rock General Store. Park my rig in back and wait."

"And then what?"

"If your story checks out, someone will eventually show up to get you. If not, you can sleep in the truck until morning. There's a blanket on the seat to keep you warm. Then you'll find your own way back to town to get your car."

"If no one shows up, I'll just drive your truck back to town."

"Heinrich won't let that happen."

"My story will check out fine. You just make sure my car is at the general store in Glenn Rock."

"We'll see."

13

Route 43, Glenn Rock

It was half past eight, and the only visible light came from the three working letters on the red neon window sign of the Glenn Rock General Store, an occasional passing car on Route 43, and the billions of stars overhead. Ray spent about an hour gazing in complete awe at the glittering black canvas above him. He didn't know why, but it made him think of a framed velvet portrait of Elvis he had once seen hanging in a vendor's stall at the International Market in Waikiki. Even with Diamond Head as part of the background and a bright yellow lei draped over the King's hula shirt, with all the Chinese-made Hawaiian souvenirs on display the large portrait had still seemed terribly out of place.

Ray turned on the windshield washer in an attempt to get a better view of the night sky, but the worn-out wiper blades only smeared the fine layer of dirt into a wet streaky mess. He wanted to get a better look at the constellations and thought about sitting in the back bed of the pickup for an unobstructed view until the quiet of the night gave way to the noises of the wilderness. The only nighttime noises he was used to were the fluttering palm fronds in his front yard and Leigh Anne's whispers of feigned annoyance followed by predictable surrender.

"*Again? Please, Ray, not again?*"

  "*Not if you really don't want to.*"

  "*Then please stop rubbing me down there.*"

  "*Do you not feel both of my hands rubbing your shoulders?*"

  "*Damn you, boy, I swear you're taking a magic blue pill.*"

  "*You're the only stimulant I need.*" *He laughed.*

  "*Pour on the syrup, why don't you. You'd think I'd know*
better by now.*"

  "*Lucky for me, then.*"

He rolled up the driver's side window, made sure both doors were locked, and settled for the view from the dirty windows. When he was a child staring up at the night sky, with just the right amount of squint he was able to create his own mythological gods. But as dark and glittery as the obscured sky was, Ray couldn't make a group of stars come close to resembling a marquee on the Vegas strip.

"Sorry, Elvis, you may be the King, but it just ain't happenin', buddy."

At nine fifteen, an SUV pulled off the road and came to a quick stop in front of the small market. Ray sat motionless, barely making out the shadows of a young couple locked in an embrace. At first he was amused by the awkward ballet of arms and legs twisting and weaving back and forth as one article of clothing, a second, and then a third came off one of the participants. When one head dipped out of view and the other one shot back into the headrest, he worried the timing of their pit stop would jeopardize his contact. He reluctantly flashed his headlights before the windows of the mobile motel room fogged over. The panic that ensued inside the cockpit was comical. While the male almost flooded the engine desperately trying to start it, his lady friend frantically searched in the darkness for her clothing. The screams and the scolding were muffled, but Ray heard them just the same. And that made him think of the time Casey was in high school and he came home to find a local hotshot named Eric Hamilton all over her. "You were sure mad at me for that move," he said to the darkness.

"How could you, Daddy? How could you do that to me?"

"Jeez, kiddo, whadija expect me to do, huh? He was all over you like an octopus."

"He wasn't raping me! Oh my god, you came barging into my room, Daddy. That was so embarrassing!"

"How was I supposed to know…wait a minute, what were you two doing in your room anyway? And with the door closed? And with nobody else at home?"

"We were working on a school project."

"What on, huh? The reproductive cycle of oversexed teenage boys?"

"This is humiliating. This will be all over campus tomorrow. How am I going to live this down? I am so ruined!"

"If he ended up having his way with you, that's what would have been all over campus tomorrow…unless you two already—"

"Daddy! How could you even think that of me?"

"After what I just walked in on?"

"Well, we didn't, and we never have, OK?"

"Good! Now how many times have your mother and I told you no boys in the house when we're not home? And even at that, you two should've been downstairs at the kitchen table doing your project, no different than when Jimmy brings a guest home to do schoolwork."

"You can't be serious, Dad!"

"Your brother follows the rules without question."

"My brother brings his jock friends home. Have you ever seen Jimmy with a girl? He's so socially awkward I'm beginning to think he's gay."

"Well, even if he were, he still follows the policy around here, and don't look at me like that. I barged into your room because I heard all this grunting and I thought you were being attacked."

"Well, I wasn't. But it was you who attacked Eric. Did you have to grab him by the neck and throw him out of the house *like that? I think you hurt him…now he'll probably never speak to me again."*

"I guess I did get a little carried away…but I was in protection mode."

"A little carried away?"

"I suppose threatening to cut off his testicles was a little much, huh?"

"You suppose?"

"Why do I now feel like I'm the one who was wrong?"

"I suppose I was wrong, too…a little."

"You suppose?"

"But oh my god, Daddy, how am I going to be able to show my face around school?"

"Unless Eric is going to lie about being carried by his neck and being thrown out the door and onto his butt, I doubt he'll be saying anything to anyone."

"I hope you're right?"

"So do I, kiddo…you don't really think your brother's gay, do you?"

By half-past nine, he began to wonder if anyone would be coming. By nine forty-five, the wait and the boredom were getting to him. Ray searched the length of the radio dial, getting nothing but static until the miracle of AM radio waves mixed with a warm air inversion layer over the Plains states brought in the soul-saving sermon of Reverend Archie Barnabas *"Die-rect from Saint Louie, Mizzourah."* That's when he decided to rummage through the glove box for something—anything—to read. *"Books! Great, now I can focus on something other than the thought of being dragged off into the woods or being dragged down into hell for not calling the 800 number to repent my sins with a large donation. So what does this guy read? I'll bet they're about bow hunting or mule skinning or something like that. Let's see…*Bargain Bride, Billionaire Groom*? *Boss with Benefits*? *All Hands Below*? *Well, I'll be…the big guy's into erotic fiction. At least it won't be boring…please forgive me, Reverend Barnabas."*

At first he didn't pay attention to the headlight beams slowly getting brighter along the asphalt of Route 43. He had seen about five cars pass in the time he had been waiting. But when the brightness of the roadway failed to increase beyond a certain point, Ray realized the oncoming car had come to a halt just west of the Glenn Rock General Store. He returned the paperbacks to the glove box, turned off the interior light, and cracked the window about an inch to listen while he watched for any movement. A few minutes passed, the roadway went dark, and he heard the crunching of gravel under rolling tires. In the darkness it reminded him of children working furiously to pop sheets of bubble wrap—then silence.

14

Somewhere in the Rockies

As Ray came to among a mix of jumbled thoughts, he wondered if he was still looking up at the sky. He thought he was, except there were no stars to be seen. *"Take it off, Leigh, and let me at least look at the stars."* His head was heavy, and he felt as though he was in a fog, but he was sure the sky hadn't been pitch black. He fought to shake the cobwebs while he thought of Leigh Anne:

"Are you saying you don't want to watch me?"

"Come on, Leigh, untie my hands and get this mask off my eyes."

"Eye mask? What eye mask?" She lightly brushed her fingertips across his chest and laughed. *"Does that tickle?"*

"Leigh, I'm not fooling!"

"'Leigh,'" she mocked, *"'I'm not fooooling.' What's the matter? Big man can dish it out but can't take it?"*

"This is different." He squirmed and laughed while trying to free his hands from bondage. *"You're not the one tied up. Besides...I was sound asleep."*

"Poor baby." She pinched his love handles.

"When I do this to you, it's different," he squealed.

"Too bad for you, mister macho. You're going to get what you give." She straddled him.

"And keep in mind you enjoy every bit of...what...I...do." His voice trailed off when she began grinding into his pelvis.

"Oh, you're going to enjoy this...I promise. Oh my god, are you perspiring?"

"It's hot in here."

"We're on the lanai and the Kona winds are blowing. It's not hot...I am. And you're just scared because right now you have no control of your future."

Her light finger strokes had a bit more nail this time. Ray arched from the sting.

"Leigh, I'm...I'm not kid...kidding. At least take this blindfold off me so I can see."

"The stars?"

"No...you!"

"Right answer but not a chance. I want your mind to see what your body is going to feel."

"Come on, stop this already...OK? OK, OK what are you going to do?" His laugh was involuntary as her hands and then her tongue randomly attacked.

"I'm going to overload every one of your nerve fibers dedicated to pleasure...and pain."

"Oh god...Leigh—"

"Praying won't help you now, boy. You can try if you want to. I'll tell you what...I'll help bring you closer to the Almighty. Yeah, that's exactly what I'll do. I'm gonna whip you into a frenzy so outrageous it'll rival any religious experience you've ever had. You'll be torn between crying out to the Lord to save you, or you'll be begging me for more."

Her laugh echoed in his head, and he jerked. He heard himself pleading, but it was dark and Leigh Anne was gone. "Just take off this mask so I can...what? Where'd she go? Leigh? Come back, you're missing the best part," he mumbled. "Leigh? What the fuck?" He couldn't tell where he was but was painfully aware she hadn't been there at all. *"But where is here?"* He looked around at the blackness. The stars were surely missing, and there definitely was no Kona wind. *"But there are no Kona winds in Colorado...Colorado...think, Ray. You were in the big guy's truck."* It was coming back to him: the headlights, crunching gravel, the sounds of the nighttime forest, gone. *"The stars aren't the only thing missing."* Gone, too, were the crispness of the night air and the thick smell of pine—save for a slight hint of it. There was now a mild odor that he could not immediately place, although it did seem familiar. It contributed to a fleeting image of food, which made him queasy. His forehead ached, which brought him back to the heaviness in his head—the weight more noticeable when tried to look around. That was when he felt the cloth-like material sticking to his hair, brushing across his face, and irritating his skin. *"I get it...I gotta be dreaming."* To be sure of his suspicion, he squeezed his eyelids closed and then opened them. *"Still dark...but this pain. This can't be a dream, the pain is too real...it's too warm and it stinks! Garlic! I gotta get some air."* The warmth he felt was from his own breath trapped inside the hood covering his head and the strange odor coming from the extra garlic pizza he'd had for dinner. But now it had a smokiness to it. He gagged at the thought of his meal. *"These people only know how to cook meat. Would've been better off ordering the roadkill. What the fuck am I talking about?"*

He tried to stand but couldn't—his legs bound to the chair, his hands secured behind his back. *"This isn't Leigh's handiwork, that's for sure."* His shoulders hurt from being forced backward, but they didn't hurt as much when he stopped trying to pull them apart, and they definitely didn't hurt as much as his forehead. The pain made Ray inch his way back to reality. *"Prisoner...but whose?"* He wanted to get free of the hood. He desperately wanted to breathe cool fresh air. He was claustrophobic and hoped his quick shallow breaths wouldn't betray his weakness. Still, as he felt himself approaching panic mode, he jerked his head around in an effort to find daylight.

"You're awake, good! That was some little dream you were having. I hope she was worth it? Now, if you keep thrashing about, you'll get whiplash, and no matter how good you think you are...in or out of bed...I doubt you can treat yourself," said a female voice.

"Then unless you're going to kill me, you'll have to cut me out of this chair before I smash it into something."

"Go ahead and try if you want." She laughed. "But if I were you, I wouldn't be so sure I'd get very far. When I secure a prisoner, they stay secure. So you can buck yourself to exhaustion for all I care, because I have no problem letting you beat yourself all night."

"If you're gonna kill me, then just do it already. Just take this fucking bag off my head so I can at least look you in the eye when you do it. Or don't you have the ovaries for that sort of thing?"

"My, my, my. You're not only comical, but you're dramatic, too."

"Well, do you have the guts or what?" Ray asked defiantly.

"Just relax. If you're good, I'll take the pillowcase off your head."

"I'd appreciate it if you untie my hands and feet as well." Ray struggled to force the tape off his wrists.

"If I was going to kill you, do you think I'd be stupid enough to free your hands and feet?"

"Then just do it already."

"Kill you or untie you?"

"Go ahead and untie me, and let's make it a fair fight."

"Wow! I hit the jackpot, didn't I? Comical, dramatic, and macho. I like that in a man...especially one who's brave enough to take on a woman."

"Then let's go." Ray tried standing again.

"Hold still, damn it, and I'll set you free...if you're ready to relax."

"Yes." He became still.

"And no funny stuff."

"Or you'll hit me again?"

"Now you're really making my night. Nobody hit you, Rambo." She chuckled. "You ran into a low-lying branch and knocked yourself out. I have to admit, for a while there we couldn't stop laughing. That is, once we realized you were still alive. It was hard to stop. I mean it was really—"

"Are you enjoying yourself?" Her laughing angered him.

"Anyway." She regained her composure. "I had to keep you bound because, as I suspected, you'd be acting like an untamed mustang."

"I'm acting like an untamed mustang because you have me bound and hooded." He pulled at his restraints.

"You know what? You go ahead and thrash about. I've got things to do, OK? So you just call out when you're ready to be calm and I'll untie—"

"I am...calm...completely calm, as you can plainly see." Ray settled down.

"Why the hell couldn't you follow instructions and stay put in the truck? Nice knot on your forehead, by the way," she said as she removed the pillowcase.

Ray took a deep breath, exhaled, and then took another. The air was somewhat cooler but not as clean smelling as it had been outside. *"Wood smoke."* His eyes darted across the room for the fireplace, finding it dark and silent before spying the glowing, crackling coals in the potbellied stove in the kitchen. Without benefit of the cotton pillowcase filtering his air, the smoke minus the garlic was now more noticeable. He looked right at Paige straddling a chair she pulled within a few inches of his face. In spite of his fog, he couldn't help but notice she was beautiful—blond-braided, Bavarian-stock beautiful. He also thought she looked tomboy rugged and guessed she could probably drink any man under the table. *"So how does she survive alone in the wilderness? No doubt by hunting down dinner and field dressing it without a second thought. But look at her...I'll bet she—"*

"Don't get your hopes up," she said to Ray's stare.

"Excuse me?"

"I've seen that look before, and I have a very good idea what you're thinking. Well, newsflash, pal, it's not going to happen here and not with me."

"You think too much of yourself, Dr. Motz? Or is it Brunhilda?"

165

She didn't answer. He continued. "Excuse the blank look on my face. I'm still a bit dazed."

"But not too dazed to be a fucking smart ass."

"The last thing I remember was the sound of a car pulling into the parking lot. Then after a few minutes I heard what sounded like a screen door open and then footsteps...two sets of footsteps coming from the backside of the store. And then it got quiet...too quiet. I figured I was a sitting target, so I just wanted to get behind some trees...to get a look at who was coming. And an ice pack would be a big help, thank you for offering."

"Stupid move. You clocked yourself pretty good on that branch. And to top it off, you fell a few feet from a prairie rattler."

"How was I supposed to know? And what's a prairie rattler doing up here in the mountains?"

"That's what they're called, and they're indigenous. And who the hell goes running into the woods at night without a flashlight or a weapon? There's a thirty-ought-six sitting on the rack in that pickup truck."

"Too bad your brother, if that Sasquatch is your brother, had it locked, and to top it off, he only left some erotic novels in the glove box instead of ammo."

"He'll appreciate being called a Sasquatch, and those books were for me. You have a problem with that?"

"I'm not going there. What you do with your—"

"Stop right there. You've already made one risky mistake tonight. Look, there's a whole lot of stuff up here in the mountains that you just don't wanna mess with." She half stood from her chair and reached over him to cut the duct tape, freeing his hands. He felt the softness of her cheek and smelled the scent of pine when she brushed across his face.

"You mean like feministas with big...guns?" he whispered into her ear.

"I'll give you this much, Ray Silver, you certainly like staring death in the face. I'm sure you can undo your legs without my help."

"So you are Dr. Motz? Paige Motz?"

"You have to ask? I've been told you once saw me in a seminar."

"I did. But that was several years ago, it was online, the lighting wasn't as dim as it is here, and if I may say, you were much heavier. You forget to pay your electric bill? Where are we anyway?"

"I'm off the grid. Strictly solar and wood for my energy, satellite for communication, and we're in a place where I may not have the luxury of grazing on junk food but at least I can be safe. That's all you need to know. Now just so we're clear and to save us a lot of time, you wasted the trip, 'cause I can't help you."

"Yes, I'd love to have something to drink."

"I've got Jack...or water."

"Water is fine, thank you very much," he said sarcastically. "And ice for my head?"

Paige dismounted her chair as if it were a saddle and walked over to the drape-covered pantry by the wood stove. When she brushed the floral-printed cloth aside, Ray could see several shelves fully stocked with mason jars of fruits and vegetables, a few sacks that looked like dried beans, slabs of jerky, and an assortment of other foodstuffs. She reached into the closet without taking her eyes off him and tossed a plastic bottle from across the room. Then she grabbed a cup from the sink, filled it with snow from the windowsill, and left it on the counter.

"Here's your ice. Now drink up and get some rest. In a few hours, just before the sun comes up, I'll escort you down the mountain...and you'll be blindfolded. Once at the main road, you can walk back to the general store. And don't hitch-hike, because I don't want you getting into a conversation with anyone."

"Hold on just a minute. I came all this way to find you—"

"Nobody asked you to come," she snapped back. "And just because you did, it doesn't make me obligated. I don't know you, and I don't owe you. You got that?"

"At least hear me out."

"I know your story. I saw the video clips and read some articles about you while you were taking your little nap." She pointed to her computer. "You got yourself in a public relations bind, and you figure I can give you the ammunition you need to make a better fight of it."

"No...not at all. You are so far off the mark it ain't even funny. And like I told your brother, that interview you saw was heavily edited, no different than the way it's been done to you. Yeah, that's right, I've seen some of the interviews of you in the mainstream press. So if it's not too much trouble, I'd appreciate it if you can give me the benefit of the doubt."

"OK, so you tell me. Besides reading articles in the alternative press, which is where you people get your information, what other data do you have?"

"You people?"

"Chiropractors, naturopaths, antivaxers...you people."

"Like the hundreds of thousands of parents of vaccine-injured children?" he added without her protest. "From books, research studies...and from whistleblower scientists like yourself."

"Touché. Which books?"

"Do you want me to list the microbiology, physiology, and pathophysiology texts that were required in school, or should I name-drop Dr. Julian Walker from Scotland. I read his book on the neurotoxicity of aluminum in vaccines and the link they have to a host of nervous system disorders."

"And you don't care that Walker's been discredited by the Royal Society of Physicians?"

"From what I read in the 'alternative' media, it was a hit job. His work has been validated by more than a dozen studies since his book was originally published. You disagree?"

"Not at all. It was a hit job, and everyone in the scientific community knows it. They just won't speak out about it because they're afraid Reggie Masterson will destroy them as well."

"Reginald Masterson from Global News Service?"

"That's right. Reggie's son, Albert, is editor in chief of the *Britannia Times* out of London. He's also on the board of directors of Wellington and Marlborough."

"The biggest maker of vaccines in Europe."

"Exactly. Walker's work began to hurt Wellington's bottom line, so Albert had one of his health reporters do a series of hit pieces on Walker. Good ol' Reggie and WM tag-teams the poor guy by threatening to pull all financial backing from medical institutions ranging from schools to scientific journals throughout the British Isles if they didn't denounce the book and all of Walker's work as fraudulent. On top of that, Wellington and other drug companies began to hint that if media outlets in Britain and here in the United States didn't include stories backing up the articles published in the *Britannia*, they were going to pull all their advertising."

"And Masterson owns the most powerful cable news network here and overseas...so you know this for a fact?"

"I've got my sources within the academic community and elsewhere. This isn't speculation."

"And you look down at the alternative media that I use?"

"Not at all, Silver. But a public brainwashed by mainstream media does, and that's who you've been trying to make your case with, right? So speaking of sources, what other stuff are you hanging your hat on?"

"There's the research done by Sherri Lightfoot."

"The one about aborted fetal cells being used in certain vaccines?"

"Yeah...reacting just like donor organs do after they've been transplanted. The fetal cells from the vaccines are attacked no different than an organ rejection, and the recipient experiences a life-threatening autoimmune response."

"I've read her work...its spot-on. The DNA of those fetal cells become incorporated into the cells of organs as well as the nervous system. The immune response treats a person's own organs as foreign invaders and attacks them. Sadly, the CDC and NIH refused to fund any research studies to back up her work. Anyway, you've got some good info, but it's not enough."

"I know it's not enough. There could be hundreds of studies and books and researchers willing to buck convention, and it would never be enough. Not when there are billions of dollars at stake here. But that's only one of the reasons why I needed to talk to you, Paige…I mean, Dr. Motz."

"Paige is fine, but I already told you I can't help."

"But—"

"I don't care. Whatever it is you need from me, I can't help you. Now do yourself a favor and go get some rest."

Paige began to walk away, but Ray grabbed her arm and got right up in her face.

"You mean you *won't* help."

"Fine, I won't help. Now if you don't mind—" She pulled herself free.

"Can I ask why?"

"Why do you think I'm up here in this cabin? The only, and I do mean *only*, reason why my brothers had you meet them was to shut you up. You were going all over the place asking about me, and I can't afford that kind of attention."

"Well, then, you're lucky, because I almost didn't read that note."

"Lucky for you that you did. There were two ways to shut you up. One was to get you off the street and talk to you, and you don't want to know about the option we didn't exercise."

"Am I supposed to be scared, impressed, or thankful?"

"Couldn't care less either way."

"Look it, I didn't come all this way because I needed testimony from an industry insider about the lack of scientific evidence on vaccine safety and effectiveness."

"You mean no scientific evidence other than those studies that have been falsified to show the desired outcomes."

"So you have proof that shit goes on?"

"I thought you said that's not the reason for your visit."

"It isn't, but having that kind of evidence would be a bonus. Both my kids were in the military…they were in Iraq."

"Recently?"

"During the past few years."

"They're sick?"

"My daughter...she's...so there's a link? Is that why you asked if they're sick?"

"I don't know if there's a link, and I don't wanna know. Like I said, I can't help you. I think it's time we—"

"You know something...I can see it in your eyes. Is that why you're hiding up here?"

"What makes you think I know anything about what goes on in the military?"

"Because you as much as said so in that seminar you gave... about experimentation on the troops during the First Gulf War. You worked for the drug company that was doing those experiments, weren't you? You either caught on to what they had done...or wait...you were working on a new project, then suddenly your conscious got the better of you, and that's why you had to disappear. That's why you're in hiding. What? They wanna kill you for all the evidence you have on them?"

Paige stared at Ray for a little bit, studying his face as intently as she examined her conscience. She went to the kitchen sink for a glass of water, hesitated, then grabbed a bottle of whiskey instead. She poured a shot for him then took the bottle and went outside to her front porch. He followed her, stopping to pick up his glass. When he got outside, Paige was wiping her lips and nodded for him to have a seat. He watched her take another drink, stuff a cork in the bottle, and set it into the small mound of snow next to her chair.

"You're partially correct. For a number of years I'd been teaching a course on infectious diseases over at the university in Fort Collins. Through my own research, I had come to realize a few things. The first was that in almost every case the antibody responses triggered by vaccines weren't a response to the viral antigen but rather a response to the more powerful chemical adjuvants and preservatives added to the shots. And that was all the drug companies were looking for...a response. As long as there was an antibody reaction to the serum, the manufacturers were able to claim the stuff was effective.

"The second thing I'd come to realize was that there had never been any safety studies performed dealing with multiple injections given to babies at one time, let alone in the different combinations they could and are being administered. The negative effects from simultaneous delivery are very real and wide ranging. Sure, if you give a single vaccine to someone, the chances are almost nonexistent there'd be any kind of reaction, and that's what they base their claims of 'safe and effective' on. They never looked at what happens when you give five, six, seven shots at once. They never looked at what happens when you repeat that procedure just a few months later, and then again a year after, and so on. And to tell parents that shooting them in different parts of the body made the injections even safer...well, that's the icing on a seven-layer cake of lies. My god, its common sense that in a little kid you're not only overloading an immature immune system, but you're also bombarding a nervous system that can't defend itself from a shitload of cancer-causing neurotoxins."

"You're preaching to the choir, Paige. But what about when a full-grown adult is subjected to a series of those lethal cocktails?"

"It's unknown because...because no one has ever studied it."

"You don't sound so sure."

"Are you calling me a liar?"

"Is that what you heard? All I said was that you don't sound sure about it not being studied."

"If they didn't do any studies with the dosages on kids, then why would they do it on adults?" she asked defensively.

"Well...when it comes to pointing out the lack of valid proof that those things are effective or safe, then I think I know just as much as anyone."

"Yes, but it's a lot different when you can talk about this stuff from firsthand knowledge and experience instead of repeating someone else's conclusions as if that makes you an authority. And that's why you got ambushed by that reporter."

"What I read...how I choose to stay informed keeps me educated. I never claimed to be an authority, and that reporter was out to get me, and it happened to you, too."

"Completely different scenario. I was set up by McTavish after I quit because of what they were doing. They wanted to discredit me so that nobody would listen to what I had to say. But you made it easy for the guy because you're outspoken about something that isn't even your specialty."

"It doesn't have to be. Are pediatricians experts in infectious diseases, no, right? Are they experts in heavy metal toxicity? Of course not? Hell, they're not even reading the literature on this stuff and they're injecting and preaching as if they're the one and only authority. At least I'm doing my homework."

"Well, it's my specialty, and I was on the inside doing the research. I saw this stuff firsthand. I'm not saying you're not knowledgeable, Silver. You probably know enough to educate your patients but not enough to lead an offensive. That reporter had you on the ropes from the outset."

"I disagree with you, because if he did, then he wouldn't have had to edit all my answers."

"I'm not going to debate it."

"Then we'll agree to disagree on that point."

"Fine!"

"Do you mind telling me what else you found out?"

"While I was still at the university, I was working with several natural healers and we—"

"My people?"

"Point taken." She sighed. "We came to the conclusion that since none of those infections are life threatening in the first place...at least not here in the United States with modern sanitation, refrigeration, clean water, and all that stuff, there were plenty of inexpensive natural remedies to help anyone get over an infection quickly and safely. All the press releases that the FDA and CDC shoot off to the media about epidemics and death rates are based on incidents that occur in poverty-stricken Third World nations, and the numbers are inflated based on worst-case scenarios. None of that has any validity in the industrialized world, especially here in America. The whole thing is one big organized scare tactic to sell more vaccines. Anyway, after I had spoken at a conference about my findings and concerns, that's when I was approached by McTavish to come work for them."

"What? Why?"

"They said they recognized there were problems with their products and they wanted me to help them formulate a truly safe and effective vaccine, one without formaldehyde or aluminum or any of that toxic shit. But in reality, what they wanted was to be able to take me out of circulation…to shut me up. You see, they promised me part ownership of the patents that would come about if I could develop such a vaccine. That's big money, right?"

"So they bought you."

"I admit I was a little blinded by the money—who wouldn't be? But the thought of having the resources to develop vaccines that actually immunized people and were safe…that was my motivation. So part of the deal was I had to sign a confidentiality agreement, which in reality was a permanent gag order."

"So you got snookered."

"I didn't realize it at first, but yeah, I got played. I really thought they wanted to do it the right way. I thought they wanted to be ethical about the whole thing. In reality, in addition to keeping me quiet, they had the added PR bonus of adding me to their research team. It pissed me off at first, but then I thought that since I was there, I was going to take advantage of every tool they had, and I really tried to develop something viable." Her eyes were laser focused on Ray.

"But I don't get it. If they know their vaccines are flawed, why wouldn't they support you in your work?

"They were, but it turns out they wanted me succeed just in case they actually had to prove they had an effective product. In retrospect, I should've known a successful outcome would've never seen the light of day."

"What are you saying?"

"Think about it, Ray. There's too much money to be made selling treatments to deal with a host of conditions that are caused by all those chemicals. Vaccines are nothing more than seeds, and the explosion of all these once rare diseases...that's the harvest, the cash crop."

"So what made you leave the company and go into hiding? What did you discover?"

"I didn't discover anything. A colleague had come to me with information that the CEO of McTavish had a secret virus development project that he wanted to initiate. If it worked, it would make billions of dollars for the company and its shareholders...on a yearly basis. There were four phases of the project: developing the actual virus, the delivery system, then the vaccine for it, and if necessary, a treatment for the disease for those who come down with it anyway."

"Wait a sec. Back up a minute here. Whaddya mean the development of the virus? You mean they were—"

"They supposedly wanted to genetically engineer a new viral strain solely for the purpose of being able to manufacture a new vaccine and have governments throughout the world stock up on it."

"How?"

"It's simple really...in theory anyway. By splicing different viruses together with other DNA, you can create a hybrid. Just like splicing the branch of a plum tree onto an apricot tree and coming up with a pluot."

"But grafting branches of different fruit trees leaves the final product up to nature. That's a whole lot different than genetic engineering in the laboratory. Shit, that's what's going on with GMOs."

"Where do you think McTavish got the idea from?"

"How were they going to test it?"

"Supposedly by aerial dispersal."

"Chem trails?"

"Not initially. They wanted it to be more controlled at first, and they were thinking of doing it either in Iraq or

Afghanistan. It was hoped that when our defense department and intelligence agencies started seeing the disease spreading in small villages, then the urgent call would go out to the major pharmaceuticals to come up with something...a vaccine to protect the troops. McTavish would've looked like a hero with its full-out patriotic research efforts while not disclosing it already had the vaccine developed."

"You've got to be kidding me. This is outrageous. They really did this?"

"The last I heard, there was one attempt to develop the virus, but the project didn't go as planned. The prototype was noninfectious, at least not by air or droplet, and in the test tube it had an extremely short life span."

"But you don't know if they made further attempts?"

"Anything is possible with guys like Moffett. I've given it some thought, about how it could be done. I mean, the possibility remains that if a hybrid could survive inside a human host, then it could still be spread through direct blood-to-blood contact."

"Like HIV?"

"Pretty much. If the virus got into the blood, then it could be delivered to any organ in the body. It could bore its way through cell membranes, incorporate itself into the DNA, and then through standard cell replication, the virus spreads throughout the entire body. And if that worked, it could then be spread through—"

"Intimate contact, needle sharing, blood and organ donations just like—"

"HIV. But there's a bigger problem that scares me to death, and that's the possibility of the virus mutating with each successive generation of cell division." She uncorked the whiskey and took a drink.

Ray leaned back against the porch railing, words such as *virus, replication,* and *mutations* repeating in his head as if on a prerecorded tape loop. "They went through with it, didn't they? Even though the results were different than intended, I'll bet anything they still did it."

"I don't know. I can't say for sure. To knowingly proceed with a project like that would be as reckless, irresponsible, and cold-blooded as...as the world powers giving the green light to the Iranians to develop their nuclear program. At least they didn't do it while I was there, but then again, they could have. They could have developed the hybrid virus and frozen it before it died. There's no way of knowing, since the lead researcher on the project disappeared just weeks after he first confided in me. To this day, there's no trace of him. Soon after, one of his assistants was involved in a freak one-car accident. They found him inside his car at the bottom of a local reservoir. And then the head of the animal lab supposedly died of a heart attack, and of course, there were rumors."

"What kind of rumors?"

"Do I have to paint you a picture? There were rumors about her death, OK? I mean, how often does a world-class triathlete just up and have a massive coronary? That's when I decided I'd had enough. I realized I couldn't be a part of a company like McTavish...and I was scared that if they thought I had any knowledge about the project, I would be the next one killed."

"So why did you begin speaking out? Now they definitely think you have information."

"That's just the thing, I really don't have anything. And yes, they've made a couple attempts."

"Paige, you've gotta listen to me. You see, this is exactly why I'm here. Deep down I feel they may have gone ahead with it."

"Why, because your daughter got sick? People get sick every day. With all of the vaccines kids get these days, there are so many more autoimmune and neurological diseases in this country than ever before. There's a reason why out of all the industrialized nations in the world, the United States is at the bottom of the list in overall health, and it isn't only because of fast food and video games...although I also have a suspicion that all these herbicide-saturated GMOs are a contributing factor. But that's not my expertise. But anyone with half a brain in his head has to acknowledge a connection between us having the greatest amounts of shots given to newborns and having the highest infant mortality rate. How anyone can explain that away is beyond me."

"I never vaccinated my kids when they were young, and just like me, they came down with chicken pox, measles, all the childhood infections, and developed natural lifetime immunity."

"Your daughter could have fallen ill for any number of reasons. It could've been from all the shots she got in boot camp or something she got exposed to in the war zone. God only knows what kind of biological agents could have been released there."

"Why couldn't McTavish have gone ahead with a test. It could've been done after you left, yes?"

"If they were going to be able to test a hybrid virus on anyone, the only way for them to do it would have been in a killed form that was slipped into an existing vaccine. Then they would have needed a captured audience, so to speak. For record-keeping purposes, the batch would have had a special lot number that could be traced to everyone receiving that shot."

"McTavish makes a lot of those vaccines, and if I'm not mistaken, they have to keep a record of batch numbers and where they're shipped. But you already know this. And since they don't tie a batch number to anyone in the general population...the best batch of guinea pigs that I know of would be military personnel."

"Then they would have needed a defense department insider willing to oversee the delivery and administration of a test lot, and then wait to see if and when troops started coming down with some strange illness...just like with Gulf War Syndrome."

"From the experiences I've had, I know that what you're suggesting can easily be accomplished. Don't you see, Paige? You can help me with this."

"No, I can't, because I have absolutely no proof. This wasn't my project. Without proof, this is nothing but conjecture. Hell, I didn't even get out of there with any of my own stuff. This is the kind of crap that gets you publicly labeled as a conspiracy nut. This is also the kind of stuff that gets you killed. And I know, because they've already tried to kill me just based on what information they think I have. And I have nothing...you got that?"

"But if they already think you have something and if they've already made attempts on you, then what have you got to lose at this point?"

"And that is exactly why I'm living in this mountain cabin."

"Yeah, I get it. I get that you're scared. I get that's why you're hiding up here and that's why you're acting like some street tough. You can help me get information that could get these people locked up for good, and you'd rather hide up here in the mountains while little children and members of our armed forces get used as lab rats, and parents around the country are ridiculed, ostracized, and pressured into conforming to a bunch of brainwashed, panic-stricken idiots." Ray's frustration boiled over.

"You're not putting this on me, so say what you want, yell as loud as you can, because I've seen what these people will do to protect their piece of the pie."

"A piece of the pie? More like the whole fucking bakery, Paige, for god's sake!"

"Exactly."

Ray looked at his shot glass, slammed back his drink, and walked the length of the porch. He stared up into the sky and looked at the constellations, taking comfort in knowing the stars remained in the night sky. *"Of course you're still there."*

"Paige, would the information...the secret project as well as your stuff...would it all still be there at McTavish?"

"If they haven't destroyed it all, yeah, it would still be there under lock and key."

"Or maybe in plain sight but masked so that a casual observer wouldn't know what they were looking at?"

"Yeah, they could do that. But don't start thinking that I could call a former coworker to look for the stuff and then send it to me."

"I wasn't thinking that at all."

"Good!"

"I was thinking that we should go get it."

"Are you fucking nuts? What are we supposed to do, walk right in and I simply say, 'Hey, remember me? I forgot some of my shit, so I'll just go on over to my office and scoop it up'? Oh, that'll go over real nice. Haven't you been listening to anything I just told you? Those people want me dead. And even if they didn't, it's been a few years since I was there. My stuff won't be where I left it."

"Maybe, maybe not. But I was thinking that we go at night when the place was closed."

"Break in? You wanna break...OK, this conversation is done, over, finished. I'm going to bed now." She grabbed the bottle of whiskey and headed inside. "There's a flashlight on the table in the kitchen. If you want, you can make your way down the mountain now. Just remember to stay to the left of the trees that have a red mark painted on them. If you don't have the confidence to make it yourself, I'll take you down just before sunrise."

"Why to the left?"

"If you go to the right, you just may step into a trap."

"A trap?"

"A girl's gotta eat."

15

Coxx News Corporate HQ
Manhattan
Early December 2007

J enna sat outside Jack Matthews's door as if she were a child called to the principal's office for having been caught violating some important school policy. And just like schoolgirls trying to hide their excitement over the latest extracurricular drama, the office staff tried to appear as if they were talking about work—as if the repetitive glances in her direction didn't reveal their gossiping. For her, the visual brought to mind the "Pick-a-Little, Talk-a-Little" number from the Broadway show *Music Man*. Jimmy had recently taken her to see the performance at the O'Neill Theater, and now that Jenna had thought of it, she knew the tune would replay in her head at random moments throughout the day.

Even if she was able to convince her boss her actions hadn't been premeditated, she was certain her punishment would be harsh—termination doubtful but not out of the question. She would be apologetic to all concerned; however, employing the "Oh yeah, well, he started it first" defense would surely show she wasn't sorry for what had happened, and she wasn't. But right or wrong, she was ready and determined to present her case and deal with the expected fallout. How the other cable stations and broadcast news channels responded to the incident, as well as viewer feedback in the days and weeks ahead, would certainly play a role in how her employer dealt with her in the long term. To make matters worse, video replays of the incident from pro and con sides of the issue would be all over the Internet—an extremely uncomfortable reminder, like salt to an open wound. It wouldn't be the first time that Coxx News got caught with its pants down, nor would it be the last. At least in Jenna's mind, her scandal didn't involve distorting a story to appease a benefactor—something that had become commonplace in news media.

She stared up at the clock—amazed that what had felt like an hour had in reality been ten minutes of listening to Patrick Moffett reading the riot act to her boss. His frantic, high-pitched, almost squealing protest—a behavior normally reserved for his inner circle of advisers—betrayed the public facade of his even-tempered narcissistic arrogance. If the situation hadn't been so serious, Jenna could have easily laughed at Moffett's meltdown, because she despised him…and she hadn't been alone. Through her work, she had come to know many leaders of industry, and while most had an air of self-importance, they were still approachable as well as charitable. Moffett was neither. He considered campaign contributions his only charity, wore his mostly honorary credentials on his sleeve, was dismissive of anyone he considered below his station, and took credit for scientific achievements so outlandish that industry contemporaries found themselves quietly questioning his claims. But each summer when he held court sailing up the Hudson River on his luxury yacht, academic researchers, congressmen, and media moguls stuffed themselves with his caviar, petits fours, and champagne, giving their full attention while he regaled them with accounts of his groundbreaking discoveries.

While the office walls echoed with his demands, Matthews's executive assistant and her staff chattered away—even wagering on the future of Coxx News's brightest on-air personality. After another five minutes of reminding the news division executives of how much money his corporation had spent advertising throughout the Masterson media empire and five minutes more of repeating his ultimatum for the head of Jenna Grant to be served on a silver platter, the door to Jack Matthews's office flew open. The speed with which people raced through the reception area startled everyone. Moffett's voice, still fluctuating in pitch, was louder and more dramatic now—perhaps because he knew Jenna had been waiting. But she was remarkably calm, making Moffett that much angrier when he saw her on his way out.

"You smug little bit—" He stopped himself. "You think you got away with something? All you accomplished today, little girl, was to end your career. Yeah, that's right. You're finished in this business. I'm going to see to it you never work for a legitimate news organization again."

Matthews stuck his head through the doorway and waited for Moffett to leave. When he did, the longtime head of the news division closed his eyes, almost as if in prayer, then waved Jenna to follow him.

"Have a seat, Ms. Grant." He offered her some water. "Interesting morning, wouldn't you agree?"

"I can explain every—"

"Shhh, not a word…not yet. Just sit there and listen. Do you hear that?"

"Sir?"

"The quiet," he whispered. "Do you hear how nice it sounds? Never in all my years in this industry has anyone ever yelled at me for anything. Not even Reggie Masterson. And he yells at everyone. You do know who Reggie Masterson is, Ms. Grant?"

"Yes, of course, he owns this news channel."

"He owns a lot of news channels, and radio stations, and newspapers, and he owns big stakes in many other companies." His voice rising. "As such, he has an enormous overhead and he counts on people like me to make sure that each of his holdings are not only covering their costs—like employees' salaries, for example—but that each of us is turning a profit. And do you know how we make a profit, Ms. Grant?"

"Mr. Matthews...Jack...I know you're mad, and I know you're mad at me, but please do not patronize me. We've never been formal with each other, and you've never talked to me like I'm some child. So if you're going to fire me, then just do it and I'll leave, but I will not sit here—"

"You're right. You're absolutely right, my apologies. But I am mad. I'm fucking mad as hell. I just sat here for twenty minutes being scolded by that self-serving, pompous sonofabitch as if I was that little child, and it's all because of that ambush of yours. What the hell were you thinking?"

"I didn't plan it that way. As much as I detested doing a manufactured interview, I was following that script, which by the way was total bull. But I'm a team player, and I was following the game plan until that self-serving, pompous sonofabitch, as you call him, ambushed me. I had no choice but to put him in his place."

Jack Matthews stood from his desk, forced a smile at Jenna, then walked over to his fully appointed bar.

"Drink? Oops, you're pregnant, my mistake. I wasn't thinking. Mind if I?"

"Go ahead, don't let me stop you."

"I don't normally imbibe before the noon hour." He dropped a few ice cubes into a tumbler, then reached for a bottle of eighteen year-old scotch.

"It's eleven. Close enough to noon."

"Some of the things I always liked about you, Jenna, are that you're a straight shooter, you're confident, you're a fighter, and you stand your ground. Those couple of years being an investigative reporter for us in DC surely taught you to stand toe-to-toe with people, which is why I brought you up to New York to coanchor the morning news. You've got a great on-air persona, the viewers love you, and since you've been up here, the morning news program has had some of the highest ratings in that time slot."

"I know, and thank you for believing in me…for everything."

"Yes, however, I don't want you to go toe-to-toe with me on this one. This is too big, and it can hurt this station's bottom line, and regardless of how I feel about you, it is the bottom line that takes precedence."

"I understand…but I sat there this morning asking all those softball premeditated questions so that guy can pimp his agenda…fine, I did it. But then he put me on the spot. He pulls out this hypodermic and tried to make an example out of me right there on live television. That's where I draw the line, Jack."

"He asked you to help him show the public how safe his products were. He asked you to get a flu shot. It's flu season, so what's wrong with that?"

"I don't like being set up by anyone, and I don't like being backed into a corner in an effort to get me to submit to any kind of medical treatment. I've never had the flu, I've never had a flu shot, I'm never ever going to get a flu shot, and I'm especially not going to get a flu shot while I'm pregnant."

"It's a simple flu shot, for Chrissake. What's your problem?"

"First off, every year they make a guess as to what strain to use, and most of the time they're wrong about it. From what I've learned, there's no such thing as a simple flu shot. Did you know they combine it with swine flu and bird flu viruses? I'm not having that stuff injected into my body while I'm pregnant, and I'm not risking putting mercury into my unborn child. End of story."

"Patrick Moffett is an expert on infectious diseases. And truth be told, he's in line to be the next head of the CDC. You heard him say with your own ears that babies can easily tolerate thousands of vaccines at one time."

"I've also heard him say aluminum is a perfectly safe brain nutrient. Now who in their right mind is going to believe that, especially when there are all those studies linking aluminum with breast cancer and Alzheimer's disease?"

"He's an expert, and he knows what he's talking about, Jenna."

"Does he? Then why did he decline my on-air challenge to take the flu shot himself?"

"I don't know...maybe he already had one."

"But if babies can tolerate thousands, then surely he could've taken a second simple little flu shot to further his own cause."

"Don't be a wiseass."

"Then tell me why he stormed off the set when I challenged him to get the entire CDC vaccine schedule right there on our show. If his stuff is that safe, then why did he run like a scared rabbit?"

"Enough! You went off script, and you embarrassed him in front of the largest morning TV audience in the nation. That stunt of yours could hurt his company's bottom line this quarter."

"I'm sure you'll give him plenty of airtime so he can defend his products and his reputation."

"He deserves it, and he's going to get it."

"He's going to get it so he doesn't pull his ads from the station."

"That's right, Ms. Grant. That's absolutely right!" Matthews was red-faced.

"I'm sorry, Jack, or do you want me to call you Mr. Matthews?"

"I told you not to go toe-to-toe with me on this...not today." He sighed, walked over to his window, and looked at the mass of yellow-and-black cars in the street below. "You put me in a very awkward position, and no doubt before this day is over I'm going to be getting a call from Mr. Masterson. Jenna, I'm going to insist that you issue a formal apology to Moffett."

"But, Jack—"

"No buts...you're going to do it, and you're going to do it on the air first thing tomorrow morning...as a favor to me."

"That guy Moffett is the devil incarnate, Jack...but I have a great deal of respect for you...OK, I'll issue an on-air apology...as a favor to you."

"Very well. In the meantime, Jenna, for your punishment—"

"Kissing his ass is not enough punishment?" she asked sarcastically.

"I'm going to have to suspend you."

"Not to sound conceited, but that will hurt the ratings and the other sponsors will—"

"Moffett's account, as well as all the other pharmaceutical accounts we have, trumps all the other advertisers combined. Keep in mind, he wanted you fired altogether. In fact, he thinks I'm doing that right now. The other sponsors might cry a little if the ratings go down, but they'll stick with us because we'll still beat the other stations."

"We always have...so that's it, then?"

"Listen to me, outside of today's poor judgment, I still hold you in high regard...plus, you have three years left on your contract. If I fire you and you end up at another station, I could lose the morning share altogether."

"If you fire me, I doubt I'll ever find work in this town."

"You will, but I don't want you to be grabbed up by the other guys."

"Thank you...I think. Can I ask how long my suspension is and how this is going to play on-air?"

"For now, your suspension is indefinite. Coxx news will issue a statement that you're taking your maternity leave early...because of a great deal of stress that you've been dealing with. And Moffett will be told that you were fired. When things calm down, and when he calms down...say, like when your baby turns one, we'll tell him that we've decided to rehire you because you've learned your lesson. Then we'll slowly bring you back in on special assignment stuff."

"I see. Well, it's better than being fired, right?"

"Exactly. And let's be realistic about this. After you gave birth, you were going to take time off anyway."

"That's true."

"So that's it, then. Tomorrow you'll do your last news show and make your apology. And then you'll begin your maternity leave, and until further notice you'll do no interviews and make no appearances on any other media outlet." Matthews nodded, then turned back to his window to watch the city below.

Jenna took her time before getting up and paused at the door long enough to hear the office staff scurrying away, opening it slowly to give them time to settle back at their desks.

"Did you ever notice, Jenna, that from up here all those cabs and limos look like a swarm of bees?"

"Now isn't that ironic."

"Ironic? How so?"

"The sting, Jack. Get one, and you may have a mild reaction to a little venom. Get stung by the swarm, and you could die." And then as an afterthought, she added, "I don't suppose this would be a good time to ask why General Griff Kelley came to see you a couple weeks back, would it?"

16

712 5th Avenue
Manhattan

The first time Jenna had been to Jack Matthews's penthouse suite was shortly after it was announced she'd be the new coanchor on Coxx's Morning News program. It was a combination news, opinion, and interview format that had been lagging so far back in the ratings that one A-list actor half joked he wanted to be paid for his appearance to promote his new motion picture. Word had come from Reggie Masterson that unless a miracle happened, the longtime anchor of the program would have to be axed. Enter Jenna Grant. The San Francisco native was a twenty-four-year-old graduate from the NYU School of Journalism when she was originally hired as a Capitol Hill investigative reporter—quickly winning fans and gaining a reputation as the fiery red-haired freckled-face congressman killer.

Jealous reporters from rival stations accused Coxx of hiring her for her looks. But tagging her with nicknames such as gingersnap and devil child only made her more determined to outperform her competition—and she did. She uncovered several scandals in the short time she worked in Washington, and lawmakers would head in the opposite direction whenever they saw her coming. Her reports on the national evening news became the most watched, and soon after the other Coxx news and opinion segments had her as a recurring guest to give inside the Beltway updates—boosting the ratings for every show she appeared on. So after two years, it was a no-brainer for Matthews to bring her up to New York to save the morning news show.

Like everyone else, he had liked Jenna. True, she was pleasing to the eye; however, he admired her persistence and respected her integrity, something he himself had compromised a long time ago. As much as it pained him to lose his morning star, Matthews had to sacrifice the morning time slot ratings or risk losing tens of millions in yearly ad revenue, which would end up hurting the entire news division. It was unwritten policy that no news anchor was to disparage their pharmaceutical benefactors, nor bring on a guest who promoted any of the natural healing arts. To do so meant instant demotion from headliner to doing human interest stories in hostile parts of the world until their contract expired. Everyone at Coxx had followed policy without question—until today.

"Looks like you're decorating for the yearly Christmas party. At least I get to see the place one last time. Mind if I take off my shoes? I've been in these heels all afternoon, and my feet are killing me."

"By all means. I never said you weren't going to be invited."

"You've got to know, the entire station is buzzing about today. It would be very awkward to be subjected to the same questions over and over, and I suspect it would also spoil the festive atmosphere."

"I see your point."

"Which I'm sure you had already considered. I'm sure you remember my husband, Jimmy Silver. Jimmy, you remember Jack?"

"Sure, I remember your husband. Good to see you again. I didn't know you were going to be joining us for this discussion."

"We had a dinner date, and this was on the way. Jenna insisted I come up." Jimmy shook Matthews's hand.

"Just as well. After all, this concerns you, too. Drink, James?"

"Jimmy," he politely corrected. "And a vodka rocks with two olives would be great."

"Jimmy!" Jenna scolded.

"Perfectly OK. Soda water for you, Jenna?"

"Yes, thank you."

"Jonathan?" Matthews called out. A tall, handsomely dressed man-servant came into the room. "Jonathan, if you would, vodka rocks with two olives for the young man, a soda water for Ms. Grant, and I'll have my usual." Jonathan nodded, then disappeared into another room. "Pardon me for not inviting you outside to the terrace. The view of the city from up here is always remarkable, and on a cool crisp night like tonight it's spectacular. Sadly, it's way too windy. But come take a look through the windows in my study. Straight away you can see the Empire State Building. I used to be able to see the Trade Towers...I saw them come down that day. Oh, and off to the left you can see the bridges crossing over to Brooklyn."

"I remember from your party last year. It's beautiful, Jack, very beautiful. Now at the risk of being rude, why was it so important to talk here and not at the office?"

"Because what I'm about to tell you." He stopped when Jonathan presented with their drinks. "Just set them down on my desk."

"Will there be anything else, sir?" he asked, tucking the silver tray tight his side.

"We're fine. Please get the door as you leave, Jonathan, and thank you." Matthews served his guests. "Where was I... oh yes...what I'm about to tell you cannot be discussed at the office because it would be inappropriate to talk about company business with a suspended employee. In my home, you're here as a friend, and this is nothing more than idle gossip over drinks."

"Understood."

"James?" He looked at Jimmy toying with an olive skewered on a little plastic sword.

"Of course, Mr. Matthews, understood."

"So about General Kelley's visit—" she began.

"Jenna, I take it you've been doing a little homework on flu shots?"

"Yes...ever since you and our less-than-healthy health producer were leaning on me to do a story on Jimmy's dad."

"Yes, Jimmy's dad. Excuse me, but I get a little confused. Is Ray Silver your father-in-law or your brother-in-law?" He laughed.

"He's married to my older sister, so he's technically both. That's why I refer to him as Jimmy's dad."

"So if I may ask, does your being against the flu shot have anything to do with Ray Silver's activism, or is it something else?"

"As I mentioned this morning, I don't like being put on the spot, but if you'll recall a few years ago there was a big media frenzy about a second swine flu outbreak, and then the very next year there was the big scare over the bird flu, and in both cases the CDC ordered tens of millions of doses of those vaccines. And in spite of several weeks of every network using it as their lead-in news story, the public didn't rush out to get those shots. Why? Because as it turns out most people still remembered all those folks who died from the swine flu shot in the late seventies, and because there was no real swine flu epidemic then, as there were no swine or bird flu epidemics this last time."

"So what does that have to do with the seasonal flu shot?'

"The CDC got stuck with all those other vaccines. So to get rid of them, they were added to the seasonal flu shot. Not only did the news media ignore that little fact, but it was the only way for the government to get rid of them...other than throwing them away, that is. And since they hold the patents on those vaccines, they weren't going to simply throw them away."

"Can you blame them? The CDC has a vested interest in those things."

"And they profit quite nicely from each one that gets administered. So let's put aside the conflict of interest for just a moment, because what's more alarming as well as ignored is that ever since they approved those combination flu shots for pregnant women, miscarriages among those vaccinated have significantly increased."

"And you don't think that's a coincidence?"

"What do you think? And either way, I'm not taking that chance. I'm not having four or five strains of flu plus all those chemicals injected into my body. Especially when there's a viable life inside me who's normal development depends on an environment that is toxic-free. Jack, too many times the media has played a deceptive role in scaring people into thinking that they're going to die from some terrible plague, and the only ones who've come out healthier for it are the drug companies and the media. So if losing my job is the price I have to pay to protect my baby, then so be it."

Jack Matthews listened to everything Jenna had to say and wished he had her backbone. He took a seat behind his desk, slowly spun his chair to get a clear view of the skyline, and took several sips of his drink.

"The reason I called you here tonight is to share with you something that I cannot share with anyone else. I'm sharing this with you for two reasons...three, actually. The first is because my wife died from that first swine flu scare back in the late seventies."

"I'm sorry; I didn't know."

"Shortly after she got the shot, she developed a paralysis. Guillain-Barré Syndrome, I think they called it. The doctor's all said it was temporary and she'd be able to walk again in a month or so. She didn't. In fact, after several weeks she developed other nervous system complications. She suffered. She had a number of seizures, painful seizures, and eventually slipped into a coma. To be honest, I was relieved that she no longer had to go through all that...after another month on the machines, she passed."

"Jack...I—" She looked at Jimmy and could tell he was thinking about his sister.

"It's OK. The second reason is because neither one of you will be able to talk publicly about what I'm going to say. If you do, every media outlet from television, radio, and print, as well as Coxx news, will paint the both of you as total wing nuts. You, Jenna, will be made out to be some disgruntled ex-employee with an ax to grind, and you'd both be lucky to find work as pushcart food vendors. It's not a threat. This is what happens to people who try to derail the gravy train. The third reason is because while you can't do anything about this, you know someone who can."

"No. Absolutely not! I am not even going to mention this to Jimmy's dad."

"Why not? He's already been making waves. If anyone is going to bring this out, then he's the best one to do it."

"And he'll be the one who ends up getting destroyed," Jimmy said. "Hell, there's already some attack dog from a local Hawaiian station who's been using him as a piñata."

"Understand this, you two: of all the products made by pharmaceutical companies, vaccines are the most profitable. It hadn't always been like that. Forty, fifty years ago, the vaccines were cheap and there were only a few...and on top of that, if a kid had a serious side effect, which was rare back then, the parents could take legal action. But that was then. Today the manufacturers can't be held liable for vaccine injury, hence the major increase in the number of vaccines. You know, I had lunch with a VP from Immuboost a few weeks back. He was making the preemptive rounds because of that little incident with their HPV vaccine program in India."

"I saw that on the newswire. Over fifty thousand teenage girls became sterile shortly afterward."

"He assured me it had everything to do with the unsanitary way the UN workers were administering the program and abso-lutely nothing to do with their science."

"No, of course not, Jack. Not after the very thorough week-long investigation they conducted on themselves," she said sarcastically. "And let's not forget the former CDC head whose influence played a major role in fast-tracking that vaccine. Now she's the head of vaccine safety at Immuboost. Coincidence?"

"All the same," he said, ignoring her remark, "and in spite of the UN's screw-up, Immuboost is voluntarily compensating each girl to show how much they care."

"With what, four hundred dollars and a nondisclosure agreement? They still walk away with a billion in profit from that fiasco."

"That's the nature of the business. More importantly, however, what events in India get covered in the news can impact the company's future."

"Is that why we never aired any stories of what happened there?"

"The sanitary conditions in India have never been a topic of concern for our audience, and as far as I was concerned, there were more pressing issues occurring during that news cycle."

"Stop insulting my intelligence, Jack!" She was growing angry.

"It's business, Jenna!" he fired back. "They've got over fifty new vaccines in the pipeline, with some for diseases no one's ever heard of before...at least I haven't. But they're worried they won't be able to sell them. They're worried because people have been growing skeptical lately, holding back from bringing their kids in to the pediatrician for their regular checkups. And do you want to know why?"

"Because of the increased rates in autism, childhood cancers, autoimmune diseases?"

"No, Jenna. It's because of rumors and innuendo saturating the Internet. It's because of people like Ray Silver who keep making noise about autism, childhood cancers, and autoimmune disorders. Not that they're wrong to be concerned, but the industry insists the science doesn't bear them out, and with all the commotion being made, it's beginning to hurt the bottom line for people like...our good friend, Patrick Moffett."

"Come on, Jack. Like Immuboost, McTavish Labs makes billions in profit every year."

"And they share the wealth...with the media as well as the government. And if they begin to see sales quotas missing the mark, their stockholders as well as everyone else in the food chain will suffer."

"So what are they planning to do, force the stuff on everyone?"

"Exactly."

"What? You can't be serious?" She looked at Jimmy, then back to Matthews, as if he were joking.

"I know you remember the recent outbreak of measles in Hawaii...those eight or nine cases? That was a trial balloon, so to speak."

"You mean that was orchestrated?"

"Not exactly. Just some very smart business executives taking advantage of the opportunity. You take a few cases mixed with a little media attention, some propaganda thrown in about unvaccinated children causing the outbreak, and you add that reporter mixing it up with Ray Silver, and soon concerned parents are raising their voices and school board members are taking up the issue. That creates more media coverage, which of course gets the debate going between people pro and against, and it snowballs. Things get a little heated, and the issue takes on a life of its own. Now, I just got word this morning that there's a bill being introduced in the state legislature over there to remove all exemptions, making it mandatory for children to receive every vaccine on the schedule. The bill will pass, Jenna, because big-pharma lobbyists wrote the legislation and small but very nice contributions were made to key players in the Hawaiian State Senate. You might say they sold out for macadamia nuts."

Maca...? Oh I get it, the Hawaii thing." She didn't laugh.

"I thought it was quite clever actually. Instead of selling out for peanuts. Anyway, the rest of the representatives will go along out of fear of being labeled antichild, antihealth...whatever. They'll go along out of fear of losing reelection. Even if the effort doesn't pass, the next little epidemic won't be so little, and it'll be on the West Coast, and the press will have a field day. The fear will really spread across the entire country. Media outlets will be carrying the story every day. Party leaders in state houses across the country, just like the politicians in DC, are already on the payroll. They've been getting contributions to their campaigns and to their favorite charities for years. But that's only the beginning. Once they get the kids, they're going to take it one step further."

"What, the adults?"

"I'm afraid so. Just think of it. Not vaccinated? Then no welfare, no food stamps, no health-care insurance. It'll become a prerequisite in order to be admitted to a hospital. Heck, the government will even start to deny air travel."

"But why, Jack? Why would they do this to us? Why would people who've taken an oath to…to uphold the Constitution sanction this kind of tyranny? Because that's what this is. And since the news media won't report this for what it really is, why would you want Jimmy's dad getting mixed up in this? You know as well as I do that no matter how much trouble he makes or no matter how many voices are raised in protest, our profession, which is supposed to be above reproach, will never give them the time of day…unless, of course, there's a concerted effort to attack them, and we all know that's exactly what will happen. I'm sorry, Jack, but after what happened to your wife, I don't understand how you could go along with this."

"You've been in this business a tad over five years now. You've gotten to know firsthand who politicians really work for, and you've met a number of your colleagues who don't even attempt to hide their bias, and yet in some respects you still have a little of that fresh-out-of-school, wet-behind-the-ears naïveté."

"I prefer to think of it as honesty and integrity, and in spite of being in this business for five years, I still have it."

"Oddly enough, that's one of your character traits the public loves, but quite frankly, it surprises me." His words were carefully chosen.

"Maybe my questions about this situation come more from my...disappointment. So if we can dispense with any further character analysis, I'd still like to know why."

"Because we're hooked...addicted, if you will. It's as plain and as simple as that. Guys like Moffett are drug lords, no different than the leaders of the Mexican cartels. But Moffett's real drug of choice is money. He and all the drug companies start us off slow, giving us a little taste of how good it is. With us in the media, they bought a little ad time, and over the years we kept pushing them for more. With Congress it's campaign contributions or sponsored fact-finding trips, complete with escorts, to the Caribbean. With universities, it's endowments that finance their research facilities and donations of million-dollar imaging machines for their teaching hospitals. For example, McTavish wants to get its latest heart drug approved, so it gets four or five researchers to sign on to a paper that had already been written. This way it looks like there was valid independent research done. The paper gets published in a prestigious peer-reviewed journal, the FDA approves the drug, and the university gets another check. Flu season is coming up, so the company sends out a series of carefully crafted press releases to all the news stations, and we all start running stories about how bad it's expected to be and how many people die each year from flu-like symptoms. We do the story often enough, and people start to panic. They run to the supermarkets as quick as they can to get their shots, along with a ten-dollar coupon for groceries, and the networks are rewarded with the sale of more ad time. A perfect example is your program. Eighty percent of the commercials are for drugs."

"Brainwashing."

"Of course, it's brainwashing. Just look at the images people are exposed to. All the actors in those ads, whether young or old, are healthy and vibrant. They're running and playing and getting frisky with one another. Since when do sick people who take those drugs look or act like that?"

"They don't."

"Exactly. But we're the vehicle that helps Visor, McTavish, Immuboost, and the rest of them trick the consumer into thinking that's the life they'll have if they take those magic pills. And that's...how...we...make...our...money."

"You're right that you've become addicted."

"Yes, I have, and so has Reggie Masterson, and so has everyone else in this business. So when somebody does something like you did today, guys like Moffett drop the hammer and threaten to cut off the cash flow. And if he does...withdrawal's a bitch, and the body count is high."

"So what you're saying is this station, as well as the others, is no better than common street junkies, willing to sell your souls for that next fix."

"It is the devil we took to the dance."

"As naïve as you think I am, I'm not shocked, Jack. I don't know why, but I'm not. I'm sad, very sad, because in the five years I've known you, I've never seen such a cavalier attitude from you about something so unethical and immoral. I guess I didn't know you at all."

"The sad thing is, when you start off this way, you don't see the harm in it. They're just another advertiser. They're selling products that have FDA approval, so your conscience is clear." He tried to justify it. "Life is good, everyone is happy, you're successful, and you keep telling yourself that it's harmless. You keep telling yourself that you're still in control and that it's your idealism that still fuels your desire to jump out of bed each morning. And then, bam, it hits you. You wake up one morning and you realize they actually own your ass. They're calling the shots, dictating content, and there's nothing you can do about it."

"They don't have to own you, Jack. You made a choice to surrender that idealism, and when you did that, you capitulated. You're enslaved because you choose to stay enslaved. You can make the choice to break those bonds, and you can walk away whenever you want to."

"And do what? Run a small-town radio station in Bumfuck, Iowa?"

"Yes, that's right. A small-town radio station. Or how about starting your own newspaper, or even running a lemonade stand if you have to?"

"It's not as easy as you think. Would I like to speak up? Sure I would."

"No, you wouldn't. That's why we're having this private meeting. You said so yourself. You'd rather have Ray Silver be your sacrificial lamb because you don't have the guts to take a stand. And who cares if he goes down? Not you, right? You're nice and safe. Well, no thanks, Jack. In fact, screw the suspension. I resign. And I'm not issuing any damned apology to Reggie Masterson or Moffett. As far as I'm concerned, they can go—" She turned to Jimmy. "Get me out of here before I throw up."

"Big mistake, Jenna. Very big mistake."

* * *

Jack Matthews relaxed in his leather recliner, listening to Mozart and nursing a second scotch. He loved looking out at the millions of glittering lights that bejeweled Manhattan, Brooklyn, Staten Island, and New Jersey as well. It gave him a sense of power, a false sense, to think that his decisions on news content influenced many of the lives of all he surveyed, as well as those beyond his view. He also felt a sense of despair, knowing his decisions were out of his control.

He sipped on his drink, then dialed his phone. "Just thought you'd like to know, the opportunity presented itself for me to do as you had asked."

"How did it go?"

"As expected."

"Did she ask about our meeting?"

"Earlier today at my office and again when she first arrived this evening. But now that you mention it, we got so involved with the main issue that she forgot about it. And I certainly wasn't going to bring it up. Oh, and by the way, she also brought her husband."

"That's even better. With any luck, in a few days Ray Silver will be heading back to Colorado, leading me straight to Dr. Motz."

"I'd be very surprised if she said anything."

"So would I. But Jimmy...he'll tell his dad. You did well, Jack, you did very well."

"Well enough to finally get the IRS off my back?"

"As we had agreed."

17

Lanikai, Hawaii

Late December 2007

With Christmas just around the corner, the decorations filling the old plantation-style house on Kaneapu Place, as well as the Kailua Center for Natural Healing Arts, couldn't keep Ray distracted as much as Leigh Anne had hoped. When he was around patients or at home with his girls, his mood appeared festive enough to pass for old Saint Nick. When he was alone with her or by himself, he became quiet and withdrawn—unless baited by an antagonist.

As much as he had been disappointed with Paige, she did provide him with information and a strategy to quickly put his attackers on the defensive: a dozen or so questions to be asked of his detractors in forceful rapid succession, a departure from the laidback aloha personality he was known for at his clinic. His confidence stemmed from the fact that none of his questions could be answered truthfully and every one of them would make an honest person question convention—admitting they knew very little of the procedure they blindly advocated. On more than one occasion, he'd overheard his wife and both Leilanis screening his calls and lying to reporters looking for an interview. But once in a while he managed to beat them to the phone.

"So let me get this straight. You're saying that the hep B vaccine given to newborns within hours of birth is absolutely vital to protect them. Otherwise, they could come down with that disease. That's what you're telling me, right?" Ray asked as if he were a prosecuting attorney.

"Well, yeah. That's what the CDC and NIH recommends. And so does the American Academy of Pediatrics. Now the science is solid on that."

"And I'm sure you've seen the science, you've read all the studies, correct?"

"Uh, no—"

"But you can produce them, yes?"

"Well...I...I don't have them printed, if that's what you mean."

"But if I wanted to see them for myself, you'd at least be able to provide the references?"

Silence.

"You do know that hepatitis B is transmitted by sexual activity or from needles used by drug addicts, right?" Ray pressed on.

"But the mother—"

"Yes, the mother. Glad you brought her up. You're aware that the mother's been prescreened for STDs and drug use, right? That's standard operating procedure, isn't it? Trust me, it is. And unless that mother-to-be is a streetwalker or a drug addict, you know she's going to test negative, and yet they stick that newborn baby anyway. You do know that the hep B vaccine still contains mercury, right?"

"Well, I...I—"

"So tell me again how many newborns, toddlers, or even grade schoolers engage in promiscuous sex and intravenous drug use?"

"I'm sure there's other reasons they give that shot."

"And yet if it came down to it, you couldn't come up with one to save your life, right?"

And while that worked great during a recent phone interview with a local radio talk show, the victory hadn't provided much satisfaction. His mental tug-of-war notwithstanding, Leigh Anne also had her struggles and had been holding up better than Ray. But she, too, had her limits, and he was well aware of that.

For the past few weeks, he could not stop thinking about Casey, Seattle, McTavish Pharmaceuticals, his trip to Colorado, and most importantly, the safety of Leigh Anne and the girls. Even though no one had been crazy enough to threaten physical harm, there was the one time he found her car pulled to the side of the road, doors opened, engine running, and no one in sight. Fearing the worst, he nearly crashed his Wrangler pulling over to the shoulder, only to find his wife and daughters in the tall grass looking for the ball little Sandy had tossed from an opened window. Leigh Anne insisted her husband played up being worried to gain sympathy and extra attention in bed—a tongue-in-cheek attempt to get Ray to laugh. And while he never turned down her advances, she couldn't help but notice he seemed somewhat distracted during his favorite pastime, opting to cuddle as if he were afraid to lose her if he let go.

"This is nice, Ray. I could stay like this for hours, but I really do need to go to the bathroom."

"Sorry, it's just that…you know."

"Hey, I've got an idea. We need to get away from all this craziness, even if it's just for a few days. I know I certainly do. Whaddya say we take a long weekend, just the two of us. We can leave the girls with Leilani, and we can fly over to the big island. Do you remember the cottage we rented up in the hills? It was like being in a time warp. The appliances were from the forties: no computer, no cell reception, completely off the grid. You know which one I'm talking about, right? The one on that coffee plantation in South Kona?"

"I loved that place, but it's in Captain Cook, not Kona."

"The one with all the mangoes and papaya…and all those banana trees? That wasn't South Kona?"

"Definitely Captain Cook. There was that mac nut farm just down the road, remember?"

"Where we got those fresh-roasted macadamias, that's right. Let's go there, OK, hon?"

"It sounds great, Leigh, but I just don't know. I'm...look it, babe, I know I've been weird lately. It's just that this thing is eating me up, and I feel that I—"

"You feel that you need to grab your lance, get on your horse, and charge at that windmill."

"Yeah."

"Yeah, and we've talked about this. You've got to be able to let this go, Ray, before—"

"You're right. You're absolutely right, and I'm trying."

And as halfhearted as his attempts were at trying to let go, they were completely abandoned when he got the call from Paige that sent him into the crushed black velvet sky of the Colorado Rockies.

"Who's this? Paige? It's two in the morning...what's going on?"

"Are you sitting down, Ray?"

"I usually sleep on my back."

"Good enough. I've decided to help you."

"Wait, what? You are? I don't get it, what's changed?"

"I just had a visitor...your son."

"Jimmy?"

"That's what he said his name was."

"Are you sure it was him? What did he look like?"

"Tall...about six two and very muscular with broad shoulders, thick black hair, olive skin...almost Italian looking. I almost didn't believe him until he showed me a picture of the two of you."

"His mother was Italian. That's him, all right."

"He looks like Jio. Well except for the eyes. Your son's eyes are brown."

"Who's Jio?"

"What? Oh...just a character in one of the books I've been reading." She was embarrassed. "Forget I said anything."

"How did he know where to find you?"

"You know damn well how he found me."

"Not from me. I never said a word about the cabin…honest, I didn't."

"Tell me again how you knew what towns to look for me?"

"Look, I admit I told him how I met your brothers."

"And that's where he was waiting for me but we can talk about that later. How soon can you get back here?"

"How soon do you want me?"

"The sooner you can get here, the better."

"I'm gonna have to square this with…give me a couple days…where do I—"

"The very same place in town where you met the boys. Go there and tell the bartender you're meeting Larson. Then wait."

"What's going on, Paige. What made you change your mind? Why the urgency?"

"It's big, Ray, very big. It's what you suspected and more."

"Proof?"

"No proof. So we're gonna have to go get it."

"Then why did Jimmy…what did he give you?"

"A warning, Ray. He came to give me a warning."

When he hung up from the call, his thoughts raced from one end of the spectrum to the other…so much so he remained lying in the dark for thirty minutes, unable to decide what to do first. It was only when Leigh Anne began to stir that he realized he'd been fidgeting.

"Who were you talking to?" she mumbled, coming out of her sleep.

"I was talking to myself. I'm sorry, I didn't mean to wake you."

"Can you do me a favor and keep the conversation in your head?"

"I didn't realize I was speaking out loud."

"And stay still, or go find something to do with all your energy…and no, I don't want to have sex again."

"I'd like to think of it as making love."

"So do I, Ray, but you've been so preoccupied that lately you've been on autopilot."

"I'm sorry. I didn't realize...let me make it up to you."

"Not now...please?"

"I'm thirsty. I'll go get some water. And when I come back, I'll make sure I don't fidget."

"That sounds like a good idea. Go drink some water...a lot of water. But, please, no more sex tonight, OK? I'm too... tired." She rolled over. "So if you have all this energy, then just...go for a jog or something."

Ray tiptoed into the kitchen for fear of waking the girls. The last time he was up this late, he'd accidentally dropped a pan, and before he knew it Ronnie, Abigail, and Sandy were up and begging for grilled cheese sandwiches.

He stared into the refrigerator, debating between all his options. Back and forth, from one to the other—thinking more about Paige's phone call than his choice of beverage. He finally closed his eyes, reached in to grab the first thing he made contact with, and stood by the open door enjoying the cool air while drinking straight from the container. When the door swung closed, he browsed the many pictures of his family hanging on fridge door until he locked on to a photo of him and Casey sucking down oyster shooters at the Pike Place Market the previous summer:

"That's it, kiddo, I'm done. I can't eat any more."

"You gotta be kidding me. There's four left. Come on, Dad, two each."

"I'm serious, I can't. I'm stuffed."

"You're either losing your touch, or that lazy island life you're living is turning you into a wuss," she baited him and laughed.

"A wuss, huh? OK, fine. I'll have one more, and I'll even finish the rest of that beer."

"Definitely a wuss."

"Two more?"

"And the beer."

"And the beer. Ready? On the count of three—"

His fingertips caressed the image of her face, and he assured her that he wasn't going to rest until he got answers. Then he noticed the to-do list pad stuck to the refrigerator door just like all the pictures, hesitating for a second before grabbing it. He rifled through the kitchen junk drawer for a pen, not realizing how much noise he was making, and sat down to prioritize—everything from packing to contacting Leilani to clear his calendar and telling Leigh Anne about his first trip to Colorado. He didn't get very far and found himself making French toast for five.

* * *

In spite of what Leigh Anne called their Norman Rockwell moments, tension at home had been high after the last round of vandalism: tire tread gouged into the lawn of their front yard, the smashed mailbox torn from its post, and now the neighbors voicing concerns after a trail of dead fish had been left along Kaneapu Place, leading up to the front door steps of Leigh Anne and Ray's house. He knew his going back to Colorado might take that tension past the boiling point. That is, if their next meeting with the preschool moms scheduled for later that afternoon didn't do it first. And since he had to deal with that before he flew east, he would certainly try to use the gathering to try and get a little breathing room for Leigh Anne. He just needed to get her cooperation, which given the latest development, was a lot easier said than done.

"Morning."

"Morning, Ray. Have you been up all this time?"

"Yeah. By the time I got the girls back to bed and cleaned up the kitchen, I was too tired to sleep, if that makes any sense. Do you want me to make you breakfast?"

"Still stuffed from the French toast. It was good. How often do you do that with the girls?"

"Not often enough. Not to worry though, I'm not in the habit of waking them up in the middle of the night. I have to admit that it is kinda fun when it happens."

"Agreed."

"I'm not going in to the office today. I wanted to prepare for that meeting tonight."

"And to pack?"

"Pack?"

"For Colorado...yeah, I know all about it."

"So you heard my end of the phone call last night?'

"I thought I had dreamed it, but then not more than fifteen minutes ago I heard you on the phone making flight reservations."

"Leigh...I meant to tell you that I went there from Seattle... after Casey...it was just for a few days."

"I thought you were going to tone things down, Ray, but since you got back from Seattle you've actually cranked it up a few degrees."

"Leigh, you know I'm not looking for a fight...not with you, not with anyone. But these reporters and radio talk show people keep calling and asking questions. I'm answering the best way I know how."

"I heard your last interview, and you nearly chewed that guy's head off."

"I'm just not giving them the opportunity to get the upper hand is all."

"There's a reason why we're screening your calls. In addition to trying to save what's left of your sanity, the moms at the preschool listen to those interviews, too, Ray. They say you sound possessed. They're getting angry, they're stepping up the pressure, and that's why I had to arrange this meeting for tonight. Tell me, did something happen when you were back there that I should know about?"

"No, nothing. I've told you everything that happened in Seattle."

"And now I think you should tell me what happened in Colorado."

Ray told her about Paige and how he was able to meet her in the first place.

"Somehow I knew you'd get Jimmy and my sister involved."

"Hold up a minute. I specifically told Jimmy that I didn't want them involved in this. Not this time around."

"And you didn't think that was an open invitation for the two of them to do just that?"

"Come on, Leigh. Your sister is pregnant. Do you really think I wanted to involve them? And besides, her meeting with her boss came out of a completely separate incident."

"OK, I'll give you that, but still, I don't want you to do this, Ray. This is all happening way too fast, and you're not thinking clearly. And I understand that."

"I've thought this out, sweetie, and I can assure you that my thinking is very clear."

"Considering what you stand to lose, I don't think so."

"Stop it, Leigh, please. I've kept my promise to you since I came home from Iraq."

"Until now...and if you remember, you nearly came home in a body bag."

"True. But haven't I been good over the past three and a half years?"

"Not exactly, but—"

"I've had nothing to do with the NSA or the CIA, right?

"Yes...not that they'll ever call you again, thank god, but—"

"I haven't raced halfway 'round the world to save humanity...I haven't even gotten so much as a parking ticket, right?"

"You know what I'm talking about."

"Yes, I do, and I've focused all of my energy on you, the girls, and my practice, yes?"

"Until recently, but for the most part, yes, Ray, you have."

"I've built up the clinic and made it everything I said I would. And in spite of the recent craziness, the Kailua Center for Natural Healing Arts is still the busiest multidisciplinary holistic health center on Oahu. And haven't I arranged my own hours so you can still teach at the university?"

"Yes, of course you have, but what was all that for? Were you doing it because you wanted to, or were you doing me and the girls a favor...just making a deposit of goodwill in order to spend it on one more wild adventure?"

"That wasn't fair. This isn't any wild adventure; this is something that needs to be done."

"I wonder, Ray, I really do. Maybe not getting so much as a parking ticket is making you go through withdrawals or something, and now you actually need to go charging off to save the world or else you'll explode."

"How can you even say that given what's happened? You surely can't be serious."

"So let's talk about what's happened and what's been happening. Do you really want to risk everything you've...we've worked so hard for? I never said anything when you began your antimedication lectures at the clinic. That was your gig and—"

"You know quite well that I teach my people about natural alternatives, and besides you're just as anti drug therapy as I am. At least I thought you were."

"I'm just not as fanatical about it as you and—"

"Fanatical?"

"Wrong word choice, but you know what I mean."

"Yes, of course, your doctorate in marine biology."

"And because of my education and experience, I'm not afraid to consider medication...if and when necessary."

"Now that's what I don't understand. In all your training and experience, every time there's a marine crisis of some sort, such as a major fish die-off, or an outbreak of some weird disease among sea birds, do you or any of your colleagues conclude that it's a genetic predisposition or perhaps a lack of some kind of medical intervention? No, you don't. Why? Because the problem always has something to do with the environment. Clean up the environment, and the marine crisis is resolved. So why isn't that the same approach with human illness? It's because of money, big money. And it's because people are easily scared into getting in line for the next miracle drug."

"Enough, Ray! I'm not one of your patients. Excuse me, I meant 'practice members.'"

"Regardless, you still do agree with me on how we choose to raise our girls, yes?"

She hesitated.

"Yes or no, Leigh?"

"I'm their mother, and I'm going to do what I think is best for them. And the way we handle it now is our personal lifestyle choice…at least it should be. I remember a time when you offered your opinion only when it was asked for and, more importantly, only within the confines of your office. Over the past couple of years and especially the past six months, you've been expanding that boundary and you know it."

"It's more than just my opinion, and the facts back me up. I have an obligation to share what I know so the people who come to my practice can make an informed choice. You know that."

"The facts, Ray, are inconclusive. You're just adamant about your point of view, and you've been proving it because you've become more vocal and much more aggressive. You've really been sticking your neck out."

"Speaking out to the community is sticking my neck out?"

"To all of Oahu and beyond, Ray! You don't realize what kind of pressure this puts on me."

"Leigh, I've been here the whole time. I see exactly what's been happening…and I know it's because the advice I offer challenges some people's reality. It makes them uncomfortable."

"Uncomfortable? Look at the vandalism to our cars, your office…and then there are the looks I get from people every time the news stations from Honolulu come to get your views whenever there's an incident."

"Like when another kid on antidepressants hangs himself or brings a gun to school to get revenge for being laughed at?"

"It's more than that. Do you know what it's like to walk into the market and people stop what they're doing to look at you? Even my sister called from New York when all the news stations back there picked up the story that reporter…what's his name?"

"Kimmel."

"Yeah, when news stations on the mainland picked up the hit piece he did on you, the news director and the health producer at Coxx pressured Jenna to do a piece about you."

"I know, Jimmy told me when it happened. And I know your sister declined."

"Of course she did, and just because she's no longer working there doesn't mean they won't send someone else."

"I'm ready for that." Ray poured himself a cup of coffee and offered one to Leigh Anne. "It's Kona."

"I'm too worked up, but thanks."

"She agrees with my position...your sister. She agrees with me."

"I don't know if she does...we've never discussed it. And whether she does or not, don't you go interfering with the way she and Jimmy decide to raise their kids."

"I won't have to. I already know how they'll be raised."

"Would you like to share?"

"Given the way I raised and educated my son, and knowing that your sister is as intelligent as you...they'll do what's best for their children."

"I think I'll have to call my sister."

"Are you saying you don't trust me?"

"With the way you've pushed yourself on the media, I wouldn't put it past you to start pressing the issue with Jenna."

"Leigh, you know that I don't go running to the news media; they come to me. And you've gotta admit that the exposure's been great for business. We're up twenty-five percent in just the past—"

"Maybe it's been great for your business, but it hasn't been great for me."

"Yeah, I know, and I'm sorry. I really thought we took care of that."

"Ray, more and more of the moms at the twins' preschool don't want our girls over for playdates."

"I thought they understood, Leigh."

"Apparently they don't. And by the way, here's the receipt from the body shop for repainting the car door. At certain angles you can still see what was written. It may need another coat."

"The police think they might know who did it."

"Yeah, well...I found this note on my windshield the other day."

"'Keep your little Typhoid Marys away from our kids.' Was this Alice Mayweather?"

"Yes...no...I don't know. I'm not sure who, but Alice and some others have been hurling insults."

"When we talk to them today, they'll calm down."

"Ray, you just don't understand. Alice is really on the war-path, and thanks to that TV hit piece, she's got them thinking you're some kind of new-age antiscience whacko."

"Antisci...now isn't that ironic? Tell me, where's the science behind giving kids antidepressants while these 'scientists' ignore the violent video games they play or or all the chemicals and sugar in the artificial food they eat all day. And how about the lack of parenting? A kid has a problem, and the parent makes 'em pop a pill, for heaven's sake."

"You don't need to convince me, but because we don't let our kids graze in the candy aisle, because we eat organic, because we don't vaccinate...look, I'm the one who's been dealing with the fallout from your crusade...and I know you can see it's getting worse."

"A crusade? Well...maybe I am on a crusade. But it's not my fault those people are ignorant about the subject. I guarantee you, not one of them has ever researched the topic, let alone questioned the advice they've been given. And they don't know or even care that I have. Come on, Leigh...I know you see the damage being done to those kids...those little medicated zombies in that preschool you bring our girls to. It makes me sick that corporations like McTavish and Visor scare the hell out of people about disease, preach lies about health, and profit from the deception."

"You feel blindsided by Casey, don't you?"

"Not by her. But I was blind, that's for sure. I didn't see—"

"You didn't want to see because her being in the military had always been part of your dream. And as far as we know, the link you talk about...it's still just a theory...your theory. You can't be sure there's a connection."

"It doesn't...change...the end result."

"But there's no evidence."

"And I say there is. And it's going to be found and made public."

"By you?"

"Yes, by me, because—"

"Because it's personal."

"Yes, it's personal. And if not me, then who?"

"You're scaring me, Ray. You should be dialing it back... I'm asking you to dial it back. Instead it sounds like you're ready to go to war."

"I just want to uncover the truth and expose it...but if a war is what it takes."

"Ray!"

"I didn't mean that, I swear. I just want the public to learn the truth about those bastards and the poisons they push on all of us. I know there's been a cover-up...I can feel it...and it has to be exposed. Otherwise, it'll never stop, Leigh."

"I'm afraid. I'm afraid that you're going to escalate this beyond searching for answers, beyond searching for proof or exposing those responsible. I'm afraid that you're going to take this thing beyond that. I'm afraid you're out to seek justice on your own terms. I see it in your eyes, I hear it in your voice, and this is who you become when your motivation is protecting your family."

"Justice? There is no justice for what they do to people. But, yes, I want to protect my family, and I want people to finally see that they've been deceived all these years. I want them to see how that deception has cost them."

"And what do you think it'll cost you? What's it going to cost us? And what if you're wrong and there is no smoking gun? How can we continue to live in this community?"

"I'm going to fix all that. I mean, *we're* going to fix all that... tonight at that meeting."

"Oh my god, you're going to start a war there, too."

"No, no. No wars. I promise. But it wouldn't be the first time I launched a grenade at those women."

"I know. But I've been able to look past those other times because those incidents were different."

"Trust me on this one, babe. I want those women out of your hair so I can focus on this other thing."

"I don't know how many times or how many ways I have to say this, Ray, but I don't want you going to Colorado. If you do what I think you're planning on doing, it amounts to an act of premeditated revenge...and if you do this—"

18

Kaneohe, Hawaii

Ray parked a few doors down from Kathy Kotter's, and he and Leigh Anne waited, watching a number of people file in. True to form, Kathy welcomed her guests dressed in her tightest, most revealing yoga outfit. They looked at each other and didn't comment but shared an eye roll and a smile. In the short time they had been sitting there, Ray had turned on the car stereo for the third time, and for the third time Leigh Anne shut it off.

"What, Leigh?"

"Could you just stop doing that?" She was agitated.

"I'm sorry, it's habit. I always listen to music when I'm in the car."

"I know, I'm sorry. I do the same thing when I'm driving... it's just that I'm...nervous. This isn't what I expected."

"Same here. I didn't know there'd be dads coming to this thing, but it makes sense given Kathy's track record of—"

"That's not what I meant."

"Oh. Are you having second thoughts?"

"I'm having a lot of thoughts, some conflicting and some not so good."

"Let's talk about it."

"We've talked enough on the way over here. I'm all talked out, and we don't have any more time. We need to go in there and get this over with."

"It'll be OK, Leigh."

"No, Ray, I don't think so."

The greetings were short and awkward, the meeting itself beginning without any formality and proceeding without any hint of organization. At times it seemed like a free-for-all; however, it was strong on agenda. It had gone much the way Leigh Anne had expected: Alice Mayweather was leading the charge, and when people tried talking over one another, the volume, unlike the level of comprehension, seemed to increase exponentially. Kathy Kotter kept making the rounds, offering crackers topped with processed cheese spread—taking time to lean over the dads so they could get a good look at everything, even the items on the serving tray, while she described the different toppings.

Ray did his best to give his point of view, calmly going over information he had presented on past occasions but this time for the benefit of the men. Not that it would do any good, because it was no different than discussing family care plans at his office— the husbands always deferred to their wives. Still, it was hard for him to complete a sentence, as Alice and some of the others kept interrupting. All things considered, Leigh Anne was impressed with Ray for keeping his composure. But unlike the other Q and A sessions, between Carrie Dunsmore's incessant head nodding to Ray or anyone voicing an objection and Arnie Mayweather's obnoxious flirting over soda crackers with cheddar-flavored cheese product while Ray spoke, they both knew they had been wasting their time. When Arnie's flirting became too much of a distraction, Ray stopped his appeal, stared directly at Alice's husband, and commented about the ongoing acts of vandalism. In response, Arnie jumped to his feet and the two men stood toe-to-toe in a standoff. Leigh Anne had had enough.

"Is that what this is coming down to?" She stepped toward the two men, and the room grew quiet. "Are you guys now going to duke it out? Look at the two of you. Ray, damn it! Because you're so, so...the whole community wants to pack us off into exile to Molokai like Father Damien's lepers once were. And you, Arnie Mayweather...everyone knows you've been doing your wife's dirty work destroying our property and leaving those anonymous notes. Yeah, that's right, Arnie, we've got you cold, so don't look so shocked. The handwriting on the notes you've been leaving on my windshield matches the lists I have on the cork board in my kitchen...I'm talking about the ones you wrote listing both your kid's food allergies, as well as the note giving me the times I have to give them their ADD medication. And now you want to stand up to my husband because he called you out on it? Are you kidding me, Arnie? If all these people weren't around, you'd be running for the hills. You're nothing but a pussy the way you always have your nose in Kathy's little camel toe. Alice should beat you silly for the way you embarrass her, for heaven's sake. For someone who couldn't punch their way out of a paper bag, you look kinda stupid puffing your chest in front of everybody right now, you know that? You wanna fight Ray?" She turned to Alice. "Go ahead and ask your wife for permission, Arnie. I'm sure she'll let you. Is it OK with you, Alice? Hell, Arnie, I'd bet the farm Ray will kick your sorry ass before you can hide behind your wife's apron strings. So unless you're ready to make good on all those threats you've been leaving in the middle of the night, I suggest you pack up that false bravado, sit down, and shut up before you get hurt!"

To say the room was in shock would be an understatement. No one, not even Ray, had ever seen this side of Leigh Anne. For the first time that anyone could remember, Alice Mayweather was speechless. Her husband slowly backed away until he found the front door. In an odd way Kathy was feeling aroused—from Leigh Anne's power surge, as well as from picturing Ray beating Arnie to a pulp.

"Now, I have to say that I'm sick and tired of all this bickering, all this fearmongering, all of the storytelling behind my back...I'm fed up with the way all you people have been acting. Grow...the fuck...up."

Leigh, I don't think—" Betty Torres started.

"Shut up and sit down, Betty. You've done nothing to help matters in any way. Now I'm going to settle this nonsense once and for all, right here and right now, and if you people don't want to associate with me anymore, then so be it. But I'm not going to put up with your childish bullshit anymore." She turned to her husband. "And that goes for you too, Ray Silver. You may have your views on health-care and prevention, and the way you run your clinic is your business, but those girls are just as much mine as they are yours. My education and experience is just as valid as yours is, and I have every right to make decisions about our children just as much as you do. And I'm telling you, as I am telling everyone else in this room, that I took our girls to get their shots."

All eyes were now on Ray. His eyes never left Leigh Anne.

"It's done, and that's that." She continued, "So you people just get off our backs once and for all. Alice, if I ever see your little spineless man anywhere near my kids, my house, or my car, I'll personally see to it that he'll never be able to reproduce again."

Everyone waited for Ray to respond. He didn't. He continued to look at his wife, noticing a slight tremor as if she were shivering from a cold wind—a result of her reluctant performance finishing long before the flood of adrenaline. Carrie Dunsmore was the first to breach the stillness, walking over to her to offer support. A visibly shaken Alice Mayweather had never been humiliated to the degree she had just experienced, yet at the same time she was happy to take the credit for getting Leigh Anne to surrender and seeing Ray get taken down as a result. A low chatter now filled the room, with the moms slowly converging on Leigh Anne. Ray walked past the group, making eye contact with her one more time, and left without saying a word. Once outside, a sustained wind agitating the tall palms and the feeling of raindrops made him take pause to look at the sky—dark and threatening. *"It's just the Kona winds."* He laughed.

"Ray?"

He turned to find Kathy Kotter behind him on the front lanai. She hesitated but spoke up anyway. "That came out of nowhere."

"Much like this storm."

"Yeah, it was just like...wow, look at that sky. It's almost as if the gods are trying to tell us something."

"It's just the Kona—" He stopped before he allowed himself to be drawn into a detailed explanation. "Yeah, Kathy, they must be pretty mad."

"Leigh Anne must've been channeling some of that energy because she was pissed! She really let Arnie have it, all right. If you ask me, that little weasel deserved it. It's so sketch how he's always creepin' on me. It just makes my skin crawl."

"Can you imagine what he'd be like if you had encouraged him?"

"Right?"

"Well, you won't have to worry about him anymore."

"Good. Hey, listen, I don't mean to be forward, but I suspect you'll be needing a place to sleep tonight."

"What?"

"Trust me, Ray, I've seen stuff like this before. You're going to need a place to sleep, and by the looks of things, you may need a place for more than just a few nights. I have plenty of—"

"That's OK, Kathy. I'll be just fine."

"It's no bother."

"I appreciate the offer, but I'll be OK."

"If you say so, but if you need a shoulder—"

19

McTavish Labs
White Plains, New York
January 2008

R ay rummaged through desk drawers and paced around
Paige's former office as she searched the McTavish
network for the files they needed and anything else
worth downloading. The process was taking longer than
the Mission Impossible scenario he had envisioned when
they repetitively reviewed the operation back in Colorado.
Thankfully, there were no precision descents out of choppers,
no choreographed acrobatics from air conditioning duct work,
no yoga inspired moves over infrared security beams. If there
had been, they would have surely been in trouble.

*"The fence line along Haarlem Avenue is the best entry point.
Specifically, this point here in the corner. Because of this tree,
it's the lowest at twelve feet, and it's not well lit."*

"Strange. Why not?"

"Politics."

"Politics?"

*"Believe it or not, between the railroad authority, the
state, the county, and the city, everyone is arguing over*

public safety and who's responsible for lighting the street. Meanwhile, nothing ever got done."

"What about McTavish security lighting?"

"When I was working there, they had wanted to light the whole fence line, but the residents on the surrounding streets complained, so a permit was never issued."

"So the government lets them produce, market, and sell drugs that kill people, but they flex their collective muscle to stop them from installing security lighting. Gotta love politics. OK...so I hop the fence here and then what?"

Paige looked up from the monitor each time Ray cracked the door to check the hallway. He glanced over at her each time she grunted her objection.

"Can you hurry it up? The chemical smell is getting worse out there."

"I'm going as fast as I can."

"I thought your friend Ambrose—"

"He's not my friend!" Paige snapped, annoyed at the interruption. "He's just a security guard, and he wouldn't be involved in a setup like you're probably thinking."

"I wasn't thinking that, but now that you mention it, let's just go over what we know. He was late letting us in, he offered up your old room, which is farther into the building than some of the other offices we could have used...think about that. An office closer to the back door or even near the old storage rooms would have been better for us. Your old access code is still valid, and blank flash drives just happen to be sitting in an empty drawer in an office that's just as empty."

"It's got a new computer and a desk, and some stuff in the drawers, so it's not empty...and maybe he did or didn't leave the drives for us, but he probably doesn't even know what a flash drive is. Would you please let me do this?"

"You're the one who said you had a bad feeling about this."

"Stop distracting me. We'll discuss this later."

Paige worked as fast as she could, but it still took her some time to navigate the new network.

"So it's agreed while I'm in the animal lab securing some reports and tissue samples, you'll meet Ambrose by this side door of the main building."

"At three a.m. sharp, right? He knows to be there at three?"

"He'll be there at three, and he'll escort you to this corridor. That's where you'll find the storage rooms. What we need should be in this one here, room 117."

"Should be in 117? Whaddya mean 'should be'?"

"Will be. The stuff will be in 117."

"You sure? It's been a few years since you've been there."

"Room 117 has been the document storage room forever. All the file boxes had number codes with dates, but they were also color coded by department. Whenever I needed to look up my stuff, I would go to the boxes with the orange stickers. In addition to that, the other stuff we're looking for will be in a box with double red stickers. You want the folders that have the initials WT and AW. Those are the guys who worked on what you're looking for. Those are also the guys who disappeared."

"What's this office down here, the one with the check mark on it?"

"That's my old office. Don't worry about it; you won't need to go that far into the building. Just stuff your backpack with the files I have marked on this list and exit the same way you came in. Hop the fence, and I'll meet you back at the car, which we'll leave over here on Cloverdale. You'll be in and out in the blink of an eye."

"Pay dirt! Everything is here: my stuff; the politicians; the list of corporate insiders at CDC, FDA, NIH; internal memos about fast-tracking...all of it!"

"Experimental stuff for the defense department?"

"There's a DoD file! No time to look at it now. I'll e-mail it, and we'll go through it all later."

She sent off the e-mails and then began downloading onto a drive.

"Forget that part; let's get going."

"No, we need these. If we were set up, chances are we could possibly get nailed before we leave the campus. That's why we'll split up. I'll go over the north-side fence that borders Bond Street, and you go to the south side of the compound and hop the fence onto Glenn. We'll meet up by the car on Cloverdale. Now, if they nab you and find the flash drive, they won't suspect that we also e-mailed the files. At least not until they have their IT guys check their servers." She pulled the drive, downloaded files onto the second one, and slipped the first into Ray's pants pocket.

"Are you kidding me? You take it."

"Ray? They could nail either one of us or both. Why take a chance?"

When she finished, she made sure the desk was exactly how they found it.

"OK, ready. Let's go."

"Uh oh…you hear that?"

"Hear what?"

"Shhh listen." A faint ringing sound echoed through the hallways. "You don't suppose—"

Strobe lights flashed, sirens screamed, and simultaneously they said, "Ambrose!"

"We gotta get the fuck outta here!" Paige headed for the door.

"Wait! What if it wasn't him?"

"What?"

"What if it's because of the chemical spill?"

"Then everyone's on their way to that side of the building. Let's go!"

"And the White Plains police and the fire department hazmat unit are on their way here, too!"

"All the more reason to get going before they get here."

She eased her head through the office door, only to come face to face with security guard Stipo and the strong stench of what seemed like several different chemicals. Ambrose Martin was nowhere in sight. She was startled at first and didn't notice the glazed-over look in Stipo's eyes until he wobbled.

He appeared intoxicated, but Paige knew that it wasn't alcohol that had the man holding on to the door frame attempting to support himself.

"What's going on? Where's Ambrose?" she demanded as if she still belonged at the company.

"He's...he's down." His face was now ashen. "They're all... down."

"Whaddya mean he's down?"

"We were...cleaning up a spill. It was pretty bad...one of the...fell and another...drum went off the—" His eyes closed, and he started to fall back. Ray grabbed him. "It hit him...he's... dead. Chemicals every...where. Vadella and Pat...passed out."

The security guard looked at Ray and then back over to Paige. She noticed the look of recognition in his eyes just as he lost consciousness. Ray lowered him to the floor and checked for a pulse. There was none.

"He's not breathing; his heart stopped. I'm gonna do CPR."

"Are you nuts? The others are probably dead, too." She began to cough from the thickening stench. "We gotta get outta here before—"

"You're right. My eyes are burning. Come on."

They raced down the corridor, then down another, and then a third until they saw the exit. Once outside, Paige collapsed to her knees—inhaling the fresh air as deep as she could. The McTavish campus was awash in flashing strobe lights and alarm bells. The wail of sirens from what seemed like every direction grew louder by the second.

"Let's go." He grabbed her by the arm, forced her to stand, and they stumbled off in the direction of Haarlem Avenue.

"Change of plans." Paige coughed." Once we get over the fence, we split up completely. You head for the train. Go into Manhattan, and we'll meet up at—"

"What? No way, Paige, that's crazy."

"Listen to me. I parked the car just off North Broadway. Every cop, ambulance, and fire truck will be coming from—"

"We stick together. With all this noise, there'll be people coming out of their houses to see the big show. We're gonna be some of those people milling around in the crowd until we can casually slip off to the car."

"Ray, look at us. We're dressed in all black. Don't you think people will notice that?"

"In all this commotion? Maybe if we're standing together."

"It's too risky."

"So suggest something better, because those sirens are getting louder by the second. Look it, we have a change of clothing in the trunk of the car, and we have no more time to debate."

20

Colorado Rockies

One Week Later

Ray leaned back against the bark of a thick evergreen to catch his breath and take a few minutes to survey the woods. The trail up the mountain was not only narrow, but at times the incline was quite steep and slippery. The broken tree limbs he used as hiking poles gave him an extra measure of stability. In addition to making sure he wasn't being followed, he tried to look for familiar landmarks. Things seemed different, and he wasn't quite sure if he had made the correct choice at the last fork.

It had been a long five days since he began the first leg of his journey, and he was starting to feel the effects of having fallen asleep on the bench seat of an all-night diner and getting the back of his head and neck chewed up by bedbugs in a road-side motel room somewhere in Ohio. He laughed at himself for having tried to be as inconspicuous as possible—coming to the conclusion that had the police been after him or if he had been tracked by McTavish people, he would have been just as recognizable no matter how he traveled or where he stayed. He longed for a hot bath and a bed with warm, clean sheets. But at this point he'd gladly settle for the stand-up shower and lumpy couch in Paige's cabin. Her accommodations might have been rustic, but at least they were clean. *"Next time you're on the run, just stay at a nice hotel."*

He forced himself to stand to ease a cramp in his left hamstring. *"Just another half mile to go. Stay to the right of the red mark going up, stay to the left going down,"* he reminded himself. The trek up the mountain seemed longer than he remembered, but then again, when he'd made the hike a few weeks ago, he hadn't been cold, tired, hungry, or on the run, and absent now was the cover of darkness that would have a least given him a measure of stealth. Now every sound in the forest or drone of an aircraft engine had him ducking for cover—his sympathetic nervous system kicking into high gear, causing his already rapid heart rate to go even faster. He'd been much more calm until a cop in Champagne, Illinois, almost ran him over at six in the morning as he was walking to get coffee. Ray had still been half-asleep, making his way to a small café, when the cruiser, seemingly coming out of nowhere, cut across his path and stopped within inches of running over his toes. When the officer jumped from his car, Ray had been convinced they had nailed him.

"Hold it right there, buddy."

"Officer?"

"Do you have any idea why I'm confronting you this morning?"

"Confronting me?"

"Do you have any idea as to why I'm making contact with you?"

"Contact? No, I don't know why you're making contact."

"Are you mocking me?"

"Mock...? No, of course not. Did I do something wrong? Did I drop some litter in the street or something?"

"I'm afraid it's more serious than that. Can I see some identification, please?"

Ray fumbled for his wallet, debating whether to run. It was a short debate when he saw the officer rest his right hand on his holster.

"Do you mind telling me what's going on, because I honestly don't know what I did?"

"I think you know...Mr. Silver, is it?"

He looked up at Ray, who nodded.

"Yeah, OK, I know. Look, officer, I'm not going to resist, honest. I only ask that you don't make the cuffs too tight. Please don't hurt my hands. I'm a chiropractor, and my hands are very important to me."

"So you are mocking me."

"No, officer, I swear I'm not."

"You think I'm gonna cuff you for jaywalking?"

"I jaywalked?"

"About two blocks back, yeah."

"But it's six in the morning. The streets are empty...there are no cars on the road."

"I don't care what time of day it is or how many cars are on the road. Do you know how fast a car can come out of nowhere and zip through that intersection? It could be clear one minute, and the next thing you know, you're flat as a griddle cake."

"Yes, sir, I see your point."

"I don't think you do."

"I do, honest, I really do."

"You say you're a chiropractor?"

"Yes, sir."

"And I'm sure you see a lot of injured people in your clinic, yes?"

"Yes, sir."

"And I'm sure you don't wanna be one of those injured people you treat, right?"

"No, I don't wanna treat myself, no sir."

"Did you treat that?" The cop had pointed to the rip and the dried bloodstain on the pant leg by his knee.

"I fell...a few days back. Was walking to get a cup of coffee and slipped on the ice. I took care of it. Just haven't had an opportunity to do a load of laundry."

"Hawaii, huh?"

"What?"

"Your driver's license, it's from Hawaii. You're from Hawaii?"

"Yes, sir."

"What are you doing way over here?"

"Cross-country vacation."

"Oh? In the middle of winter?"

"Yeah. Stopping in on friends for the holidays...I've got none here in Champagne, though. I just stopped for the night. I got my car back at the hotel down there. Gonna grab some breakfast, then continue on my way...to Davenport. Big chiropractic school there...in Davenport...Iowa. Hey, look, I'm really sorry I jaywalked, but I'm a little behind schedule. Are you gonna ticket me or something, 'cause I really—"

"I'm gonna let you off with a warning this time. Good thing for you, I like you chiropractors. I go to one, you know?"

"That right?"

"Yeah, every once in a while I need to go get my neck cracked. Hey, maybe you know my guy, Doc Wakefield?"

"I wouldn't know anyone here, I'm sorry."

"Yeah, OK. Just be careful, understand?"

"Yes, sir, and uh...thanks."

Ray rubbed the bandage-covered gash on his knee, and stretched out his hamstrings once more before diving back into the snow at the sound of a helicopter fast approaching from the east. He lay motionless, listening for the thumping noise to pass overhead and fade off. He remained lying in the snow. It felt good to stretch, out even if it was for just a couple minutes. Save for a light wind that played with the trees as it ebbed and flowed, it was peaceful. He tried to allow his mind a moment to be quiet—something that had been escaping him recently. He closed his eyes to listen to the music of the forest, but the internal chatter kept him wondering about many things—especially Paige. Before splitting up in Manhattan, she had warned him to stay vigilant throughout his journey back to the cabin. "I'm doing my best," he said to the sky above.

"Even though it's unlikely it could happen, you still have to be very careful."

"I know, Paige, I know."

"If you suspect you're being followed, don't explain it away. It's probably not your imagination running wild. You've got to take a detour and keep on it until you're sure you've lost them. The last thing we need is for someone to follow you back."

"I'll be careful...I can do this, so stop worrying."

"I am worrying. I've been living like this for the past few years. I've had to plan every time I ventured out. A two-hour round trip into Fort Collins took me three and a half, sometimes four, because there were people tailing me and I had to take so many different detours to confuse and lose them. You can't even begin to imagine the precautions I had to take. One mistake, one slip up, and they got you. So, please, Ray, I'm serious about this."

"I know you are."

"I surely hope so. I can't...we can't afford any mistakes."

"Do I look like I'm treating this lightly? Trust me, I'm on top of my game here. The last thing I wanna do is lead someone back up that mountain...you got that?"

"Yeah...yeah, I got it, I got it."

"Are you OK?

"I'm fine. I just can't stop thinking about Amby...but I'm fine. You?"

"Yeah. Got my route plotted out. I should meet up with you in about four days."

"I'd make it five or six unless you're planning on living on energy drinks."

"I don't, and I plan on being there in no more than four. I'll grab a bus, maybe even a train. I'll even bum a ride if I have to. One or two good rides with a trucker, and I'm there in no time."

"Wanna bet you'll be walking a lot?"

"No. Now don't lose my kid's number. We're agreed that if we can't reach each other, for whatever reason, we're to call him to let him know we've lost contact. This way either one of us can leave messages he can pass on."

He had doubts she would contact Jimmy if the need arose. Ray had complete trust in his son, but he'd seen the apprehension in Paige's eyes. After all, Jimmy did work for the government. Although press coverage of the chemical spill and accidental deaths had made no mention of a data breach, let alone a break-in, there were times during his journey when Ray couldn't help but think that company officials were aware of the file download, as well as who was responsible. He rationalized that given the incriminating evidence stolen by Paige, the company would keep that news from the media, which also meant keeping it from the authorities. That way they could dispatch a team of their own people to track, locate, and dispose of the two of them.

It was while taking a nap in the back of a Greyhound bound for Pittsburg that he had dreamed of Harrison Ford in the *Fugitive* movie. It became his motivation for staying clear of airports, railroad stations, or any more bus depots—opting instead to hitch or if necessary walk back to Colorado. At one point, when he caught a ride at an Illinois truck stop, he heard an anxious dad calling after his son: "Richaaard." From that moment until he crossed into Iowa, he kept imagining Tommy Lee Jones running through a water tunnel in hot pursuit, yelling: "Raymuund! Raymond Silver! US Marshall! Stop, or I will shoot!"

His cheeks burned a little, but it was not from the cold. He picked up a handful of fresh powder that had blanketed the already snow-covered mountains and pressed it into his neck and jaw to soothe his skin—irritated from sweat, dirt, and scratching at his five-day-old beard. He scooped up another handful and sucked on it for the water. *"If I hafta drudge through this stuff all the way back to the cabin, at least it serves a purpose. But I guess if I was hunting for dinner, the animal's tracks would—"* He turned around and saw his footprints as far as his dilated pupils could focus. His heart pounded so hard his chest hurt. "Stupid, stupid, stupid, Ray," he said aloud. He punched the ground in frustration, and once again heard Paige's voice:

*"One mistake, one slip up, and they got you. So, please, Ray,
I'm serious about this."*

"I know you are."

"I surely hope so. I can't...we can't afford any mistakes."

*"Do I look like I'm treating this lightly? Trust me, I'm on
top of my game here. The last thing I wanna do is lead someone back up that mountain...you got that?"*

"You're on top of your game?" He started to double back to
clean up his mistake, and just as he was convinced he'd made
the wrong choice at the last fork, he lost his footing on an
exposed section of ice. His makeshift hiking poles went flying
as he furiously worked his feet in an effort to stop sliding. The
harder he tried to stop them from moving, the faster they kept
slipping in all directions—his arms waving, his body twisting
back and forth and from side to side as if he had studied dance
under Twyla Tharp. His weight shifted, and he found himself
veering off to his left—sliding closer toward a crevasse.

In a panic, he decided to let his legs slip out from under
him and threw himself backward into the snow. Instead of
this ending his ordeal, he found himself sliding down toward
the ledge faster than before. He feverishly worked his arms,
pushing backward as his body continued to pick up speed. He
noticed a tree coming up on his right, but so, too, was the crevasse. He stuck his right arm out into the snow, keeping it as
stiff as he could—using it as a rudder. Ray's body veered off
toward the tree, his right arm catching it. He jerked to a hard
stop.

* * *

By the time the sun set, Ray had regained lost ground and
then some. In spite of the shadows overtaking the field, he was
able to make out the cabin sitting just ahead in a small clearing. Using a large pine branch, he continued to sweep the
snow behind him until he got about fifty yards from the front
door. His cleanup effort had been a process that included

leaving footprints going off in misleading directions, which was repeated from the trailhead all the way back up the mountain. He figured after five days on the road, a few more hours to ensure their safety was worth the effort.

The cabin was dark. There was no sign of smoke coming from the chimney, and the door was bolted closed. He knocked a few times just in case Paige might have been asleep. He peered through some of the windows and wondered if he had simply arrived before her or if perhaps something had happened to her along the way. As far as he could tell, and unless she arrived before the most recent snowfall, there were no other footprints around besides his and what looked to be those of a bear. He studied the large paw prints and forced himself to keep from laughing, but as hard as he tried, he still lost his composure. Once the thought of the bear chasing Paige entered his head, he couldn't shake the image of her dressed as Goldilocks.

"Poor Paige, she'd be dinner for sure...unless there was a salmon around. Bears love salmon. But then again, if she was Jewish and her name was Golda Lox—" He laughed even harder. *"Oh god, please forgive me. I can't bear the thought of her on a bagel...Ray, you moron, stop it."*

When he had checked in with her thirty-six hours prior, just before his cell battery died, Paige was in Saint Louis, hoping to spend the night with an old friend. Ray now hoped she did hook up with her friend and she was taking advantage of having a hot shower, warm food, and a comfortable place to sleep. Again he scratched at his beard and vowed to shave it off as soon as he got inside—*if* he got inside. He walked back and forth, more for warmth than anything else, while debating breaking a windowpane or attempting to kick in the front door.

"Who am I kidding? Her brother couldn't even kick that thing open, and Paige would kill me if I damaged anything. I'm tired...cold...hungry. Don't think about that, it'll just make it worse. But I am hungry. Should've grabbed something to eat at the general store. The guy had some really nice-looking sausage buns and hash brown...potatoes." His mind began to wander:

*"Do me a favor. While I'm braising this venison, go down
into the root cellar and grab a bunch of potatoes."*
"Root cellar...really?"
*"Yeah, of course. Great place to store a lot of stuff. Spuds,
beets, guns, ammo."*
"You're kidding, right?"
*"No, not at all. And it makes a great emergency exit.
There's a door that opens up—"*

"At the back of the cabin, of course!"
He raced around to the back—stopping dead in his tracks
as he looked at the mounds of snow all along the length of
the cabin. Ray tried to picture the location of the cellar rela-
tive to the entry point inside the kitchen, then began stomp-
ing and listening for a change in sound from the dull thud
of solid ground to the echo of empty space underneath a plywood door. The minute that sound changed, he dropped to
his knees and began digging, shoveling with his hands until
he felt the hard surface. He brushed away some more of the
snow until he found the U-shaped handle and pulled. Nothing
moved. He pulled harder and still no movement. *"Too much
snow on the door...too heavy!"*
He dug and shoveled some more, his hands becoming red
and numb from the cold—cursing now about the fleece gloves
he'd accidentally left at a truck stop in Nebraska. He blamed the
heavy fat-laden Midwestern meal of shoe-leather steak and french
fries that tasted more like strips of sponges soaked in grease. He'd
been thankful he only ate half, stopping because of the nausea
that had started to build in intensity. He had laid his head down
on the table waiting for his stomach to settle, and the next thing
he knew a trucker was shaking him awake by his shoulder.
"The guy over there says you're lookin' for a ride to Colorado."
"What? Yes, yes, Colorado. You going there?"
*"Yeah, and right now. So if you want the ride then you
better get a move on it...and leave your food. I don't need that
pile of shit smelling up my truck."*
"Not taking the food. That's for sure. Thanks."

"I left it, all right! I left my fucking gloves, too."

After exposing another third of the plywood, he grasped the handle again and pulled as hard as he could. This time it flew open, almost hitting him in the face. He quickly gathered himself and inched his way down the eight steps into the dark. He slid his hands along the dirt walls as if by some miracle he was going to find a light switch. But then he remembered the one time he'd gone in to retrieve potatoes, he had used a lantern to guide his way. Without a light, he would have to feel his way to the other set of steps that led up to the kitchen, and he hoped that door wasn't locked as well.

Ray inched forward, sliding one foot at a time and moving his hands along the wood-framed storage bins filled with what felt like russets. *"These have to be turnips, definitely sugar beets... and a gun."*

He couldn't see, but he did feel the cold steel of a gun barrel press against the back of his head and heard the unmistakable ratcheting sound of a hammer being cocked.

21

The Cabin

Ray slowly wiped the fog off the bathroom mirror and methodically stared at the contours of his face. Although he had never complained to anyone, he had always been somewhat critical of his own appearance, often dismissing a compliment as nothing more than a throwaway line—much like a "how are you" that people never expect to be answered. He stared at the gray in his temples and wondered how long they had been like that. He imagined Leigh Anne running her fingers through his hair and laughing at his display of vanity while assuring him how distinguished-looking he was. He thought he looked old. Like war paint, the dark circles under his eyes seemed intimidating and advertised the level of fatigue he had been experiencing for several days. Having burned so much adrenaline just hours before, he was surprised he was still able to stand, but the anticipation of going through the McTavish files gave him energy he didn't know he could still muster.

"How much longer are you gonna be in there?" Paige called out.

"Almost done...sorry."

"I sure as hell hope you didn't use up all my water."

"I'm sorry, OK? It was my first hot shower since New York."

"I know high school girls who don't take this long."

"Get off my fucking back already." He then mumbled, "Now I know why she lives alone."

"What was that, Ray?"

"I said I can't wait to get back home," he yelled back.

He leaned in toward the mirror once more and thought his cheeks still looked a little raw, but they felt clean and smooth nonetheless. Ray squeezed a little more coconut oil onto his fingertips, carefully applying it across his face as if he were getting made up for a big date. Then he inspected the sink one more time, making sure not to leave a single whisker.

"I can't believe you use that razor to shave your legs. The blades are so dull it irritated my skin more than before."

"Ray, damn it...that was my last blade!"

"So thank me for saving you from butchering your legs... and thank you for the oil."

"Is that stuff helping?" Paige asked. She had been glued to her computer, going through one folder after another while he cleaned up.

"Absolutely. It's really taking care of this raw patch along my jaw. I guess I didn't realize how much I was scratching. I'm surprised you have it. I use this all the time back home. It's amazing how many commercial products this stuff can replace."

"Keep that to yourself. The last thing we need is to be in the cross hairs of another industry," she joked. "I left a set of my brother's clothes for you. See it?"

"Sasquatch?" He laughed. "I'll get lost in those things."

"My other brother, you jerk."

"Jerk? Who put a gun to the back of my head?"

"Who broke into my root cellar? How was I supposed to know it was you?"

"I broke in to get out of the cold. I broke in because you were hiding in—"

"Sleeping. I was sleeping, not hiding."

"Sleeping, hiding, whatever. If I had unleashed my martial arts expertise on you in that cellar, you'd still be lying with the spuds."

"OK, now you're just plain full of shit, and you should be thankful I didn't hit you over the head with the damn gun... or worse."

Ray threw on the jeans and flannel shirt—impressed they fit—and then examined what was simmering on the stove.

"Smells great, may I?"

"Help yourself."

"Doesn't smell like venison."

"So now you're an expert, huh? It's bison."

"You hunted down a bison?"

"My brother's did...at a local market. Grab a bowl, and pull up a chair. You're gonna be amazed at what's here. It's a gold mine, Ray...the mother lode."

"Let me see." He set his dinner down and pulled a chair alongside her.

"This is prime. You'll be able to use all this stuff...assuming you continue to do battle with that reporter in Hawaii...or anyone else. Check out this list here. We're both right about the revolving door between the drug companies and the regulatory agencies. The connections are deep, and the corruption is widespread. See all those names in the CDC hierarchy? I recognize every name on that list. Jackson was a VP at Sterling Biologics, Edwards was a former top exec with Visor. Oh my god, Lyons? You've got to be kidding me. She used to be head of safety testing at McTavish. What a joke. When she was there, her department had more screw-ups than any other. Ray, these guys are all stockholders in these companies. Talk about a conflict of interest. They make tons of money every time they approve another drug."

"It makes me laugh that the public thinks these agencies are all about consumer protection."

"That's because the press plays it up whenever the government removes a drug that's been causing a lot of injuries. But that, too, is a sham. Take that five-hundred-million-dollar fine assessed on Visor for its anti-inflammatory drug Co-Loxx."

"That made big headlines a few years ago. Didn't Visor make something like six billion dollars on that drug?"

"Yeah. They still walked with a five-and-a-half-billion dollar profit. Talk about a slap on the wrist. Tens of thousands of people suffered heart attacks or strokes from Co-Loxx, and thousands more died. And on top of that, the patent was about to expire so they were going to stop production of it anyway."

"I'm glad I got that other flash drive. This stuff will come in handy."

"I...I took the other flash drive from your backpack...when you were in the shower." She held up the drive for him to see, then placed it into a small manila envelope she took from a cupboard near the sink.

"Why? This is all good stuff, Paige. Didn't you just say that I'll be able to use this?"

"There's stuff on here that I can't let you see. I'm sorry, but that's just the way it's gotta be. Don't worry, though. I'll make a copy of all the documents that you'd want. Take a look at this other list. Check out Jackie Gerber, the head of Immuboost's vaccine division."

"You could've asked me for the drive, I would've given it to you. You didn't have to go through my pack."

"I'm sorry, Ray. I didn't mean to—"

"It's done, so don't worry about it. I'm just letting you know that you could have asked first." They stared at each other. "Jackie Gerber? Isn't she a former head of the CDC?"

"That's right. I remember she had recommended Lyons for a post at NIH, but it was shot down because of the poor performance reviews she had received. I wonder how she ended up at the CDC."

"Seems like Gerber owed her a favor." They both nodded.

"Anyway, Gerber was also the one who championed the approval of Immuboost's HPV vaccine. She swore up and down how safe it was before testing was ever completed."

"I remember that. It was right after the FDA approved HPV that she announced her retirement from government service."

"Only to show up six months later working for Immuboost and getting a two-million-dollar bonus for coming onboard with them. You know as well as I do that compensation package was a payoff for that vaccine getting approved. And now that the FDA's Pompeo is getting ready to retire, he's all set to approve that same shot for use on young boys."

"And no doubt he'll end up with Gerber in some capacity, right?"

"See how they play this game, Ray?"

"It's what I thought all along."

"Yes, but this is hardcore evidence that it actually happens."

"We're going to have to release this to the media."

"I'm surprised you'd even suggest that. You know they won't do a single thing about it. You know as well as I do that they'd sit on this information."

"Let's check out this folder." Ray grabbed the mouse and clicked. "It's an old internal memo from Moffett to his head researcher on the measles vaccine. Look at...can you believe this? They knew it was largely ineffective. And look...recipients of the shot actually do shed the virus for up to four weeks after being injected. Independent researchers had been saying this all along, but they get attacked and discredited in the press."

"Hellooo, I'm one of those researchers, Ray. That was why Moffett wanted me onboard in the first place...to shut me up."

"And once you were on the team, didn't you discuss this with him? With anyone? How about the lead guy on that study?"

"We discussed it. We discussed it ad nauseam. They wanted me to show them the evidence. I didn't have any."

"What about McTavish's own studies? You certainly read those, didn't you?"

"As quick as they were distributed for review, the company VP ordered all copies and internal memos returned to his office. Then Moffett ordered them rewritten to exclude large portions of the study group in order to make the results more favorable. One study was actually done over so that the control group wasn't given a shot of sterile saline but rather a solution containing the same amounts of toxic preservatives and adjuvants. This way they could report that the test group didn't experience any more adverse reactions than the control group, and they didn't have to lie about the results. Don't look so shocked. It goes on all the time." She clicked on another file. "Look at this one with polio. The makers of the killed injectable version and the company that makes the live oral version are accusing each other of having a product that actually causes polio in people, which we know they do. They also claim that the other's product caused many adverse reactions."

"Look here: SV-40. I knew it. For years they all denied it, and they knew it all along. This live virus vaccine was cultivated on brain and kidney tissue of simian monkeys."

"Which had been found to carry a virus...the SV-40. And that's the same SV-40 that's been showing up in the DNA of human brain cancers. The government knew it, too, and never said a damn word."

Ray stared at the computer monitor, but his mind flashed back to his childhood:

"Stop pulling, Raymond! Now be good and let Dr. Weiss give you this vaccine."

"No, Ma, no! I don't wanna get no shot. They hurt."

"It's not a shot, Raymond. It's new. You drink it."

"That's right, Raymond" said Dr. Weiss, who held up the vial and smiled over his reading glasses. "Your mother is absolutely right. This new polio vaccine is a sugary drink that tastes really good. So no needles, no pain. And we all know how important it is to keep you healthy."

"The government knew it all along," Ray repeated, "and instead of saying anything, they quietly changed the recommendation to go back to the killed version. Nothing was ever said to the public. Every child of the sixties and seventies who had been given the live virus vaccine is walking around with SV-40 as part of their DNA. Why? Why would they do such a thing?"

"You make me laugh, Ray. Sometimes you sound so naïve. Did you know the live virus version is still manufactured and they still use it?"

"I know...in India."

"In Africa, India, and other underdeveloped countries. There are charities who are buying that stuff by the shipload, and they've made it their mission to vaccinate the world. There are service organizations that hold big charity auctions and donate to the foundations that manage these operations."

"But if it's known to contain a cancer-causing virus, then why?"

"In my opinion? As sinister as this may sound, if they disclosed it prior to the 1986 NVICA, it would have opened them up to one hell of a class-action lawsuit. And after the Injury Compensation Act became law, they were free from all liability. So now they can continue to sell a cheap vaccine to the Third World where life is just as cheap, make tons of money, and avoid litigation."

"I've read...in the alternative media...that over twenty-five thousand children in India became paralyzed after receiving that shot. Is it true?"

"I'd heard from a reliable source that it was more like forty-five thousand. But in a country of more than a billion people, I guess those numbers are acceptable." Her sarcasm was obvious.

"Especially when it's not your child or when you can't be held accountable." Ray watched her circle the mouse pointer over a file labeled "Friends." He said, "Go ahead and click on it."

They read through several pages before Ray grabbed a legal pad and began scribbling. "So let's assume 'jgerb' is Jackie Gerber, but why is there an x next to the name and why would she be grouped with 'genred dod,' 'con5c,' 'con3d,' and 'confl'?" Paige looked at Ray.

"What if 'dod' is Department of Defense? You said it yourself that McTavish does a lot of military stuff."

"Then 'genred' is General Red somebody?"

"Yeah, but who?"

"Well, then, let's assume this has something to do with that special project you're concerned with. General Red at the DoD has to be someone dealing with military health services."

"Then since we're making assumptions, let's assume 'con' stands for Congress or, better still, stands for congressional district. 'Con5c' could be Fifth Congressional District of California or Connecticut."

"Makes sense. 'Con3d' could be the Third District of Delaware," Paige said, then began a search on the Internet and was quickly deflated. "Delaware has only one congressional district."

"But I'll bet California has more than five, and the same for Connecticut or even Colorado." He pushed his way in on the keyboard and began typing. "Bingo! I was right. All three have a fifth district." He typed some more. "The guy from Cal. Fifth is on defense appropriations. 'Con f1' has to be the Florida First."

"So what's 'D3'? There's only one state that begins with—"

"It's gotta be a city. A large city that makes up a congressional district or at least a large portion of one. Give me some cities."

"Denver?"

"Look it up."

"No, it's not Denver. Dallas! I'll bet its Dallas." Paige typed away and found that the northeast portion of Dallas, Texas, was part of the Third Congressional District. And the representative was also a member of the Defense Appropriations Committee.

They took turns at the computer reading page after page throughout the night. They found multiple lists of campaign contributions, donations made to the favorite charities of key congressional leaders. There was the McTavish "top twenty" list of the Washington power elite who got invited to the pharmaceutical company's private Caribbean Island, and a blacklist of congressional representatives and senators they would be actively working to defeat in the next election. There was even a "gift list" for media executives and news anchors across the country. But there was nothing to be found regarding a plan to manufacture and disseminate an experimental virus.

By four o'clock, Paige was ready to go to sleep. By all appearances she had given up and wished Ray would accept that his theory was simply that, a theory.

"Is there any more coffee?" He yawned and leaned back in his chair.

"I would have to make some, but why? It's not here. What you're looking for...it isn't here. Shut off the computer and come on...the sun will be up soon. I'm gonna get some sleep. You should, too."

"Well, maybe you just didn't download it," he said, not wanting to accept defeat.

"Or maybe it never existed? Maybe there was no plan to sell a vaccine for a hybrid virus."

"Then why would your colleague have told you there was?" He continued to press. "When you were working at McTavish, you said you had a colleague who'd been working on a secret project to create a new virus."

"Then wouldn't the information have been there? Maybe I was lied to." She was dismissive and walked away.

"Then what caused my daughter's nervous system to short-circuit and burn up like an overloaded electrical panel?"

"I don't know, Ray. I don't know. Whaddya want from me?"

"But, Paige, you said they had made an attempt. I remember you said that."

"I said that I had heard they made an attempt. I didn't say they had actually gone through with it."

"But I was standing right out there on your deck when you said it. I heard you."

"I know what I said, and you heard what you wanted to hear."

"What I wanted to hear? I can't believe I'm hearing this now."

"Look, I'm sorry, OK? I don't know what else to tell you."

"Then why did you call me? Why did you tell me you wanted to help me? Help me to do what?"

"I called you because your kid paid me a visit."

"Yes, that's what you said on the phone. You told me that you wanted to help because he paid you a visit and that this thing was bigger than you thought. You said he came to give you a warning. What, Paige? What was the warning?"

22

The unmarked corporate-style jet carrying General Griffin Kelley and Jimmy Silver touched down at a private airstrip on the outskirts of Colorado Springs at 6:00 a.m. and taxied to the far end of the runway, where it was soon joined by a similarly painted helicopter carrying four NSA assault commandos.

"Before we join the others, I want to go over this one more time, Lieutenant Silver."

"Before I met Dr. Motz at the Ram pub I had placed a transponder on her brother's pickup. That gave me a general idea of where the cabin was. Then a couple days ago, she called me when she lost contact with my father. That's how we knew she was back."

"And you've been able to confirm the location of the cabin?"

"Affirmative. When she called me, we were able to triangulate the cell phone signal to get the exact position and the coordinates of where she was calling from. That structure is right here." Jimmy pointed to the red circle on his map. "She confirmed they had breached McTavish security, retrieved information from their computer system, and then split up to make their way back here to Colorado."

"And you're sure they had nothing to do with the chemical spill?"

"Absolutely. She was emphatic it was an accident caused by one of the guards."

"And he was found dead in the loading dock?"

"Along with several others, that's correct. He had been drinking heavily; that was confirmed in the tox screen. It was a coincidence that it happened at the same time they were there."

"Isn't it always?"

"Sir?"

"Nothing...well, OK, then, let's get on that chopper and get over there."

"You promise my father won't get hurt, yes?"

"That is my standing order, but if things get out of control, then it's out of my hands. You understand that, right, son?"

"He has no idea what's about to happen, and that's what worries me. You've seen him in situations like this before."

"Then the sooner we get there, the better for all of us. Lock and load, lieutenant."

* * *

Paige knelt low by the window, scanning the tree line just beyond the open field in front of her cabin. During her time in hiding, her senses had become so fine-tuned she knew, even with less than two hours of sleep, that they weren't betraying her now. She had yet to see any movement or hear any unusual noise, but it was the absence of noise from the forest inhabitants that spoke volumes.

"Ray...Ray, get up," she called out without shifting her focus. "Ray."

He stirred a little, then was motionless.

"Ray!" Paige was louder, and again he stirred, this time trying to open his eyes.

"I thought you didn't want any more sex tonight, Leigh, but if you insist."

"Wake up, damn it, and get over here!"

With the smile now gone from his face and eyes fully opened, he realized he wasn't at home in Lanikai. He glanced over to see Paige positioned just below the window.

"What is it?"

"We've gotta get outta here."

"Somebody there?"

"I can't see anyone yet, but there are several of them."

"How do you know?"

"Trust me, OK? You dressed?"

"All except boots and stuff like that."

"Get dressed and quick. Leave your backpack and anything else that'll slow you down."

"But what about—"

"No time for questions. Just listen. You good with guns?"

"Nine mil and others."

"Go out through the root cellar. Grab a nine and some additional clips. They're in the third bin on the left, under the sack of black beans. When you go out the back entrance, you'll be facing west. Head that way into the woods for about fifty yards, then cut south for about fifty, and then head down the mountain till you get to the road. Remember the rule about the trees."

"Stay to the right of the red marker."

"To the left! Stay to the left when you're going down."

"To the left. Got it."

"As soon as you know there's no one on your tail, you call my brothers and tell them what's going on."

"And what about you?"

"I've got my hunting rifle and my crossbow. I'm gonna play a little hit and run with these guys."

"Let me help you."

Before she could answer, a tear-gas canister crashed through a window.

"Shit! They're coming from the north. They must've come up during the night and settled in behind the north tree line. Ray, get the fuck out."

"But—"

"Get! Don't worry about me. We'll meet up somehow."

Ray flew down into the root cellar and dug his hands under several food sacks until he found a weapon and extra ammunition clips. The thought of someone waiting on the other side of the plywood storm door had him hesitant enough to advance a round into the chamber of his gun. Flipping the door open as fast as he could, he stepped back into the short stairwell and waited—peering out like a jackrabbit coming out of its burrow, surveying the back of the house as best he could before sprinting into the trees. *"Wait for Paige. Make sure she gets out."* He stopped after a few yards, using the trees as cover, and waited until she made her exit. She headed south, then disappeared into the woods. He wondered if that was the last time he'd ever see her.

Ray glanced back at the cabin and noticed smoke rising up out of the cellar. It wasn't white as it had been coming out of the tear-gas canister. *"Shit! The cabin caught on fire."* He remembered the burning canister had landed on an area rug by the kitchen sink, and that made him think of Paige putting the second flash drive in an envelope and stashing it in the cupboard. He ran back inside.

* * *

Dressed head to toe in white commando gear, four men moved in for the assault. Two advanced on the front of the structure, while the other two headed for the back.

When Ray and Paige didn't emerge from the smoke-filled cabin, one of the men tried to kick in the bolted door, which only resulted in a twisted ankle. They opted to clear out the glass from the busted window, remaining focused on the main entry in case the door did fly open. After another minute, the hobbled one was hoisted through the empty window frame. Around back, the other pair had split up—one man heading off to follow Paige's footprints and the other briefly debating whether to follow the set of prints heading into the woods behind the structure or the set of prints heading back into the cellar. He went into the woods.

* * *

Ray covered his nose and mouth as he inched his way through the thick black smoke—stumbling his way to the top of the root cellar stairs. Other than the heat and the orange glow of flames, he could make out a few pieces of furniture but not much of anything else. *"Just a few steps more...gotta get that envelope."* He heard glass shattering, the whoosh of air as smoke was pulled from the kitchen as if by vacuum, and then a dull thud. His eyes burned and watered, but he was finally able to make out the cupboard by the sink—the wood cabinets turning black as the old paint curdled and bubbled from the heat. When he reached out for the metal knob, two hands shot out of the smoke and fastened onto his neck. The force of the contact pushed Ray backward at first, but his recovery was reflexively quick and surprised them both. He lunged in the direction of his attacker, whose bad ankle made him lose his grip. Once free, Ray moved back toward the kitchen cupboard, but again his advance was interrupted with a hand grabbing and squeezing his face. This time Ray dropped to his knee as the cloth he used to filter the smoke also dropped away. He felt the weight of a heavy body forcing him toward the flames. He collapsed into a ball, and the attacker's ankle gave way so that Ray now had the advantage. He rolled on top, making sure to dig a knee into the man's groin while simultaneously punching anything he could make contact with. He tore off the man's ski mask, bringing it to his face to help him breathe as the fire raged on.

Ray became dizzy from the lack of oxygen, staggering just long enough to be blocked from his objective once more. Fortunately for him, his disoriented opponent reached out for a cupboard door knob too hot to touch, and his hand clenched in a burning spasm. What was left of the cabinet door separated into several pieces as he fell back to the floor screaming,

"Sonofabitch motherfucker!" He grabbed his hand while Ray grabbed for the envelope and dove to find breathable air—disappearing into the smoke.

* * *

Paige crouched behind a thicket and adjusted the sight on her crossbow. She moved with calm mechanical precision, no different than if she had been lying in wait for a caribou. She watched the one assassin sitting to the side of the front door. When he stood in response to his partner's screams, her trigger finger tightened with enough pressure to send the Teflon-coated projectile into the throat of the assailant. His snow camouflage now stained with dark red, he grasped his neck while choking on his blood—his futile last breaths nothing more than a gurgle. "Take that, you piece of shit!" she said and reached for another arrow. The one who had entered through the window had exited with less care than he had entered. The smoke and heat too much for him to endure, he fell face first onto the shards of window glass he had created minutes before. He lay bleeding in the snow trying to soothe his scorched hand until he noticed his dead companion. As fast as he tried to crawl off to the tree line on the north side of the clearing, Paige was already reloaded and carefully following him in her cross hairs. She watched him struggle for every inch, waiting until he was within a few feet of cover. The arrow ripped through and exploded the back of his head as if it were a watermelon.

Not known for being sentimental, Paige took a moment to watch her home go up in flames, and then she was gone—off to regain the advantage of surprise.

* * *

Ray stumbled up the steps from the cellar and dropped into the snow, sucking in as much fresh air as he could. He briefly studied the singed but intact envelope and squeezed it—confident the lump in the package of papers was the extra drive—not questioning the handwritten *"JS for your eyes only—Dr. PM"* on its face. Stuffing it into the side pocket of his cargo pants, he looked deep into the trees and surveyed all that he could see. It didn't take him long to notice two men converging on his position: the one who had followed Paige's tracks and the one who had followed his. He had to act. Right or wrong, he opted for the trail that took them down the mountain. He cut around the north end of the cabin and headed east toward the trail.

As he made it across the open field and approached the trees, he heard the firecracker pops of an automatic weapon. Shards of tree trunk exploded on his right, a chunk of bark tearing through his thick flannel jacket. He didn't break stride nor look behind him to see where it came from—he already knew. Another burst of pops, and he heard the multiple thud of bullets hitting the layered snow behind him. He briefly debated making a stand with his 9 mm until he saw a tree with a red marker. *"OK, boys, let's have a little fun."* He ran to the left of the tree, and again there was an explosion of bark, but this time he escaped injury. The two men stayed on his tail. *"Go to the right of the tree, damn it. To the right."* He prayed they would take the telepathic advice. Another forty yards of weaving in and out of trees, and he came upon another red marker—again cutting to the left and praying they'd go to the right. They didn't. *"What the fuck?"* He continued downhill until he came upon a third marker. This time he dared fate and went to the right of the tree, but unlike him, his pursuers stayed to the left, remaining within striking distance. Ray didn't feel the metal trigger plate underneath the snow; however, the sound of steel jaws snapping shut to capture nothing but air had him giving thanks as he ran. That's when he caught another little break as one of his hunters got tangled and tripped over a fallen branch.

"Clayton!" he called out to his partner. "Help, I'm stuck."

His partner stopped and turned long enough for Ray to duck behind a thick evergreen—waiting and hoping he hadn't been seen, nor had the condensation of his heavy breathing betrayed his position. While readying his pistol, he pressed his lips into the bark in an attempt to diffuse his breath. Clayton ran past without a clue. *"Shoot now...no, don't. Only if he comes back. Take out the other guy first."* He clicked on the safety and cocked his arm, timing the arrival of the second guy as if he'd rehearsed the ambush a hundred times. *"Take this guy out as quietly as you can, then ambush the partner when he comes back this way."* The sound of heavy rubber soles on the hard pack drew closer, then stopped. It was eerily quiet, and then he heard the slow crunch of snow. One crunchy step, then silence. A second slow crunch, and Ray sprung back onto the path like a mountain lion on the attack. The flat surface of the gun made pinpoint contact with the surprised face of a predator turned prey. He was stunned and wobbled but didn't go down. Ray struck him again, this time breaking the man's nose. His eyes glazed over, blood poured down his face, and he dropped his weapon, but he still he didn't go down.

"You stupid fuck," Ray said. He shoved his handgun into the side pocket of his pants and grabbed the automatic weapon from the snow, quickly swinging the shoulder strap over the head of the dazed man and twisting the braided harness over the carotid arteries with so much force that within seconds the man went limp. But that wasn't good enough for Ray. He gave an extra twist and a quick snap, listening for the Velcro-like rip he'd wanted to hear.

That struggle didn't go unnoticed. When he glanced down the trail, the fourth attacker, Clayton, was on his way back— indiscriminately firing along the way. Had Ray taken the time to untangle the assault weapon from the body, he wasn't sure if he would've had enough time to take a clean shot, but he had no doubt he would have been on the receiving end of a few well-placed rounds. He took off up the mountain path, remembering he still had his 9 mm. He tried to dig it out of his pocket without sacrificing his lead. Again he wove in and out of the trees. It slowed his ascent, but the trees aided in deflecting bullets.

* * *

The chopper pilot called out to Griff Kelley as they closed in on the coordinates from Jimmy's map.

"Off to the right, General. Do you see it?" he said, pointing beyond the nose of the aircraft.

"That's the cabin?"

"I believe so, sir. Doesn't look good. Whaddya want me to do?"

"Set her down in the clearing." Kelley turned to Jimmy, then over to his four commandos. "It looks like the lieutenant was right. Be prepared for anything."

"What now?" Jimmy asked as he too watched the thick black smoke rise up out of the trees.

"Nothing's changed." Again Kelley looked at his men. "If you come up against any resistance on the ground, you know what to do. If her body isn't in or near the cabin, we look for her until we find her."

"Don't you mean *them*? Don't you mean we look for them until we find them?"

"That's what I meant, Jimmy."

* * *

Ray came up to the same fork he had encountered the day before. The path to the left led back up to the clearing and the cabin. The path to the right was the one that had led him to the steep, narrow, winding trail. He weighed his options, and it made him think of the deep crevasse. He turned to see how much of a lead he still had. The way he saw it, he had three choices: take the left fork back up to the nonexistent cabin in hopes of meeting up with Paige, take the right fork and somehow ambush the guy, or take cover where he stood and shoot it out. When he heard the beating sound of helicopter blades, the thought of a second wave of killers had him take off up the right fork—heading for the most dangerous portion of the trail. *"Not good!"* he thought as bullets peppered the snow behind him. *"This is not good at all."*

No different than the day before, the seldom-used trail had a layer of ice just underneath the snow pack. The harder Ray tried to gain ground, the more his feet slipped out from underneath him. Several times he lost his footing, fell to his knees, and backslid several feet, one time almost losing his gun. He stuffed the pistol into a pocket, freeing both hands for better control—now grabbing at rocks and branches. His arms and legs grew heavy as he tired.

Wearing studded hiking boots, the remaining hit-man had no such trouble and gained ground easily. He was close enough that Ray—finally depleted of adrenaline and struggling—heard him load a new ammo clip. When Ray lost his footing again, he didn't try to get up but rather turned onto his back to watch the hooded reaper confidently walk to within a few feet. Ray prayed for Paige to be lurking in the woods, crossbow trained on this guy's heart.

"Wait...don't shoot...not yet. Please." Ray watched as the assault rifle was raised up toward him.

"Stalling? That's a nice touch. Almost like on those TV shows. But trust me, no one is coming to rescue you."

"I know no one is coming, and I...I'm not trying to stall. I...I just wanna stand up. I just want...to stand up and do this like a man. Would you allow me that?"

Clayton nodded, and Ray stood to face him. The weapon was raised, and before Ray could say another word they both heard a click. The new magazine had ice in it, and the bullets wouldn't advance into the chamber. The executioner pulled the trigger again and still nothing. Ray took a step toward him, and the automatic was quickly discarded in exchange for an eight-inch serrated hunting knife.

"I see you still have a little fight left in you. Don't make this harder than it has to be. You wanted to die like a man? Then let's get this over with."

Ray looked over Clayton's shoulder, giving a slight nod as if someone had been there. That was enough to get the attacker to look behind him. Ray lunged into a baseball slide, striking just below his assailant's knees. One of Clayton's feet came out from under him, and the other, sticking firm because of the studded shoes, snapped at the ankle. He fell backward into a split, lost the grip on his knife, and reflexively grabbed for his injured leg. With equal panic, they both tried to recover and regain the advantage; however, the steep slope of the icy path had both men sliding downward at increasing speed. The crevasse was coming up on the left, and Ray remembered the young tree that had saved him just hours before. He looked for it and, like the time before, stuck out his right arm to act as a rudder. It wasn't working. His feet were tangled in Clayton's arms, who was heading straight for the ledge and was determined to take Ray with him. He kicked at Clayton as hard as he could. Twenty feet to the ledge, and Ray kicked harder until he broke free. The tree was coming up fast on the right, and this time he slammed his right arm into the snow, his body jerking toward the tree. He grabbed it and came to a hard stop.

Ray lay still for a moment. Except for his breathing, it was quiet. He looked down the length of his body toward the ledge, toward the crevasse. There was no Clayton to be seen. He leaned his head back into the snow and closed his eyes, wanting to laugh and scream at the same time. And then he heard the groan. He lay there and listened for it, hoping he'd heard the wind in the trees, and then it came again. He pulled his body back up against the thin tree trunk until he was in a sitting position and listened for it one more time. This time is was more of a grunt.

"Oh, please no," Ray said, looking up at the sky.

He reached down to the side pocket of his cargo pants, checking for the envelope and his gun. He inched his way over to the ledge, making sure he was a few feet above the slide marks. The last thing he wanted was to have a hand reach up to grab him.

"You win, OK? I'm done. Please help me up before I lose my grip...before I...fall."

"That tree branch looks pretty strong. Besides, do I look that stupid?"

"You got the advantage on me, man. Come on, OK? I can't hold...this much longer. Get me up."

"Who sent you, and how did you track us?"

"Pull me up, and I'll tell you."

"Fuck you, man. I'm outta here."

"No, wait...please!"

"Who sent you?"

"I have no idea."

"Bullshit!"

"I'm serious. We never know...we never know who the job is for. We just get contacted by...told to pick up instructions at a neutral site...envelope, money, instructions. That's it. Please, I'm slipping."

"How'd you know where to find us?"

"It was in the instructions."

"Fuck off, asshole! Have a nice ride down."

"OK, OK, don't go, don't go, man...your download and e-mail...it was tracked to an IP address...help me up, man, come on."

"Then what? Tell me, or I walk."

"The IP address gave us a general location, so we staked out area airports. We saw the girl fly in...from Saint Louis, so we followed her back to Fort Collins. I'm slipping, damn it!"

"Then I suggest you let go of that pistol and hold onto the branch with both hands. And be careful, because I've got this 9 mil pointed right at your ugly face."

"Pistol? What pis—"

"I see it behind your back, you fuck."

Clayton let the gun fall away and reached up for the branch.

"Happy? Now help me up."

"So you traced the IP address. The only way you were going to get that address was from McTavish."

"I don't know what you're talking about. I told you, damn it, we just get instructions."

"Your instructions wouldn't tell you about an IP address. Who gave the order? Who gave the order to take us out?"

"Shit, man! What the fuck is wrong with you. I told you—"

"I'm gonna come over there and stomp on your damn ass fingers. Who gave the fucking order?"

"I...don't...fucking...know!" he screamed. "Now, please... I can't hold on anymore!"

As he inched his way over to the ledge, Ray saw the ghost-white fingers begin slipping from the tree branch and the fear in Clayton's face. A hand shot up in desperation for Ray to take, but he just stared at it. Clayton looked up at his would-be rescuer, pleading with his eyes, but Ray was having none of it. He pushed himself back away from the edge and stood. Without saying another word, he baby-stepped over the ice, making his way back down the trail.

* * *

Paige watched the helicopter touch down from the safety of the tree line. Four men in tactical assault gear exited the craft and, with weapons at the ready, took up positions around the perimeter of the aircraft. She took aim, and then Griff Kelley emerged and scanned the woods for movement. Just one more pound of pressure on the trigger, and the federal agent closest to her position would have been dead. She flipped on the safety and raised her crossbow into the air.

"She's here," he yelled over the rotor noise so that Jimmy could hear him and then waved her in.

* * *

Ray got back to the fork and realized the chopper had set down. Although muffled by the trees, the thumping noise of the rotor blades were steady—not changing in volume or pitch as if they were gaining or losing altitude, nor getting closer or farther away. *"The best thing to do is to head down the mountain, and the right thing is to go help Paige...assuming she's still alive."* He continued straight down the trail to retrieve the automatic weapon and the white camouflage jacket from the man he had killed earlier. He wanted the firepower, but more importantly, he wanted to get out of the red flannel jacket. As much as he wanted to address the wound in his right arm, he knew the shard of bark had only left a superficial cut, with the thick flannel absorbing most of the impact.

He checked his new weapon, grabbed an extra ammo magazine off the dead body, and then headed up the left fork toward the eastern edge of the clearing. Once there, he spied the four men keeping vigil around the perimeter of the chopper. From his vantage point, they looked no different than the four who had just attacked them. Then he saw Paige come out of the woods on the opposite side of the clearing—crossbow held in the air, moving without hesitancy for the helicopter. He immediately checked his weapon and was ready to fire on the two commandos closest to him, but their lack of response and her casual approach surprised him. He didn't know what to make of it. *"Is she surrendering, or is she—"* That's when he saw Griff Kelley walk out to meet her. Words ranging from betrayal to patsy raced through his head. And then he saw his son.

His legs felt weak, almost rubbery, and he allowed his knees to buckle. He reached into the side pocket of his pants and pulled the envelope. *"JS for your eyes only—Dr. PM."* Confused, he desperately tried to gather his thoughts, to analyze and to decide on a course of action. He let the voices echo in his head, searching and trying to pick up clues:

"Is there any more coffee?" He yawned and leaned back in his chair.

"I would have to make some, but why? It's not here. What you're looking for, it isn't here. Shut off the computer and come on...the sun will be up soon. I'm gonna get some sleep. You should, too."

"Well, maybe you just didn't download it," he said, not wanting to accept defeat.

"Or maybe it never existed? Maybe there was no plan to sell a vaccine for a hybrid virus."

"Then why would your colleague have told you there was?" He continued to press. "When you were working at McTavish, you said you had a colleague who'd been working on a secret project to create a new virus."

"Then wouldn't the information have been there? Maybe I was lied to." She was dismissive and walked away.

"Then what caused my daughter's nervous system to short-circuit and burn up like an overloaded electrical panel?"

"I don't know, Ray. I don't know. Whaddya want from me?"

"But, Paige, you said they had made an attempt. I remember you said that."

"I said that I'd heard they made an attempt. I didn't say they had actually gone through with it."

"But I was standing right out there on your deck when you said it. I heard you."

"I know what I said, and you heard what you wanted to hear."

"What I wanted to hear? I can't believe I'm hearing this."

"Look, I'm sorry, OK? I don't know what else to tell you."

"Then why did you call me? Why did you tell me you wanted to help me? Help me to do what?"

"I called you because your kid paid me a visit."

"Yes, that's what you said on the phone. You told me that you wanted to help because he paid you a visit and that this thing was bigger than you thought. You said he came to give you a warning. What, Paige? What was the warning?"

"Like me, you're on a hit list, Ray."

"What?"

"It wasn't long after I began working at McTavish that I had heard rumors of hybrid viruses and all that stuff. There was a researcher there who liked me...we dated a few times. One night after dinner, we went back to my apartment. He had a little too much wine, and he started talking about plans for such a project, but there was nothing in the works. He started telling me other things that were too shocking to believe. That's when I contacted a friend who works for the government. The next thing I know, I'm working for them."

"Who, what agency?"

"Does it matter? Listen to me: my role was to get whatever information I could...rumored or real, it didn't matter to

*them. They wanted everything and anything. I was able to get
some data to them, but then Moffett and others were growing
suspicious. I couldn't get anything else out. And then people
started having accidents, disappearing, stuff like that. The
guy I was seeing was found two hundred miles away from his
home...in a drainage ditch with a gunshot wound to his chest.
That's when I knew I had to get out."*

* * *

"How many were there, Paige?"

"Four."

"What convinced you it wasn't me?"

"If it had been your guys, Ray and I would be just as charred
as that pile of logs behind us."

"We tried to get here first, to stop them, of course, but we
didn't know they were coming so soon."

"Nothing ever changes, Griff," she said to his annoyance.
"Moffett's boys, no doubt."

"Yeah. But you had to know it would be coming from him,
and had you kept in contact with me, I could've stopped this a
long time ago."

"So you say now. Regardless, I'm without a home."

"You're lucky you still have your life. Where's Silver?"

"Out there." She made a sweeping gesture. "He had two
on him, but from what I was able to see he took one out, and
then I had to break off my pursuit when I heard the chopper.
If I had known it was you guys, I would have stayed with him."

"There will be others, you know. If Moffett knows his guys
failed, he'll send more. That's why I want you to come in. You'll
be safe with us."

"No. I told you a few years ago that I'm done with you guys."

"Paige, the information you were supposed to get for us...
when you worked at McTavish...it was important. It's still a matter of national security and—"

"Don't worry, I recovered it." She handed a flash drive to
Kelley. "When Silver first contacted me, the thought of going

back there was out of the question. But when his kid found me," she looked over at Jimmy, "it made me realize that either you or Moffett's men wouldn't be too far behind. That's when and why I decided to take Ray back there with me. It was important for us to strike first. I not only wanted to get this stuff as an insurance policy for me, I wanted him to get the information he was looking for."

"And now you're willing to hand over your insurance policy?"

"I made enough copies. They're nice and safe as long as I am."

"Paige...we're not the ones you have to be afraid of. We're not gonna do anything to you."

"You got what you came for, yes?"

"It is what we paid you for in the first place."

"And I'll take that bonus now, thank you very much."

"I'll see that you get it. In the meantime, this will be interesting to say the least." He held up the drive.

"There's a list, Griff...a list of about a hundred or more of the world's best microbiologists, infectious disease experts, and others who had worked for a number of...they're being killed off...he's having them killed, Griff. They were working on some serious biological shit that's gonna change the face of this planet if it's ever put into play. But the guys working for Moffett, the guys working on the hybrid...the bastard had them killed because they either knew too much or they were going to sound the alarm. Some were shot during home invasions, street muggings, carjackings. Some had suspicious accidents, like hunting accidents or car crashes. Some just simply disappeared without a trace. Hell, one gal from McTavish drowned while scuba diving in the Caymans. She couldn't even swim, Griff. She was deathly afraid of water!"

"So he went through with it?"

"No, he never went through with the hybrid. Not yet anyway. It's still too volatile, and they haven't figured out a way to neutralize it. Whatever they've developed up to this point is stored in their cryogenics lab, which is—"

"Smack in the middle of Manhattan. We'll get a team on that, but I still need to figure out why we've got about two hundred military personnel who've experienced a complete neurological system collapse. I've got reports going back three years of guys fully functional one minute then completely brain dead the next. If it's not Moffett—"

"It is Moffett, and it is vaccine related"

"Whaddya mean?"

"When you originally contacted me, you asked me to keep my ears open about a joint project between McTavish and the CIA."

"He doubled the doses...the adjuvants, the preservatives, everything?"

"Exactly. It's all in there. Everything you need to know."

"Are you telling me he actually did this? He actually went ahead with a human trial after what happened with the animals?"

"From what I read, it looks like he did. You'll also find the name of a doctor, a general at the Pentagon, who was overseeing drug procurement. He was Moffett's connection to get this done."

"And I take it he's since retired?"

"That information isn't on the drive. It was, but it was redacted. Nonetheless, you've got his name, so I'm sure you'll figure out where he is."

"And Silver has a copy?"

"Yes. Well, at least I think he does. Hopefully, he retrieved it before the cabin went up in flames. I made sure he'd have everything he needed. The flash drive as well as the stuff in the envelope."

"Everything, even this information?"

"Yes. I hid all that data in my personal file, so if he got the envelope, then I'm sure he'll find the info once he's had a chance to look. It's in a folder marked 'quarantined computer viruses.'"

"And what makes you sure he'll go through that one?"

"He's a man, isn't he? I'm sure he'll be going through every document that's on the drive, and then—"

"Find him, and call him off, Paige. I'll take care of what needs to be taken care of...do you understand?"

"No, I don't. Why does the head of the NSA want to deal with a CIA or military issue?"

"I might be NSA, but I'm also a retired brigadier general and—"

"Yeah, I get it."

"OK, then. So now please find him, and then it's time for you to come back in...do you understand? For your own good, you need to come back in."

She quickly scanned a face void of emotion, but it was his energy that caused her uneasiness.

"Let me think about that...coming in, that is. I'll give it some thought, then let you know."

"Just don't wait too long. It's not safe."

"No kidding."

"I'm serious, Paige."

"I know, I know."

"Then why the hesitancy?"

"I said I know, OK?" She tensed, and Griff nodded. She continued, "And do me favor and hold off on doing anything about Moffett. What little I know of Ray Silver, I think he'll be on his way back to White Plains, and isn't that why you wanted him to have that envelope in the first place?"

Griff didn't answer.

"Then let him do this, Griff. He needs this...he's justified, and you know it."

"And I suppose you'll be helping him?"

"Have a safe trip back to Washington...and don't forget to send a crew for these bodies."

Griff signaled his men, and as they boarded the helicopter, he watched Paige disappear into the forest.

23

Castlewood, New York
One Week Later

Perched alone atop a hillside in this small northeast hamlet known for its rich Revolution-era history and million-dollar mansions, the views from Patrick Moffett's estate were the envy of his guests and neighbors alike. On a clear day one could see as far west as the Hudson River, and to the east was Long Island Sound. Unlike the traditional colonial design of the village shops and area homes, Moffett's compound had more of a bucolic Southern feel to it in more ways than one. During the humid summer months, when the sprawling acreage was busy with an assortment of overworked groundskeepers, arborists, electricians, and pool boys, the large old plantation-style architecture evoked *Gone with the Wind* imagery.

The seasonal house staff was kept busy from sunrise to sunset preparing for and catering to visiting politicians, foreign dignitaries, captains of industry, and university presidents. While detesting the need to entertain his strategic partners, Moffett did enjoy the power and attention he received from those willing to do his bidding for the relatively few pieces of silver he deposited in their pockets. He had once bragged: *"Of all my investments, this mundane activity easily yields the greatest return...not to mention the raging woody I get watching these guys fight over who gets to kiss my ass the most. But I do love the politicians. Now right there you've got a bunch of people who produce nothing and contribute nothing of any value to humankind unless people like me lead them by the nose."*

For all the work his staff did—from chauffeuring his guests to and from the nearby airport or country clubs to providing nonstop hors d'oeuvres and alcohol service while they spent weekend afternoons playing bocce ball and croquet—Moffett was richly rewarded with government contracts, tax breaks, fast-tracked FDA approvals, favorable research studies, and continuous positive media coverage, which in and of itself was equal to every penny spent on marketing. And marketing was something his industry had been extremely good at: seventy-five million dollars a day good at.

It was truly a scene out of the old South as Moffett's guests strolled the lawns and sipped mint juleps at his annual Kentucky Derby party. But while many of his day laborers made the one-hour trip north from the South Bronx stuffed into aging minivans, some of the undocumented domestic help, Moffett's favorites, got to live on site—using the turn-of-the-century guest cottages on the far end of the property as their refuge from the occasional independent-minded immigration official. And in exchange for a modest deduction from their under-the-table wages, family members were also allowed to stay. Moffett's refuge was the young upstairs maid who'd earned the scorn of her coworkers, aware of her above-and-beyond requirements for the privilege of being allowed to live in the private quarters situated by a back staircase leading to the kitchen—convenient for Moffett's midnight hunger pangs on evenings when his wife was staying at their beach house in the Hamptons.

Guests and historians visiting the estate had marveled at the rolling green fairways, rainbow-colored gardens, and imported Spanish moss—freely making comparisons to the grounds at Jefferson's Monticello. Moffett, himself an avid practitioner of horticulture, had often boasted during charitable functions how the third president would have been envious of his expertise in cultivating many varieties of medicinal plants in his climate-controlled greenhouses—his personal use of herbal medicine and essential oils among some of the many contradictions of his life.

* * *

If it had been summer, it would have been extremely difficult for an intruder to access the oft-occupied grounds. But in the dead of winter, there were no weekend fundraising parties for the childhood diabetes, arthritis, cancer, or autism foundations to which McTavish Pharmaceuticals had been a regular contributor. And while local and national media were always quick to highlight the company's generous philanthropy, the irony wasn't lost on anyone searching the database of injury awards given out by the Federal Vaccine Court—especially the hypocrisy of the McTavish "Back-to-School Wellness" campaign, which pledged $1 to autism research for every child producing an up-to-date vaccination record.

Ray thought about that, as well as how to gain access to the estate, while sitting in his rental car across from the main gate of the Moffett compound. Without the constant presence of workers performing post-party cleanups or other warm weather maintenance, Ray's main concern now was the number and placement of private security guards. During the twenty-four hours he had spent surveilling the gated entry, he didn't see one camera, one guard, not even one patrolling Doberman.

Not only did the lack of security surprise him, but he was further amazed when several hours earlier Moffett had driven himself off the property. When he was certain no other cars were coming down the long driveway to shadow the excursion, Ray decided to follow. He briefly thought about approaching Moffett when he stopped at the pastry shop on Main Street or at the service station located at the edge of town. But he knew that wouldn't have accomplished anything other than people bearing witness to any kind of exchange between them. He opted to watch from a safe distance as Moffett berated a young attendant at the gas pumps for allowing a few drops from the nozzle to drip onto the side of his Range Rover. He felt sorry for the high-school-aged girl who was on the receiving end of a tirade the townspeople had seen once too often. *"Maybe everyone at the gas station would applaud and feign amnesia if I drove up there right now and took a tire iron to that bastard's head."* He was amused that a man of such small stature could be such a big a prick. And at slightly over five feet four inches tall, Ray saw firsthand that Paige's description of him was spot-on. *"He definitely has a Napoleon complex."*

Following Moffett down Route 22 toward the McTavish laboratory in White Plains, he wished he still had Paige's 9 mm automatic—one of the consequences of having grabbed a flight out of Denver meant leaving the weapon with the Motz brothers in Fort Collins. He fantasized pulling up alongside the SUV and popping a few rounds into the vehicle. He would have loved to have had the opportunity. Then he thought about swerving into it and forcing the car into a ditch. But the winding icy road offered little opportunities to pull this off. Since the southbound roadway bordered the shoreline of the Kensico Reservoir, the heavily reinforced guardrail kept cars from crashing through. On the northbound side, the flow of traffic was unpredictable. As bad as he wanted to see Moffett's demise, Ray didn't want to risk hurting innocent people. The other deterrent from acting rashly was his need to have a face-to-face confrontation. He not only wanted to physically hurt this guy, but he wanted to mentally and emotionally terrorize the living daylights out of him. Ray wanted to see the fear of death in Moffett's eyes when the realization hit home that he was not going to be able to bully, bribe, or barter his way to getting what he wanted—in this case, his life.

While Moffett was inside the McTavish facility, Ray had patiently sat across from the Haarlem Avenue entrance and studied the grounds. He looked up at the fence where he had gashed his knee. He could see the red brick face that had scratched the back his head in his attempt to press himself into the shadows. He watched and heard the steel service door open up and remembered that moment when Ambrose's red swollen nose came peering through. It was the first time he had gotten a chance to see the place in broad daylight, and once again he was surprised: this time at how old, run-down, and dirty the buildings were, a far cry from their new world headquarters in midtown Manhattan. Heating and air conditioning units and chemical storage tanks were heavily rusted, as was the perimeter fence. In addition to the visible decay and filth, Ray also thought about the haphazard way poisonous and volatile chemicals were stored at a facility where research involving health and disease was actively conducted. *"I'd bet my last dime you wouldn't see so much as a layer of dust on the crown molding in Moffett's house...his house, of course! I should drive back up to the house while he's here. With no security patrolling the grounds, I can get up to the house and...wait, the house could still be alarmed. And if it is, I wonder how much time I'd have before the local police got there?"* After a brief internal debate, he decided to take a ride back up to the estate.

24

U pon his arrival back in Castlewood, Ray realized that except for the town's small business district, there were no good places to leave his car. It was a rental after all, and while it wasn't yellow this time, it was still a basic American sedan. Had it been an older model covered in dents, duct tape, and bumper stickers, locals would have assumed it belonged to hired help come to shovel the snow from a driveway. If it had been an older sedan sans the economy bodywork and added decorations, they would have assumed it was the INS looking for that hired help. But the rental was new, undamaged, artwork-free, and recently washed. That alone would make it stick out like a sore thumb in this exclusive neighborhood of imported luxury cars and SUVs.

The only other domestic cars ever seen on the seldom traveled outlying lanes belonged to the local police who would venture the few miles from the center of town to investigate one of the many false burglar alarms usually triggered by an improper code setting, heavy winds, or even the occasional forgetful homeowner who stepped out to retrieve the morning paper before deactivating the system. Even then it usually took the patrolman about twenty minutes to show up, which, contrary to accusations, was an unofficial planned response among the rank and file to allow ample time for any real intruder to get away and minimize the chance of a dangerous encounter... hence the frequent comparisons to Keystone Cops or Barney Fife from Mayberry. On the rare occasion they did come face to face with an "armed" burglar—four by the latest account—it never ended up in the intruder's favor. The shootings were consistently found to be justified.

As Ray reviewed the nuances of town law enforcement recorded in the notes he'd found in the manila envelope, he tried to piece together a plan of action that would allow him to accomplish his goal. No matter how many different scenarios he managed to invent, not one yielded a positive outcome for him. He would have loved to have been able to get into the mansion with enough time to search for any incriminating evidence before ambushing Moffett. Triggering an internal alarm system, however, would give him twenty minutes at best before encountering a trigger-happy police officer. *"I don't think I'd be getting a jaywalking ticket for this one. If only there was some way I knew when Moffett was close enough to the estate. That would give me the time I needed."* And with that thought, the sound of rolling tires crunching through the snow made him look into his rearview mirror. It was Moffett's SUV. Before slumping lower in his seat, Ray noticed that Moffett had a passenger. *"Not quite perfect, but it'll have to do. When he heads up the driveway, I'll sneak in behind them before the main gate shuts. No alarm and all the time in the world...but there are two of them now."*

The crunching of snow stopped by the side of Ray's car. As low as he slumped, he was still visible. *"Damn it! The car is out of place. He's gonna check it out or call in the plate number. Shit!"* He looked over at the SUV but couldn't see through its tinted windows. *"I broke down. That's what I'll say. If they ask any questions, I'll just say I broke down and I'm waiting for the tow truck."* And then he heard his name.

"Ray! Roll down your window."

He looked over, and his ears didn't deceive him. It was Paige sitting in the passenger seat holding a gun at Patrick Moffett. Without waiting for him to say a word, she directed him to bring his car up the driveway behind them. She turned to Moffett, jabbed the barrel of the gun into his rib cage, and ordered him to proceed.

* * *

Moffett's head bobbed a little as the sedation began to wear off. The chiropractor in Ray took over as he watched the head repeatedly creep downward, then abruptly and unconsciously rebound back. He pictured the relaxing neck muscles and ligaments easily stretching forward, then reflexively snapping the head upright, causing multiple microtears in the soft tissue. He'd seen thousands of similar whiplash-type injuries over the years, from those patients who had fought dozing off on long plane trips to those surprised they were injured in rear-end auto collisions so minor there hadn't been so much as a scratch on the car. He watched Moffett's head slowly decline and then snap back up, and knew by the time he woke that his head would surely be pounding as if he'd been hit with a club, the beesting-like pain in his arm a residual from the shot Paige had given him as he tried scaring both of them with threats that his maid Rosie or one of the other help would surely call the police once they heard the struggle coming from his library. In the two hours he lay half-slumped in his chair, at times mumbling incoherently, no one had come by to investigate. Rosie had been the only other person in the main house, and Paige had been quick to neutralize her.

Drugged and drooling all over himself, Moffett didn't look anything like the tyrant he was known to be.

"If you could only see yourself right now," Ray said with building frustration. "Helpless and weak, you servile scum. Wake up, you little fuck. I've got some business to settle with you."

Exhaustion was catching up to him, and at this point, sitting and staring at Long Island Sound while Paige searched the library in Moffett's private study was the last thing he wanted to be doing. Unlike Moffett, he didn't need a drug to do battle with his eyelids. In his struggle to stay awake, their closing was his white flag of surrender.

"Hey! Wake up over there!" Paige yelled. "I need you to keep an eye out to see if anyone is coming."

"I'm awake, I'm awake!" Ray jumped. "I'm just resting my eyes."

"Uh-huh. When was the last time you slept?"

"I don't remember. I think I got a few hours on the plane."

"You wanna check the kitchen for coffee?"

"No."

"Then grab some of this dark chocolate. It's pretty good."

"If you got that from his desk, then I'm not touching it."

"Why? You think he planted it? That's crazy. He would've known we were coming."

"He knew we breached his database."

"So you think the chocolate was tampered with? Seriously, you think he tampered with it?"

Ray nodded and laughed when Paige spit it out.

"Well, just don't fall back to sleep."

"I wasn't sleeping."

"You were out for fifteen minutes."

"I'm wide awake now, so go...go finish what you were doing. I'll keep an eye on the driveway and on our pint-size dictator over here. And by the way, I'd like more answers about what went on up at the cabin. You still haven't explained this whole thing between you, Griff Kelley, and my kid."

Moffett stirred from the noise. He was slowly coming to, and as he fought to clear the fog, he again mumbled his warning about Rosie. The ongoing discussion between Ray and Paige echoed loudly through the cloud of his semiconsciousness.

"If you two don't mind, I've got a splitting headache."

"Does it hurt real bad?" Paige asked with insincerity.

"You know it does."

"Too bad. Now be quiet and stop interrupting us."

"What the hell did you give me?" he persisted, with saliva clinging to his chin.

"I have no clue. I found it in the animal lab, and it was marked experimental," she lied, then turned her attention back to Ray. "I don't know how many times I have to tell you: I had to do it this way."

"Because it was Griff Kelley's idea?"

"No. Once I learned about what this jackass was up to," she pointed to Moffett, "I made sure you knew where I stashed the envelope. I wanted you to have it, but I didn't want you to see that stuff in the condition you were in. I didn't think it would be good if you went off half-cocked and exhausted."

"You mean like I am now?"

"You better not be blaming me for that attack...and it was Kelley who didn't want you in on this part of the whole thing."

Ray thought about his encounter with Clayton:

"Who sent you?"

"I have no idea."

"Bullshit!"

"I'm serious. We never know who the job is for. We just get contacted by...told to pick up instructions at a neutral site... envelope, money, instructions. That's it. Please, I'm slipping."

"How'd you know where to find us?"

"It was in the instructions."

"Fuck off, asshole! Have a nice ride down."

"OK, OK, don't go, don't go, man...your download and e-mail...it was tracked to an IP address...help me up, man, come on."

"Then what? Tell me, or I walk."

"The IP address gave us a general location, so we staked out area airports. We saw the girl fly in from Saint Louis and followed her back to Fort Collins. I'm slipping, damn it."

He decided not to mention it.

"But he didn't mind that I was in on it when Moffett sent his killers after us. He was OK with that, right?"

"Wrong again. Once he and Jimmy got intel that a team was hired to take us out, they made every effort to stop it."

"Their timing sucked."

"They did the best they could."

"Fine. Just tell me, how long have you been working for them?"

"Yes, Dr. Motz, tell us both how long you've been working for the NSA." A slightly less woozy Moffett joined in. "And if it's not too much trouble, can you untie me from this chair?"

Paige ignored Moffett, continuing to look at Ray.

"Well, Dr. Motz, your friend and I are waiting. I knew you were gathering information and stealing company secrets while you were working for me. I made the mistake of thinking you were working for one of those militant vegan organizations. I never would've guessed you were working for the government. Which, if you think about it, is kind of funny, because in a way I've got most of everyone in the government working for me...I mean, for all the drug companies, that is."

"Yes, we know." Ray joined in. "You, Immuboost, Visor, Thompson and Thompson, and the others have paid off enough senators and congressional representatives so that your people get hired to important positions within the CDC, the FDA...heck, you've even got people in the Department of Agriculture."

"Are you two really going to spend your time here lecturing me? I told you my maid—"

"Yes, your little plaything, Rosie." Paige scowled. "You know, it took the same amount of the sedation I gave to you to put her under. She's a tough little Latina. I just hope I didn't give her too much. It'd be a shame if she had to pay a price for your sins."

"Are you two crazy? I've got people coming here for a dinner party tonight. When I don't open the gates to let them in, they'll be calling the police."

Feeling a little more awake, Moffett struggled in vain to free his hands.

"You tied him better than you tied me, Paige."

"No, Ray, I tie everyone the same. You're just stronger than this little pussy. And my guess, Moffett, is since there's nothing cooking in the kitchen, no place settings put out in the dining room, and no staff on duty shining all the serving platters—except for little Rosie, who wasn't quite dressed for kitchen work—we'll be long gone before anyone shows up. As a matter of fact, if anyone is going to come to the house, it'll be your wife." Paige laughed. "After all, I did send a bouquet of flowers out to your beach house on the island. The card was quite romantic, too."

Moffett struggled harder as Paige went on.

"If I remember correctly, you told her that with the icy winds blowing off the ocean, it would be nice, very nice, if she came home to get warm. And if she does take the bait, she'll find your purrsonal maid tied up in your bed. She's quite a hot little number in those thigh-highs and heels."

"I'm thinking we ought to put him right beside her."

"That's pretty kinky, Ray, but I like your thinking."

"You two are fucking nuts. Motz, I understand your motivation, but what's with this guy, huh? What's your beef with me?"

"The list is long, Moffett. Shall I go through it for you? How about one in eighty-eight children with autism? How about SIDS and leukemia and other cancers? How about more childhood diabetes and a host of autoimmune diseases than we've ever seen before, and food allergies, and how about—"

"Are you fucking kidding me, Motz? You brought one of those cult-following antivax nuts with you?"

One look at the expression on Ray's face, and Paige walked away—deciding to turn her attention to what seemed like endless volumes of leather-bound books carefully alphabetized and neatly lined up on the handcrafted redwood shelving throughout the library.

"You know, it's funny," she said, scanning the books, "but I don't see a Bible here in this amazing collection of yours. At least it's not with the *B*s. Perhaps you keep it under science fiction like some of those research studies you fabricated. I know, you keep a copy by the side of your bed so you and Rosie can do a little Bible study before your evening prayers. Tell me something, Moffett, do you pray for forgiveness, or a good hard erection? No, wait, don't tell me, let me guess...you use one of your erectile dysfunction wonder drugs. Oh better still, you don't take any of the products you make, do you? You've got that extensive organic herb garden. Check this out, Ray, the same medicinal herbs and essential oil extracts the FDA confiscates and destroys because they work so well...this son of a bitch cultivates for his private use."

"I'll take hypocrisy for a thousand, Alex." Ray walked toward Moffett and shook his head. "I don't think you'd find a Bible in this house, Paige. Not with a guy who already thinks he's God. Isn't that right, Moffett? You think you're God, don't you? You get off on it. With every untested drug and vaccine that you peddle, for every mandated shot that's sold without any viable research behind it, you're playing God with every one of those people who believe that you really care about their well-being."

"I knew it! You are one of those conspiracy, antiscience, religious whack jobs. The science has long been settled and—" Before Moffett could finish his sentence, Ray's fist landed on the side of his head with a force so hard it almost knocked him over.

"Go ahead and say it again, you coldhearted fuck." Ray raised his arm for another strike. "Go ahead and tell me the science is settled. Go ahead, I dare you. I don't know who the hell you think you're talking to, but don't you dare insult me or Dr. Motz by telling us the science is settled. You fucking know there is no science behind the claims you make. You know damn well that since the '86 protection act, you guys have been pumping out more untested vaccines because you're not liable for the damages they do to people. Scumbags like you keep turning out more unnecessary vaccines, because with government mandates forcing kids to be poisoned, you have a captured customer base and you're raking in billions in profit every year. Go ahead and deny it. Go ahead and tell the hundreds of thousands of parents who've buried their babies that the science is settled. I dare you. But that's not the half of it, is it?"

"I don't know what you're talking about. Vaccines save lives. Vaccines have saved—"

Once again Moffett took another blow to the head, and he and the chair flipped over. And this time, the tape around his ankles snapped apart. Paige watched from the far end of the room. Ray pulled him upright and noticed he had been steadily working to loosen the tape on his wrists. He signaled Paige, who came over to redo her work.

"Vaccines save lives? How many people my age have died from brain cancers that are tied to the simian monkey virus in those fucking polio vaccines? Tell me how your industry tried to publicly destroy the reputations of the researchers who discovered that tonsils are not only part of the immune system but they make the antibody to fight the polio virus. How many innocent children die within hours or days after receiving a hepatitis B shot? Tell me, God, can little kids really tolerate thousands of shots at once? Yeah, that's right, I saw that interview you gave. I heard the way you belittled the parents whose daughter died within hours of receiving six shots at one time. How do you sleep at night making such an outrageous claim? How do you look at yourself in the mirror telling moms-to-be that breastfeeding doesn't provide natural immunity or that it's perfectly safe to inject all that mercury from a flu shot into their bodies, as if that poison doesn't flow through the blood of the umbilical cord into that little baby? Are you going to sit there and tell me that all that mercury and aluminum is safe for a developing brain?"

"So you're here to kill me, is that it? Your child has a learning disorder, perhaps some kind of behavioral issue…oh wait, little Johnny has a peanut allergy and you want revenge?"

Ray was about to hit him again, but he looked at Paige instead.

"I see what you mean about his small penis syndrome. This guy is on death's door, and instead of pleading for his life, instead of atoning for his sins, he wants to get the shit beat out of him first. He is an arrogant bastard for sure."

He turned to walk away, but just as Moffett let out a sigh of relief, Ray turned and backhanded him across the face so hard that blood flew from his mouth and nose. He looked at the back of his hand with disgust and forcefully wiped it across Moffett's white silk shirt.

"You two are not going to get away with this," he slurred through swollen lips. "Of that I take great comfort."

"You're not going to see us get caught. Of that I take great pleasure." Ray smiled at Moffett, and without turning to Paige, he asked, "The more I think about it, do we have to let the maid be a victim in all this?"

"No. I didn't really give her that much, and she never got a look at me. She should be waking up soon. What are you thinking?"

"Let's leave her tied up. Take the hypodermic with the remnants of the sedative and leave it on the nightstand by his bed. In Moffett's suicide note, we can say that he wanted to kill her because she told him she was going to tell his wife."

"I guess we can do that. Look, Ray, it's getting kind of late. Let's finish this thing and get going."

For the first time since he'd woken from his chemical-induced sleep Moffett was in total panic. He wanted to stall them as long as he could. He'd bluffed about the dinner party, but he still hoped one of the estate workers would come by for something. As much as they detested Rosie, they often thought of an excuse to come to the main house for a glimpse of her in the maid uniform she wore when Theresa Moffett was away—the short black skirt with matching gartered stockings revealing just enough cheek to excite them.

"Do you two think this whole thing ends with me?" he asked in desperation. "Do you think that by killing me you're going to stop the biggest money-making machine in human history? Collectively, we are bigger than too-big-to-fail. We're the ones who fill the troughs all those pigs belly up to. We own the media, we own the banks, we own the universities...we own the fucking government, for Chrissake! You kill me, and you're not even cutting off the head of the snake. Sure, we make a ton of money off vaccine sales. But that's only a part of it. For every disease, every disorder, every syndrome that develops as a result of all the toxic chemicals that get injected into every body, there has to be a treatment. And we've got those treatments," he yelled at Ray.

"And those treatments last a lifetime because you're not in the business of developing cures. You just want to develop customers," Ray yelled back. "You don't want to make cures for anything, because to do that would be counterproductive. And not that you could cure anything, because if you could, you wouldn't be cultivating all those natural herbs in your own garden, you lousy hypocrite. It's people like you who've got your jackbooted FDA storm troopers shutting down legitimate natural healers."

"Because there's no profit in healing people, you naïve idiot!"

"Not naïve. Me and my colleagues have been saying this for years. We've been teaching our patients this for years. And you know what, they get it. And that's what scares you and the rest of your drug cartel. If you guys lift your boots off our necks, even just a little, the ripple effect will build into a tsunami."

"Bingo, genius. You got it; you get the prize."

"Well, isn't that ironic…God comes to confession."

"You'll never get a chance to use it."

"Whaddya mean?"

"Who's gonna listen to you?" He laughed nervously. "Who can you go to who isn't on the payroll? You think the four guys I sent to get you two is the last of it? Hell, don't you read the newspapers? Hey, Paige, I'm sure you remember your researcher boyfriend who told you about our little secret project. Do you think he's the only potential whistleblower who's had that kind of unfortunate accident? You two will never live another day without wondering when and where your accident is going to happen. I hope your motivation was worth it."

Ray charged at Moffett and pushed the chair over. His head hit the floor, but it was Ray landing on top of him that caused him more pain as several of his ribs cracked on impact. He grabbed Moffett's head intending to slam it against the hardwood a few more times but halted his assault when he felt a hand on his shoulder. He turned to tell Paige to back off, but she was still by the bookshelves. He inhaled deeply and pulled Moffett's head up toward his chest as if latching the string of a crossbow. Just as he was about to explode his arms forward, slamming the bloodied head into the floor, he felt the hand pull back on his shoulder, a whisper in his ear: *"Don't, Dad. Not you...not in my name...not like this."* Ray gently released his grip.

"You wanna know my motivation, you piece of shit? You wanna know? It's my daughter. She was an officer in the United States Navy who unselfishly served her country. So tell me why her life was in more danger from a scumbag like you than the bullets and mortars she dodged in the hostile wasteland of Iraq. Don't bother, we already know why. She's my motivation, and you fucked with the wrong dad. You wanna know what you fucking did to her? Vaccines with double and triple the amounts of toxic adjuvants to speed the onset of chronic disease in adults."

Moffett didn't say a word, but his eyes grew wide.

"What's the matter, you heartless sonofabitch. People weren't getting sick fast enough for you? I hope your motivation was worth your life, you motherfucker."

"It's time, Ray," Paige said. "We gotta finish this."

He got up and moved off to the side and watched the first hypodermic needle pierce Moffett's thigh. That was all he had to see, and he walked outside to wait for Paige to complete her task.

"What was that? What did you just put in me?" Moffett's legs and hands trembled with fear.

"It was a sedative...like the one I gave you earlier but not as strong. I want you relaxed enough so you can't fight but awake enough so that you can comprehend how you're going to die." She placed a black medical bag on his desk. "Like Dr. Silver mentioned, you made numerous claims that little babies can easily tolerate thousands of vaccines all at once. That's a lot of formaldehyde, and acetone, and aluminum, and mercury... and the list of toxic chemicals is a long one. But of all the people, especially you, claiming this stuff is safe, not one of you is rolling up your sleeves to prove it, are you? Well, congratulations, Moffett, you're taking one for the team...the equivalent of a couple of hundred actually," she said as another needle pierced his thigh. "The suicide note I'm leaving on your computer will state that considering how much pain, suffering, and death you've knowingly caused to countless innocents, you could no longer live with yourself."

"Please, don't...you're making a big mistake. I've got money. You know I've got money, lots of money. It's in my safe. It's yours; you can have it. I won't say a word."

"Here's one that you'll like. A triple dose HPV shot. Three times the aluminum, three times the mercury," she said, squirting a little into the air.

Moffett became rigid, and Paige pulled back.

"Relax, Patrick, relax. The science is settled...you said so yourself. Tell you what I'll do. I'll use different limbs so that it's even safer."

* * *

Ray stared down the long driveway and out across the snow-covered treetops. Long Island Sound was nearly frozen over, yet one medium-size cargo ship plied its way east, heading toward the Atlantic. It made him think of the Gordon Lightfoot song, "The Wreck of the Edmund Fitzgerald"—a tune he had sometimes thought of when he and Casey would venture down to the fishmongers of Seattle's Pike Place Market to suck down oyster shooters as they watched the freighters heading north in Puget Sound.

"OK, that one over there. Whaddya think?"

"She's not bringing anything in, that's for sure."

"How can you tell?"

"Well, first of all, she's riding high in the water, so she's empty."

"You're getting pretty good at this. What else?"

"She's slowing, and it looks like she's turning to port. See the activity picking up over at the grain elevators? She's gonna take a load of wheat to Asia or something like that."

"You'd be pretty good if you ever did sea duty, which makes me want to ask if you're sure you want to do this, kiddo?"

"The Navy ROTC, or the nursing thing? Hands off, that big guy is mine. I earned it."

"That's my oyster! You had the other three really big ones... the navy and the nurse thing."

"Well, I gotta do the navy, you know that. It's the family tradition."

"I told you that you really didn't have to."

"I know you're feeling guilty, Dad, but like Jimmy and I have told you, we want to do this. You didn't talk us into it, and yes, it is a family tradition and we want to uphold it. Is that so terrible?"

"No, it's honorable and admirable. But I've thought about it, and quite honestly, one day I'm going to hang up these magic hands and move to Hawaii. It'd be nice to have someone in the family become a chiropractor and take over the practice. Since your brother wants to go into law and has already committed to the navy, I was thinking—"

"First off, you know Mom hates Hawaii. You guys would end up getting a divorce if you start talking about moving there. And as far as taking over your practice, you know as well as I do there are no chiropractors in the navy."

"Exactly."

"Original family tradition first…and then maybe later on we can revisit my going to chiropractic school."

"But nursing?"

"I'll be a surgical nurse. At least I'll be focused on saving lives. Now get. Your hands. Off. My oyster."

Ray didn't hear Paige come up behind him until she spoke. "Hey, wake up."

"I'm awake. All done?" He studied Paige's face. She looked pale.

"Yeah…he began crying."

"No kidding?"

"Yeah. About halfway through he started whimpering like a baby, begging me to reconsider."

Ray laughed a little. "My daughter would've said, 'Sucks for him.'"

Paige turned away. She didn't want Ray to see she was nauseas, but he had seen that look before.

"It's OK if you have to—"

"I don't." She tried to fight the pressure making its way up from her stomach into her throat.

"Don't resist. It's not good to hold—"

"I said I'm OK." She lurched forward and heaved into the snow.

Ray placed his hand on her back for reassurance, and for the first time since he had met her, she allowed herself to be vulnerable.

"It's OK, let it out."

"I'm sorry, I didn't mean to."

"It's the adrenaline, Paige. It's still surging. Perfectly natural."

"It's not as if it's the first time I ever killed," she offered freely. "I'm a hunter. I've taken down deer and caribou and—"

"And some of those guys who hunted us down?"

"Yes...but that was different. Moffett was a prisoner. I took my time, and he couldn't fight back."

"Like the hundreds of thousands of innocent children who died a slow torturous death from his toxic cocktails? Like the millions more across the world who've been permanently disabled and suffer every day they exist? Fuck him, Paige. He hunted you down for years. How will you ever get that time back? He got what he deserved, so fuck him."

"It's that easy, huh? It was that easy for you the first time you—"

"No, not exactly."

"Then how?"

"Because it was justified...just like it is now."

"Justified?"

"Absolutely. And if you start telling yourself anything different, then you're gonna end up in counseling...if you're lucky."

"Is that what happened to you?"

He smiled, pulled her in for an embrace, and whispered into her ear. She closed her eyes and nodded.

"So, Dr. Motz, what are you going to do now?"

"I told Griff I'd think about coming back in."

"Are you? Going back in that is. Hell, maybe you do need counseling."

"I don't know, to tell you the truth. I'll go back to Colorado for a while...check in with my brothers and see what's going on there. I gotta think about it. What about you?"

"I've got some unfinished business in Seattle. Then it's back to my little girls in Lanikai and my practice in Kailua... see what's going on there. I've got a lot to think about as well."

"He used us, Ray. Griff used the both of us."

"He's part of the government, and it's what they all do."

"All? That's pretty cynical."

"Think about it. It's a business. The US government isn't a representative body of the people. It's nothing more than a business. It's just another corporation trying to make a profit at any cost, and it'll consume anything and everything in its path in order to grow. And just like most corporations, the government has absolutely no regard for the health, safety, and welfare of its customer base. And why should it? After all, there's a load of new consumers born every minute to take the place of the ones injured or killed in the quest for the almighty dollar. You know what I'm talking about. You've seen the callous disregard for humanity. Hell, just take a good look at Moffett. If he ain't the poster child for all this, then I don't know who is. But with the government, there's a bit of a difference. You see, they're so inept, corrupt, bloated, and self-serving, they'll never make a profit...well, except for the individual politician or the decision makers at the different agencies. They get to fill their pockets thanks to the lobbyists, but the government as an entity...you know as well as I do that they lose hundreds of billions every year from the waste, the fraud, the abuse. And then there's the overall lack of accountability because they don't have a board of directors or even stockholders they have to answer to. They just stick it to you and me.

"And they'll continue to get away with it as long as the public remains complacent."

Ray looked up and watched the tiny dot of an aircraft drawing a thick white line across the sky. "Complacent, apathetic... drugged is more like it."

Paige didn't comment. Ray continued.

"Drugged as in medicated, sedated, dumbed-down... drugged. Drugged as in the average citizen in the United States being on ten to twelve prescription medications at any given time throughout his or her life. Look how many kids are on some sort of antidepressant, anti-anxiety, or attention deficit medication. It's freaking mind control is what it is. The food we eat is full of pesticides, herbicides, growth hormones, and antibiotics. The water is fluoridated. Prevent cavities? My ass! Hell, Paige, that shit is a known poison to the nervous system. I mean, what the fuck are these people doing to us?"

"Oh, Ray," she sighed, "you don't need to tell me...you don't. I know all about it."

"Yeah, I'm—"

"Very angry?"

"Yeah."

"If it'll make you feel any better, there's a few more shots left on Moffett's desk. You can go back in and give him a jab... or two."

Realizing that his diatribe was a way to blow off the tension built up throughout the day, he now laughed at himself for proselytizing.

"I was preaching...I'm sorry." Ray looked up at the sky and pointed to the white trail of smoke stretching from one end of the horizon to the other. "Why doesn't anyone take notice of how that shit up there slowly spreads across the sky? What kind of chemicals do you think they're spraying on us?"

"I'll bet you a million dollars it's not vitamin C, Ray."

"People need to wake up and connect the dots, for Chrissake." He looked over at Paige. "Yeah...Griff used us. He's the government, and that's what they do. You feelin' any better?"

"Yeah...drive me to the airport?"

"Sure."

25

Seattle, Washington

Ray and Leigh Anne sat in the car watching the raindrops sprinkle over the windshield until the lettered awning of the red brick building across the street was just a blur. When enough water accumulated across the top of the glass, the heavier drops began to inch their way down the sloped window—growing in size and speed as they absorbed the smaller droplets in their paths. He briefly wondered what magical force influenced the slalom-like course of travel rather than a straight beeline to the finish. He thought of other useless things as well—anything to avoid thinking about going inside the building across the street. He cleared his mind of the random chatter, finally allowing himself the bittersweet memory of Casey:

"Come on, kiddo. You need to get out of the car, or you'll be late for school."

"But it's raining too hard, Dad."

"Excuse me, but did you forget this is the Pacific Northwest? It rains here, and you've been dealing with that every winter for all of your sixteen years. Now get going, because I'm already late for my first patient."

"Then call Mrs. Butterbutt and, like, tell her you're running late."

"Mrs. Butterfield. And how many times have I told you to stop making fun of her weight?"

"I didn't say anything about her weight. You did. And since you brought it up, don't you think she's, like, extremely large? I mean, she may be a great office manager and all, but how can you tell your patients about healthy lifestyle choices when Mrs. Butterbutt—"

"Butterfield!"

"Is always snacking on junk food in the office."

"What? How can you say that about her?"

"Because I've seen her do it. She does it when you're not there. I even know where she hides her stash."

"I can't believe you snooped around and that you're tattling on her."

"I didn't snoop. One of the other assistants showed me."

"Which one?"

"If I told you, that would be tattling. You should really talk to her about it, Dad. It doesn't look good. I mean, like, she does it in front of your patients."

"Never mind, young lady. Now get out, 'cause I'm late."

"But I don't wanna get my book report all wet. I forgot to put it in one of those plastic covers, and the pages will get, like, soaking wet."

"Casey?"

"I'm sorry, OK, I had too many last-minute things to get done."

"But you can't just sit here. Look it, kiddo, it's a twenty-yard sprint to the awning and from there a dry walk to the front door."

"Don't you have, like, a bag or something?"

"Nope. There's nothing back there except your brother's sports gear."

"That explains the locker-room smell."

"Tell me about it. Come on and stop stalling. Get, before it starts to rain even harder."

"Could you tuck it under your jacket and run to the awning with me? Please?"

"But I'm already late."

"Pretty please? If you help me now, I'll go with you for oyster shooters on Saturday."

"Hmmm, sounds tempting. Here in town, or in Seattle at the Pike Place Market?"

"Pike Place, of course."

"Give me your paper. On the count of three, you ready?"

For the third time since they'd pulled up and parked, he turned on the radio and Leigh Anne turned it off before his hand could return to his lap. They looked at each other and smiled, hers being more of an "I caught you" and his from having been caught.

"I'm sorry, Leigh, it's just—"

"Habit, I know."

"I just wanna listen to the news."

"I know. You've still got a good ten minutes. I haven't seen or heard from you in a few weeks, and outside of a few words since you picked me up at the hotel...Ray, don't you think we should talk?"

"You're right, I'm sorry."

Knowing what awaited him inside, he was fidgety—praying to get it over with but wanting to be able to put it off indefinitely. Ray knew to even think of such a thing was selfish and pointless. Once again he went to turn on the radio and then quickly diverted his hand to flip the wiper control when Leigh Anne caught the attempt and shook her head."

"Ray!" she laughed. "Be patient, please!"

The dried-out rubber blades stuttered across the glass, leaving thick, dirty streaks.

"You can tell this is a rental." He shook his head. "You'd never see this happen on our cars."

"It was easier to see before."

"Like a lot of things, Leigh, like a lot of things."

"But I think we've got one thing settled. Everything back home is back to the regular level of abnormality. The vandalism has stopped, the moms at the preschool are off my back,

Alice Mayweather was so embarrassed by the slap down she and her husband received she's left the preschool altogether... your plan worked, Ray. That little act we did at Kathy Kotter's really fooled them. And speaking of Ms. Kotter...I never got a chance to tell you, but after you left that meeting, I had her drive me home."

"That must've been interesting."

"I figured that since I was still in character and fired up, I should take that opportunity to have a little talk with her."

"Oh?"

"You can rest easy. She won't be hitting on either of us anymore."

"You did put on an award-winning performance. And I have to admit, you actually had me worried there for a bit."

"And I admit I had my doubts about the whole thing, but they all bought it hook, line, and sinker. They all think I went against your wishes and got the girls vaccinated."

"I hate to say this, but it proves my point that people don't ever look past the packaging...on anything. They just wanna live in a world that shows them what they wanna see and tells them what they think they wanna hear: that everything is all right, and if it's not, it's because someone else is at fault. And as long as someone doesn't come along with a set of facts that fly in the face of a false reality, then all is right with the world. Any problems with the preschool?"

"No, no problems. I had called Patty Mclean's office like you said. I told the receptionist I was your wife, and she got me right in. I wish there were more pediatricians like her. I wish she had been in practice when I had Mahina. I have no doubt in my mind she'd be a healthy and thriving young woman today."

"And with the abundance of love that you have and share, I have no doubt about that. There are plenty of docs out there that wanna be just like Patty. They're just too afraid to think for themselves...too afraid to practice in any way not dictated by the American drug cartel. And if they weren't hurting so many children, I could almost feel sorry for them."

"Feel sorry for them? Really?"

"What kind of life is it to live in constant fear? Look at those researchers who had the evidence of an MMR and DPT link to autism. They were trying to get the word out, and look what happened to them. Murdered...assassinated in order to silence them." He turned to Leigh Anne. "So you brought the girls in and—"

"She did a basic exam and then began filling in their vaccination records as you said she would. She also wrote a letter for the preschool saying the girls would be 'up-to-date' within the next few months. Is this how you did it with Jimmy and Casey when they were that age?"

"Pretty much. I mean, at that time the vaccine schedule was about a third of what it is today. I practically filled out that stupid little trifold card myself."

"You forged it?"

"Yeah." He laughed. "It was as valid as those shots."

"Dr. Mclean won't get in trouble for doing the same thing?"

"Nah."

"She said if the rest of her patients were as healthy as our girls, she'd have more time for surfing."

"Well, hopefully I'll be sending more parents with their *keiki* to her for the same service."

"It's so sad that this is what we have to do. I can't believe this is what has become of our country. And as much as the facts are on our side, Ray, I still get the feeling that the way this is being done is all wrong."

"It does have that feel to it...kinda. Almost as if we were living in an enemy-occupied country and we're resistance fighters...kinda like the French underground in Nazi-occupied France. Many of the civilians back then were really resistance fighters sneaking around the shadows and carrying out covert operations in an effort to win their freedom."

"That's pretty extreme, comparing us to them, don't you think?"

"Maybe, but based on the path this country is traveling, I'm afraid it could get to that point. Just look at the frenzied hysterics we had to deal with. Those people are so totally brainwashed by an orchestrated campaign of misinformation and fear, they can't think for themselves."

"I'm wondering now since we put on our performance in front of everyone that night...is it going to be harder for you to continue speaking out?"

"Not at all, if you think about it. Even though they all think you came to their side on this issue, I never compromised, and therefore, I can still carry on as usual."

"But how can you tell people our kids aren't vaccinated when a whole bunch of people around Kailua town now think they are?"

"The only time those people will hear me is when I'm being questioned on the news, which you should know...I am taking a solemn vow to adopt the phrase 'no comment.' Even if it's Mileka Johnson. And even if I should have anything to say outside the office, I can still honestly say that I never brought my kids to the pediatrician to have it done. And if you think about it, neither did you."

"And people who know us won't think it strange there's no friction between us?"

"That group thinks everything we do is strange, and who really cares what anyone thinks?"

"Mileka's bosses cared."

"Whaddya mean, Leigh?"

"She got fired from her job because she managed to air the unedited interview you had done with Josh Kimmel. It was almost as if she wanted to get fired for taking your side."

"I'm not surprised. She said she wanted to work on a documentary. If she ever gets it made, then something like this would certainly be good PR for it."

"Did you know that she and Leilani Blacque are—"

"Sisters? Yeah, I knew all along. That was one of the reasons I wanted Lani hired."

"What are you talking about, Ray?"

"Don't get me wrong, Lani is more than qualified for the position. When she first interviewed for the job with Leilani, she did what all good office managers do and ran a standard background check. She does it for all the applicants. Anyway, when the connection to Mileka Johnson popped up, I thought it was a good opportunity to get some better press coverage. Little did I know that Ms. Johnson's motivation to do a documentary film was her own sister."

"Vaccine-injured?"

"Yeah, from the HPV shots she received while on active duty. That's why she gets the full disability pension. I'm thinking we should introduce Mileka to your sister."

"Maybe we shouldn't. At least not until after she has her baby."

Ray sighed, looked at the dashboard clock and then across the street. The raindrops were building up again. He could still read the letters spelling out "OF PUGET SOUND" on the awning, but the first two words were now blurred. He wondered if the dirty streaks would alter the path of the drops when they began to roll again.

"It's the top of the hour, Leigh. Mind if I put on the radio to hear the news?"

"Not at all. I know it's important to you."

It had been several years since he'd lived in the area, but holding the scan button to locate the news stations was second nature—the dial numbers instantly recalled without a second thought. He picked one at random, slouched back into his seat, and patiently listened to the lead story, the next two after that, and then the commercial break. He turned to Leigh Anne.

"Everyone is here already, right?"

"Jimmy, Jenna…Leilani came with me to help with the girls. They're all inside."

"You know what I wanna do when we get home? I mean besides jumping your bones?"

"Will you ever stop thinking about sex?"

The radio crackled:

"And now here's a follow-up on the sudden death of longtime outspoken McTavish Pharmaceuticals chief Patrick Moffett. We go to our sister station in New York for this update. Peter?"

"Yes, Tammy and John, on the surface it seems that this is wrapping up, but I suspect the fallout will be far-reaching, and here's what I mean by that. Shortly after the FBI concluded its investigation, we received two formal statements today: one from Moffett's wife Theresa, and the other from the chairman of the board of McTavish. Both letters confirm that Patrick Moffett had been battling a rare form of cancer for quite some time. While he was strongly urged by company scientists as well as the board of directors to submit to FDA-approved treatments, Moffett felt it was his duty to humanity to once and for all settle the notion that alternative treatments had any validity. Sadly, he felt he had to sacrifice himself for the overall common good. And while Theresa Moffett as well as everyone here at McTavish are deeply affected by his loss and vow to make sure his bravery and sacrifice is not forgotten, Congressman Chuck Schotman from the New York district where Moffett resided announced he will be leading an effort to get the FDA to tighten its control over these unconventional therapies, getting many of them off the market and putting the snake-oil salesmen who peddle these products behind bars where they belong."

"It sounds like you have pretty strong feelings about this, Peter."

"Yes I do, Tammy. I've had a number of relatives and close friends, as I'm sure every American has, who've had their battles with cancer, and I've gotta tell you how comforting it is to know that when they died they were under the care of some of the best oncologists this nation has to offer."

"Uh...yes, of course. Tell us, Peter, has there been any official comment from the CDC or the FDA?"

"Yes, John. In fact, all the news crews gathered here at the Moffett estate were handed an approved joint statement from both those agencies, and it reads as follows: 'When people's health and welfare are at stake, we cannot allow pseudoscience charlatans to get in between the sick and their medical professionals. It's simply unacceptable to hijack the vulnerable for the sake of profit. Each day this traveling medicine

show is allowed to continue, tens of thousands of lives are at risk.' And as we have seen time and again, Tammy and John, unsuspecting consumers are preyed upon all the time. Hopefully, the government will get the message that it is time to take serious action on this. Back to you guys."

Ray turned off the radio, wondering what Paige might have left in that suicide note that deterred them from disclosing the actual cause of death. *"She must've uncovered the mother of all incriminating evidence to have given birth to the piece of propaganda we just heard. If so, I hope Griff is going to help her. Otherwise, she's gonna be hunted like she's never been hunted before."*

Regardless, he thought the story that Moffett had been battling cancer was a stroke of genius—a brilliant coupe on their part. "Brilliant, simply brilliant! Now anyone, be it consumer, columnist, or congressional representative who was against natural healing won't even consider the fact that there is no mainstream medical cure for cancer. Billions of dollars spent every year on chemotherapy and radiation for nothing more than the hope that a life would be extended by a year or two."

Leigh Anne offered her hand. He took it—gently squeezing, he brought it to his lips. He took the clear plastic container with the bright yellow lei from her lap.

"I'm ready," he said.

26

Before going inside, Ray stopped briefly to look up at the words on the awning. Although they had been partially obscured by the smudged windshield, he didn't have to see them now but still stared up at them and wondered if he had been selfish to prolong what he had known should have been done weeks ago. *"Selfish? No, not at all. Hopeful, I was hopeful."* He took a deep breath, looked up, down, and across the street, and was bothered by a familiar uneasiness. He unconsciously tightened his grip on Leigh Anne's hand.

"What, Ray? What is it?"

He looked over at the rental car parked just a few yards away and felt a slight quiver in his legs. The sensation grew, the energy almost overpowering, but he couldn't quite put his finger on it. *"Is it? No way, not here, not now. He wouldn't,"* he thought. Again he scanned the street. As if an afterthought, he looked past the car toward the veterans' hospital to the south—the massive aging campus sitting high atop North Beacon Hill.

"Far from being a beacon of hope," he said.

"What, Ray? What's a beacon of hope?"

"I'm sorry, Leigh, I need a moment. Please…go on in and tell them I'll be up shortly."

Leigh Anne embraced her husband, brought her lips to his ear, and whispered: "I love you, Raymond Silver. With every fiber of my being, with every beat of my heart, I love you." She gently kissed him, then left him alone with his thoughts. He looked back at the medical center with disdain.

"What do you think you're doing, Ray? You can't take her out of here like this!"

"It's not your call, Stella. She's still my daughter, and I'm going to do what I think is best."

"Well you can't have her."

"I can't what? I can't have her? Who the hell are you, and who the hell is this hospital to tell me what I can and cannot do with a member of my family?"

"We're her caregivers, and she is still in our charge. That's who the hell we are!"

"Caregiv...are you out of your fucking minds. You call this backwoods butchery caregiving? Take a look at her. Take a good long look at her, damn it! It's your holy paradigm that caused this. What the hell can that paradigm do to fix this?"

"And what the hell are you going to do for her, Ray?"

"I'm going to give her the love, respect, and dignity she deserves."

"Come again, Ray? I didn't catch that."

He didn't have to turn around to know that the voice belonged to Griff Kelley. He didn't have to turn around, but he did.

"I knew you were here. I felt you...I swear I felt your energy. Even though I couldn't see any trace of you, I knew you were close by."

"That bad, huh? My energy that is...it's that bad?"

"It just is. I know we have our differences, Griff, and you certainly have your agenda, but tell me...was she in the test group? And please don't pretend you don't know what I'm talking about."

"She was one of two hundred and fifty."

Ray studied his eyes. It was one of the few times he had come face to face with the man where his face hadn't been hidden by a pair of government-issued sunglasses. It was the first time he saw a hint of compassion in those eyes. Griff continued:

"From all the data reviewed by my docs at the agency—"

"You guys have your own docs?"

"It's been a long time since we've been able to trust anyone at the CDC or the FDA. Too much conflict of interest, if you know what I mean."

"All too well, Griff. I know all too well. You had them review all her tests, her labs, all of it?"

"Yes."

"But why?"

"It's a long story."

"I've got a few minutes. Give me the crib-note version."

"A certain general at the DoD was nicely compensated to allow the experiment to happen. You'll be happy to know he's been dealt with."

"So there've been others."

"Yes, but the shots were shipped to a few dozen bases throughout the country. The recipients were picked to minimize any chance of there being similar health challenges in any branch of service or in any geographic region once enlistments were finished."

"So what happened to Casey would appear as a random thing."

"That's right, Ray. And just so you know, as far as your daughter's condition…Stella was in the dark." He continued despite Ray's skeptical look. "Unlike what you think, she doesn't have access to everything that goes on at that medical center. And she doesn't have an agenda. There was a good deal of information about Casey's condition that wasn't disclosed to her. What she did have access to…let's just say she had her doubts about the test results and what she was being told by her superiors. She finally got the nerve to call and ask me if I could have my guys review her stuff."

"Stella?"

"Yeah. At the risk of losing her job, she sent us copies of reports and was even able to secure some tissue samples. Had she been caught, she would've been in deep shit, Ray. And another thing, everything she did or said after that point…it was because of me. She was doing me a favor. I'm sorry, but I needed you to help me find Paige. It was me, Ray. I'm the one who used you."

"Again! As if I should be surprised by now. Tell me, Griff, am I that easy?"

Griff laughed. "Everyone is easy. You just have to know what motivates a person and it's...I'm getting off topic. The point is, it was me, not her. She didn't want anything to do with this. She didn't want you to think she betrayed you in any way. But I needed her to get to you. I needed her to fuel that fire that's always inside you, Ray. And who better to do that than someone who knows your emotional triggers. Stella reluctantly played along because she understood the importance of what needed to be done. And as we both know, she didn't need another reason to hate me. So you just might want to cut her some slack on this."

"I'll...call her. I promise, I'll call her and—"

"No *and*. Just call her. She'll know why."

"So how was it that my daughter became a victim of this experiment? How was she picked? Why her?"

"She was in the wrong place at the wrong time."

"That's it? She just happened to be in line and that crap was in the next series of hypodermics."

"Yeah, it was that random."

"When? How long before she began getting sick did it happen?"

"We estimate it was about six months before her first tour. So about four years ago."

"And the others?"

"Some had serious reactions within a few weeks, some a few months, and some...they're still out there."

There was no satisfaction knowing he had been right all along. He could only think of the mental and physical torture his little girl had endured. He could only think of the countless others who had gone through the same suffering or had yet to begin to experience the cascade of symptoms. But he did know that like their past encounters, Griff Kelley had once again managed to diffuse any thoughts of retribution he would have for the spy chief.

Ray nodded at Griff, stuck his hand into a pants pocket, and fingered the two-inch-long flash drive.

"What's the agency's business with McTavish and Moffett? Why are you involved, or can't you tell me?"

"Are you telling me you don't know? Paige said she left everything for you on a memory stick. I can't believe you didn't open and scour every file on that thing."

"I never got a chance to look at it. I lost it up in the mountains when I was fighting with one of the guys sent to kill us. The only thing I can think of is that it came out of my pocket during the struggle and went into the crevasse. Your guys didn't find it when they recovered the body?"

Now it was Griff who stared into Ray's eyes but didn't say what he was thinking.

"The wildlife got to it before we could. Ray...you know I can't tell you anything about my interest in this. It's... highly classified. And anyone unauthorized to view that material runs the risk of serious harm, if you know what I mean. The agency, however, has had no connection to Moffett or McTavish."

"This was personal, wasn't it?"

"On a certain level. You already know about my loyalty to the troops. When I got word that Moffett was using our men and women as test subjects, I decided to get involved. He crossed a line. So, yeah, it was personal. And for your own good, that's all you need to know."

"OK, I'm OK with that." Ray pressed his fingers onto the memory stick. "So I guess were done here?"

"No. Ray...I'm going to give you a piece of advice for free. You're playing a very dangerous game. And what's more, you know it. For your own sake...for the sake of your wife and your kids, even Jimmy and Jenna...don't you think it's time you stopped? Don't you think it's time to live that laidback Hawaiian family life you've been bragging about?"

"I thought I already was."

"Sure, you're there, you've got your nice little house near the beach, you've got your natural healing arts center, and you're eating your tropical fruit every day but—"

"But you keep pulling me back in."

"You want to be pulled back in, and you know it. Just look at what you've been doing over the past year. This whole activist thing against the drug industry...not that you're wrong about them. In fact, you couldn't be more right, but you were all but begging for something to come along like what just happened. But I've got to tell you that you're fucking with the wrong people. Not me, not the NSA, but with a bunch of powerful people. Look, Ray, you're not protesting against some bad tax policy. You're going after an industry's pot of gold, and if you think that what my NSA or the CIA does is bad, these drug guys are more vicious than any of the cartels in Mexico."

"They make poison, Griff. Their poison is like the poison of a snake, and their very survival depends upon people being sick. Even if it means seeding the population with the precursors of all those diseases. Those vaccines, Griff—"

"Sure they're bad, but you've got to get it in your head that the only thing worse are the people who make them, push them, and profit from them. Whistleblowers like Paige and people like you, Ray...you're the guys who are getting people to wake up. In an ideal world, that's a good thing, but do you think the drug industry is going to sit idly by and let you do it?"

"I hear what you're saying."

"But you're not going to stop, are you?"

"I can't, Griff; it's not who I am."

"I kind of knew that's what you were going to say."

"And I doubt you flew out here from DC just to tell me that."

"I came out of respect. Not just for you, but for your daughter. I came to tell you something about Casey you didn't know. Something that she never told you...because that's the kind of person she was."

"Griff, I'm sorry, but I gotta get inside. Can we do this another time?"

"You'll want to hear this, so please…just another minute."

"OK."

"Days before your raid on that old village outside of Fallujah—"

"You mean the one that saved your life?"

"Yes, the one in which Casey and others saved *our* lives… that one. Some days before that, your daughter's medevac unit had made a number of hops—I mean, medical evacuations—in the middle of an ongoing firefight. After one of the other chopper units got blown out of the sky, she still strapped herself into a harness and demanded her pilot lower her down into the battle. She made a total of a half-dozen drops over several hours that day, providing first aid and bringing wounded up into the helicopter using her own harness. She was shot at while dangling in the air and even attacked on the ground. I'll bet she never told you she had to shoot an insurgent at point-blank range."

"I didn't know that—I never heard any of this before."

"She didn't want to talk about it. That's just the way it is with almost everyone who's been over there. They keep it bottled up inside, Ray. It's not something people want to keep thinking about. You should know that."

"But yet they do. They keep it bottled up, or they medicate the memory." For a brief second, Ray saw himself standing in the Iraqi desert facing down a Taliban fighter frantically pulling the trigger of a jammed AK-47 pointed his way. "Why didn't her pilot or anyone else ever say anything about it?"

"He did. He wrote up a full report and submitted it for medal consideration."

"She wouldn't have wanted any—"

"Medal of Honor, Ray."

"What?"

"Yes…he recommended her for the Medal of Honor. But the military being what it is…anyway, he contacted me a few months ago because he found out that Casey had also been working for me. He was upset that there had been no action on his recommendation. Not only that, he was also being heavily pressured into withdrawing his request. He thought I could help. Long story short, after I read the report and learned the full details of what she had done that day, I made a few phone calls. I can't and won't promise anything, but you should be hearing something. It may take a year, but you should be hearing something. I'll do my best to keep the pressure up."

"I don't know what to say, Griff. I don't know what—"

"You don't have to say anything. She earned it. She deserves it."

"Thank you, Griff...look it, I gotta get inside."

"Sure. I'm going to be calling you, Ray."

"Griff—"

"You know you want me to. It's in your blood, and you're just afraid to admit it."

27

I n defiance of the emotional burden he carried, Ray straightened his shoulders, took a deep breath, and then entered the hospice. All morning long there had been a hollow feeling in his stomach as well as a knot in his throat, but it had been manageable due to a conscious effort to think of anything other than this moment. The heaviness of sadness, regret, helplessness, and hopelessness that filtered into the corridors from rooms filled with family members and friends of the soon-to-be-departed pushed against him like a pounding surf. He felt the knot tighten; he had difficulty swallowing. He was just a few steps from Room 206 but chose to sit on the bench just outside the door, looked down at the bright yellow lei, and closed his eyes:

"Daddy, come quick. Hurry before they swim away!"

"I'm here, I'm here."

"Do you see them? Look at all the fish, Daddy. They're so colorful. Look at all the red ones, and the ones with blue and black, and oh, Daddy, look at the yellow ones! They're my favorite!"

"You really like them, huh?"

"Yes, I do. I really like the yellow ones, Daddy. They're as bright as the lei I got at the airport. Can we catch some and *bring them home? Can we? I wanna have a big fish tank in my room, and I can watch them all the time."*

"No, we can't bring them home. I'm so sorry, Casey."

"Why not? There are so many of them. Why can't we just take a couple?"

"Because if we take them, then everyone will want to take some, too, and then pretty soon there won't be any left."

"Hmmm, I guess you're right. Oh, I know what we can do, I know what we can do."

"I know: take some pictures and make posters for your room?"

"Oh, we can do that, too, but I was thinking that we could come back to Hawaii every year to see them. I just love it here, Daddy. I love it, I love it, I do! I love Hanauma Bay, Daddy!"

"I do too, kiddo. But I don't know if we can come back every year."

"But, Daddy!?"

"But we can take pictures, and I can get you a bright yellow lei like the one you got at the airport."

"For my eighth birthday?"

"Every year on your birthday. OK?"

"Oh, that's so wonderful, Daddy."

"Daddy!"

Ray came back from his memory to the sweet chorus of voices belonging to his little girls: Ronnie, Abigail, and Sandy. They climbed up onto the bench seat and crawled over one another competing for hugs. He didn't hesitate, scooping all three into his arms and squeezing them tight. Kisses showered his face until Leigh Anne and Leilani swooped in for the rescue he didn't want. Leilani ushered the girls down the hallway to the visitors' lounge, while Leigh Anne picked up the plastic clamshell holding Casey's yellow lei from the floor. Ray nodded and went into the room.

The sight of his eldest daughter caught him off guard. He hadn't seen her since having her transferred over from the veterans' hospital. It hurt him to see her lying there, slowly wasting away—a lifeless shell of her former self. *"At least you're not in any pain, kiddo. At least you're not feeling any of this."*

Jimmy and Jenna stepped over to comfort him. He smiled and hugged them, and they left him to wait down the hall. He looked at Leigh Anne.

"I can stay with you, if you want, Ray."

He looked at all the wires and tubes going in and out of his daughter, the heart rate monitor showing the slightest activity. The monitors measuring brainwave activity could have been turned off and utilized elsewhere, but he had insisted they be hooked up from the moment he had her brought to the facility. *"Just because your instruments aren't sensitive enough to show activity doesn't mean there isn't any,"* he had stated, more from denial than optimism.

"Ray?"

"I'm sorry, Leigh. I'll be all right. Go ahead and wait with the others."

She handed over the lei and kissed him one more time before leaving.

He sat down on Casey's bed, brushed the hair away from her face, and leaned in for a kiss. Her once soft cheeks were now dry, hollow, and absent of any color. Ray's vision blurred with tears. The tissues from the nightstand helped, but his nose remained stuffed. He kept snorting back the flow and started to laugh.

"Blow out, Casey. Blow out!"

"I am blowing, Daddy."

"No, you're snorting it back in."

"I can't blow out; you're pinching the tissue too tight on my nose."

"Well, it must be a little piggy nose, because you're snorting."

"Oink-oink, I'm a piggy, I'm a piggy."

"OK, OK, stop. Let's try again."

"OK, but let me do it myself."

"Just get over here and blow."

"I wanna do it myself. You pinch too hard."

"Nope. Not after what you did the last time."
"Jimmy's a tattletale."
"And with good reason."
"I'll do it myself, and I promise I won't wipe my hand on his back, OK?"

"You certainly were a piece of work, young lady. What am I gonna do without you?"

Ray looked down at the lei, opened the box, and brought the flowers up to his nose. Even stuffed he could still smell the sweetness.

"You got me a lei...and yellow, too. But it's not even my birthday."

"I know it's your favorite, and I wanted you to celebrate with me. You see, we got the guy, kiddo. We got the guy who did this to you. It may not stop what's going on, but at least he'll never hurt anyone again."

"Oh, Daddy. You gotta stop doing things like that. You can't keep doing things like that. If anything happens to you, then who'll take care of our girls, huh?"

"I wish I could have taken care of you a little better."

"You did just fine."

"You think so?"

A doctor and nurse entered the room and stood at the foot of the bed.

"Yes, Daddy, I know so...Daddy...it's time."

Ray looked at his lifeless daughter and prayed for her to open her eyes while placing the lei over her head to rest across her shoulders. He picked up his daughter's hand and watched machines being turned off, electrical plugs being pulled from the wall sockets, and tubes being disconnected from his baby.

28

Honolulu

May 2008

There were so many people who had come to voice their opinion on Senate Bill 1941, the committee members were forced to move the hearing from Room 229 to the full senate chamber down the hall. Under normal circumstances, they wouldn't have changed the venue; however, the topic of forced vaccination raised the ire of a citizenry known for fighting government overreach. Hawaiians, both Kama'aina and transplants, were a laidback people, but just like Ray, when there is a threat to the family they make a stand—very rarely backing down. And as much as the ten-member Committee on Health and Welfare tried to get the hearing out of the way with little to no community participation, word had spread faster than a tsunami warning. Parents came to Oahu from all the islands in the chain—the Maui moms making up the largest and the most vocal contingent. The rumor of Ray Silver coming to testify before the committee not only generated the biggest buzz but brought the full Senate and every house member to watch the anticipated theatrics promised by news reporter Josh Kimmel.

Ray sat quietly among the others, patiently listening to those both pro and against—the arguments were what had been expected from either camp. In each two-minute allotted speaking time, public health officials, pediatricians, and school officials warned of massive outbreaks of life-threatening diseases and endangering the herd versus holistic doctors, independent researchers, and parents of vaccine-injured children arguing everything from the violation of their civil liberties to the ridiculous need to vaccinate newborns for diseases contracted through unprotected sex and intravenous drug use. Each side wasted no time charging the other with fearmongering. In spite of the passion from both camps, the testimonies were remarkably calm and respectful—something Ray took note of while he waited his turn.

In between listening to the speakers and reviewing his handwritten list of talking points that coincided with his pile of documents, he couldn't ignore the energy directed toward him. He glanced around the auditorium at the standing-room-only crowd—surprised at how many eyes were focused on him. He found Josh Kimmel and Setsuko Yamata talking to each other at the back of the chamber. *"No doubt plotting an ambush."* Off in the far corner, Jenna and Mileka were filming away for what had become the beginning of a joint project—their four-hour interview of him the previous night had helped him hone his message.

One by one, the citizens of Hawaii took to the podium, introduced themselves, and read their prepared remarks. For some, two minutes seemed like two hours as they nervously spoke their piece. Ray could empathize and appreciated their effort. For others, the allotted time felt like a few seconds as they barely got through all of what they had wanted to convey.

At first Ray didn't feel Leigh Anne's arm wrap across the top of his shoulders—he was lost in the moment, even flashing back to the time he had testified before Congress:

"Dr. Silver, did you hear what I just said?"

"I'm sorry, sir, I was thinking about something. Could you please repeat?"

"We're ready to resume, and as you were told this morning, this is an exploratory committee, the purpose of which is to see if there's enough evidence of wrongdoing, such as misappropriation of government funding, violation of international law, piracy, or murder committed by CIA operatives. We are not here today to accuse or prosecute you or anyone else involved in the operation that took place in January 2003 but rather to determine if a further, more detailed investigation is warranted. Regardless, doctor, I remind you that you have been sworn, and while under oath any false or misleading statements knowingly made by you can and will be used against you at a future date. In other words, sir, you could be charged with perjury in addition to being held in contempt of Congress. Is that understood?"

"Yes, congressman, I understand."

"Good. Now earlier this morning Representative Francine Manetti yielded the rest of her time so that she may be able to conclude her session with you this afternoon. Ms. Manetti, you have the floor."

"Now, Mr. Silver," she said, *peering over her reading glasses, "prior to your appearance here this morning, we had the opportunity this past week to meet and question John Walters, Steven Scott, Charles Shimkin, and Dennis Warren. Do you know each of these gentlemen?"*

"Yes, ma'am, as I said in testimony earlier today, I do know each of them."

"Mr. Silver, I know this may seem trivial to you, but could you please address me as 'Congresswoman Manetti'? The word 'ma'am' is very derogatory."

"I use the term in a manner of showing respect. I don't see it as derogatory."

"Well, I do."

"Yes, ma'a...uh, I mean, congresswoman."

"I want you to understand that I'm not being nitpicky here. It's just that I've been in Congress for many years, and I've worked very hard to rise to the positions I now hold."

"Yes, congresswoman."

"Can you understand that to address me as anything less than 'congresswoman,' especially in a setting such as this, is disrespectful and dismissive of all I've earned?"
"Yes, congresswoman. I see your point."

"Ray? Are you listening to me?" Leigh Anne gently shook his shoulder.

"I'm sorry, Leigh, I was—"

"Worrying about talking in front of all these people?"

"Surprisingly, I'm not. I'm actually feeling quite calm about this."

"Good, so I guess you see my point...about not making this about yourself and just presenting the facts, right?"

"Right."

"Good, because they just called your name."

"What?"

"They just called your name. You're up; it's your turn."

Ray took a deep breath, looked at Lani Blacque, who had the bulk of his documents placed in her lap, and then looked back at his wife.

"Go! And be respectful," she said with a wink and a smile.

The low rumble that had filled the room came to a stop as Ray, pushing his office assistant's wheelchair, approached the podium. Some of the senate members chuckled when they saw the stack of documents in Lani's lap.

"Good morning, Dr. Silver."

"Good morning, Senator Okamato, and good morning to the other senators on the panel."

"Before you begin, doctor, that's a significant amount of paper the two of you have there. I'm sure you're aware that you only have two minutes to state your case."

"With all due respect, senator, among all the people who signed up this morning to testify, there are six who have graciously yielded their time to me. And with any luck, I hope there might be a few more who decide to do so as well. So I believe that as of right now I have a total of fourteen minutes to state my case."

The senator shielded her microphone while she skimmed through a few of her own documents, then turned to her colleagues, who acknowledged Ray's claim.

"Very well, doctor, you may proceed. Even though you are known to this panel, I'd still like for you to state your name and occupation for the record."

"Thank you. My name is Raymond Silver, I am a chiropractor and the owner and director of the Kailua Center for the Natural Healing Arts located here on Oahu. We are a multidisciplinary natural healing arts center, and I come before this committee today to voice my opposition to your pending legislation Senate Bill 1941, a bill that will strip away certain parental rights, namely that of informed consent, meaning a parent's right to decide when, where, or if a specific type of medical procedure can be performed upon his or her child."

A thought popped into his head, and without understanding what now possessed him, he decided to take a brief detour.

"Now before I actually start, I'd like to say to this committee that I take great ease that I get to state my case in front of a group of individuals whom I consider *O'hana*—family."

The committee members looked at him with some suspicion.

"The reason I say that is because whether by blood history or by immigration to these small islands, we are all Hawaiians. And you know what I mean by that. We may be the fiftieth state in a much larger union, but we sit alone here smack in the middle of this vast Pacific Ocean isolated in ways technology can never bridge. In times of disaster, in times of great sorrow, in times of need, we turn to one another for help, for support, and for comfort. We rely on one another to do the right thing. That's not just the meaning of *aloha*, that's *O'hana*, that's family. We're next-door neighbors. You know where we live, just as we know where your homes are as well. We see one another at the grocery store. We worship in the same churches. We fix your cars, we mow your lawns, we deliver your mail. Our *keiki*, our children, go to school together, play together, grow up together. We celebrate our successes and mourn our losses together when we pay our respects with a paddle-out to spread the ashes of our departed. Now, I admit that it's not as close-knit as all that, but deep down this is who we really are. This is why I am comforted that I stand before this panel today instead of a detached and isolated group of politicians, like we have all seen in larger states such as California where time and again outsiders and special interests have been allowed to write legislation and influence lawmakers to turn on their neighbors because of financial incentives."

Now the committee members exchanged looks among themselves.

"So while it's true that all families may have that rare black sheep or even have their differences of opinion over hot-button issues, I know that all of us here in this room today take great ease in knowing that we stand up for one another and that none of us, especially those of you who asked us for the privilege and responsibility to represent us in these chambers—to look out for our best interests, to see to it that the foods we eat, the waters we drink, and the health-care we receive are the safest they can possibly be—would purposely risk the health, safety, and welfare of their fellow Hawaiians in exchange for the few pieces of silver offered by individuals or corporations who have no stake in our community."

Ray paused a moment and put his hand on Lani's shoulder before returning to his notes. "I think it's safe to say that the majority of the people in this room can agree that the United States of America has the greatest health-care in the world. Is that not true?" he asked, and received unanimous nods from the panel. "And because of that belief, it is my opinion that people are willing to assume that long-administered interventions are safe and effective. Well, I've gotta tell you, I'm not convinced we have the greatest health-care, and I can assure you that there have been many mainstream medical practices that have been abandoned after quiet acknowledgment of the damage caused by those interventions.

"While it's true the medical profession has twenty-first-century space-aged high-tech tools that can diagnose almost every disease, disorder, and dysfunction known to humankind, a diagnosis and subsequent course of treatment does not correlate with a cure. The statistics I've obtained from the federal government clearly show that in our country today we have more health challenges than ever before. If we were to just focus on our children and compare the state of their health to all of the other industrialized nations, it's easy to see with the current US schedule of forty-nine doses of vaccines by the time a child enters kindergarten and at least sixty doses by the time they graduate high school, we are by far the most heavily vaccinated nation on Earth, and yet one in six American children now have a neurodevelopmental disorder, over fifteen million of our next generation are enrolled in a program to deal with learning disabilities, one in four kids are using prescription inhalers for some sort of respiratory disorder, and in the past ten years the amount of children with food allergies has doubled. Kids are having seizures and dying from peanut butter sandwiches, for crying out loud.

"But that's not all. Today we have more children on prescription medications for a smorgasbord of health issues that were for all intents and purposes nonexistent twenty years ago. We have more childhood cancer than ever before in our nation's history. There are more children with diabetes, more asthma, more behavioral disorders, and more autoimmune diseases. Out of all the industrialized nations on this planet, the United States...with the greatest health-care system in the world"—he said with a tinge of sarcasm—"ranks among the highest in infant mortality. How can that be?

"Ladies and gentlemen of the committee, our country makes up only five percent of the world's population, and we consume sixty percent of the world's drugs. Each year over the past fifty years, our country has steadily increased the amount of doctors, nurses, hospitals, and diagnostic centers, and yet we have more people taking more drugs for more illnesses than ever. Is that the hallmark of a good health-care system, or is it just a good business model for an industry that is the poster child for Munchausen syndrome by proxy?" He paused for effect. "Back in the early eighties when the vaccine schedule was a third of what it is today, the myriad diseases of childhood and young adulthood alike were a fraction of what they are now. A coincidence? Autism was one in ten thousand. Today, it's one in eighty-eight, by 2016 it's projected to be one in fifty, and by 2025 the projection is one out of every two children. A coincidence? Better diagnostic techniques? I think not."

Ray turned to look at Leigh Anne and then to the back of the room to Jenna and Mileka. Before continuing, he did a double take—thinking he had just seen Paige. It made him smile. "So a thinking person...a reasonable person has to ask, 'Do we really have the best health-care, or do we have the most utilized profit-motivated disease-care system in the world?' And why are we in a position to need it so much? Genetics? Chestnut's work has clearly established that our genes have changed very little if at all over the past forty thousand years. In that case, a thinking person must also ask him- or herself why this is not happening in nations with half the amount of vaccinations. I'll give you this much: the carcinogens in all those vaccines are definitely altering cellular DNA, and there are some studies that suggest the damage to reproductive cells will have a significant effect on the health of the offspring of the children exposed to all those chemicals. A thinking person has to ask why the American Amish, who do not vaccinate their children—why is it that autism is practically unheard of within their society. And an honest person will acknowledge that countries like Japan, Germany, Sweden, and others are not experiencing the outbreaks of the diseases that American health officials scare us into believing will happen to us if we adopted the less-aggressive vaccination schedule that those nations employ. People who are advocates of the current program and individuals like the late Dr. Moffett from McTavish Labs have repeatedly stated that vaccines are completely safe, but if that were truly the case, then the enactment of the National Childhood Vaccine Injury Act would have never been necessary.

"Think about this: of all the products drug companies make...products that come with a laundry list of adverse effects...products that have caused death...products for which the makers are regularly sued because of the injuries they've caused...why is it that for all those products these companies have liability protection provided by private sector insurance companies, but yet they had to go running to the federal government for liability protection for their completely safe vaccines? And may I add that, to date, the federal vaccine court has paid out almost three billion dollars to children injured by vaccination? Even with that information, people will still say the science is settled. So if any member of this committee is willing to vote for this bill because he or she believes the science is settled, I'm willing to wager that not one of you has even seen the science, because it doesn't exist. And I say this with confidence, because after spending a significant amount of time doing my homework, I'm here today to oppose this bill for a number of reasons, the first of which is the absence of any safety studies, short- or long-term, performed on multiple-dose vaccines given at one time and repeated within short intervals of time. As evidence to that claim, I present this testimony from the congressional record...an admission of that very fact made just this past year by the head of the CDC in sworn testimony before the United States Congress. I present this as exhibit number one."

"Excuse me, doctor...you don't have to present your evidence so formally."

"My apologies, senator."

"And I'd like to ask if you are conveniently forgetting all the work done by universities that regularly perform medical research? Are you saying that they too haven't looked into this?"

Ray thumbed through his stack of documents—divided by a rainbow of colored tabs—and pulled out a thirty-page paper. He held it up to show the panel. "Probably one of the most significant indictments ever put forth about the American pharmaceutical industry comes by way of the former editor in chief of the prestigious *North American Medical Journal*. In Dr. Mary Albright's expose called "Ghost Writer: How the

Drug Companies Write University Research," she goes into great depths of how a pharmaceutical company will write up a 'research' paper, add the names of university researchers to that paper as if they were the ones who conducted the studies, and then submit the paper to peer-reviewed medical journals for publication."

"And the universities go along with this?"

"According to Albright, university administrations stay out of the loop so they can claim they are not aware of any wrongdoing. Those researchers who go along with this scam do so because, with their names on those papers, they have the prestige of being published and they also receive a financial reward for their cooperation. But the big bonus goes to the university, as it ends up getting million-dollar endowments." Ray nodded to Leilani Onakea. "My office manager is bringing you a list of approximately one hundred fifty research universities that have built or are building new laboratories, lecture halls, and even sports venues, along with the list of pharmaceutical donations that make all that possible. Make sure you check out the picture of the new state-of-the-art Visor Pharmaceutical Intramural Sports Center. It's beautiful."

"And you no doubt have a lot more information to share?"

"My apologies, senator. However, with your permission, patience, and open-mindedness, I would still like to present as much as I can of this stack of research and this stack of statistics from our own CDC, NIH, and FDA that I obtained through the Freedom of Information Act. I'd also like to present this package of sworn affidavits from both military and private sector vaccine researchers and infectious disease experts. After all, I did come to make my case."

"Even with your fourteen minutes—make that ten minutes now—I don't think you'll be able to present your whole case, even if another dozen scheduled speakers yielded their time over to you."

"Well, ma'am, with all due respect, can we ask?"

And with that a half-dozen hands from the audience shot up to donate their time.

"It looks like you just got another twelve minutes, Dr. Silver."
Ray smiled. "In that case, if I may continue without interruption I will talk as fast as I can, and then whatever I don't get to present to this committee I can still make available to each and every one of you, as well as to our good friends in the media. And when I'm done, I would appreciate the serious consideration of this body as well as the entire state legislature to vote to deny passage of a law that would remove an individual's right to informed consent, whose children would be subjected to an invasive medical procedure whose safety and effectiveness has never been established, as you will surely see." He placed his hand on the stack of documents resting in Lani's lap in full view for all.

Senator Okamato surveyed the quiet room and then turned back to Ray. "We're listening."

About the Author

Richard I Levine is a native New Yorker who was born and raised in the shadows of Yankee Stadium. After working in the auto parts business for several years and a one year wanderlust trip that took him coast to coast and back again, this one time North White Plains, N.Y. volunteer fireman, North Castle, N.Y. auxiliary police officer, and bartender returned to school and eventually became a chiropractor. A cancer survivor who opted for natural intervention he is a strong advocate for the natural healing arts as well as an environment free of man-made chemicals that are not congruent with the health of the planet or its inhabitants. New York remains in his blood but he's called the Pacific Northwest home since 1991

Made in the USA
San Bernardino, CA
01 May 2016